Praise for

A Heart of Joy

A Heart of Joy is a wonderful and refreshing book of life. It would help one to remember how beautiful and fragile life can be. I found myself drifting back on many occasions just thanking the Lord for all he has done for us. From a simple glance or expression, to the full understanding that no matter what happens God is and will always be in control. Jesse and Olivia may only be storybook figures, but they represent a true meaning of God's unconditional love. Thank you for the good read.

—Dr. Hubert W. Russell

Donna sets the stage for us as readers to experience the warmth of love and the anticipation of what is to come. *A Heart of Joy* is a compelling story of true love and a passionate desire to follow Christ's direction. I loved reading *A Decision of the Heart* and now *A Heart of Joy* is a breath of fresh air.

—Faye Thomas

One word penetrated my mind as I read *A Heart of Joy*: Trust. Olivia learns to trust in God's predetermined path. Her parents so completely trust in a young man's promise to shelter and love Olivia. And the new marriage that evolves eventually centers on the kind of trust God intended for all of us. *A Heart of Joy* tickles the senses, excites the mind, and evokes the heart's deepest emotions. The characters' Christ-centered relationships inspired me to bring even more love and happiness to my own young marriage, and to completely trust in the Lord's love, purpose, and power.

—Jessica Colvin

A Heart of Joy is a wonderful recipe of love and devotion where the Father, the Son, and the Holy Spirit permeate the recounting of each moment in these memorable characters' lives. If you believe that a family who prays together stays together, the story of Jesse and Olivia will become yet another reason why your belief is so well founded.

—Dr. Robert McTyre

A Heart of Joy

Donna Rhine

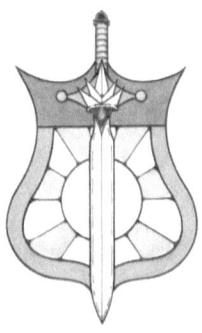

A Heart of Joy Donna Rhine

© 2008 Donna Rhine
© 2011 Donna Rhine

Published by:
Armoury House Publishing
P.O. Box 60
Addison, MI 49220 USA

ISBN-10: 0-615466-06-0
ISBN-13: 978-0-615466-06-4

All scripture quotations, unless otherwise indicated, are taken from The King James Version of the Bible.

Author: Donna Rhine
Cover: Steve Rhine, James Dunayski, Chamira Jones
Editor: Rebecca Hayward, Robert McTyre, Jessica Colvin, William Abbott

First U.S. Edition 2008
Second U.S. Edition 2011

Library of Congress Cataloging-in-Publication Data

Rhine, Donna, 1958-
  A heart of joy / by Donna Rhine. -- 1st U.S. ed.
      p. cm.
  ISBN-13: 978-1-934363-31-7 (pbk. : alk. paper)
  ISBN-10: 1-934363-31-6 (pbk. : alk. paper)
  I. Title.
  PS3618.H56H43 2008
  813'.6--dc22

                          2007046553

A heart of joy / by Donna Rhine. -- 2nd U.S. ed.
      p. cm.
  ISBN-13: 978-0-615466-06-4 (pbk. : alk. paper)
  ISBN-10: 0-615466-06-0 (pbk. : alk. paper)

Summary: Historical inspirational romance--a powerful moving saga of faith, adventure, and romance that develops in the midst of overwhelming circumstances.

For current information about releases by Donna Rhine or other releases from Armoury House Publishing, visit the author's Web site: http://www.daisytales.com

Printed in the United States of America
tv2 05JUN20
#cv2 23APR11

In Loving Memory
of Mom

Carolyn Elizabeth Williams

Thank you for the testimony of the
power of God's grace in life.

Your life will live on for generations
in the hearts and lives you have touched.

Until we meet again in glory.

"Wherefore seeing we also are compassed about with
so great a cloud of witnesses, let us lay aside every
weight, and the sin which doth so easily beset us, and
let us run with patience the race that is set before us ..."

Hebrews 12:1

Acknowledgements

*Now to him who is able to do immeasurably more
than all we ask or imagine, according to his power
that is at work within us ...*

Ephesians 3:20 (NIV)

I love to sit back at the end of such a journey and consider all that had to take place in order for this novel to come to fruition. The Spirit of God flowing through the body of Christ is a wonder to behold. You see, to me this is not just a story. My heart and life are interwoven in the pages. How could I ever take lightly all that God has brought me through—all that He has shown and taught me through His Word and others—all that He has laid on my heart to share with you? It is to Him the glory belongs. Without His presence in my life, I could not and would not be writing.

To all who have been praying for me along the way, I will always be thankful. You and I know that prayer changes everything. May God bless you abundantly for the way you have blessed and encouraged me.

To my husband Stephen—my cherished friend, who loves me just because I'm me ... you know how much you mean to me.

To Pastor Rocky Barra and Pastor David Stephens, thank you for allowing me to weave your life giving messages into this book. Your input was, is, and always will be invaluable.

To Doctor Hubert Russell and his wife Kim, cherished friends and fellow servants. Thank you for the many ways you have ministered life to me.

James Dunayski, thank you for sharing your illustrating gift, I've been so blessed by your efforts.

To the creative staff at Armoury House, the cover is astounding.

Chamira Jones, your finishing touches are amazing.

Krista Kimani, thanks for allowing me to use your image on this cover.

To my editors, Rebecca Hayward, Doctor Robert McTyre, William Abbot, and Jessica Colvin, thank you for all your input and hard work. Your expertise gave this novel the finishing touches it needed.

God Bless all of you.

Love,

Donna

A Heart of Joy

A Heart of Joy Donna Rhine

Contents

A Heart of Joy   Donna Rhine

The Michigan Chronicles

The Michigan Chronicles are a collection of stories from the days of yesteryear. The adventures begin in the nineteenth century, with two families farming in a small pioneer community nestled along the Huron River. The site, now known as Ypsilanti, is where the old Indian trail crossed over the Huron River. Come travel to a place in time where life was simpler ....

He Loves Me!

Prologue

August 20, 1830

"YOU'D BETTER FIND yourself a wife and get back here as soon as possible, Jesse Somers! My children need their uncle in their lives, and besides, your sister misses you way too much already!"

As Jesse reached to caress Elizabeth's damp cheek, his heart went out to her. This time of separation would be difficult for all of them. While he understood his family's reluctance to say good-bye, knowing they supported his reasons for leaving eased his mind, if only to a degree.

"Lizzy, the winter break will be here before you know it. We'll have a nice long visit." Jesse sat next to his sister on the bed, hugged her tight, and pressed a kiss to her brow. "You've got my best friend at your side. What's more," he added after taking Brenae from her arms, snuggling the baby close and taking a long hard look, "my niece and nephew need an aunt who will love

1

them as much as I do." Having watched Cameron grow by leaps and bounds over the last two years, he knew Brenae, born only yesterday, would change considerably over the next four months.

Jesse turned to his brother-in-law. "As soon as I get settled I'll write, but, Kaleb, you and Elizabeth had better keep in touch." Jesse kissed Brenae's soft pudgy cheeks before handing her back to Elizabeth and standing to his feet.

"Writing has never been my strong suit," Kaleb admitted, "but I suppose I can make an exception ... as long as you don't send them back corrected."

Jesse chuckled. "Now, what kind of a teacher would I be if I didn't offer a few pointers?"

Kaleb shook his head. "All kidding aside, know that our prayers go with you."

"I'm counting on that. Have fun with these little ones."

"We will."

Jesse hunkered down, tussled his nephew's hair and whispered in his ear, "You give your momma and baby sister lots of hugs for me while I'm gone, will ya, Little Man?"

Cameron giggled when Jesse tickled his sides. "You silly, Uncle Jesse!"

"So are you!"

There was so much more Kaleb wanted to say to his lifelong friend, but his wife was struggling and he had no intentions of adding to her despair. Kaleb and Jesse shared a brotherly hug before he headed toward the door.

A sparkle tweaked Jesse's eyes as he glanced back at Elizabeth. "Keep my sister out of trouble, will ya?"

Kaleb sat on the bed next to his wife and lightened the weight of her brother's departure with a flippant response. "I gave up trying to control your sister a few years back."

"I know. Quite freeing, wasn't it?"

"You know it! Besides," Kaleb added as he tucked Elizabeth's stray wisps behind her ears, "I kind of like this feisty beauty just the way she is."

Jesse turned to leave, saying as he walked out the door, "I'll see ya in a few months."

Kaleb and Elizabeth knew from experience that winter storms in this Michigan Territory could alter the best-laid plans. Even so, God had a purpose for this time of separation. They would pray for Jesse continually and leave his future in the Lord's hands.

Jesse's long morning ride had been uneventful, but the sultry air held a foreboding presence. Thunderstorms were common occurrences in this area, and as much as the dry earth could use a good soaking, he would prefer that the storms hold off until he reached his destination. Regrettably, that was not to happen. When Jesse was about an hour south of Ann Arbor, the clear blue skies darkened to hazy gray, and the torrential rains that began falling would continue over the next two days. Although the temperatures remained warm, plodding along the muddied trail was anything but pleasurable. What he wouldn't give for a cup of hot coffee and a home-cooked meal!

Jesse laughed, recalling how much he'd been looking forward to having this time away from his ordered life. *Funny*, he thought, *the grass really does look greener on the other side—*

until ya get there and reality hits. Even so, he was determined to fight against the loneliness creeping in.

Jesse had prayed long and hard about accepting this position. He needed to take this step in faith. So why was he discouraged? *I know this is what You want from me, Lord. Help me not to lose sight of that. You've shown me time and again that nothing will rob me of my joy faster than wallowing in self-pity. Besides, who am I to think that serving You and others won't cost me? You're expanding my boundaries, aren't You, Lord? You've taken me out of my comfortable surroundings. Help me to keep my eyes on You and what You've called me to do. You never promised that I wouldn't struggle, but You did promise to be with me. Knowing you are gives me the courage to press on.*

Jesse's lids slid shut, and he tried not to breathe as he passed through a swarm of gnats. The pesky little insects were annoying. Fortunately, they disappeared as quickly as they had come. The moment he opened his eyes his weighted heart soared. Shimmers of light peeked through the trees as if guiding him to the edge of the forest. When he rode into the next clearing, nothing could have prepared him for his first encounter with the oak openings. With great abandon, Jesse sighed as he drank in the magnificence of God's creation. The grand view the countryside presented was nothing short of breathtaking. When he tried to envision how he would describe what he was seeing to others, the only memory he could liken the endless expanse of trees to was the vastness of the great lakes.

His father had said that when he reached the oak openings, it wouldn't be long before he'd come to a small town. Nudging

Shadow on, he could only hope his father was right. He had no way of knowing if accommodations would be available, but he refused to allow uncertainty to keep him on the trail any longer.

As Jesse rode into town, he noticed a large hound sprawled out on the boardwalk in front of the country store. Some guard he turned out to be. The dog never budged as he passed by.

The banker, a tall, thin man with graying hair, was locking his door. He flipped the open sign over before he turned, glanced Jesse's way, and greeted him with a welcoming smile. "Good evening, young man. New in town?"

"Yes, Sir." The massive courthouse down the street caught Jesse's attention. Turning back to the banker, he said, "Now that's an impressive building."

"They did go all out, didn't they?"

Jesse nodded in agreement. "I'm looking for a meal and lodging for the night. Could you point me in the right direction?"

The gentleman lowered his chin and peered above his spectacles. "Livery's on the far end of town. The owner's son is working tonight. He'll know if anything's available at the boarding house. I've had the pleasure of sampling Mrs. Sisson's cooking—quite satisfying. Evans or Ketcham's Inns are along Chicago Road. A bit pricey if you ask me, but they'll have rooms available if Sisson's is full up."

"Thanks." Jesse tipped his hat and continued on.

A piano playing an unfamiliar tune rang out from Green's tavern, and although voices were coming from within, most of the inhabitants of this small community seemed to be settled in their homes for the evening.

The streets were a sight from the heavy rains. In fact, they were so laden with mud that Jesse waited to dismount until he rode into the livery. A boy, introducing himself as Joey, took Shadow off his hands. He also directed Jesse to a nearby house that welcomed well-mannered borders for a nominal fee.

Chapter One

Dreams or Reality

"WELL, BLOW ME down!" Jesse Somers exclaimed, as he rode out of the livery the next morning. In the midst of folks scurrying about, trying to get to their destinations, a tall, slender woman in a pale blue dress stood out like a beacon in this otherwise dreary day. Jesse was captivated. Her body in motion was the essence of femininity, and just as he was about to get a clearer image of her face, she stopped and turned toward the muddied street. For seconds she stood in contemplation. Her dainty finger rose to the brim of her bonnet, tilting it back so as not to obstruct her view. His brow arched when she ever so slightly lifted her skirt and began her graceful trek across the boards, which were staggered on the mucky road. He sighed deeply. The way the bright sunrise brought out the red highlights in her long brown hair took his breath away. Unaware of anyone except this intriguing young woman, Jesse moved toward her, fully intending to get a closer look. His heart skipped several beats when the heel of her boot slid into a knot on the wood plank. She tried to wiggle it out—wavered—and lost her balance, falling face first into the sticky bed of mud.

Jesse's forward motion was stopped by the sound of laughter. Her friends, who had already crossed safely, were greatly amused by their companion's mucky plight. Without bothering to help her in any way, they offered to inform her teacher that she would be late and went on their way.

Appalled by their lack of concern, Jesse would have said something, but the poor young lady was failing miserably in her attempt to stand. She needed help—now.

Jesse maneuvered Shadow alongside of her, reached down, plucked the unsteady maiden off the street, and sat her across his lap. The front of her dress was heavily laden with sludge, and her face, hands, and arms were not much better. "Are you all right, Miss?"

Awed by his selfless act, Olivia nodded, as a man she could not see proceeded to wipe the muck from her face.

"If you'd like to try and open your eyes, Miss, you should be able to see a little better."

As if the sound of his deep masculine voice was not enough to send shivers up her spine, she lifted her cumbersome lids to find herself in the arms of a fine-looking man with dark brown hair and eyes bluer than any she had ever seen. *I must be dreaming,* she concluded. While anything was possible—it was not probable. At a loss for articulate words, she rambled apologetically, "I can't thank you enough, Sir. Oh my, look what I've done. Your clothes ... they're all soiled. I am so sorry. I'm ... I'm such a klutz. Please,

I beg your forgiveness."

Jesse couldn't believe his ears. Here she was, covered with muck, and her own condition did not bother her in the least—her concern was for him alone. "No need to apologize, Miss. I'm glad I could help. Here," Jesse offered. Feeling somewhat flustered himself, he handed her the hanky. "Maybe this will assist you." Had he been paying attention, he would have noticed that the amount of mud dripping from the fabric rendered it useless.

Her efforts were ineffective. When she tried to return the soiled cloth, he insisted she keep it.

"If you tell me where you live, I'd be happy to take you home, Miss ...."

"You're too kind. You can let me off at the end of the boardwalk. I should be able to make it the rest of the way on my own. My house is just a short distance from there." Curious, she asked, "Are you new in town, Sir?"

"Yes and no. I'll be teaching in Frenchtown this year. I stopped overnight so I could rest up before continuing my journey."

"I see, Mr. ..."

"S. I've been informed that my students will call me, Mr. S."

"Then I'll pray for you, Mr. S, as you begin your new teaching position." She paused for the space of several seconds. "I hope you won't find me presumptuous in saying so, but concentrating on my studies would be nearly impossible if you were my teacher."

Jesse, finding her straightforward honesty a complete delight, laughed aloud. "Then it's best I'm not teaching here. I wouldn't want to be the cause of putting a halt to your education."

She shook her head and rolled her playful green eyes in such a way that she reminded him of Elizabeth. The memory made him smile. "Do you think there's a chance I might capture a glimpse of the real you when I come back through town before Christmas?"

"That is a possibility. I'm sure my parents would be pleased to meet the kind gentleman who took such good care of their daughter. I must warn you though—you could be running a great risk."

His brow furrowed. "Oh! What risk would that be?"

"For all you know I'm as ugly as a mud fence, and you're none the wiser."

His grin went from ear to ear. "True, but what lies beneath the surface has me captivated."

She lowered her head, taken aback by his compliment. "A chivalrous knight tends to bring out the best in a clumsy maiden, My Lord."

He chuckled softly. With wide-eyed curiosity, Jesse just had to know, "Tell me, Miss, how do your parents respond to a daughter with such a vivid imagination?"

She shook her head. "You don't know the half of it, Mr. S!"

"You might not surprise me as much as you think. I have three sisters. The oldest, Elizabeth, is a character like you. I'm sure the two of you would be good friends if you ever had the pleasure of knowing her."

She cracked a muddied smile. "I am quite sure that anyone related to the daring knight, who so gallantly rescued me from the dreaded bog, would be well worth knowing."

Again, he laughed, a deep hearty laugh.

Olivia was impressed with this kind man. In the few minutes they spent together, he had altered the way she would perceive men in the future. *Surely*, she mused, *few men exist who would so graciously rescue a clumsy maiden from such a terrible plight.* While the thought of ending this enchanted moment was nothing short of dreadful, if she allowed him to go much further she would be knee deep in the mire trying to get home. Although time spent with him might be worth it, she had an inkling that he needed to be on his way.

"Mr. S, I'm afraid we've arrived at my destination. As much as I would like to kiss you for your benevolent gesture, I am sure you would not thank me for the extra mud. Instead, I offer my most sincere thanks, along with my heartfelt prayer that God will richly bless you in your endeavors—whatever they may be."

"Do you have a name young damsel, or would you prefer to remain anonymous? I'm not sure I would recognize you if I were to see you walking down the street. Unless," he said with a twinkle in his eyes, "there are no other young ladies in this town with sparkling green eyes and red highlights in their long brown hair." Jesse didn't miss the smile that crossed her face nor the glint of light that danced in her emerald gaze. So fascinated was he with this new acquaintance, he found himself wishing he had time to know her better. The reality of it was, though, he needed to be on his way.

"You may call me Lady Maryse, Sir Knight."

Jesse lowered her long slender frame to the boardwalk, removed his hat, offered a knightly bow, and said with a radiant smile, "I do believe you and I were born in the wrong century to be talking such nonsense. Even so, I have thoroughly enjoyed this little diversion. For now, I must bid you farewell, Lady Maryse. If God be willing, I would find great pleasure in gazing upon your lovely face at another time."

With deep appreciation, she called out as he moved away, "Goodbye, Sir Knight, I will remember you always with fondness in my heart."

As the tall, dark-haired stranger with the cobalt eyes turned to wave one last time, she did the same. Although the chance of their meeting again was slim to none, he would forever hold a place in her whimsical heart. After all, doesn't every young maiden dream of the day when her knight in shining armor will appear on a magnificent steed to rescue her from a terrible plight?

"Mama! Papa!" Olivia called out as she came in the front door dripping with mud. "You'll never believe what just happened. It was destiny, I tell you—destiny!"

Josiah merely shook his head. His daughter's imagination had apparently run away with her again. "From the looks of you I'd say you fell in the mud. I'd hardly call that destiny, Livia!"

"Oh, Papa, that's not what I'm going on about. Of course I fell in the mud. I'm talking about what happened *next*. A handsome man on a black horse rescued me when I lost my balance on those wobbly boards. My friends went on to school, so if it wasn't for him I'd still be trying to make it home."

Josiah groaned. "I'm not too sure about these young people you call friends, Livia." A coughing spell took him unawares. He reached for his glass of water to soothe his throat before going on. "In my day a friend was someone willing to stick by your side no matter what."

Olivia glanced at her mother who affirmed, "Your father's right."

The paleness of her mother's gaunt face troubled Olivia, but she kept her worries to herself. It was rare to see her mama out of bed, enjoying her morning tea and she had no wish to remind her of her weakened state. Turning back to her father, Olivia attempted to ease his mind. "Don't be upset with them, Papa, I really didn't mind. If they had stayed, I would have missed the opportunity to meet this kind stranger. One minute I was struggling to stand on my feet. The next, I was being lifted off the ground and seated atop his magnificent steed."

The humor in her ailing parents' eyes did nothing to discourage her from continuing her tale. She would explode if she didn't tell someone. But her father was right. Her friends were not friends at all—not in the true sense of the word. If she were to tell her friends what this man did for her, they would dismiss her, insisting she had made the whole thing up.

"So where is this fine gentleman? I'd like to thank him for taking care of my girl."

"You can't, Papa." Olivia said, sadness exuding from her tone. "He's on his way to Frenchtown. More than likely, I'll never see him again."

"I'm sorry to hear that, Honey. He obviously made quite the impression on you."

"He did. I'll never forget the kindness he showed me."

"I'm sure you won't." Josiah lovingly patted her shoulder. Life experiences had a tendency to touch his daughter so deeply that many viewed her as an eccentric. He saw her creativity as God's way of directing her inward thoughts. While Josiah understood her artistic mind, he couldn't help wondering if she would ever find a husband who could accept and love her for who she was. Josiah had to believe that his Heavenly Father had those details all worked out. He would cling to the hope that this dreadful lung disease would not take him and his lovely wife before they could see Olivia happily wed.

Sensing her husband's pensive state, Maryse hurried her daughter along. "Olivia, if you don't want Miss Blackmar to penalize you for your tardiness, you'd best get cleaned up and be on your way."

Her response was a bit too dreamy. "I will, Mama, but I'm sure my mind will not be on my studies today."

Josiah's chiding brought her back to reality. "Save your dreaming for at night, Olivia. Your grades suffer enough as is."

"I know, Papa, but ..."

"No excuses. Now get changed and off to school!"

On Wednesday night Jesse camped along the Raisin River, taking the time to relax, clean up, and wash his clothes before making his way into Frenchtown.

As he scrubbed at the dried mud from his recent rescue, thoughts of this remarkable young lady brought a smile to his face. Although he could not see the woman behind all the muck, Maryse's looks had little to do with his reaction to their meeting. In those few moments together, she had altered the standard by which he would perceive other women. Most females would find such an experience humiliating at the very least. Maryse acted as if it were no great misfortune—just another sticky situation that life sent her way. Should God in His infinite wisdom see fit to give him a wife, he prayed she would be much like Maryse.

Allowing his thoughts to wander could get him into trouble,

but he couldn't help taking them one step further. Maryse, unless he read her wrong, was just as taken with him as he was with her. For some unknown reason she intrigued him—greatly. *Perhaps, he thought, we will meet again. It can't hurt to dream, but the reality of this is that only God knows for sure—I need to trust Him!*

Daisytales

He Loves Me!

Chapter Two

The New Teacher

*H*EARING A KNOCK at the side entrance of the church, Richard Jamison rose from the chair he had been occupying far too long and stretched his weary bones. As he opened the door, the cool breeze tussled his graying hair. A welcome relief from the stuffy room he called his office. "Hello, Young Man, is there something I can do for you this fine morning?" The dark-haired gentleman he greeted had to be at least six-foot three, and the deep blue eyes that met Richard's held a gentleness that warmed this pastor's heart.

"I'm hoping so. My name is Jesse Somers. The notification I received suggested that I contact a Pastor Jamison when I arrived."

A smile crossed Richard's face as he welcomed Jesse with his outstretched hand. "It's good to make your acquaintance. I am Pastor Richard Jamison. My wife, Rebecca, and I have been looking forward to meeting you."

Jesse nodded. "I would have been here sooner, but I ran into some bad weather. Spent the night at a boarding house in a small village along the way."

Richard went back to his desk and picked up a single key. "I could use a dinner break. Come on, Jesse, I'll show you around."

As they walked down the main street, several folks stopped to introduce themselves, and Pastor pointed out several tidbits of town life as they continued on their way.

"The postmaster's name is Jed. He's on the school board and knows your full name, so he'll make sure you get your mail."

"That's good to know. My family members weren't too pleased when I accepted a position this far from home." A cat screeched, swirled around their legs, and took off running in the opposite direction. A small, yapping fur ball was in hot pursuit.

Jesse chuckled. "Is there always this much excitement in the morning?"

"Can be ... the watch dog belongs to the folks who run the hotel. They call him Ambush, and rightly so. He lies in wait for the next critter daring enough to come within ten feet of him. I saw him chase a dog four times his size. That little spitfire has no fear."

"Either that or no brain!"

"Could be ... So tell me, Mr. S, is Ypsilanti taking great strides or is it still as uninhabited as it was the last time I saw it?"

"I'm not sure how long ago you were there, but the town's coming along. About three years back, the Stewart family built a hotel on the northwest corner of Michigan and Washington.

They call it Hawkins House. His father-in-law uses it as a trading house of sorts. Since their stock is limited, we still get most of our supplies from Ann Arbor or Detroit. We finally got around to building a schoolhouse last year."

"Sounds like they're making progress."

"Not what I'd call taking great strides, but it's progressing."

Richard smiled in remembrance. "I'm not sure if Pastor Williams told you, but I had the pleasure of spending a week with him in Detroit a few years back. At the time, they were looking to adopt some children. Were they successful?"

"Just before Christmas two years ago they adopted a young boy and his little sister. Theodore and Mikayla are thrilled to be with them, but that goes both ways. I'm afraid their situation was rather grim. Their mother passed away just before the children were brought to the Williams'."

"Then it's good they have each other. I really should take the time to write to him more often."

Jesse nodded. "I'm sure he'd love to hear from you."

Thoughtful, Richard asked, "You can tell me if it's none of my business, but I'm curious. How is it that a handsome young man like yourself hasn't found himself a wife yet?"

Although the question took Jesse by surprise, he could not withhold a smile when he noted the sly grin on Rich's face. "I suppose I'm waiting for that special someone."

"Then I'll commit it to prayer."

"I appreciate that. Tell me, Pastor, do you know where I'm supposed to hang my hat for the school year?"

"I do. In fact, you have two options. I hope you won't mind, but when the school board asked my opinion about your living quarters, I suggested our home. Our children are all married and living on their own, so you would have the entire top floor to yourself. And, there is another benefit to our offer. My wife is a wonderful cook. We'd love to have you take your meals with us. Now mind you, if you decide you'd rather be on your own, Rebecca and I won't be offended. There is another place available."

Jesse grinned. "My mother would be pleased to hear that I'm not trying to survive on my own. You see, I have three sisters, so there has never been a need for me to help in the kitchen. I'm a mess without coffee in the morning, and to be honest, I have no clue as to how to make a decent pot—never mind an entire meal."

Richard chuckled. "I think most men are in the same boat. I can make a pot of coffee, but my skills end there."

"Your wife won't mind having another mouth to feed?"

"Are you kidding? Rebecca was elated when I mentioned my thoughts. She'll enjoy your company more than you know."

They turned down a side street, and Richard stopped in front of a two-story house. "This is home."

Jesse nodded and followed Richard through the gate. An array of purple flowers decorated the walkway leading to a large covered porch. Off to the right, a double swing hung from chains, and a pair of rocking chairs sat in front of the large picture window. As Rich opened the front door, a mid-sized dog, white as snow, with a large golden patch over her left eye and many more scattered across her body came out onto the porch. Her welcome came complete with a wagging tail.

Richard offered, "Rebecca told me she wanted a lap dog to keep her company while I was at work. Duchess may have been a lap dog when she came as a pup, but now she's an overgrown pest. We love her, but if you don't care for dogs, be firm and she'll leave you alone."

"Actually," Jesse admitted as he leaned down to pet Duchess, "I love dogs. My sister Elizabeth has one that would dwarf this one. Brutus weighs as much as I do."

With wide-eyed curiosity, Richard asked, "Your parents don't mind having a dog that big?"

Jesse shook his head. "Lizzy doesn't live with us. She married my good friend, Kaleb White, about three years ago. I'll have to share their story with you when we have more time."

"That would be nice." Pastor heard footsteps coming toward them, looked up and smiled as he reached for his wife's hand. "Rebecca, I'd like you to meet Frenchtown's new teacher, Jesse Somers. Jesse, this is my wife, Becky."

"It's nice to meet you, Mrs. Jamison. I can't thank you enough for your generous invitation to stay with you folks. I'm from a big family, so to be honest, I wasn't looking forward to living alone."

"Then I'm glad we made the offer. We want you to feel at home, so if you don't mind, can we dispense with the formalities. Rich and I understand that we're to call you, Mr. S, in public, but when it's just the three of us we'd prefer to be on a first name basis."

"Then Pastor and Becky it is."

She nodded and turned to her husband. "Rich, if you'll show Jesse around, I'll put dinner on the table."

"Sounds good."

Rebecca turned back to her houseguest. "Would you like lemonade, coffee, or tea?"

"If you have coffee that would be great. I'm still feeling the effects of going without this morning."

Rebecca smiled and turned to leave.

"Jesse," Rich asked as they moved up the stairs. "Am I correct in assuming your horse is at the livery?"

He nodded. "I made sure Shadow was settled in before I came by the church."

"Good."

"Is the schoolhouse here in town? I didn't notice one on the way in."

"Actually, the sanctuary doubles as a school house for now."

"I see. Do you happen to know how many students I'll have?"

"I believe the count is up to nineteen. You'll be pleased with the group. I taught for a while at the end of last year and found that the older students are willing to help the younger. Your biggest problem will be the older girls. Especially when they get a good look at their new teacher."

Jesse looked back at him and grinned. "It's strange you would bring that up. As I was leaving town yesterday morning, I helped a young woman who had fallen in the mud. I mentioned that I'd be teaching here and she made it quite clear that if I were her teacher, she'd have a hard time paying attention to her studies. I thought her comment was funny at the time, but now I'm beginning to wonder if she was warning me."

Concern etched Rich's face. "Just keep your head about you and you'll do fine. I think it's only fair to tell you—the last teacher had to be let go because he took a shine to one of his older students. Although they married and moved out of town, I wouldn't recommend falling into the same trap."

Jesse's eyes met his. "I appreciate your honesty."

Rich opened the first door they came to. "Here we are. You have three bedrooms to choose from, and there's a comfortable sitting room in the middle on the left. The kitchen is at the far end should you decide to get daring and try your hand at cooking."

Jesse shook his head. "I can almost guarantee you that won't happen. I really do appreciate you and Rebecca opening your home like this. When I know how the school board plans to pay me, we can set up payments for room and board."

"Room and board comes with the job, Jesse. As far as your pay goes, after dinner we'll head over to the bank and set up your account. I have your money for the remainder of August. If you're in agreement, on the first of every month your salary will be deposited directly into your account."

"Sounds good to me."

"I'll leave you to look around. Come and join us for dinner as soon as you're settled."

After a filling dinner, Richard and Jesse left to run a few errands. Jesse had the pleasure of meeting the banker Ted Walters, his soft-spoken wife Lois, and their two small daughters who were pleased to inform him that they would be in his class Monday morning. From there they stopped by the dry goods store. Pastor introduced him to the proprietors, Ernie Parks and his lovely wife Mary. They were members of the church and longstanding friends of the Jamison's. Their four boys would also be his students.

Pastor and Jesse were about to leave the store when a young child darted out from where he had been hiding behind a large barrel and tugged on Jesse's pant leg. He stooped down to question the frail child.

"Hello there little man is there something I can help you with?"

"Are you ... are you my new teacher, Mister?"

"I believe I am. My name is Mr. S."

The boy, appearing overwhelmed by Jesse's size and deep voice, looked as if he could use some reassurance. "You wouldn't be willing to do me a big favor on Monday, would you?"

The timid child nodded, albeit hesitantly.

"Since I'm new in town, it would help me out a great deal if you could introduce me to the other students in the class. Would you be willing to do that?"

The child turned to his mother, who had come to his side, and grinned from ear to ear. "Did you hear that, Mama? The new teacher needs my help."

His mother's eyes held a tenderness for her young son and the look she sent Jesse's way told him he had read the boy's apprehensions correctly.

"If you're going to help Mr. S, don't you think you should tell him your name?"

His little hand flew to his mouth. "Oh yes, Sir, I mean, Mr. S. My name is Jacob Adler, and this here is my mama."

"I'm glad to make your acquaintance, Mrs. Adler. Now don't forget, Jacob. I'll be counting on you, so don't be late."

"Thank you, Sir. See ya!" Jesse watched as the dark haired boy strutted out of the store clutching his mother's hand.

As they moved out of earshot, Richard said, "You certainly made his day. I don't think I've ever seen Jacob Adler so excited. He's usually quite somber."

Jesse's brow furrowed. "What would such a sweet little boy

have to be sad about?"

Rich grimaced. "Let's just say his father isn't a happy sort. He's not around very much, but when he is, he tends to make life rough for his wife and six children."

"I'm sorry to hear that."

"All I can say is continue to show him that you care. With Jacob, a kind word goes a long way."

Taking Richard's advice to heart, Jesse chose not to question him further.

❀ ❀ ❀

"Jacob Adler, would you like to come up to the front of the room and introduce me to your fellow classmates?" Jacob wasted no time coming to stand beside his new teacher.

"This is Mr. S, our new teacher. He comed all the way from Yip-c-lanti." Jesse gave Jacob a pat on the shoulder, thanked him, and watched him skip back to his seat.

When Jesse looked out over the classroom, he found eighteen sets of eyes glued to him and wondered how long it would be before they would all be working smoothly together. Realizing that much of that was up to him, he opted for an icebreaker.

"Since all of you are as curious about me as I am about you, I'll start by telling you some things about my family. When I'm through, I'd like each of you to introduce yourself and tell me something you find special about your community."

Daisytales

He Loves Me!

Chapter Three

God's Timing

HE FIRST HALF of the school year flew by in a whirl of hard work, laughter, and minimal struggles. A close bond now existed between Jesse and his students, and he was looking forward to the second semester. Although he loved teaching and all that it entailed, he missed his family terribly. Unfortunately, his plans to go home for Christmas did not look promising.

As Jesse stood staring out his bedroom window at the billowing winter storm now covering Frenchtown in a pristine white blanket, he made a decision. His family's disappointment would be as great as his, but he knew they wouldn't want him traveling in this storm. Pastor and Rebecca made it clear that he was welcome to celebrate Christmas with their family. As he moved down the stairs to take them up on their generous offer, he attempted to shake off his despairing mood.

The aroma of roasted chicken greeted his nostrils as he moved into the kitchen to find Rebecca rolling out what he assumed was pie crust.

"Can I help with anything?"

"I suppose you could set the table."

Jesse, hearing hesitancy in her voice said, "Rebecca, you're something else. You live with two men who can't toast a piece of bread without burning it, and yet you feel like you're imposing when we're the ones who offer to help."

She looked up at him and smiled. "I love what I do, Jesse. I don't see it as work."

"Well, I hope Pastor knows how blessed he is."

"I do." Rebecca and Jesse turned to find Rich standing in the frame of the kitchen door. He grinned at the surprised expressions on both faces.

"If I ever marry, I pray my wife will know your contentment, Rebecca."

"Drawing close to the Lord is the key, Jesse."

"I know."

Rich slipped his arms around his wife and kissed her cheek.

"Honey, we didn't hear you come in."

Jesse poured the coffee and joined Richard at the table, while Rebecca finished the pie she was working on.

"Since it's just the three of us, and you brought it up, would you mind my asking a personal question."

Jesse shrugged. "Ask away."

"The first day you arrived in town, you mentioned that you were desirous of finding a wife. I see you sitting with different women at church and dancing with a few at socials. Are any sparks flying?"

Jesse couldn't help but chuckle as he took in Pastor and Rebecca's inquisitive looks. "My father said I'll know when I meet the right woman, but I'm beginning to wonder if I'm doing something wrong."

"I doubt that."

"I enjoy Belinda's company, but no more than my sister's. Truth is, there's only one young lady who has ever sparked my interest."

"Can you tell us about her?"

"Do you remember me telling you about the girl I helped out of the mud?"

"Yes ... do you still think about her?"

Jesse nodded. "More often than I care to admit."

Richard's curiosity peaked, "Are you going to pursue her?"

Jesse shrugged as his hands went up. "How would I find her again? Because her face was covered with mud, her features were unclear. The town folk would have me arrested if I started going door to door asking about a woman with green eyes and long brown hair who fell in the mud last August. No," he conceded. "I need to put that whole experience behind me and see where the Lord leads."

Rich and Rebecca shared a knowing glance but remained silent.

Jesse grew quiet as well. "Suppose I don't have to fall head-over-heals for a woman to consider marrying her, but I'd like to hold some sort of a fondness for her."

"I couldn't agree more. God will lead you, Jesse; just keep an open heart."

"Most men would probably settle for a pretty face. I'm more concerned about her heart. I want a wife who loves the Lord— who shares my faith." Jesse lowered his head. After a brief pause, he looked up at Richard and winked. "Now if she happens to have a playful spirit as well, I'd count myself blessed beyond measure."

"I'm almost afraid to ask what you mean by that."

"Someone with a touch of sass. If you knew my sister Elizabeth, you'd understand why this is important to me."

Richard's brow furrowed. "The sister who married your best friend?"

When Jesse nodded, Richard added, "You never did tell us her story. Would you mind?"

"Not at all. My mother would say that Kaleb and I have been best friends since the day I was born. He's three years older than me, and Lizzy's two more years younger. She spent most of her childhood tagging along with Kaleb and me. So the three of us have always been close. Elizabeth was coming home from Ann Arbor during a whiteout when her horse got spooked and threw her. She was stranded with a broken ankle and would have died if Kaleb hadn't found her when he did. He took her to an abandoned cabin to get her warm and wait out the storm. Unfortunately, the snow fell for two days, and a week passed before he could get her home. When folks began to talk, Kaleb was willing to make her his wife, so my dad insisted that she marry him. It took her a while to adjust, but eventually she came around. They were doing well until Elizabeth became ill with her first pregnancy. Kaleb was so afraid of losing her he allowed his fears to come between them. Then, as if Elizabeth hadn't been through enough, intruders took her from their home. The injuries Kaleb sustained that day forced him to begin trusting the Lord where Elizabeth and their unborn child were concerned."

"It is unfortunate, but our trials often strengthen us in ways nothing else can. What convinced her captors to finally release her?"

"She passed out while one of the men was beating her. When she woke up the next morning, they were gone. To make a long story short, she ran into some friends of ours from Detroit. Kaleb's grandma was their neighbor at the time, so they dropped Elizabeth off at his grandma's house and sent the letter Lizzy had written to Kaleb explaining her whereabouts. Needless to say, Kaleb and I were on our way to Detroit right after he received the letter. Lizzy's something else. When Kaleb told her he wanted to see her marred back, she asked him not to look at her wounds with anger in his heart. She wanted him to see them as she did—the price of freedom for her and their unborn child. The men who took her planned to sell her to a man who owns a string of bordellos."

Tears were streaming down Rebecca's face when she asked, "The baby wasn't harmed in any way, was he?"

"No, Cameron is fine."

Rich wondered, "How did all this affect their marriage?"

"Healing began from the minute they were reunited. Lizzy's ability to find the good in every trial she went through is what impressed me the most."

Rebecca said, "She sounds like a remarkable young woman."

"She is. Not perfect by any means, but a true testament of

what God can do in our hearts if we allow Him. So, you can see why I'd like the woman I marry to have a bit of my sister's spirit."

Rich nodded. "God knows the desires of our heart, Jesse. Be patient. Wait on Him. In His time He will open that door."

December 1830

"Olivia," Pierre asked as he slipped his heavy overcoat on and wrapped his scarf around his neck, "I'd like to escort you home and join your family for tea today. Would you mind?"

Her smile exclaimed her pleasure. "I'd like that. Can you give me a minute? I need to say goodbye to Nicole. We won't see each other until after the holiday."

Olivia was looking forward to having time to pamper her ailing parents. They both had terrible colds and their coughing spells were growing worse all the time. Although the doctor had been out on several occasions, nothing seemed to be helping. She could understand her parents' desire to guard her from the truth, but the days of being coddled were over. She fully intended to have a heart-to-heart talk with her father over the Christmas break.

"Are you ready, Pierre?"

He nodded, smiling attentively as he offered his arm.

Olivia had noticed Pierre Beaudette casting his big brown eyes her way on several occasions and today was no different. He was acting a bit strange, and while she wondered what he had on his mind, she didn't question him. Her father had made it clear that he did not approve of Pierre because of their religious differences. While she agreed with her father, she saw no harm in being Pierre's friend. If only he wasn't so handsome. In truth, she found him difficult to resist. "So tell me, Pierre, what are your plans for the holiday?" He took her by surprise when he captured her hand.

"I suppose that depends on your father's response to what I need to speak with him about."

"Oh?" Olivia racked her brain for what that might be. Although she knew what her father would say to any request Pierre would make, she did not have the heart to tell him. Besides, what could he possibly want? Perhaps there was a party coming up that he wanted to take her to, or a dance. She could only pray that her father would know a moment of weakness and allow him to escort her this one time. Curious as to why he evaded her question, she pressed him further. "You didn't tell me, Pierre, how does your family plan to celebrate the holiday?"

"We're going to Canada to see my grandparents."

"How exciting. Will you be home in time for school to resume?" They were walking up the snow-covered trail to her home when he dodged her question again.

"Since we're already here, let me speak with your father and then we'll go over the details of our trip."

The way he said 'our' made it sound like he was talking about the two of them—not his family. Thinking she heard him wrong, she let it pass. Her father must have seen them coming up the path and opened the door to greet them.

"Thank you for walking my Olivia home, Pierre. I hope you have a nice holiday."

She couldn't understand why her father was so rude to him. She knew he wasn't feeling well, but that had never stopped him from inviting her friends in for refreshments. "Papa, I invited

Pierre to stay for tea. He has something he'd like to talk to you about."

"Very well. Go to the kitchen and start the water while I speak with him, Olivia." After hanging Pierre's coat and hat from the hook, Josiah led him to the sitting room.

"Have a seat, Pierre."

"Thank you, Sir."

"Now," Josiah said as he sat down on the couch and looked up at Pierre, "what can I do for you, Young Man?"

Pierre squirmed just a bit, cleared his throat, and began, "I know this is short notice, but my family is moving back to Canada by week's end, and I'll be going with them. My grandparents were aware of my reluctance to return to Canada, so they sweetened the draw by offering me a plot of land with a small house on it and enough funds to get me off to a good start." He hesitated for a moment before continuing, "I think you know that I'm very fond of your daughter, Sir."

Josiah was not aware of his fondness, but he allowed him to continue.

"I am here to ask you for Olivia's hand in marriage."

Josiah, stunned by his inquiry, took a moment to collect his thoughts. "I can appreciate your interest in my daughter, Pierre. She has mentioned that you're good friends, but I would never consent to a union between the two of you."

His brow furrowed. "Can I ask why?"

"You're barely sixteen, am I right?"

"I don't see what that has to do with anything. I am capable of supporting Olivia in a manner to which she's accustomed."

"I don't doubt that you are, but as her father, I have other things to consider. To begin with, Olivia has never mentioned holding a fondness for you, and secondly, I would never encourage her to enter into a union with a man who does not share her faith."

"I see ...."

The expression on Pierre's face told Josiah he did not. Well aware of Olivia's emotional state, Josiah was convinced she should marry someone stable—someone more mature—someone who could help her through the grief she would soon face. "If you're truly seeking a wife, I will pray for you, but let me assure you, Olivia is not the woman for you."

Disappointment filled Pierre's eyes. "I can't say that I agree with you, Sir, but I can see that your mind is made up. Would you allow me to say my farewells to your daughter?"

Josiah nodded. "Go ahead and join her in the kitchen." Josiah wasn't feeling well, so he excused himself and went to lay down with his wife, who's health seemed to be getting worse every day.

Pierre joined Olivia for tea, but out of respect for her father, he never mentioned his offer of marriage. He did tell her that he and his family would be moving, and while she said she would miss seeing him at school, she did not seem greatly affected by his news.

As Pierre walked away from the Ordan's home, he had an assurance that things turned out as they should have. *Olivia's father must know her well. She didn't shed a single tear over my leaving.*

❀ ❀ ❀

"Papa," Olivia inquired after he prayed over their evening meal, "Mama's been in bed for a week now, and you aren't doing much better. I know you're keeping the truth from me so I won't worry, but it's not working. I'm a grown woman, Papa. I need to hear the truth, no matter how hard it is to take."

Josiah, taken aback by his daughter's insight, had planned to tell her after they spent their last Christmas together. But her persistence told him the time had come. Maryse's health was failing fast. He would need to help Olivia work through her uncertainties before they would have to part.

"You're right, Olivia, we have been keeping the truth from you. I'm afraid that outside of a miracle, your mother and I don't have much time left. Doctor Tower has tried every remedy he knows and nothing seems to be helping. I've learned of a sanatorium that specializes in caring for those afflicted with this disease. Doctor Towers is hopeful they will know more than he does. If nothing else, they'll be able to make us more comfortable in our final days. I know this will be hard for you to accept, but when the time comes for us to leave, Olivia, you won't be going with us."

"What?" Olivia burst into tears.

As much as Josiah's heart was breaking for her, he and Maryse had discussed this at length. They were convinced there was no other way for her to move on with life.

"I won't leave you and Mama ... I can't ...."

Josiah's hand came up to caress her damp cheek. "When the time comes, your mother and I are at peace with going home to be with the Lord. Before that happens, we have every intention of seeing you happily wed."

She sobered quickly on this announcement. "What are you talking about? I haven't even met anyone I'd consider marrying."

"You leave all that up to me, Olivia." Josiah patted her hand, trying to reassure her.

"Papa, you can't ask me to share my life with a man I don't know."

"Honey, come here and let me hold you." Although she complied without hesitation, this time her father's arms held no comfort.

In a moment of weakness, Josiah wondered if he should have accepted Pierre's offer. However, the thought had no more crossed his mind when he reminded himself that God's peace flows from obedience to His leading. Josiah had to believe he would know when the right man came along.

"You're hurting, Olivia. As much as I'd like to take this from you, you're going to have to lean on your faith. God will be with you. Just take His hand and allow Him to lead you through. We don't always understand why things happen, but God does. He sees the greater picture. He loves you more than anyone else ever could."

"But I need you and Mama too ...."

"Your Mother and I won't always be with you physically, but the memories of our times together will remain in our hearts."

"I know that, Papa." As hard as it was, Olivia made a conscious effort to pull herself together. This had to be as difficult for her parents as it was for her. How could she add to their despair? "Did Doctor Tower say when?"

"That depends on how we do this winter. Traveling in cold weather would be hard on your mother. We'll try to wait until spring."

The severity of her parents' illness plagued her. As she

began to realize how much her life could change over the next few months, she spoke her thoughts aloud. "A husband, Papa? I don't know if I'm ready to be married. I won't be sixteen until September. What kind of man would take such a young wife?"

The uncertainty in her soft green eyes was disheartening. "We don't want you worrying about this. I have a plan to find you a wonderful husband. One who shares our faith. I need you to trust me in this, Olivia. Concentrate on learning all you can from your mother. And, by all means, enjoy the time we have left together."

"I'll try," she said as another onslaught of tears spilled down her cheeks. "Forgive me, Papa. I can't promise I won't struggle with this."

"That's to be expected. Just remember what Pastor Olsen is always telling us: God's timing is not our own—be anxious for nothing, Livia."

Chapter Four

Divine Appointment

1831

*J*ESSE STOOD IN front of the students he had poured so much of himself into over the last year. Their final day was coming to a close. Recalling an article he had read in the *Sentinel Newspaper* that morning, he said in closing, "For those of you who haven't heard, the Governor of the Michigan Territory, Lewis Cass, is expecting a visit from President Monroe any day now. In honor of the president, the governor will be changing the name of Frenchtown to Monroe." The children's excitement over having this news confirmed, diverted their attention, making their final parting so much easier.

Jesse had received a letter from his father, requesting that he be home by harvest time. The spells his father had been having with his heart were coming more frequently, and Doctor Taylor was insisting that he slow down as much as possible. Jared and Joseph could handle the planting season without him, so he encouraged Jesse to take his time coming home.

Although Jesse was disappointed to be going home without a wife, he was not discouraged. The year had given him the time he needed to grow in the Lord. Having the opportunity to truly give of himself to others, not only in his classroom but in the community as well, had changed him. The Jamisons had become his good friends, and knowing them had broadened his vision. With greater clarity Jesse could see that the various seasons we walk through in life help us to grow into individuals God can use. He didn't need to know where the Lord would lead him from here. Just knowing that God has a purpose for every experience, good or bad, eased his heart as nothing else could.

Richard had stopped by his classroom earlier in the day and asked Jesse to meet with him after school. Jesse, assuming his pastor was only curious about his plans, ambled into Richard's office, greeted him, and slumped into the extra chair.

Pastor picked a letter up from his desk, handed it to Jesse, and offered a heartwarming smile. "I received this in today's post and immediately thought of you. Pastor Olsen is a good friend of mine. We've actually spoken about your desire to find a wife, so I'm sure that's why he forwarded this letter on to me. You need to understand that although Pastor Olsen sent this, the young woman's father, Mr. Ordan, wrote it."

"Is it for me?"

"Not specifically ... I don't want you thinking that because I'm sharing this with you, I'm suggesting anything. God will lead you, Jesse, but I will say this: I've prayed about it and I feel relieved knowing you have this letter.

Jesse's curiosity was peaked as his eyes fell on the written words.

Dear Pastor,

This letter comes to you with a heavy but hopeful heart. My wife and I have been suffering with an illness for some time now, and our doctor has encouraged us to leave our home in Tecumseh in order to seek further medical help. Although we are at peace with doing as he suggested, the thought of leaving our daughter alone is unbearable. As much as we would love to be with her during the time we have left, doing so would not be in her best interest. Our greatest desire is to see her married and starting a new life before we begin our journey. With that in mind, I am prayerfully sending out this inquiry.

If you know of a young Christian gentleman seeking a wife, please contact Pastor Olsen in Tecumseh to set up a meeting with me. Thank you for any help you can offer in this matter. Please understand there is urgency in our request as my wife's health is failing fast.

In Christ,

Mr. Ordan

"You look surprised, Jesse. What are you thinking?"
He looked up at his friend and said without an ounce of

hesitation, "I'm not sure why, but I've got to go."

"Would you like me to write to Pastor Olsen?"

He shook his head. "That won't be necessary, but ... if you're willing to write a letter of introduction that I can take with me, it could be useful. Would you mind helping me pack so that I can leave right away?"

"Not at all."

"I hate to run off in such a hurry, but I feel strongly that I must. The long ride will give me time to pray."

"I understand. Listen, Jesse, you head over to the bank and close out your account. I'll go home and have Rebecca pack up some food before I head over to the livery to get Shadow ready. I'll meet you back at the house. I couldn't agree with you more about the urgency. Just promise you'll write and let us know how you're doing. Rebecca and I will pray that all goes as it should."

"I can't thank you enough for the special times we've had together."

"Trust me, Jesse, it goes both ways."

In stunned silence Olivia Ordan walked out of the home she had shared with her parents for most of her life. Sinking into the swing on her front porch, she began to rethink the events in her young life leading up to the conversation she had with her father only moments before. Neither the familiar creaking of the swing in motion nor the calmness of the sunny spring morn eased her overwhelming feelings of hopelessness and despair.

If only she had listened. Her parents had tried to tell her the day would come—the day when they would be forced to leave her.

Like a giddy child, she had refused to believe it would ever come to pass, clinging to the hope that by some miracle they would get well. She understood the extent of their illness, lived with it every day. But losing them? How could she prepare herself for this? It was all too much for her to endure.

Her father informed her that he had sent out letters to neighboring churches asking if there were any young Christian men seeking to take a wife. *Oh, Papa!* she wondered, *what were you thinking? Don't you see how terribly humiliating this is? I feel like a prize to be awarded to the best available contender.*

Despite her uncertainties, she could appreciate her parents' reasons for wanting to see her wed. They were all she had in this world. Facing this loss on her own would be horrible. She didn't doubt that. But how could she find comfort in the arms of a man she had never met? It all seemed so unreal. As reality took root, she refused to give in to her spiraling emotions. Her parents' welfare had to be her first concern. She would do nothing to add to their grief—even agreeing to a loveless marriage—if doing so would give them peace.

Her Papa told her that on Saturday he had spent most of his morning with a young man he was confident would be perfect for her. "I invited Jesse Somers to join us for dinner. Mama and I will share a meal with the two of you, but I would like you and Jesse to spend some time alone, so you can get to know each other. Doctor Tower was here yesterday. Honey, he made it clear that if we don't leave right away, the long journey will be too much for your mother. The last thing I want to do is pressure you into making a decision, but I've checked into passages. The next available transportation isn't for two more weeks. You know we can't wait that long. If you decide after spending the day with Jesse that you could share your life with him, Pastor Olsen will marry you in the morning."

Her tortured mind was still screaming for answers. *Papa, how can I marry a man I don't know? You said he's been looking for a wife for some time. Surely that could only mean one thing: he's a sorry sight to behold!*

Father God, give me the strength I'll need to get through this. I know You're in control in spite of my wavering faith. Help me to accept what I cannot change.

Her father went on, and she knew that his heart was breaking, "Olivia, leaving you will be one of the hardest things we've ever had to do. I wish that time was on our side, but you know it's not. To drag this out would only make our leaving that much more difficult. Knowing you'll be starting a new life with a young man who has a relationship with the Lord will greatly ease our minds. We need you to trust us this one last time."

Olivia, seeing the pain in her parents' eyes, could not deny them this last request. She had to believe that God would sustain her through this dreadful time and give her the strength to carry on.

Life as she knew it would change forever—tomorrow. Her parents loved her. She could only hope that her father, in choosing a husband for her, thought about more than the words that came out of Jesse's mouth.

Olivia sat up, dried her tears, pulled her shoulders back, and came to a firm resolution—sitting on the porch and fretting about this impossible situation was not going to change a thing. She needed to go back in the house, make herself look presentable, and create a meal that might be pleasing to this man her father would like her to call *husband*.

Olivia was putting the finishing touches on dinner when she heard a knock at the door. Her heart fluttered and then sped out of control. Her father turned to her, offering a reassuring smile as he went to welcome their guest. She remained in the kitchen long enough to start the coffee and to give her thundering heart a chance to ease.

Earlier her father had said that he would take Jesse straight to the sitting room to join her mother. Olivia could come when she was ready. Would she ever be ready? Everything within her told her to leave this house and run for her life, but she refused to give in to desperation, or fear. As impossible as her situation was, curiosity propelled her feet forward. For a long moment she stood just out of sight, entranced by the depth of this stranger's voice.

Olivia checked her appearance in the hall mirror one last time. She had decided on the soft yellow calico, and wisps of her long brown hair were pulled back with a matching ribbon. This dress, she knew it was her father's favorite, and today she wanted to please him.

She had no more peeked around the corner when she quickly withdrew. What she saw stilled the flow of blood through her veins. *How can this be?* There was no mistaking the identity of this tall handsome man who dwarfed her mother's rocking chair. *Does he know who I am? Papa, do you know who he is?* Olivia, after a moment's consideration answered her own questions. *Of course not, how could they?*

A smile lit her face. *What a wonderfully odd twist of fate!* The words had no more run through her brain when she corrected her thought, *This is not fate, Olivia—this is divine appointment!*

Her heart leapt. *My, but he's a sight to behold!* His long jean-clad legs stretched on for miles, and the cream shirt he wore accented his tanned skin. Given the chance, Olivia was sure she could lose herself in those glorious blue eyes. After a moment's contemplation, she thought it best to keep their prior introduction to herself—at least for now.

Her eyes slid shut. *If this is Your way of comforting me, Lord, I thank You, it's working well. I know You love me, but I never would have thought You'd go to this extreme.* Taking a deep breath, she took the next step. Seconds ticked by as she stood, unnoticed, in the frame of the parlor door.

Jesse fidgeted with the black wide-brimmed hat on his lap as his thoughts questioned, *Where is she?* Josiah had introduced his wife. But while Jesse enjoyed chatting with the frail woman, his anxious mind found it difficult to concentrate on what they were saying. In fact, their words became a blur. The mysterious young woman he had heard so much about held his thoughts captive.

Olivia's expression when she first laid eyes on Jesse was all that Josiah and Maryse could have hoped for and then some. They didn't miss the way Jesse kept glancing at the entrance. His eagerness to meet their daughter pleased them. Their gaze was fixed on Jesse when he caught his first glimpse of their Olivia.

Jesse's mouth turned up at the corners as he stood, hoping against hope that this lovely young woman with the twinkling green eyes was indeed Olivia.

Josiah, sensing their runaway thoughts, rose to make the formal introductions.

"Jesse Somers, we would like you to meet our daughter,

Olivia Ordan."

Without hesitation, Jesse reached for the slender hand she so graciously offered and brought it slowly to his lips for a fleeting kiss. "It's a pleasure to meet you, Miss Ordan." Her timid smile warmed his heart.

"I'm pleased to meet you as well, Mr. Somers."

Olivia and Jesse, all too aware of the reason for their introduction, held each other's gaze, as if searching for answers to the questions running through their heads.

Josiah and Maryse shared a knowing glance, thrilled with the obvious attraction. Josiah made a suggestion. "Since dinner is ready, why don't we move to the kitchen so we can get better acquainted."

Olivia gladly took the arm Jesse offered, and Josiah did the same for his wife. Maryse had not been out of bed in days, and while her weakness concerned him, Josiah understood that she wouldn't have missed this meeting for the world.

When the circle of hands were joined around the table, Josiah returned thanks.

After the food had been passed, Jesse looked at Olivia and asked, "Has your father told you much about me, Olivia?"

"He hasn't had time ... you could tell me."

Jesse nodded. He was about to speak when the kettle boiled and Olivia stood to make the tea. After filling her mother's cup and then her own, Olivia returned to where she had been seated next to Jesse on the bench. Reaching for the butter, her arm brushed softly against his. Strange sensations fluttered through her as their eyes met.

Jesse could not look away from the woman beside him. His

heart soared as the realization struck him. *She could be my wife within days!*

Forcing himself to look away, Jesse stuck a forkful of tender pork into his mouth and savored its flavor. He needed a moment to regain control of his scattered thoughts. After several sips of coffee, he turned back to Olivia. "About a year ago I left my home in Ypsilanti to take a position in Frenchtown. I received a note from my father last week. He's having spells with his heart, so he'll be counting on me to be home in time for fall harvest. My pastor was aware of my desire to find a wife and didn't hesitate to share your father's letter with me."

Olivia nodded, thinking, *This is so awkward.*

"If we do agree to marry, we'll be moving to Ypsilanti within a couple of months, Olivia. You might like to know that I have a very large family ...."

Her timid eyes rose to meet his deep blue gaze.

Sensing her unease, he tried to reassure her, "They'll welcome you with open arms, Olivia."

"Jesse," Josiah explained, "Olivia didn't know about the letter I sent out until today. She wasn't even aware of our meeting."

"I see."

"I told you on Saturday that my wife and I would be moving on as soon as possible. I've done some checking, and I'm afraid the only ship that will grant us passage in the next two weeks leaves tomorrow. If the two of you decide you're willing to commit to this union, Pastor will perform the nuptials in the morning. Immediately following, we'll be taking the stage to the waterfront."

Jesse turned back to Olivia and for a while just watched her. When she met his gaze, he said, "I understand that we'll need time to get to know each other, but I would have to know you're as committed to this union going into it as I am. I want a real marriage, Olivia. If you're not ready to make this kind of commitment, you should say so before we proceed any further."

Olivia lowered her head in thought.

He didn't wish to discourage her, but ...

Her eyes, filled with apprehension rose to meet his hopeful gaze. "I'm well aware of the huge commitment marriage involves, so you can rest assured, Mr. Somers, I would never enter into this lightly. I ... I won't lie to you. The thought of entrusting my life to a complete stranger frightens me, but my father speaks very highly of you. Knowing he has always been a good judge of character gives me a measure of comfort. We would both be taking a step in faith ... but, isn't that the life God has called us to?"

"Yes, He has." Jesse couldn't have been more pleased with her response. He didn't know why, but he was drawn to Olivia—drawn in ways he found difficult to grasp. A peace about moving forward settled over him.

Jesse, recognizing that time was of the essence, looked to her parents. "If Olivia is willing, I'd like us to spend some time alone, talking. Would you object to my taking your daughter for a walk?"

Josiah nodded his agreement.

As Josiah and Maryse watched their only child walk out the door, their thoughts held a mixture of joy and sadness. Inasmuch as they wanted this for Olivia, actually letting her go would test their faith as nothing ever had before. They had to believe that God would give them the strength they'd need to walk through what was sure to be the hardest day of their lives.

He Loves Me!

Chapter Five

A Bit of a Tease

A RUSH OF UNFETTERED SENSATIONS transfused her body and soul as Jesse led Olivia down the street toward the open field just outside of town. Not a single cloud cluttered the clear blue sky, and the beautiful spring day warmed her in ways she found difficult to define. It was as if God Himself were smiling down on them and offering His promise of new beginnings—not only for the blooming foliage, but for Olivia and Jesse as well.

Jesse, irrepressibly drawn to Olivia's profile, smiled as he recalled the description he had given his sister a few years back of the woman he would like to marry. Olivia was all that and more. From the shimmering red highlights in her light brown hair, to her tall willowy frame that moved along with the grace of a dancer in motion. He reveled in her soft smile and youthful beauty.

In a moment of boldness, Jesse reached out and captured

Olivia's hand. While he had no wish to frighten her, her deepening flush and her tremble at his touch told him that he had. He understood her apprehensions, his own heart thudded to the beat of an unfamiliar drum, but he could not release her.

"Olivia, forgive my forwardness. Will you allow me to explain?"

In her reluctance to look his way, she offered a hesitant nod.

"We barely know each other, yet tomorrow we could be saying vows that will join us as husband and wife. I, well, I just thought it would be comforting to know each other's touch. Do you mind?"

"No ..." she conceded as her gaze fell on his oversized hand. "It's just that you surprised me."

Jesse, growing uncomfortable with the silence that hung between them, said, "I've been open to taking a wife for some time, Olivia, but it wasn't until I met a rather delightful young woman on my way through your town almost a year ago that I gained a truer picture of what I was looking for in a wife."

Swallowing hard past the lump in her throat, she asked, "Is there a reason you didn't pursue a relationship with her?"

"It was only a brief meeting. I came to her aid after she fell ...."

Olivia fought to contain a smile. The deceitfulness of her silence pricked her conscience, but she had her reasons for not exposing herself.

"Her selfless spirit left a lasting impression on me. I'm finding more and more that God brings people together—sometimes under the *oddest* circumstances—to encourage and help each other. While this young woman made it clear that she appreciated my help, she lifted my spirits as well."

"I see ...."

"Do you? If you decide to become my wife, I want you to know that I will do all that I can to help you through this difficult time." Although he could clearly see that she was struggling, he didn't know her well enough to say more. When she squeezed his hand, her wordless response eased his concerns.

"I know this is kind of sudden, but I'm curious. Do you think there's a chance you could spend your life with a homely wheat farmer from Ypsilanti?"

His distorted expression made her giggle. She gave him her undivided attention as he continued.

"In all fairness, I should warn you. With you being a city girl and all, you'll have to put up with some heckling from my siblings until you learn the ropes."

Olivia really didn't think that would be a problem. *Who knows*, she thought, *maybe being a part of a big family will keep me so busy I won't have time to dwell on my loss.* She refused to contemplate all that she would face tomorrow. If she allowed herself to fully process her circumstances, thoughts of tomorrow's separations would prevent her from considering all that Jesse was offering.

When the silence lengthened, he wondered if his comment worried Olivia. Her solemn expression prompted him to add, "There is no question in my mind that my family will love you, Olivia."

Her long lashes, dampened by tears, swept up. "How can you be so sure?"

"I know my family."

"But you don't know me, and neither do they."

His sudden laughter startled her. "Your father and I spent several hours together on Saturday. I'm afraid I have you at a disadvantage."

"Oh?"

"Yes! I learned much about you while you know so little about me. Your father shared many of your strengths and some of your weaknesses. At times I got the impression he was trying to shock me. You know, see if I'd jump on my horse and high tail it out of town? I assured him that I have younger sisters. Elizabeth is very much like the young woman your father described. Trust me, Olivia, after growing up with Lizzy at my side, there is little you could do that would truly surprise me."

"I don't know J ... um, Mr. Somers."

"Olivia, please call me Jesse."

The thought of calling a teacher by his first name amused her. Then she reminded herself that teaching was no longer his profession. He may be a farmer from Ypsilanti, but homely? There was nothing homely about this man. Since he could be her husband tomorrow, she made an attempt to let down her guard and be more at ease in his presence. As they continued to walk and converse, some of her anxieties dissipated. *Besides*, she kept telling herself, *Papa wouldn't steer me wrong—he loves me too much!*

"Having siblings is only something I've dreamed about. My parents talked about having other children ... it just wasn't meant to be."

A gust of wind swept Olivia's hair across her face. She didn't so much as flinch when Jesse reached to put her silky lengths to rights before releasing them behind her. He recaptured her hand, and they moved on as if they had been courting for weeks and nothing were out of the ordinary.

"A few hours ago my father told me that he had met with a very special young man last Saturday and that he was convinced I could share my life with this man. As if that weren't enough to digest, he went on to say that you would arrive in time for dinner. You had barely arrived when you were informed that should we come to an agreement, we will marry in the morning—the same morning I will say goodbye to my parents for the rest of my life." Olivia made no attempt to look away when tears flowed down her cheeks with great abandon. "I understand their wisdom in not telling me before now, but I may never understand why they're being taken from me. They've suffered so much, Jesse. I could never add to their suffering by challenging Papa's advice. My father has never given me cause not to trust him, so I will do as he asks, provided you are in agreement. I'm not sure why a handsome man like you, who could probably have any number of women, would want to marry a complete stranger, but I believe God has His hand in all of this."

Olivia's tears were almost Jesse's undoing. He would love to take her in his arms and somehow ease her mind, but he held himself at bay. His actions could frighten her and add to her despair.

"I want to trust you, really I do. I'm willing to accept all this marriage will bring, yet I'm frightened. Tomorrow will bring with it so many changes. I'm not sure how … I'm not sure how I'll hold up."

"I understand … I will be there for you."

"I don't doubt your sincerity, but I'm not sure you do understand."

He looked confused.

As humiliating as it was, she lowered her gaze and tried to explain. "Marriage is a big step for me. We don't know each other, and in truth ... the thought of intimacy with a stranger, well ... it's ... it's a bit scary." Timidly, she admitted, "I've never even had a beau, my father wouldn't allow it."

"I see ...."

Do you?

She was so sweet, yet so incredibly vulnerable. *Father, am I wrong to want ... a real marriage?* He didn't think so, but if he truly believed that love was not self-seeking and expected nothing in return, he would have to love her and leave all else in the Lord's hands. Glancing her way, Jesse sensed Olivia's struggle. He had to say something, anything that would alleviate her fears. Patience had never been one of his stronger suits. *Perhaps this is part of what marriage is all about. Thinking of her needs above my own.* As hard as it was to speak the words, he saw no other way. "Olivia, you're going to have enough to deal with over the next few days. I see no need for us to rush into anything."

Her eyes shot up. "You don't ...." Her puzzled expression made him chuckle.

"No, I don't. I'm hoping we can spend a month or two at the trapper's cabin my father and his friends go to. We'll both need time to get to know each other before sharing the intimate side of marriage."

"But you said ..."

"I know what I said. I've never done this before. Some things cannot be written in stone. This union's not just about me—it's about us."

Though strengthened by his offer, she didn't know how to respond. His reaction told her much about Jesse's character. As she glanced his way she realized this was awkward for both of them. "Would you be willing to give me a week or so?" A month is what she had in mind, but compromise needed to go both ways.

"Absolutely!"

She breathed a huge sigh of relief, until she heard that three-letter-word.

"But ..."

Without giving him a chance to finish, sparks flew in her mind. "You either will or you won't. Don't tell me you're willing to wait and then change your mind!"

He actually had the audacity to smile—chuckle was more like it.

When she opened her mouth to call him on it, he spoke. His consoling tone soothed her fretful mind.

"When you have the time to get to know me, you'll learn that I strive to be a man of my word. I can't promise that I'll never change my mind. But in this, Olivia, you can rest assured. What I was trying to say is that there is only one bed in the cabin."

"Oh ..."

"And ..."

"And ... what?" Her flush deepened.

His cheeks warmed as well. "I come from a long line of huggers, Liv, and I can't guarantee that I won't try to steal a kiss from time to time."

She wasn't too sure about the kissing part, but hugs weren't so bad. What choice did she have? These seemed to be his terms, take it or leave it. Staring into his big blue eyes, she conceded, to a degree, "I suppose, I'm used to hugs ...."

What about kisses? He would have asked, but she grew pensive as her eyes fell on the distant field.

A flock of mallards flew overhead before landing in the marshy pond—the same pond where she had fished with her father on numerous occasions. As cherished memories transfused her mind, she wondered, *Will my memories fade as quickly as my parents' lives are fading, or will they forever give me something to look back on?*

Jesse, sensing her despondency, said nothing for a time. He was content to watch this delicate lady who walked beside him hand in hand, as if doing so were an everyday occurrence, and they were both right where they belonged. *Does she feel as I do? Have I found her, Lord? Is this the woman I'm to share my life with? Please let it be so.* Jesse was captivated by the way her long flowing tresses curled up at the ends and flounced against the backdrop of her slender frame. Her pale yellow calico dress enhanced the green of her luminous eyes, and her cute little nose turned up ever so slightly at the end, giving emphasis to her plucky disposition.

He smiled as he recalled the way her stubborn chin went right in the air the moment she thought he would renege on his agreement. No doubt she would hold him accountable, and he saw this as a good thing. Even in her troubled state, she didn't hesitate to give him a piece of her mind. He could be sure, life with Olivia would hold its challenges, but the thought of facing them thrilled his soul.

Olivia was awed by the way Jesse's long legs stretched across the path. He had to be holding back his stride, or even she at five-eight would be struggling to keep up. For almost a year, she had thought about this man, hoping against hope that she would see him again. Never in her wildest dreams did she imagine that her Mr. S would be her arranged husband. Laced through hers, his long fingers had not relinquished their firm hold. The slight curve of his thick lips exemplified the kind-spirited man he had shown her thus far. Was he being himself? Or was it a pretense to gain her approval? She thought not.

Feeling her intense gaze, Jesse looked her way. Their eyes collided and held, as if trying to decide what a future together would hold. They were growing more at ease with one another. Although at times Jesse's thoughts were scattered, his determination to proceed was crystal clear.

The afternoon air had cooled immensely by the time Jesse and Olivia turned back toward the town of Tecumseh. They had been walking for hours. Awkward or not, they needed to continue chatting if they were going to come to a decision that could alter both of their lives, forever. With their future in the forefront of his mind, Jesse brought up what he thought would be a lighter topic. "Olivia, I was twenty-one on April tenth, how old are you?"

Her scrunched expression made him smile, but she was hesitant to answer and that concerned him.

"I'll be sixteen on September seventh."

"Wow! I was going to say eighteen or nineteen. Fifteen you say? Are you sure you're ready for this kind of commitment?"

Olivia wasn't surprised by his reaction; she expected it. In truth she was hoping to avoid the subject altogether, but he did have a right to know. "I'm sure we both have insecurities, Jesse. Mine have little to do with the actual commitment. I suppose you will have to decide if you can keep up with such a young wife during your advanced years."

The tender smile that brightened Jesse's face was reassuring. "What you lack in years, you make up for in fortitude. Since you'll need that quality to mellow out this old man, I suppose I'll take my chances. Truth is, I'm glad you haven't had time to get too set in your ways."

A single brow arched. "I'm not so sure that's true, but I am open to change. I do have a *few* qualities you might find advantageous."

"By all means fill me in."

"I've been told I'm an excellent cook, so you won't starve. I am quite handy with a needle and other household chores. But, it is only fair to warn you that I know nothing about farming. In fact, I've never even ridden a horse alone." She held her breath, wondering what he would say.

"That shouldn't be a problem as long as you're willing to learn."

"Please! Anxious would be more like it." Her enthusiasm tickled him.

"How do you feel about having children ... some day?" Jesse casually inquired.

"Fine."

Her short response and deepening flush kept him from pushing further. Besides, they were almost to the edge of town, and Jesse had noticed a patch of daisies in full bloom. He released her hand just long enough to pick a bouquet.

Emotions she had never before felt swirled inside her as Jesse came toward her, offering his gift of flowers. He dropped to one knee in front of her and reached to reclaim her hand. For a long moment she lost herself in his tender gaze.

"Olivia Ordan, I believe God has brought two people together who desperately need each other. I long to take a wife, and you need a husband. If you would do me the honor of becoming my wife, with God's help, I will cherish you all the days of my life. Will you marry me?"

Olivia's glassy jade eyes sparkled like precious jewels. "Are you sure?"

"Positive!"

"Then yes, Jesse Somers, I will marry you."

Leaping to his feet, he held on to her shoulders and stared straight into her eyes. He asked again, just to be certain. "You will?"

"Yes!"

"Tomorrow morning you'll become Mrs. Jesse Cameron Somers?"

Olivia nodded, and as she did a wave of happiness flooded her soul. She had so many reasons to be sad, but becoming Jesse's wife didn't have to be one of them. Hope was renewed as her knight in shining armor lost all control. Sweeping her off the ground, he joyfully swung her around and around. Laughing in delight, they shared this enchanted moment, holding onto one another with expectancy in their hearts.

It was with great reluctance that Jesse set her down. When he looked up, Mr. and Mrs. Ordan were standing on their front porch, and Jesse was sure they had witnessed their entire exchange. The swell of uncertainty that struck him dissolved into thankfulness as a peaceful elation filled their tear-drenched faces. It was a picture he would never forget. Knowing their daughter would be loved and cared for meant the world to them.

Jesse and Olivia joined her parents on the porch and plans were set for the following day. Since Jesse had already checked into the boarding house, he would stay there for the night. A team and wagon would have to be purchased so Olivia could bring furniture and other treasures from her childhood into her new life with him.

Jesse agreed to come back early in the morning to pack up Olivia's belongings before the ceremony which was scheduled for ten o'clock.

Sensing that Jesse would like to have a moment alone with their daughter, Josiah took Maryse by the hand, said their farewells, and went into the house.

Jesse pulled Olivia to her feet, slid his hands around her slender waist and drew her to him. Her nearness was having a wonderfully strange effect on him. While he relished her closeness, she seemed to be leery of her position. He wondered if stealing a kiss would intensify her discomfort, but he had to try. As his long fingers trailed slowly down her face his eyes beheld her comeliness.

She licked her lips, unsure of his intent and growing more uncomfortable with each passing second.

Every nerve in his body came alive as he leaned in to claim her sweet lips—a split second more and they would be his—except she turned her head and willingly offered her cheek instead.

Jesse sent her a lighthearted wink before releasing her

with his assurance that he would see her bright and early the next morning.

He couldn't help but chuckle as he strutted down the street. It would seem that his fiancé was a bit of a tease. "Yes!" he exclaimed as he kicked up his heals. *Very soon, Olivia, you'll be mine indeed!*

Olivia giggled out loud as she witnessed his elation, knowing that while she evaded his kiss this night, Jesse Cameron Somers would not be denied for long.

He Loves Me!

Chapter Six

Sorrow Into Joy

*J*ESSE AND OLIVIA stood before Pastor Olsen with a small cluster of caring friends who had come to witness this monumental moment in their lives. All, including her parents, had gone out of their way to try and make this marriage ceremony a joyous occasion, but the awareness of the Ordan family's impending separation prevailed. How could it not?

Mildred, Pastor's wife, had the voice of an angel, so when she stood to sing, a soothing presence settled over the small gathering. Even Jesse was held captive by her exquisite resonance, and Olivia was thankful for the reprieve.

The magnitude of what Olivia was about to do weighed heavily on her mind. Before glancing at her betrothed, her eyes fell on the lovely bouquet Jesse had picked for her earlier that morning. His distraction gave her a moment to really look at him without feeling self-conscious or rude. There was so much about this man she didn't know. Could she love and honor him the way a wife should? She had to believe that in time she would. For now she would have to trust in the Lord and not try to lean on her own understanding—because she didn't understand. Perhaps she never would.

Your Word says that You do everything right and on time. It doesn't feel that way right now, but I trust you, Lord. Papa has always said that faith cannot grow if it is never put to the test. Forgive my impertinence, Lord, but this is one test I'd rather not take.

Father, help me to remember that this is just a season and joy cometh. What I wouldn't give for a big dose of Your joy right now, Lord, for I know from experience that Your joy is my strength.

A smile bubbled up from within as Olivia recalled Jesse's arrival at her home this morning. *Papa had been staring pensively out the picture window and called out to hurry me along. "Livia! Jesse's coming out of the livery with his black horse tethered behind the new team and wagon. He should be here any minute." I listened as Papa greeted Jesse warmly and ushered him in. When I was confident my lilac ribbon was tied in a perfect bow, I turned to leave my room. Jesse must have heard my footsteps because the moment I came around the corner his face lit with pleasure. His eyes danced as they met mine. The way he went on about how pretty I looked made me feel special. He insisted that I spin around so that he could take in every inch of my new lilac dress, before drawing me into his arms for a comforting embrace. Perhaps it is vain, but knowing*

he likes the way I look on our special day is important to me.
In truth he looks very handsome himself, standing beside me,
dressed up like he's going to a Sunday meeting.

The apprehensions assaulting Olivia's mind had nothing to
do with the way Jesse presented himself or the gentle spirit he
had shown her thus far. They were more about the things she
didn't know. She agreed to marry this kind stranger after such a
brief encounter because of her extreme situation—and to please
her parents.

Now she was seeing things through different eyes that could
see more clearly. *Once my parents board the stage, this union*
will no longer be about them and what they want. It'll be up to
Jesse and me to make this marriage work. Can I let go of my
past and find contentment and a sense of belonging as Jesse's
wife? While she had no way of knowing for sure, she would
certainly give it her all.

Her parents' illness was beyond her control. There were no
guarantees that the vows she was about to take would someday
bring her happiness. Her father had reminded her that marriage,
even to someone you think you know and love, is a step in faith.
Happiness, however, is a choice.

Oh, Father God! Will I ever understand why all this
is happening?

Last night, her papa had told her, *"Nothing happens by*
accident, Livia. If we love God, the things that occur are all part
of His plan. We as his children need to trust, not question." He
read her the passages in Ecclesiastes that say there is a time for
everything, and a season for every activity under heaven. Would
this marriage be God's way of turning her sorrow into joy? She

had no way of knowing and no assurance that the passing of time would bring answers to her many questions.

Father God, You've promised to never leave me. Help me not to fear what life will bring. Show me Your purpose in all of this. Help me to open my heart to love my husband.

When Olivia felt Jesse's warm hand caress her cheek, her soft green eyes rose to meet sapphire blues. Their gazes held as he reached for her hand and slowly brought it to his lips. His kiss and then the tenderness he showed as he pressed his cheek where his lips had just been, gave her the reassurance she needed to go on.

Witnessing Jesse's gentleness with their daughter went a long way toward easing Josiah and Maryse's aching hearts.

Pastor Olsen, while he did his best to make the ceremony pleasant, kept it brief. After saying goodbye to their friends, Josiah, Maryse, Jesse, and Olivia, somberly stepped out into the street.

As they moved toward the waiting stage, Olivia couldn't help wondering if the heaviness in her heart would ever ease. The weight of her burden made every breath difficult—every step laborious. She fought to be strong for her parents' sake, but she was losing ground quickly.

The driver came out of the post office and announced that it was time for all passengers to board. Maryse hugged her daughter as much as her weakened state would allow. She reminded her to think of all the special times they had shared and lean on her Heavenly Father and husband for support. Maryse sent her an endearing smile as Josiah helped her into the coach. Olivia knew her mother had wanted to say more but held back as they were both struggling. No amount of words would ease their despair.

Josiah pulled Jesse aside to speak with him privately before taking his daughter into his arms and telling her again how much she was loved. After seeing Olivia secure in Jesse's embrace, Josiah climbed aboard and took a seat next to his wife. Once again, Jesse reassured them both that he would cherish Olivia all the days of his life.

Josiah and Maryse waved as the stage pulled away. Although it broke their hearts to let Olivia go, they had the Father's peace—a confidence that they had made the right choice.

Jesse lifted his sobbing wife into his arms and headed toward their wagon. He thanked the Lord for small favors—Olivia was unaware of the onlookers who had stopped to gawk. Since he couldn't bring himself to put her down, he simply held her in his lap, snuggling her close as he drove the team out of town. Not ten minutes had passed when sleep came mercifully to claim her.

Jesse stopped long enough to settle her beside him on the wagon bench, resting her head in his lap. He tenderly tucked her flyaway hair behind her ear before continuing on. He could only hope the rest would do her some good.

"Maryse," Josiah said to his wife after they were settled in their small stateroom aboard the ship, "Olivia gave me this package before we left the house this morning. It came with strict orders that we were not to open it until we were on board. She said it would bring us joy."

Maryse smiled. "If I know Olivia, it's a portrait."

"But she hasn't had time for even a sketch."

"Hmm ... now I'm really curious."

"Would you like to open it, or shall I?"

"I will, Josiah." As she pealed back the paper, the painting that came into view made their hearts stand still. Jesse was sitting atop his horse, fully garbed as an English knight. On the front of his mount, secure in his lap was none other than their beautiful Olivia, with a huge smile illuminating her face. The town and buildings surrounding the muddy bog in which Jesse's mount stood was Tecumseh. Olivia did not appear as she had the day in question. Instead of the blue dress she wore the pale yellow calico Josiah so loved. "Are you thinking what I'm thinking, Josiah?"

"I am. Look, Maryse. She included a note."

Dearest Papa and Mama,

Although Jesse is unaware of our prior introduction, I thought you might find it comforting to know that the kind man who pulled me out of the mire almost a year ago was the same man you asked me to marry. I was sure I'd have to let go of my dream of ever seeing Jesse again. Because of your willingness to follow God's lead, you not only brought Jesse back into my life but have also given me the strength I will need to go on. Thank you for the example you have always been. Try to be happy in the days you have together. Find comfort in the knowledge that God alone has sent my knight in shining armor to rescue me from the depths of utter despair. In time He will turn my sorrow into joy.

This gift comes complete with all my love. Never forget

that I hold you forever in my heart and constantly in my prayers. I can't thank you enough for all the joyful years we've spent together.

Until we meet again at the pearly gates of Heaven, never forget how much you are loved,

Olivia Maryse Somers

※ ※ ※

Olivia, feeling somewhat disoriented, opened her eyes to find her husband smiling down on her.

"Hi, sleepy head ... feel any better?"

"More rested." Sitting up, she lifted her arms in the air and stretched, allowing the radiance of the sun to heighten her awareness. "Where are we, Jesse?"

He pointed up the way. "If you look over there to your left you'll see the barn. The cabin sits on the side of the hill just behind it."

Stunned, she asked, "We're already here?"

"Yes ..."

"But, why didn't you wake me?" Disappointment filled her.

"You didn't miss a thing ... Liv, you needed the rest."

Olivia, embarrassed by sounding petulant, turned away. "I suppose you're right." She had spent most of the previous night, standing in the frame of her parents' bedroom door, watching them sleep. She had to be sure their faces would be etched in her mind forever. It wasn't until exhaustion overtook her that she went back to her bed. If she hadn't she would have crumpled to the floor.

Tears that seemed to have a will of their own filled her sore eyes. Gently brushing them away with the back of her hand, she made a conscious effort to keep her mind off her woes.

As her gaze fell on the ascending fields, she immersed herself in her new environment. The wild flowers intermixed with flowing grasses swayed in the gentle breeze. And the landscape was rich in vibrant shades—flourishing. Massive pines framed the picturesque cabin, and the swing on the porch awaited occupants, reminding her of the one at home. Her heart warmed. Time spent in this peaceful place could only bring healing to her tattered soul. She would have to remember to thank Jesse for bringing her here, for now she only wanted to take it all in and bask in the splendor of God's creation.

Jesse, having been here so many times before, suddenly realized how much he took for granted. Taking in the view through his wife's eyes was an adventure in and of its self. She delighted in every discovery. How could he not be enthralled with her wonder? Curious, he asked, "Olivia, did you and your parents travel much?"

"No ... I've never been further than the pond you and I walked to outside of town." Their gazes held.

"We'll explore the world outside of Tecumseh together, Liv. I promise."

"I'd like that." No one had ever called her Liv before and she wondered if Jesse even realized he was doing it. *No matter,* she thought, *he can call me anything he wants.*

He pulled the team to a halt in front of the cabin and glanced her way. "What are you thinking?"

"I'm in awe, I suppose. I lost so much today, but I gained a kind-hearted man for a husband. I'm beginning to see my parents' wisdom in all of this."

He set the brake, jumped down from the wagon and came to Olivia's side. Ignoring her warm blush, Jesse scooped her into his arms, climbed up the steps to the porch, and carried his bride across the threshold of their temporary home.

She was so busy taking in her new surroundings that she withheld her objection—until he boldly lowered his head. Fortunately, he had loosened his grip, so she leapt from his arms before he stole a kiss.

Jesse, while he found her shyness sweet, was growing weary of her evasions. He would never force the issue, but they did have an agreement and this groom wanted a kiss. For now he swallowed his wounded pride and did what he could to put her mind at ease.

"Welcome home, Mrs. Somers. I know it's not much," he admitted as he looked around the small dusty cabin. "Do you think you can tough it out for a month or so with this homely farmer?"

She captured his gaze. "I don't know ... the cabin's nice enough, but ... putting up with an aging farmer from Ypsilanti might be too much to ask of a young city gal like myself."

While he was pleased to see her spirits lifted, he refused to let her intonation pass without an equal response. "You might get more than you bargained for in this aging husband if you continue to be such a tease."

With feigned innocence Olivia declared, "A tease? Me? I would never!"

His eyes narrowed.

Unnerved, she asked, "What is that look supposed to mean?"

His brow arched. "Wouldn't you like to know?"

She squinted, scarcely peeking up. "I might!"

"That, *My* Dear Wife, is for me to know and you to find out."

A response ran through her head, yet the way he stared at her mouth sent warnings off in her head. *Kisses! Is that all you think about Jesse Somers?* She blanched when he took a daring step toward her. A quick peek to the right revealed a way of escape, but unfortunately, her deflection had cost her. He was now only inches away. She wanted to flee. Like a frightened bird she stood frozen in place. Her thoughts begged, *Oh, Jesse, please go away!* Wishing he would leave did not make it happen. Her eyelids flipped up when his warm hands captured her face and then slid ever so slowly over the surface of her silky hair. He was toying with her. Even so, his blue-eyed stare sent prickly shivers up her spine. She had to say something, anything to shatter the intensity of the moment!

"So this is how the game will be played is it, Mr. Somers?"

"Yes, Ma'am, it is."

Olivia simply had to distract him. He was far too serious and making her nervous. "You'd better watch yourself, Jesse Somers. You might be in over your head when I get to feeling more like myself." She stepped back, needing to put space between them.

"I doubt that ...."

Olivia, thinking this could go on for hours, let it drop. Besides, her stomach had begun to growl and everything would have to be unpacked before she could even begin preparations for a meal. She scanned the room, taking in their simple yet ample furnishings. The mantel above the stone fireplace was filled with various treasures that she would have to investigate later. Two fluffy chairs sat on either side, and a large braided rug added warmth to the room. Parts of the small kitchen could be viewed from where she stood. For a split second, her eyes fell on the closed door that must lead to the bedroom. Turning back to her husband, she said, "I don't know about you, but I'm starving. Should we get unpacked, so I can make supper?"

"In a minute. Let me show you around first." Jesse latched onto her hand, and before she could grasp his intent he had pulled her into the bedroom.

"Olivia, this will be our room while we're here."

His touch sent prickly heat up her arm.

"The armoire in the corner is empty. You can put ..." His words trailed off the second her crimson face came into view. Her timidity spoke volumes. So, with as much tact as his rambling thoughts would avow, he released her hand and backed off. "Look at the way I'm carrying on. You decide where you'd like things to go. I'll do the hauling and get the horses settled."

Olivia sagged with relief.

When he returned, she started unpacking the first crate; unfortunately, it put her back in their room. It did feel odd to be putting Jesse's things amongst her own, but ... she would have to get used to it. After spreading the clean linens and quilt on the bed, she made her way to the kitchen.

This job would take longer than she had hoped, but she didn't let that discourage her. Olivia found her apron, put it on and pushed up her sleeves. She began by removing the layer of dust covering everything. She could really use that water Jesse had promised to fetch, but she made due with the dry rags. Olivia thought she'd better wait for him to light the small cook stove, it didn't appear to have been fired up in months. She was pleased to see the nice supply of cookware and utensils on the shelf by the back door. They would certainly come in handy; she loved to cook.

She had been so intent on her cleaning, her heart flipped when the back door flew open. Thankfully it was only her husband with the first buckets of promised water.

"Jesse, will you make sure the flue is critter free before I light it?" Her face scrunched up as she added, "I don't like surprises."

He shrugged. "I'll start it for you this time."

The way he said, *this time,* told her she'd better get over her uncertainties. Begrudgingly, she offered, "Thanks."

The crook of his long finger touched the tip of his wife's nose, his blue eyes taunting her as he walked out the back door to collect firewood. The temperatures in the hills had a tendency to drop in the evenings, so when he came back in he built a fire in the fireplace as well as in the cook stove. By the time he came in with the last pail of water, Olivia had the meal on the table. He was pleasantly surprised.

Jesse held out a chair for Olivia and then sat in the one beside her. Since she had assumed he would sit across from her, his place setting was there. She was about to remedy the problem when he did it for her. Their eyes met as they joined hands. When they bowed their heads, he prayed so long over the meal, their marriage, and her parents journey she was sure the food had to be cold.

"Olivia, this looks wonderful." Since he had missed his noon meal, he thought the supper, consisting of fried ham, potatoes, cinnamon apples, and corn muffins, looked like a king's feast.

She hummed as she bit into her first piece of ham.

"Does taste good, doesn't it, Liv?"

"Yes ... I can't remember the last time I had ham."

The wood popped in the cook stove. "Why is that?" When no response came, he reached for her chin and gently turned her face to him.

Her cheeks warmed. "Other needs ... they took precedence."

"I see ..." *How could I be so daft! Her father hasn't been able to work in who knows how long. Of course they struggled.* He had assumed that their sickness attributed to their gaunt frames, but now he wasn't sure. His heart wrenched. Why did he not think to offer them money for their journey? The thought of her parents going hungry tore at his heart. *Oh, Father. Please send a kind soul across their path. Provide for their needs until I can send them a portion of Your bounty.*

Jesse's eyes fell on his wife's frail arms and wondered if she would fill out during the coming months. The thought brought a smile to his face. He had no complaints about the way she looked, but a few pounds here and there might do her some good. One thing he knew for sure, he would make it his personal mission to see that she never went without ham again.

Daisytales

He Loves Me!

Chapter Seven

Windows of Her Heart

"OLIVIA, THERE'S A nice-sized tub hanging on the back of the cabin. If you'd like to take a bath, I'd be glad to haul the water."

A good soak sounded wonderful. Had she been home she would have indulged, but the thought of putting herself in such a vulnerable position kept her from accepting Jesse's gracious offer. As much as she wanted to trust him—her trust was something he would have to earn. Knowing she would be expected to sleep next to him taxed her mind enough. "I'll be fine. I took a bath this morning."

"In that case, I'll head down to the creek for a quick scrub."

"Okay ..." The thought made her shiver. The air was cool which meant the water would be cooler yet.

"When I come back I'll show you around before it gets too dark."

"Sounds good." Olivia washed the dishes, dumped the dirty water outside at the edge of the forest and took a moment to glance around. As she slipped in the back door, she removed her apron and went to retrieve her shawl from the hook in their room.

Movement outside the bedroom window caught her attention. She stopped to take a quick peek and was held captive by two squirrels leaping through the trees from limb to limb in what appeared to be a game of hide and seek. One would spot the other, and they would take off on a merry chase. For a time they were content with only the chase. She got a case of the giggles when a plump rabbit invaded their play space, causing both of them to stand at attention.

She wasn't sure how much time had lapsed when she turned away from the scene in the yard. Lost in thought, she ran smack dab into a bare chest. Her heart took flight as her bone-chilling scream pierced the silence.

"Olivia, it's me." Jesse's arms came about her. "I'm sorry, Liv. I thought you heard me come in."

It took a while, but her racing heart finally eased. When she found the courage to look up, she couldn't fathom the depth of devotion she saw in his eyes—nor could she accept it. In fact, this half-naked man left her feeling so unsettled she slithered out of his gentle hold and made haste for the door. She needed to get away—she had to put distance between them.

Jesse smiled at his wife's fleeing back. He really didn't mean to frighten her. It would seem that her reluctance to be in his arms was worse than he thought. Did his missing shirt add to her discomfort? *No matter*, he thought, *in time she'll understand that I only want to love her.*

He pulled his shirt on and caught up with her before she reached the barn. Capturing her hand, he led her through the big door.

"So, Olivia, you've never ridden a horse before, right?"

"I was on one but not by myself."

"Then I suppose you know nothing about them?"

"Other than the fact that they stand on four legs and they're covered with hair, very little."

When Jesse opened the first stall he came to and clicked his tongue, she stepped behind him. His massive black mount came out of the darkness and nuzzled up against him. Using Jesse as a shield, she stood on her toes and peeked over his shoulder. "Olivia, Shadow's been my horse for seven years, he won't hurt you."

At first she was not convinced, but eventually she came out of hiding.

"Open your hand and let him nuzzle you."

She complied. "His nose is so soft."

"Would you like to ride him?"

Her wide eyes met his. "Oh, I don't know, Jesse."

"I'm not trying to rush you ... I just thought ..."

"I'd like to."

His hand slid down her arm, his expression telling her that whatever she decided was all right with him.

"I suppose I'd better buck up and learn all I can. I'd hate to make a complete fool of myself in front of your family."

"There's really nothing to it, Liv."

Her head lowered in contemplation. When her eyelids rose, she met his tender gaze. "Are you sure he's not too tired from our journey?"

Jesse chuckled softly, reveling in her sweet innocence. Everything was so new to her. "Shadow's fine. Stand aside and I'll bring him the rest of the way out."

Olivia was awed by the way Shadow just stood still while Jesse brushed him, threw a blanket over his back and bridled him. He was more like a faithful dog than a typical spirited mount. She had just begun to wonder how she would go about getting on him when Jesse lifted her off the ground and placed her on Shadow's back. Somewhat panicked, she asked, "Isn't he supposed to have a saddle on?"

"You won't be on long enough to bother."

But I need that thing to hang on to .... Her voice trembled as she looked down at the ground and confirmed, "I'm awfully high." Only her pride kept her from wrapping her arms around Shadow's neck and hanging on for dear life.

Jesse did not miss the way her eyes skittered about. "Olivia, I won't let you fall. Here," he said as he handed her a clump of mane, "hang on to this if it helps you feel more secure."

If only it did. Every step Shadow took heightened her awareness of the sheer power this magnificent creature possessed. Every nerve in her body was on edge. His sudden movements had their effect, from the twitching of his ears—to the swishing of his tail—and the way he threw his head without warning.

"Why do Shadow's ears do that?"

Jesse, hearing his wife's voice quiver, peered up. Her pale features startled him. She was apparently scared skinny and unwilling to tell him.

"Liv, do me a favor and move forward."

"Why?"

"I'm tired of walking."

"Oh ..." To her complete stupefaction, he leapt off the ground and mounted behind her. After sliding his arms around her and snuggling her close he took up the reins and nudged Shadow forward. Having her close suited him just fine.

Her relief knew no bounds.

"Now, tell me again, what were you asking about his ears?"

As the questions ensued over the next half hour, she visibly relaxed and even enjoyed their ride.

"Jesse, what's on the other side of the hill behind the cabin?"

"Mostly forest."

"Oh."

"Olivia, since you slept the whole way here, you're unfamiliar with our surroundings. We're out in the middle of nowhere, so we'll have to take some extra precautions."

"Like what?"

"I'm sure you're used to wandering around town alone, but I don't want you doing that while we're here at the cabin."

"You're being silly. I've been on my own for years now. I'm perfectly capable of taking care of myself."

"I understand that, but out here it's different." When she offered no response, he offered an explanation he was sure would end all arguments. "Olivia, we've had problems with bears, wolves, even wild cats from time to time. If you want to go exploring, that's fine, but we'll go together."

She craned her neck to look at him. *Why do men have to be so ...*

"Olivia, let me assure you, I am not exaggerating. I've waited a long time to find a wife and I have no intention of losing you because you're too stubborn to heed my warning. I don't mean to come across as being overbearing, but I need you to trust me in this."

She was shocked by his insight. Her husband had exposed her thoughts, yet she had never said a word. "All right," she conceded, muttering as she turned away, "but you don't have to be such a grouch about it."

An irrepressible smile crossed Jesse's face. "I won't be a grouch, if you'll promise to trust me."

"I married you, didn't I?"

He wrapped his arms around her and kissed her cheek. "Yes, Liv, you did, but I'd still like to hear that promise."

"I promise."

"While I've got your attention, there are a few more things you should be aware of. We'll have to keep the barn door closed at all times. So if you use the lantern put it back on the hook when you're finished with it. I need to know where it is in case I have to come out in the dark."

She nodded, but her thoughts plagued her as Jesse led Shadow back into the barn. *He's obviously not as agreeable as I originally thought. Then again, you're not so agreeable yourself, Olivia, so knock it off!*

She had barely gotten her attitude under control when Jesse shut the stall door, latched it, and turned back to face her. "You, my dear wife, are entirely too serious!"

If only you knew!

Without warning, Jesse threw Olivia over his shoulder like a sack of feed.

She was about to protest when he cleared the barn door and

began spinning her around and around. Laughing, she squealed and begged him to stop. By the time he set her on her feet, they were both so dizzy they fell to the grassy field. Husband and wife were lying on their backs, sprawled out like a couple of children, blanketed by the heavens.

The light of day was diminishing, and the radiance of the yellow sun had mellowed, appearing like a golden coin slipping ever so slowly into varying shades of orange, purple and blue.

Minutes passed before Jesse sat up, and his long arms straddled her slender frame. As cobalt eyes longingly scanned her face, a surge of emotions spiraled through her—through him too as he closed the distance between them.

His silky lips, brushed ever so softly across her brow, kissing her cheeks, leaving her breathless—confused. If only he would have stopped there. As the intensity of his gaze deepened, surrendering to her husband's advance seemed inevitable. However, at the last second, she made her narrow escape, foiling his plan once again. For a scant moment accepting his kiss felt so right, but in the end fear won out.

Sighing, he informed her with much tenderness, "You will not avoid my kisses for long, Olivia." Possessively, she was lifted off the ground and encircled in his embrace. As quickly as the moment came it ended, and once again she was left somewhat unscathed.

"Olivia," Jesse asked as he lunged up the porch steps, "I brought along a checker board. Would you like to play a few rounds before we call it a night?" He chortled with glee when she curtsied, as if addressing royalty and responded with much decorum.

"I am willing and able my husband. But in all fairness I must ask—are you sure you are a worthy opponent?"

He was laughing when he returned her playful glance and informed her with confidence, "I have a good chance."

After losing to his young wife for the third time, Jesse found himself looking at her in a different light. She, like Lizzy, was a master of the game. Standing to his feet, he humbly entreated, "You're welcome to have mercy on me and teach me some of your skills, My Lady. As you can see, mine are in great need of sharpening."

"You must forgive my insolence, My Lord, but I refuse. Your lady will not teach you how to defeat her. As a knight of the realm, you must pay close attention and sharpen your skills on your own." She relished her victory, but it was short lived. Jesse's next suggestion sobered her quickly.

"Olivia, if you'd like to go ahead and get ready for bed, I'll join you in a minute."

While going to bed was not on her list of things she would like to do, she felt certain he was not asking, but telling.

As she propelled her feet forward, she could feel the heat of his eyes on her back. Without a backward glance, she closed the door and hastened to undo the long row of buttons trailing down her back. Hanging her dress from the hook, she pulled her nightgown over her head and took the time to secure every loop from navel to chin. After adding her robe as an additional layer, she removed the lavender ribbon from her hair, picked up her brush and methodically ran it through her snarled tresses. She had barely finished her braid when Jesse knocked.

"Are you ready, Olivia?"

Ready for what? She took a deep breath to ease her apprehensions as she stepped to the door and opened it. She made an attempt to glide past him.

The day had been long and Jesse was tired. Since he anticipated Olivia's defection, his arm came out to detain her. He couldn't be sure if her actions were based on fear, defiance, or a little of both. Either way, she was his wife, and she would have to get used to his closeness. "Where would you be going in such a powerful big hurry?"

"I thought I'd read for a while."

"You thought wrong. Now go warm up the bed."

He turned her back toward the bed, but she stood perfectly still. She couldn't possibly comply. Not yet! "I'm not tired," she said in a rush. "Reading relaxes me."

He fought against the smile that threatened to erupt. "I wasn't born yesterday. I know you're trying to avoid me."

She saw no need to deny it. "I'm not ready to share a bed with a complete stranger."

"I'm not a stranger; I am your husband. Up till now I've allowed you to evade my kisses, but you will sleep alongside of me."

Can't you see what your closeness does to me? "I made that agreement before I knew what I would be up against."

He scowled. "What is that supposed to mean?"

"Maybe I don't want to tell you." How could she explain? *The desire oozing from the depth of your sapphire eyes makes me feel like a small prey about to be devoured.* She couldn't tell him that—he would laugh!

"That works for me because I'm exhausted. This discussion

is over. Climb into bed before I blow out the lamp."

The extent of her insolence was no mystery to her, but her excuses were well founded—undeniably clear—to her way of thinking anyway. *Two can play this game. I can be just as stubborn as he is domineering.*

Her lack of movement told him she was not about to comply, so he helped her along. With a firm hand at the small of her back, he ushered her into the room. He had his hand on the door and was about to shut it when she breathlessly announced, "The closet!" *That's it!* "I need to use the water closet!"

His brow furrowed. "Do you mean the outhouse?"

"Yes!"

Jesse pulled to the fore what was sure to be the last of his endurance. "Olivia, do you really?"

"Some things can't be helped."

He reached for the lantern and followed her out of the room. As she stuck her feet into her boots, he did the same and she wasted no time declining his aid. "I'm capable of handling this alone, Jesse."

He merely laughed and shook his head.

Infuriated, she droned, "I can't imagine what you find so funny!"

"You, Olivia! It's you I find delightful. If I didn't know better, I'd swear I married my sister's long-lost twin. You don't look alike, but your personalities are almost identical. Whenever she's faced with difficult circumstances, she manages to come up with every excuse in the book to deter the inevitable."

"Oh ..." was all she could say as she turned and made her way to the small wooden structure. In the lantern light, she could see a fair-sized spider up in the corner weaving his web and taking up residence where he was not welcome. She brought her hand to her mouth to suppress her own shrieks, should the dreaded eight-legged creature decide to move too swiftly. Her original plan to take her sweet time would have to be altered. She finished what she had come for and got out. Tomorrow morning she would bring the broom along and rid the necessary room of such creepy crawlers.

Jesse held the back door and followed her in. She moved to the counter and took her time getting a drink of water. Jesse's hand rubbed slowly at his evening shadow as he watched in silence. If this had been one of his siblings, she would be in really big trouble about now. Jesse was trying his level best to give her some leeway, but her pluck amazed him. That she would chance being so bold and brassy this early in their relationship boggled his mind. She was a tall woman but willowy. Pound for pound, he had to be twice her size.

Olivia was on the prowl again. When she snatched her book off the table, he had a strong inclination as to where she was going. She skillfully avoided eye contact as she set the lantern on the small table in the sitting room, plunked herself down in one of the big chairs and began to read.

Jesse didn't so much as pause on his way to the room. Without shutting the door, he removed everything he was wearing, except his under drawers. He turned down the bed with one full swing and went to retrieve his daring young wife.

Olivia heard him coming and cringed when he took her book, sat it on the small table, blew out the lantern, and snatched her from the chair.

She squealed, "Put me down, Jesse Somers!" But her insistence was roundly ignored.

Jesse kicked the door shut, then sitting on the edge of the bed with Olivia in his arms he inquired, "Tell me, if you will, what is a tired groom supposed to do with his obstinate, yet oh-so-lovely bride?" The uncertainty in her wide green eyes was almost too much for him to bear. Pensively, his long finger ran slowly up her arm and over her shoulder before outlining her narrow jaw. He tried for the life of him to understand her reaction to his closeness. "I would never hurt you, Olivia. What has you so troubled?"

"You."

He looked confused, wounded almost.

"Jesse, I told you, I've never even had a beau, and now I find myself with a husband. My parents ... they tried to prepare me, but they said nothing about my insides being all in a whirl."

"Mine aren't exactly stable either, Olivia. I desperately want to kiss you, but the fear in your eyes keeps me from pressing you."

"I can't help it. I agreed to let you ... before—well, before I knew how scary it would be. Can you try to be patient?"

He offered a sideways grin. "Let me think about it. We need to discuss what went on here tonight, because it can't keep happening. If you have a problem with me, then by all means tell me."

She lowered her head. "Easier said than done ...."

"I think it's only fair to warn you that I have a surefire method of exacting compliance, one that my siblings would assure you works like a charm."

Her thoughts were anything but rational as his words ran

precariously through her mind. She didn't have a clue as to what he was getting at, so the deviant smile he sent her way, settled everything. "I won't fight you anymore, Jesse. We did have an agreement. I'll just have to trust you."

"A wise decision. Unfortunately, I can't let you off so easily. I think a small sampling is in order, don't you?"

Her abashed expression turned to surprise the second his hands came to her sides. She squirmed in his hold and her best effort to contain her mirth failed miserably. She burst into uncontrollable laughter. "Quit!" she begged as he tickled her bare feet, her neck, and then went back to her sides. Only a minute had passed when he stopped, though it felt much longer. She could only hope her debt had been paid in full.

"For a kiss, I'll forgive all."

Her green eyes widened. "But I thought ..."

"That I would be patient?"

"Yes."

"I will be very patient. But if you're ever going to get over your fears, you need to work through them. I did not say where to kiss me, I only asked for a kiss."

She sighed with relief. "So your cheek is all right?"

"A kiss on the cheek would be wonderful." Jesse turned in profile, savoring her fleeting penance.

Although she found his skin quite prickly, she survived the ordeal. Now if he would just let her go, she might breathe easier.

"Which side of the bed would you prefer, Olivia?" Without waiting for an answer, he added, with a mischievous glint in his eyes, "I should warn you. There are creatures living in these forests that devour only the first person they come to when they open the door."

She punched him in the arm and declared, "Jesse Somers, you're trying to frighten me!"

"You're right. Forgive me. Which side of the bed do you want?"

She rolled her eyes and shook her head. "Not next to the door, thanks to you!"

Jesse laughed out loud as he lay back on the bed. "I prefer to sleep next to the door, and that little story works every time."

"Don't tell me. You've used it on your siblings and it works like a charm."

"How did you know?"

"Just a wild guess." She scooted to the far side of the bed as Jesse blew out the lantern. She prayed that he would forget the holding part, but no such luck was hers!

When she stiffened to avoid his embrace, he reminded her of the cost of defiance, and she moved quickly into his arms. After praying together, her husband whispered softly in her ear, "I can see why God says that finding a wife is a good thing." Snuggling her close, the exhausting day caught up with him. He was asleep in no time.

Olivia, on the other hand, was wide-awake with nothing except the dark room to keep her mind from wandering.

She reflected on her last hours with her parents and wondered how close they were to their destination. Her father had been concerned, and rightly so, that she would panic and try to follow them. He refused to tell her where they were going. Her mother assured her that this was best and promised to send a letter to the farm with their address. After that, she would be able to correspond with them.

Thoughts of meeting Jesse's family brought a mixture of apprehension and joy. He was certain that they would love her, and although she prayed it would be so, that was yet another unanswered question floating around in her brain.

Her mother had said it would be up to her to begin opening the windows of her heart and allowing the love that Jesse offered to fill her up. If only it was that easy. He was quite understanding of her fears, not to mention the way he combated her willfulness with his moving fingers. His ingenuity astounded her! How could she be unsure of a man who took pleasure in making her laugh? Oh sure, he could be annoying, but he was silly and wonderful too. They both came to this union complete with their own imperfection. Could they accept each other as is, and someday come to love each other as a husband and wife should? Perhaps in time she would have answers to her questions. In the meantime, she would have to find a way to open the window to her heart, even if it was only a crack at a time.

As the moonbeams cast their gray shadowy hues about the room, she closed her eyes. Snug in Jesse's arms, Olivia was lying on his chest and picked up the beat of his heart. After listening for a time, she asked herself, *Is it only his heart that I hear, Lord, or is it both of ours learning to beat as one?*

Daisytales

He Loves Me!

Chapter Eight

Anything is Possible

OLIVIA WOKE TO warm lips ever so lightly kissing the nap of her neck. She tried not to move, but it tickled profusely. Shivering, she pulled away. "Jesse, I can't stand it."

"I should have known." He sounded terribly disappointed.

"How could you have known my neck would be ticklish?"

"I didn't. Elizabeth reacts the same way when Kaleb tries to kiss her neck. I had hopes that it was only my sister who found this intolerable, especially now that I understand why Kaleb keeps trying. Do you know how soft your neck is?"

She started to laugh. "No!"

He wrapped his arms securely around her.

"Jesse," she insisted, "nature is calling. You have to let me go."

"I will in a minute. Liv ..."

"Hmm?"

"With everything that happened yesterday, I failed to mention a slight flaw in my character. You really should be made aware of it."

She stiffened in his grasp, wondering what he might say or do next.

"I tend to be a bit of a grump until I get my coffee."

"Then get up and fix it!" She couldn't imagine why he would tell her when he could see to the task himself. Her father made his coffee everyday and never once complained about the chore. It became clear that her response was not what he was looking for when his long fingers came to her sides and began moving. "Jesse!" she squealed. "I promise, you do not want to do that first thing in the morning."

"Then don't be so plucky." The silence ticked on. Desperate, Jesse groveled. "Please be a good wife and make my coffee."

She craned her neck around, staring at him. *Oh my, he's pitiful!* "You don't know how to make it ... do you?"

"Now you know one of the reasons I needed a wife. My mom and sisters have me spoiled rotten."

"I can see that. You'd be in a real predicament if my father had never taught me."

"Olivia, do you really think I'd leave something that important to chance?" His pathetic scowl brought on a case of the giggles.

"You asked my father if I could make coffee?"

"Yes, outside of your having a personal relationship with the Lord, it was second on my list of importance."

"I'm almost afraid to ask about the third."

"That's simple, I needed to know if you could cook. I couldn't very well ask for your hand and then let you starve."

"And the fourth?"

"I had to be sure you were sassy. Let me tell you, your father wasted no time in letting me know that you were all that and then some!"

She rolled her eyes. "I find it hard to believe that a man as domineering as you would find sass an asset." She sounded wounded, but a touch of sarcasm was woven in her tone.

He couldn't resist a baiting response. "Kaleb once told me that as much as he tries, it's impossible for two people to live in the same house and not squabble over something. After spending a day together, I can see the truth in his words. He also said that following the Scriptural principle of not allowing the sun to go down on your wrath has its advantages. His favorite part of disagreeing is making up." When she turned back to face him. He winked at her playfully and added, "Maybe it will be mine as well."

She shook her head, unwilling to give in to his ploy. Being an honest man, her father would have warned Jesse about her tenacious spirit, and as far as she could tell, Jesse was not exactly the type to back down either. Although God was at work in her heart, she had by no means neared perfection. Her father had often reminded her that she needed to be the calm in the midst of life's storms, not the storm itself. He said a strong marriage must be built on selfless acts of love. It all sounded so good coming from him; however, accomplishing such a feat was yet to be seen. Thinking she could start slowly, she gave in to Jesse's plea.

"Let me up and I'll make your coffee." At those words, he released her immediately. Since she hadn't removed her robe last night, she merely slipped her feet into her boots before moving through the kitchen and out the door.

The coolness of the dawn was dissipating and the warm summer sun had begun its assent in the eastern skies. A choir of birds sang their merry tunes as a fuzzy brown rabbit nibbled on a clover bloom. Oh, how Olivia would love to lose herself in the wonder of this forest—perhaps another time. Right now she had a husband to attend to, who was completely at her mercy. The knowledge of it made her smile.

Olivia returned to the kitchen with the extra kindling she collected on her way. To her surprise, Jesse had come as far as his chair at the table. Although his jeans were on, his shirt was not. She found his bare chest a bit of a distraction. Her eyes trailed up his manly form and stopped. His head was propped on his hands distorting his face, and his droopy eyes seemed to have a will of their own. His deep brown hair was no longer neat; it was going every which way. This picture was too much to endure. She burst into gut-wrenching laughter!

"You'd better not be laughing at me," he snarled, adding, "Are you going to make my coffee, woman, or does the torture commence?"

She threw her long braid over her shoulder and tried to control herself long enough to light the stove. If she hadn't chanced another peek, she might have succeeded. Tears clouded her vision, as she grabbed her stomach and dropped to her knees on the wooden floor. Olivia couldn't remember the last time she had laughed so hard.

Without warning, Jesse lunged toward her, pinning her to the floor with ease. Unable to fight him in her weakened state, he tickled her until she was sure she could laugh no more. Before he released her, he drew close—so close she could feel his warm breath on her face. Again he asked what was apparently the question of the hour, "Are you going to make my coffee, woman?"

Though speech evaded her, Jesse must have accepted her nod because he reclaimed his place at the table.

Once the mood-altering liquid was brewing, Olivia snuck a quick peek. Jesse's head lay on his arms, and while he might be feigning sleep, she was not about to disturb him.

She started breakfast, going out of her way to be as quiet as possible. Thoughts of her new husband ran through her mind. What were his favorite foods? More importantly, what were his dislikes? And what about her did he like or dislike? The list could go on for hours. She smiled, wondering who the lucky soul was who had the pleasure of waiting on him during the year he taught school. Perhaps in time she would ask.

In so many ways, her husband was like no other man she had ever known. Yesterday he was full of surprises, and now this. *No matter,* she thought, *I could get used to all this laughter with no effort. No wonder Papa liked him.*

Thank You, Lord, for bringing this man into my life. Help me to continue to find joy in this time of discovery, to accept what he can bring to my life, and to give of myself in the process.

With a full mug of coffee, she cautiously approached her grumpy knight. Olivia had no more set it down when Jesse inhaled deeply and let out a contented sigh.

"You're welcome." She smiled as she moved back to the stove and flipped the last two pancakes before dishing up the fried ham. Her mother's recipe for apple and cinnamon sugar syrup was bubbling nicely when she poured it over the stacks on their plates. Olivia joined her husband at the table and he reached for her hand. He sounded much more coherent when he returned thanks.

"This smells wonderful, Olivia."

"I hope you like it. I'd be terribly disappointed if you didn't. It's one of my favorites."

He savored several bites. "If you keep cooking like this, I could be in real trouble."

"Why?"

"I'll end up spreading out."

She didn't for a minute think that would happen, though she didn't expose her thoughts. She merely took pleasure in watching Jesse devour everything on his plate. In fact, he scraped until even the smallest morsel was gone. Having eaten her fill, she pushed her food aside and sipped at her tea.

"Aren't you going to finish yours, Liv?"

"I'm too full." When he finished what she could not, she offered, "Jesse, if you're still hungry, I'd be glad to make something else. I didn't really think about it, but I'm sure you have a bigger appetite than my father."

He squeezed her hand. "I'm fine for now."

He had chores to do in the barn, so Olivia took advantage of the time alone to get dressed. After making the bed, she removed her nightclothes, washed up, and slipped into her tattered skirt and blouse before sitting on the bed to pull on her worn socks. She would have to do some mending soon. For now she took care to position the holes so that her toes and heels would not stick out. Her father wanted to buy her some new things before they left her, but he had already spent too much on the lilac dress. She was content making do, but she had her work cut out for her if she was going to make herself look presentable before meeting Jesse's family.

Olivia, determined to get her baking out of the way, started a batch of bread that she hoped would tide them over for a couple of days. She had a hankering for something sweet, so she made sugar cookies as well. Her mother had given her a nice selection of herbs, spices, and other ingredients that would come in handy, like vanilla and nuts and such. Jesse had gone shopping the day he asked her to marry him. When she took inventory of what he bought, she wondered if he had ever gone for supplies before. The excessive surplus of beans, rice, oats, flour, sugar, potatoes, onions, and apples would surely last them six months instead of the two they had planned to stay alone at the cabin. The items that peaked her curiosity the most were the large amounts of lemon drops and chocolate. There were also two big packages wrapped in brown paper that she assumed were gifts of some sort for the folks at home. She took care to put them out of harm's way.

The morning flew by in a whirlwind of chores. She was pleased with all she had accomplished. The cabin was fairly clean, a few dozen cookies were ready to be eaten, and the bread was cooling on the table. When she stepped out the back door to shake the flour dust out of her apron, she looked up the hill with open curiosity. Jesse didn't think she should go up there alone, so she would heed his warning. But, if she wasn't mistaken, there was a patch of berry bushes up the way. Maybe the thought of a nice pie would entice him to take her climbing.

Olivia turned away from temptation and followed the banging sound into the barn. Since she entered unnoticed, for a time she watched her husband at work in the loft. His shirt had been discarded and beading sweat trickled down his muscled back as he pounded nail after nail into the dry timbers.

Olivia's attention was drawn away when Shadow stuck his head out of the stall and whinnied as if calling her to his side. She moved to stand in front of him and giggled when his soft nose rubbed against her cheek. "Hi there, big boy. I'll bet you're tired of being in that little room, aren't you. Let me see what I can do." She looked around the barn for the brush Jesse used on Shadow the night before. She found it hanging on the wall, close to his saddle.

Without thought for her safety, she opened his stall. Fortunately, Shadow only followed her like a puppy. She brushed him for a time, but she felt sorry for the other two horses. She was about to let one of them out when Jesse's deep voice stopped her.

"You don't want to do that, Olivia." He came to where she stood and secured the stall door.

Her questioning gaze met his. "Why not? I'm sure those horses would like to get out so I can brush them too."

She really doesn't know a thing about them. "You're so sweet."

Feeling awkward and embarrassed, Olivia looked away.

Jesse, noticing her flush, reached for her slender hand and gently pulled her to him. His kind words were enough to bring her eyes back to his. "Feel free to take Shadow out and spoil him as much as you'd like. I'm confident he would never purposefully hurt you. But just like people, Liv, not all horses are alike. The team hasn't given me any trouble so far, but I don't know them well enough to allow you to handle them. For all I know, they might have plowed right through you when you opened their stalls."

Her eyes widened. "You're not teasing me, are you?"

"No," he said as he pulled her closer. "Not when your safety's at stake. I have every intention of teaching you how to handle them, but let's take things slow. I don't want you getting hurt."

"You really don't mind that I got Shadow out?"

"Not at all." Jesse ran his finger down the soft skin of her cheek, leaving a trail of dirt where his finger had been. He didn't tell her. "Would you like to ride him in the barn while I finish my work?"

"Could I?" she asked, elated with his offer.

"Of course. I'll even put the saddle on." Olivia's eyes danced as she watched Jesse get Shadow ready. When she stuck her foot in the stirrup and attempted to mount without knowing how to throw her weight, her determination tickled him. After several tries, he gave her a slight boost and she was on.

Jesse tapped on the top of her boot. "We'll be going through Ann Arbor on our way home. As long as it's not a Sunday, we'll pick you up a hat to keep the sun out of your face and better boots with a thicker heel for riding. I don't want your feet sliding around in the stirrups like they are right now. Maybe if you're real good I'll even confiscate an old pair of Joseph's jeans for you to wear when we go riding on the farm."

"Are you serious?" Her look was incredulous.

"Why wouldn't I be?"

She started to giggle.

He was about to ask why when her reason bubbled out, "Oh, Jesse. If my parents ... if they knew you were going to lead me down such a sinful path, they might have changed their minds about us being wed."

Jesse's brow furrowed. "Your parents would agree that farm life is much different than living in town and exceptions have to be made. Besides, you're my wife, Olivia. You answer to me now."

At first she wasn't sure what to say, so she smiled and said the first thing that came to mind, "I don't know, Jesse, that's an awfully tall order for someone like me. I'll have to see what I can do."

He smiled. She was proving to be full of surprises and in truth that suited him just fine. *Besides,* he thought as his father's counsel came to mind. *Men and women were created with their distinctive differences and reactions for a reason. If a husband delights in loving and caring for his wife, she will willingly submit to him. And a husband's natural response to a wife who seeks to please him will be to love her more and more.* For now he would show her his newly-formed love and leave all else in the Lord's hands.

Jesse was pleased to see that Olivia's fear of Shadow had dissipated. More than likely her inquiries from the previous day had eased her mind. After showing her how to use the reins, she was off on this new adventure, and Jesse went back to work.

When the heat of the day made it impossible for him to continue, he moved to the edge of the loft. As he descended the ladder, Olivia was loosening the cinch strap. Apparently she intended to put Shadow away by herself. As she proceeded to slide the saddle off Shadow's back, her knees buckled against the unexpected weight. She recovered nicely, until the saddle bumped the pitchfork handle and she tripped over it. As hard as he tried, Jesse could not reach her in time to break her fall. When she dropped to the clay floor, some of the prongs from the fork slid into her leg. Her hand came to her mouth to stifle her cries as she quickly pulled it out.

He rushed to her side and without thought lifted her skirt to assess the damage.

"What are you doing?" she bellowed.

It wasn't until Jesse looked at Olivia that he realized the effect he was having on her. The red flush on her paled face slowed the beat of his heart. If he wasn't mistaken, his wife felt as though she had been assaulted. He would have to handle this with care.

When she attempted to get up he insisted, "Olivia, stay where you are until I get Shadow back in the stall."

Why do I have to be such a klutz? Her leg throbbed, but her resolve to hide her pain prevailed. She did fine until thoughts of her parents flooded in. Without warning, tears filled her eyes and spilled slowly down her cheeks.

Jesse stooped down to lift her off the barn floor. "Olivia, don't cry. Honey, we'll get you soaking in the creek and have you fixed up good as new."

"I'm not ... it's just that ... I miss my parents."

"Of course you do." He snuggled her close and headed toward the water. "We have each other now. I'm going to take care of you." She was bound to go through emotional times; he expected that. "Liv, you have to give yourself time."

She didn't know if she could accept the help he was offering, but his caring words and gentleness touched her despairing heart.

Warm blood was seeping into her skirt as Jesse lowered her to the creek bank. Although she wanted to look, she was not about to with him so close.

After removing his own bluchers, socks, shirt and jeans, Jesse sat beside Olivia and unbuttoned the back of her blouse and skirt, as if he had done it all her life. After removing her boots, he set them aside. When his hands slid up her leg to remove her socks, she about jumped out of her skin.

"Jesse, I'll do that. Please, you have to go." The mulish look in those deep blue eyes told her he had no intention of going anywhere. There was no pretense in his actions, but she was not one of his sisters. She could not—she just could not accept his help!

His wife was making too much of this. She needed him, even if she was too stubborn to admit it. "I'm your husband, Olivia. You have nothing to be embarrassed about."

After the initial shock wore off and her heart calmed to a steady beat, she managed to say, "I won't take my clothes off in front of you."

"I didn't think for a moment that you would."

"Then what do you propose?"

"I'm sure you go swimming all the time in your shift. You can do that now. We'll tend your wounds after you have a good soak in the deep water."

He was digging his heels in, unwilling to budge, so she conceded. However, she removed her own socks and skirt.

Jesse could feel her trembling as he lifted her into his arms and walked slowly into the water. The further they moved into the creek, the tighter she clung.

Her initial contact with the water burned her injured skin, but after a time it felt soothing. She hid her fear well until he began moving again into deeper water. In a near state of panic she buried her face in her husband's chest. "Jesse, that's far enough!"

"You're sweating, I just thought you'd want to get cooled off."

"I'm fine," she affirmed. He looked confused, so she softly

added, "I'd just rather stay here."

"Why?"

Olivia shivered, and Jesse, totally missing her look of terror, assumed she was cold. "Our farm is on the Huron River, Liv. You'll need to get used to the cool water. I love to go swimming, and I'll want you with me."

She lowered her eyes but not soon enough.

"Olivia," he asked, his tone unwavering, "what aren't you telling me?"

Although his inquiry brought her gaze back to his, she attempted to make light of it. "It's nothing really."

He wasn't buying it. "Your expressions tell me otherwise. Tell me what's troubling you." He thought he knew, but he wasn't sure until she spoke the words.

"I can't swim."

"You don't know how?"

"My father never learned. He was afraid I would drown if I went with my friends, so I made my excuses when they wanted me to go."

"We have the perfect spot for you to learn while we're here." She didn't seem enthralled with the idea, so he added, "You need to accomplish this, Olivia. Most of the creek is fairly shallow, but the deep spot we're heading toward should work nicely."

"Maybe I don't want to learn."

"You'll wish you had the first time Jared and Joseph take a notion to throw you in the river."

Her eyes widened. "You won't let them, will you?"

"You're going to learn, My Dear. We'll wait until your leg is feeling better. But I promise to be a very attentive instructor."

Her brow rose. "It doesn't sound like you have swimming on your mind."

"Olivia!" Jesse exclaimed in feigned shock. "I'm offended. How could you even think I'd have ulterior motives?"

"Please! I'm not as naive as you think. My father taught me much about the nature of man—purely out of a need to protect me. He was afraid my trusting nature would get me into trouble if he didn't enlighten me on certain issues. You're my husband. I know in my head that God created us to enjoy each other, but I've yet to find this knowledge comforting. Papa assured me that you were a man of integrity. I believe him until I see a certain look in your eyes that makes me leery of what I've gotten myself into."

"I'm your husband, Liv. There is nothing wrong with the way I look at you. Surely you don't expect me to hide the fact that I find you desirable."

She thought about the joy that her parents found in each other and realized that Jesse's was a natural response. "You shouldn't have to try to hide your feelings. I'm just not used to this kind of attention."

"There's no need to fret about such things. Do I press you when you evade my kisses?"

"No ..."

"I'm not going to force you to do anything you're not willing to do. We have doors that need to be opened, but we'll open them slowly—together. Will that work for you?"

She nodded, unable to look away.

"Olivia, there's a big rock we can sit on under the surface of the water. I'll have to swim to it, but it's close. I won't let your face go under water. Can you trust me?"

She hesitated. "It doesn't sound like you're giving me a choice."

"The deeper water is cleaner. It'll be better for your wounds. Besides," he teased, "we'll call this your first lesson. Your single task is to trust your husband." Jesse didn't wait for an objection before moving further into the water. He knew the creek bed well and stopped just before the drop. "I'm going to let go of your legs so that I can wrap my arm around you. We're almost there. Close your eyes if it helps."

She forced herself to relax against him like she did on Shadow. Before she had a chance to think otherwise, they were sitting on the top of the flat rock Jesse told her about. Unfortunately, her insecurities were pressing in.

Jesse sensed her alarm and never let her go.

The sounds of the babbling creek worked to soothe her every care. It really was such a peaceful setting.

Father, You knew how much I needed this place, didn't You? Of course You did. You know me inside and out. You love me in spite of my many faults. As Jesse and I continue to walk through the days ahead, draw us closer together, Lord, to You and to each other. May Your purposes be accomplished in our lives. Thank You for carrying me through this time of sorrow—this time of discovery.

It wasn't long before the coolness of the moving water began to ease the pain in her leg. Feeling more at ease, she said, "Jesse, we should have brought the soap from the cabin. While we're here, we could get cleaned up."

"If you think you'll be all right, I'd be glad to go and get everything." His eyes never left her as she looked cautiously around.

"Are there snakes in the creek?"

Her look was so solemn that he chortled with glee.

"It's not funny! They give me the creeps!"

"I'm sorry, Liv. Your expression ... it was too much! Snakes *usually* prefer still water that isn't so cold."

The word *usually* offered no guarantees. "Will you hurry?"

Jesse pressed a kiss to her cheek and was off. The moment he was out of sight, Olivia attempted to get a better look at her leg, but she came all too close to slipping off the rock. Needless to say she gave up trying and put her time to better use. Unbraiding her hair, she swirled her feet in the deep water and wondered, *could my father have been wrong about learning to swim? I'd love to be able to glide through the water like Jesse without fear of drowning—especially in all this heat!*

Jesse appeared at the top of the embankment and called out, "Olivia, I brought your hair soap, do you want to wash it?"

"If you don't mind helping."

"Not at all."

Jesse slipped the bottle in the small burlap sack that hung from his neck by a string. He dove under the water, and she felt him tickle her toes before his head popped up. "Hi!"

"Jesse, how deep is that water?"

"I'm not real sure, probably ten feet or so!"

"Oh?" Her eyes widened.

"Don't look so worried, Liv, I won't let you drown." Jesse came out of the water and sat beside her.

She lowered her head. Peering up she admitted, "I lost my balance while you were gone and almost slid off the rock. You wouldn't have been here to help me."

"What were you doing?"

"What do you think?" She bumped his arm purposefully. "I was trying to look at my leg before you came back."

"And?"

"And nothing. I got scared and quit trying."

"All the more reason to learn to swim, don't you think?"

She stared at the man before her, trying to decide if her desire to learn outweighed her fears. "Is it hard?"

"No, but you have to be relaxed and trust the person teaching you."

"Maybe after we wash up, we could start."

Jesse wondered if that was such a good idea. He had no way of knowing how severe her leg wounds were. "Are you sure you're up to it?"

Had she known what he would ask her to do, she might have changed her mind. As it turned out, the rock they were on was much larger than she thought. Jesse had her move to the center of it.

"Liv, you're in a foot or so of water. I want you to lie on my arms until you feel as if you can float on your own. Remember what I said: you have to relax or you won't succeed." After much laughter and several failed attempts, she finally got the hang of it. Jesse noticed, however, that her movements were increasing the flow of blood coming from her wounds and put an end to the lesson.

When they were back in the cabin, he retrieved a dry set of Olivia's underclothes and a nightgown. "I'll turn around while you slip out of your wet things. Put your camisole on and wrap the dry toweling around your waist." Ignoring her rose-colored flush, he averted his eyes until she had finished.

Two of the prongs had torn and severely bruised her thigh, but he had no way of knowing how deep the punctures were. "You'll have to take things slowly, Olivia. The bruising will bother you more than anything, so you won't be riding anytime soon."

She shook her head. "I'm sure I'll be fine by tomorrow."

He gently captured her stubborn chin and affirmed, "You'll take things slowly."

Her father was such a passive man; it might take her some time to get used to Jesse's assertive ways. "You don't have to be such a grouch about it!"

Her impertinence astounded him, but it wasn't as if he hadn't been warned. "You'd better watch yourself, Young Lady. You dish out too much of that sass and it might come back to haunt you!"

Her eyes narrowed in on him. "Tell me, Mr. S, did all your students do exactly what they were told, or did you annoy them as well?" Her flippant words were out before she could stop them. She wasn't prepared to tell him yet. She was hoping against hope that he didn't catch on, but he did!

His mouth gaped open. "There was only one person in the town of Tecumseh who knew that name. How did you hear it?" She was chewing on her bottom lip as if she had no need of it, when he pressed her further. "Tell me, Olivia, did you know Maryse? Did she tell you my teaching name?"

"Well ... yes and no." *So much for my secret!*

"She either did or she didn't!"

The intensity of his gaze told her it was time to explain. "Since the day you pulled me out of the mud I've dreamed of seeing you again." With that revelation, his deep blue eyes came all too close to bouncing out of his head.

"You! That was you?" He was so confused—befuddled was more like it! "How can this be? Your name—did you lie to me?" She was shaking her head, but it made no sense.

"My middle name is the same as my mother's. Since everyone called her Mrs. Ordan, you couldn't have known that her name is Maryse. Papa didn't like me giving my first name to strangers."

"Oh."

"Jesse, you were so wonderful that day. I was devastated when my father told me he had invited a man over with whom he was sure I could spend the rest of my life. I knew it would mean letting go of my dream of finding you. But Papa was adamant. "It's not a woman's place to contact men," he said. "I had no choice. I had to trust him."

"I knew when I first saw you at your parents' house there was something familiar about your eyes and hair. Why didn't you tell me?"

"It was difficult not to." She started to giggle. "Especially while we were walking. You mentioned the woman you met. When I saw you in the sitting room, I couldn't believe my good fortune. At that moment I knew without a doubt that God was bringing us together. He used the bond we had formed to comfort me through all of this. In truth, I was terrified until I realized that the terribly handsome man my father had chosen for me was my knight in shining armor. Once again you came to rescue me—this time from the depths of utter despair."

His fingers touched her cheek. "I still don't understand why you didn't tell me."

"I didn't think you would marry me if you knew I was the klutz you pulled out of the bog. I convinced myself that if you really wanted that woman for a wife you would have come back for her."

He looked so forlorn.

"I can't help it, Jesse. Think of the conversation we had that day. I'm a hopeless romantic. I wanted you to want me for me. I couldn't bear to think that you married me because you felt sorry for me." Her eyes slid shut. "Maybe you did anyway."

His hand came up to caress her face. "Nothing could be further from the truth. I've thought about that tall girl with the red highlights in her long brown hair every day since. It was because of our meeting that no other woman in Frenchtown could measure up. So you see, my dreams have come true as well. It was only because I found you so much like her that I believed we could be happy together. I gave up on her just like you gave up on me."

"Do you really mean that, Jesse?"

"With all of my heart!"

Tears blinded her. She could no longer see the man who caressed her face with his warm hands, covered her cheeks in soft kisses, and then held her gently within the shelter of his arms.

"I'm so glad you told me."

"I should have told you sooner."

Olivia caught the blood dripping down her leg with the corner of her towel, reminding him that his wife still needed his care. After bandaging her wounds, he helped her into a worn out gown. He wanted her to stay in bed, but she was too excited to concede. In truth, he understood.

"Olivia," Jesse asked as he gave her a hand with dinner, "did you tell your parents?"

She grinned. "I told them in the same way I planned to tell you."

"How was that?"

"If you go into our room, there's a package under your side of the bed. Don't open it until you come back in here, okay?"

"I will if you sit down until I get back. You're kind of tipsy, Liv."

"It hurts too much to sit. Go ahead though. I won't move around, I promise."

Jesse wanted her close when he sat down to open the package, so he helped her sit on his leg, avoiding her sore spot. As he peeled back the paper, he couldn't believe his eyes. The painting was a perfect likeness of the two of them, but he was dressed as an English knight sitting atop Shadow with Olivia perched in his lap. "This is amazing. Who did this?"

She nudged his chest. "I did, silly. No one else saw you, remember?"

"All too well ..." he said, awed by her portrayal. "When—when did you start painting this?"

"The week after I met you. I wasn't willing to chance your face fading from my memory."

"I can't believe your father never told me how talented his daughter is—or," he added with much emphasis, "that he had seen my portrait before."

She shook her head. "You don't understand, Jesse. My parents never saw this. The smell of wet paint made their coughing worse, so they never went into my room. Even after they were dry, something kept me from showing them." Smiling, she added, "This way God gets the glory for bringing us back together. I can see that so clearly now. They didn't know you were the man who rescued me until after they left us. I sent a portrait just like this with them and a letter thanking them for following God's lead."

He could feel goose bumps forming on his arms. "Seriously?"

"Yes, but you should know, Jesse, although your wife may be gifted in this area, she's as graceful as an ox." Her admission made him smile in remembrance.

"The day we met ..." he paused for a moment to correct himself, "for the second time, you were so nervous you would hardly look at me."

"I couldn't help it."

"I really didn't mind. It gave me the chance to gawk at the beautiful woman whom I was hoping would be my wife."

Their eyes met. "I know you see yourself as a klutz, but I don't. The way you move reminds me of a dancer in motion."

The smile that brightened her face told him how much his words meant. "As long as nothing gets in my way, I'm fine. It's those knots in the wooden beams and the pitchforks that tend to throw me for a whirl." They laughed, remaining in each other's embrace for quite some time.

"I'm so glad I know, Olivia. You have to admit, it is amazing to see the way the Lord works. Because we were willing to take this step of faith, we now have each other."

"I know you're right. Just don't set your sights too high. I'm still clumsy Olivia, complete with all my many imperfections."

"But you're my Olivia, and with God at the helm, anything is possible!"

He Loves Me!

Chapter Nine

Molding Us for Eternity

OLIVIA WAS NOT at all pleased. Her dear sweet husband had insisted on her taking it easy for several days now. His request had been reasonable. The bruising in her leg was a terrible sight and while the pain was subsiding, one of the puncture wounds kept breaking open. Since she was unaccustomed to such a leisurely lifestyle, boredom set in at a rapid pace.

Had it not been for her plaguing thoughts, she might have welcomed the break. Never having been away from her parents, she missed them terribly. Not knowing if the trip had taken its toll on them left her in a state of turmoil. What she wouldn't give for a moment with them, a hug, or a single kiss. As hard as she tried to get a handle on her spiraling emotions, nothing worked.

It wasn't as if she didn't have *things* to occupy her time. Handwork did have its way of helping her work through her anxieties, so she wiled away the hours on the porch swing with her mending. Unfortunately, her efforts did not have the usual calming effect, but her tattered wardrobe was certainly benefiting from her situation.

Regrettably, her annoyance with the tall man giving the orders had gotten out of hand. Several times she strayed from the path she should have taken—became the storm instead of the calm. She apologized to Jesse, and asked him to forgive her every time. So why did she feel so awful inside?

"Olivia," Jesse had suggested, as he snuggled her close after her last outburst, "I want you to do something for yourself." Filled with conviction, her green eyes rose to meet his deep blues. "Ask the Lord to show you what's really making you to feel like this. Are you angry with me, or is it the Lord? Are you trying to carry your burden alone instead of entrusting it to God? I'll be here for you no matter how long it takes you to sort this through, but you alone can begin to release your grief. You can't pretend it's not there. Grieving is a process you have to work through. Will worrying about your parents change the outcome?"

"No ..."

"As hard as it is, you have to accept what you cannot change. Pray for your parents, yes, but leave them in the Lord's hands."

"I'm trying, Jesse ... but it's not easy."

"In and of your own strength it is hard. Lean on Christ. Listen to what He's trying to tell you through this time. Expect Him to deliver you, Honey. He won't let you fall."

What Jesse said made perfect sense. Her heart was in utter turmoil, but not because of Jesse. It wasn't anyone's fault that her parents were ill, but she did need to quit taking her frustrations out on him.

She had just dried the last pan from breakfast, tucked it away, and was hanging her apron from the hook when Jesse stuck his head in the back door.

"Would you like to go riding?"

She, determined to alter the direction her thoughts were going today, responded to his inquiry. "Can you give me a minute to change?"

His brow furrowed. "What's wrong with what you have on?"

Olivia looked down at her burgundy skirt. It was the only one she had left without a frayed bottom. "I suppose if I'm careful it'll be alright."

Jesse reached for Olivia's hand and led her out the side door. His touch, like the gleaming yellow sun, had a wonderful warming effect. Never having noticed it before, her gaze met his. She was still trying to sort out the changes taking place in her heart when Jesse released her and went into the barn. He came out, kissed her cheek, and handed her Shadow's reins. Her puzzled look made him smile.

"It's time you got used to riding alone, Liv. See if you can get on him while I put a bridle on Mable."

Confused, she asked, "Can you ride Mable?"

"I sure hope so!"

She wasn't questioning his ability, but it didn't take an expert in horsemanship to see that Mable lacked training. Since he was determined, she watched in silence as the huge mare skittered about, spun in circles and stood on her hind quarters several times. Olivia's concerns were mounting, so she offered her recommendation, "Jesse, Mable's not in a very agreeable mood.

Maybe you should put her back and ride with me."

He chuckled softly. "Mable will be fine once we get going, she's just antsy—she needs a little work."

Little, my eye! While Olivia did not agree, she kept further doubts to herself.

Jesse reined Mable in as they came to the open field. Adjusting his wide-brimmed hat, he asked, "Liv, I need to let Mable stretch her legs for a while. Can you keep up?"

Uncertainty washed over her. "I won't have a choice. Shadow won't listen to me if you take off."

"He will if you're firm with him."

When she rolled her eyes, he laughed out loud.

"I'm not sure what you find so funny, Jesse Somers, but I'll try. What should I do if I can't keep up?"

"Just remember what I told you. You're in command. Pull back on the reins if you want him to stop." At her hesitant nod, Jesse made a clicking sound with his mouth, and Shadow, hearing his master's call, leapt into action.

At first Olivia was frightened. She had never ridden at such a speed and wondered what Jesse was thinking. Her hair took flight, and Shadow's hooves barely touched the dry earth as he ran on and on. She prayed that her wounds not rip open. The thought of being confined to that porch another day did not bode well. Keeping her wits about her, she managed to slow Shadow down to an acceptable gait, and in truth she enjoyed the ride immensely! She was lagging behind, but she could see Jesse up ahead and wasn't concerned. The leisurely ride she had anticipated was anything but that. She spied several rabbits leaping through the tall grass. They were probably running from her. Wildflowers decorated the rich lands in abundance, but she sped by them too fast to enjoy their vibrant blooms. Maybe Jesse would allow her to collect a nice bouquet on their way home.

Olivia's eyes flew up when she heard Jesse yell out. He didn't sound hurt, just frustrated. Mable had just reared up and dumped him on the ground. While it took all the restraint she could muster not to laugh as the scene played over in her mind, she managed to marshal her face into a concerned expression. Thankfully, only Jesse's pride had been wounded, but she had a sneaking suspicion he would not appreciate her making light of his circumstances. Regrettably, Mable was long gone.

"Liv, I need to go after Mable. Wait for a while—if she takes me on a wild-goose chase, can you find your way back to the cabin?"

"I'll be fine," she assured him as she slid off Shadow.

Jesse mounted, sent her a playful wink and took off in the opposite direction they had come.

Olivia watched her husband ride out of sight and then slowly scanned the surrounding area. The more she saw, the more unsettled she became. Had she spoken too soon? Nothing looked familiar. Her only thought had been to follow Jesse. Since he would probably come back for her, she tried to set her concerns aside.

Olivia's legs felt strange—wobbly as she paced back and forth. She could only assume the odd sensation had something to do with their morning ride. Thinking it best to stretch them a bit, she ambled around before seeking shelter from the glaring sun under the shade of a huge maple. Settling herself on the hard ground, she leaned against the wide trunk and prayed for Jesse.

It wasn't long before the warm breeze lulled her to sleep.

Olivia awoke with a start. Surely hours had passed and still there was no sign of Jesse. Could she have missed him?

Standing to her feet, she stretched her cramped muscles and realized that her empty stomach was gnawing on her backbone, her parched throat was making it difficult to swallow, and other than wanting to kick herself for sleeping for so long, she was just peachy.

From the position of the sun, she guessed that it had to be at least three, if not four, in the afternoon. She whispered a prayer as she headed in the direction she had come. Her heart rejoiced when she came to the clearing, she assumed that would take her back to the cabin. After walking for what seemed like miles, she stopped and really looked around. Her feet were killing her. Her surroundings, though familiar, were different. The hills were now on every side. Surely they hadn't come this far, had they?

A feeling of dread washed over. She could be lost. No ... she was lost! How would she ever find her way home?

As her thoughts tumbled within, the words her parents spoke whenever she was saddened by their illness, brought peace to her anxious mind.

Who holds our lives in the palm of His hands, Livia? Worry is a sin. It is not our place to question, but to trust. God knows our every need. Lean on Him and He will give you peace.

Dropping to her knees, Olivia began to pray. She prayed for her parents, for Jesse, and then for herself that her Heavenly Father would lead her back to the cabin.

As she surrendered her anxious mind to the serene resonance of God's creation, she heard crickets chirping, birds singing, long grasses swishing in the gentle wind. And then it came to her, as a ray of hope in the midst of her dispiriting circumstances, the reverberation of rippling water. Like a choir of angels raising their voices in praise, the sound was sweet—reassuring.

"The creek!" she shouted. Her spirit quickened as she leapt to her feet thanking the Lord for answered prayer. With a tranquil heart, she followed the timbre of the babbling stream. After taking the time to quench her insatiable thirst, she followed the creek bed upstream. Again, she walked for what seemed like hours. This time was different. She knew she was heading in the right direction.

The light of day had fallen by the time she reached the familiar swimming hole. Only the orange-gold sphere of the setting sun remained to guide her way as she moved up the path that led to the cabin.

Exhausted from her journey, Olivia's heart soared the moment she saw Jesse standing in the yard. He must have heard her approach because he was coming toward her.

She would've thought he'd be glad to see her. His dark look told her otherwise. In fact it was so severe she wanted to flee—but where could she go?

As he came close, angry words flew from his lips. "Where have you been?"

Irritated, her temper flared. "You have no right to be angry, Jesse Somers!" It was the worst thing she could have said. He came toward her so abruptly she backed away. Not quick enough. His strong hands wrapped around her arms and drew her to him.

"I have every right! I've been looking for you for hours!" He shook her gently, needing to be sure he had her full attention. Was she merely exploring and lost track of time? Did she not know the dangers lurking in these woods? His thoughts had been running rampant for too long. "Tell me, where have you been, Olivia?"

Swallowing hard past the lump in her throat, she trembled in his hold. Willing herself to calm, she offered her meek response, "Lost ..."

Her single word said it all. His wife was innocent of all that he had imagined. He was calling himself every kind of fool! Jesse closed his eyes, trying to make sense of it all. "Olivia, I'm sorry." *What's wrong with me?*

She wrapped her slender arms around her husband's waist. She understood his frustration. If he hadn't cared, he wouldn't have been so affected by her absence. Desiring to ease his mind, Olivia admitted, as she rested her weary head on his chest, "I fell asleep waiting for you. I tried to find my way, but everything looked the same. I'm sorry I made you worry. I heard the creek while I was praying and realized I could follow it back." Looking up, she waited for his response.

"I'm so glad you're safe. Please forgive me." Jesse held Olivia's face in his hands and gently dried the tears trailing down her cheeks. As his eyes beheld her, the forgiveness emanating in her emerald gaze soothed his despondent heart. With a hopeful spirit, his searching lips brushed softly across her mouth. Finding no resistance, he drew her closer still.

Olivia's willingness to yield stirred within her emotions she could not define. Responding to his tenderness felt so right.

This was not a fleeting kiss; in fact, minutes passed before

Jesse relinquished his bride—his bride who now stood safe in the shelter of his all-encompassing arms. Sensing her diminishing strength, he scooped her into his arms and carried her into the cabin.

He sat in the chair with her in his arms, and his softly spoken prayer eased both of their hearts—both of their minds. "Thank you, Father God, for guiding Olivia's steps and bringing her safely home. Thank you that Your grace truly is sufficient and Your strength is made perfect in our weakness! Forgive my lack of faith—in You—in my wife."

"Jesse," she admitted after several minutes had lapsed, "it's late ... I know you're tired, but I need to go down to the creek and wash up." Her eyes begged him not to question her further.

After all she had been through, he couldn't possibly deny such a simple request. "I think we could both use a nice cool swim. If you collect our night clothes, Liv, I'll grab the soap and toweling."

He brought along the lantern, but left it at the top of the hill. Having grown up with a sister so close to Olivia's age, he had a feeling his wife would appreciate the cover of darkness to take care of her needs.

"Jesse," Olivia asked as she sank into the cool water, "will you bring the bar of soap? I left it next to the towels." She watched as his towering form waded toward her in the darkness and wondered about the peacefulness that had come over both of them. Was it merely relief, knowing they were safe and together again? Or was it his wonderful kisses she wouldn't have denied him for the world?

"If you turn around, Liv, I'll wash your hair."

She complied without hesitation. "In all the confusion, I forgot to ask if you found Mable."

"She took me on a wild goose chase, all right, but eventually she ran herself into a cove on the side of the hill."

"What do you think scared her?"

Although he wasn't so sure he wanted to tell her, she was waiting for an answer. "A snake."

She shuddered. "I often wonder what God was thinking when he created such creepy crawlers."

"They have their purpose, Liv." Jesse handed her the soap. "Enough talk about creepy crawlers. You won't sleep if we keep this up. And by the way, I think it's only fair that you wash my hair too. Since mine is short and not nearly as much work as yours, you can scrub my back as well!"

"Oh, you think so, do you?"

"Yes, Ma'am, I do!"

She waited until he turned around and squatted down. Feeling ornery, she stood to her feet, jumped up a bit, and pushed on his shoulders. Unsuspecting, he lost his balance and slid under the water.

She knew she was in big trouble when he slithered out of her grasp. He was lurking somewhere under the water. Her eyes darted every which way as she shivered in anticipation. The cover of darkness hid him well. Before she realized how close he was, she felt herself being propelled out of the water. Completely at his mercy, sitting atop his broad shoulders, she pleaded, "Jesse, please put me down."

Not in a compliant mood, he asked as he hung on to her legs and began swaying back and forth, "Tell me, Liv, what's a husband supposed to do with a wife who seeks to drown him?"

"I would never!"

"Ah, but you tried." His chiding words continued as he swayed faster and faster. He seemed to be trying to dump her off, yet he held her legs tight, not allowing her to fall.

Losing her sense of balance, she wrapped her arms around his head. She was giggling so hard she unwittingly covered his eyes.

"Now you not only seek to drown me, you're blinding me as well."

"Jesse, put me down. I promise to be good while I do my chores."

"Chores!"

"Well, you did say that doing my hair was work, so I can only assume that washing your hair and scrubbing your massive back will be an even greater chore." His response was to lean forward and dump her face first into the creek.

After righting herself, she came up spewing water, muttering as she pushed her hair away from her face. "What's a wife supposed to do with a husband who steals her horse, yells at her when she gets lost, gives her several rather amazing kisses, and now tries to drown her as well?" She paused before saucily adding, "You'd better be nice, Jesse Somers, or I'll have a nice long talk with your mother and tell her just how abusive you've been."

Without warning, he reached out in the darkness, pulled her into his arms and silenced her threats with another indescribable kiss!

"Is that nice enough for you?"

"I don't know," she teased, hesitating just long enough to

summon the courage to add, "maybe you should do that again so I can be sure." Jesse chortled out loud—all too happy to oblige.

"You keep this up, you'll be my wife in earnest sooner than you thought." Noting his wife's timid response, he immediately regretted his words.

Olivia turned away, embarrassed by her forwardness. She should tell him. "Jesse ..." she began, but the words would not come.

He reached for her hand, and she turned to face him. "Talking about such things can be awkward, but we have no need for secrets. I had a feeling something was up when you wanted to come for a swim. When did you start?"

"I didn't yet, but the way my stomach's cramping, I know I'm going to. Sometimes it last seven days ... I'm sorry."

"I'm not, Liv. A week ago I thought I'd be going home without a wife. I've been blessed with the woman who has filled my dreams. I'm in no hurry. God's timing is everything."

"How well I know ...."

She sank into the cool water, moved behind her husband and gladly washed his hair and back. It pleased her to know they could speak so freely. Without her parents around to confide in, she needed a confidant. Jesse was like no other friend she'd ever had.

Papa was concerned that no man would understand or put up with my unusual ways. In many ways she was holding herself at bay. Even so, Jesse seemed to be taking things in stride. Coming to love this man might be easier than she had thought. Only days had passed since their nuptials and already the adventures and wondrous pleasures he had shown her surpassed her expectations.

Climbing up the steps, she hung their wet things over the porch railing. "Jesse, look at this, I've ruined the only skirt I had left without a frayed bottom. Your parents are going to take one look at me and think you've married a street urchin."

He wanted to laugh, but the gloomy look on her face told him it would not be wise. "Olivia, my family won't think that, not for a minute. Besides," he flippantly added, "if you're that worried about it, make yourself some new clothes."

She looked up at him and rolled her eyes. "And how do you propose I do that, Mr. Smarty Pants?"

Now he did laugh, a deep hearty laugh that he found difficult to contain. "I haven't heard that expression in years!"

"If you keep picking on me, you'll be hearing it quite often, Mr. Smarty Pants!"

That was it; he wrapped his arms around her, sat on the swing, and tickled the sass right out of her!

"Jesse, quit!"

He kissed her cheek. "Give me one good reason why I should."

"'Cause I'm tired. I need to go to bed."

"Not with wet hair, you're not. You'll be ill."

"I can't stay awake that long."

He smiled. She did look like she would fall out at any given moment.

"I'll compromise. Let me brush out your hair, and I'll hold you in the chair next to the fire until it dries. If you fall asleep, I'll carry you to bed."

She would have argued the point, but frankly she didn't have the energy. Besides, with his determination, she had an inkling she'd be fighting a losing battle.

"Jesse," Olivia asked as he continued to brush through her tangled mass, "I know my father told you where they were going. Do you think they arrived?"

"No ... not yet."

Since she agreed with her father's reasons for not telling her their destination, she didn't question him further. "I got to thinking while I was walking: you haven't been fishing since we arrived. Is there a reason?"

"Just haven't gotten around to it. I have a couple of poles in the barn, we could fish tomorrow if you'd like."

"I would."

Olivia had no more laid her head on the overstuffed arm when she drifted into a peaceful slumber. For a time, Jesse stared in wonder at the beautiful woman now curled in his lap. He loved the way they were coming to depend upon each other. In truth, he had never expected to feel the way he did so soon in their relationship.

Her expression when she commented about meeting his family in her tattered clothes brought a smile to his face. How could he have forgotten to tell her about the purchases he made for her? He would have to check with her tomorrow and see where she had put them.

Jesse was struggling to stay awake, so he snatched his wife's Bible off the small end table and turned to Second Corinthians, the first chapter. As he began reading, all the little notes she had written along the margins attracted his attention. He couldn't help being drawn in by her understanding of this passage. Down by verse nine, he read, *This happened that we might not rely on ourselves, but on God.* Then by verse eleven he continued: *Life is a test, a preparation for Heaven. God in His great love for His children made a way for us to enter Heaven through Jesus Christ. He uses the experiences we go through in life to mold our character into servants He can use. He is molding us for eternity.*

This, he thought with awe and wonder, *is powerful stuff. If we as believers could go through life and keep these thoughts ever before us, we could accomplish so much more for God's kingdom.*

Father, may we ever look to Your Word for strength and guidance in this journey. Comfort my wife in her loss, and help us to give thanks in every circumstance.

❀ ❀ ❀

"Mom," Lizzy asked as she came in the back door to her parents' house, "where's Dad?"

Elizabeth's daughter Brenae was in her arms. Brenae smiled the minute Jayne came into view. Cameron, Elizabeth's son, ran toward his grandma with outstretched arms.

Jayne lifted Cameron, kissed him and Brenae as well, before responding to Elizabeth's question. "He's in the sitting room, Honey."

A huge grin brightened Elizabeth's face. "Mom, I got a letter from Jesse. He was married the morning after he sent this missive. Since you don't get to town as often as you used to, he asked me to pass the letter on to all of you."

Jayne was shocked. "He didn't even tell us that he was courting someone. Let's go out with your dad and we'll read the letter together."

Lizzy found her father fast asleep in his chair. She hated to disturb him, but this couldn't wait. "Dad," Elizabeth said, as she laid her hand on his warm cheek.

George looked up at his oldest daughter and grinned from ear to ear. "Hi, Honey, what brings you and my grandchildren out so early this morning?"

"I would have come last night, but you know what Kaleb's like when he thinks a storm is brewing. Mr. Worrywart couldn't come with me, so he insisted we wait until today."

"Well, you're here now. Tell me, Honey, what has you all fired up?"

"I got a letter from Jesse, Dad. Would you like to read it or shall I?"

"You go ahead, I left my spectacles upstairs." George smiled knowingly. Elizabeth's love for her big brother had not waned in the time Jesse had been away, and the knowledge of it warmed George's ailing heart.

Elizabeth took a seat next to her father, opened the letter and began:

Hello to all in Ypsilanti!

This letter comes with all my love and much joy over my coming marriage. While I don't have time to give you all of the details, I'll tell you what I can and we'll catch up when I get home, which will be no later than harvest time.

I met a very remarkable young lady in Tecumseh, and I have no doubt that God has brought us together. Her name is Olivia Ordan and she has agreed to become Mrs. Jesse Cameron Somers in the morning.

We are overjoyed to be joining our lives together, but tomorrow will hold a mixture of joy and sadness for my dear Olivia.

After the nuptials, her parents will be leaving to seek medical support in their remaining days. They are both suffering from tuberculosis. Mrs. Ordan is in the final stages of the disease and suffers a great deal.

Olivia and I will be going to the hunting cabin. I thought about bringing her home right away, but I feel strongly that she will need time to grieve over her loss. This will also give us a few weeks to begin depending on each other.

I can hardly wait for her to meet everyone. She has no other family, so we are it. I have no doubt that you will make her feel welcome when we arrive.

Lizzy, I have to tease you a bit. Do you remember telling me on the way back from Detroit that I couldn't be too specific, or I might miss the woman God has for me? Olivia is living proof that it really is okay to dream big. She's tall with long spindly legs, and she has red highlights in her long brown hair. Now about her personality, I must warn you! My mind has been totally altered in that respect. I decided before I arrived in Frenchtown that I wouldn't know what to do with a woman who was too agreeable. I'd say she's about as sassy as they come, so you two should be great friends!

I'll be picking up a new team and wagon so Olivia

can bring a part of her past into our new life together. I'm just kicking myself for not finishing our house before I left. God knows all that. I'm sure she'll enjoy living with our big family for a while.

Her parents are going to write to us when they arrive at their destination. Pray not only for us as we begin our lives together, but also for Olivia and her parents.

Take it easy, Dad, and know that all of you are in our thoughts and prayers. I'll be back to help soon.

Until we meet again, I love you,
Your son or brother, Jesse (whichever applies!)

Lizzy looked up at her parents, who both had tears running down their faces. "Now stop that you two or you'll have me crying again. What do you think, Dad?"

"I think it's wonderful. Sounds to me like they needed each other, and that's a good thing."

"That's what Kaleb and I thought too. How about you, Mom?"

Jayne sighed with relief. "I think it's grand, but we'd best get their quilt started or we'll never have it done in time for them to arrive."

"Kaleb said he'd take me into Ann Arbor tomorrow for supplies. If we can decide on a color scheme, I'll pick up the fabric."

"That would be good. Do you mind picking up the other supplies we need while you're there?"

"Just make me a list."

"So tell me, Dad, how are you really doing?"

"I wish I could say I'm fine, Lizzy, but the spells are coming more often. The good Lord may be calling me home sooner than I would have thought."

Tears flooded her eyes as she wrapped her arms around him. "Don't talk like that, Dad. I can't bear the thought of your leaving us. Maybe it's selfish, but I need you here to spoil my children."

"I'd love to be here too, but His will isn't always ours. Besides, you know me. I'll be up there singing and rejoicing with the saints who've gone before me."

"Well, until that time comes, if you promise not to talk like this and make me cry, I'll tell you a secret."

"Oh?"

"You didn't promise, Dad."

"All right, I promise, so tell me!" Lizzy's glassy eyes were twinkling, so George had a pretty good idea what she was about to tell him.

"Now you can't mention this to anyone else, but Doc says we have another baby on the way."

George caressed her face, grinning as he did. "That is good news, Honey. Are you feeling okay?"

"It's strange, but I feel great this time. Doc seems to think I'm already three months along."

A huge smile spread across her mother's face. "That means you'll be getting fat just in time to meet your new sister-in-law."

"Thanks for the reminder, Mom!"

George put in, "Now! Now! Now! God's keeping you humble. All part of His plan, you know."

"How could I forget? The rumors that followed me being

stuck in that cabin with Kaleb were humbling enough. When you insisted that I marry Kaleb, I didn't think I would ever be happy again, but look at me now. If you weren't willing to walk in obedience to the Lord, I would have missed out on so many blessings. I may be fat when I meet my new sister-in-law, but I'm glad God cares enough to keep this servant humble. I know how blessed I am!"

"And so are we, Lizzy—so are we!"

Chapter Ten

Grandpa and Grandma

"HEY, LAZY BONES!" Olivia cajoled as she shook her husband's shoulder trying to wake him, "breakfast is ready." When he didn't budge, she saucily added, "I'm starving, so are you eating with me or not?" After her third try she stood at the side of the bed, tapping her foot to an impatient beat. "Fine! Stay in bed all day. See if I care!" When he didn't even flinch, she issued a baiting remark that was sure to get a reaction. "I'm going berry picking on the hill behind the cabin ... see you later."

"No, you're not!" he bellowed as he flew out of the bed and ran after his squealing wife.

"Now, Jesse," Olivia implored, managing to stay just out of reach on the other side of the kitchen table. "You have to be nice; I was merely goading you."

"You'd better be!" He countered as he dashed around the table, capturing his defecting wife and drawing her into the circle of his arms. "Now what are you gonna do, Mrs. Smarty Pants?"

Squinting against his imminent response, she coyly intoned, "Feed you so I can go ... berry picking?"

She was always wide-awake, full of vim and vigor first thing in the morning. He was not. Jesse stared intently at his spirited wife, wanting desperately to kiss her. His long fingers ran ever so slowly down the side of her face and earned him her full attention. "Don't forget what I told you, Liv, or the wolves and coyotes will be the least of your worries."

The tenderness in his eyes and the amazing kisses that followed made it difficult to believe he could ever be harsh with her.

Thoughtfully, Olivia moved towards the stove. She dished up the ham and potatoes before filling a plate with muffins and setting it on the table.

Jesse, lost in his own ponderings, poured her tea and his coffee. After praying over the meal, he questioned her. "Last night you wanted to do some fishing, so I suppose the choice is yours: fishing, or berry picking."

"Why can't we do both?"

"We won't have time, Liv. The meat supply is getting low, and the way those clouds are changing, we'll be getting rain tonight or tomorrow. The hunting can't wait. Would you rather me go this morning or after dinner?" His wife wasn't enthralled with being left alone, but he refused to take her. If she was anything like his sisters, she'd never let him shoot a thing, and frankly, he didn't have the patience for such nonsense.

"Will you be gone long?"

"That depends on how well I do. Your father told me you

don't like staying alone, but this time it can't be helped. Just stay in the cabin and bolt the doors—you'll be fine."

She was about to offer a simple solution when out of the blue he asked, "There were a couple of packages in brown wrap from the store. Where did you put them?"

"On the top shelf in the pantry."

He stood to retrieve them, quite pleased with himself when he returned and placed them in her lap.

"These are for you. I wasn't teasing last night when I said you could make yourself some new clothes, Mrs. Smarty Pants!"

"Are you serious?" Her smile went from ear to ear.

"The proprietor in Tecumseh was very accommodating when I told her who these things were for."

"Mrs. Weihe's a sweet lady. She had been hiring me to make clothing to sell in the store for the last year or so."

It shouldn't have surprised Jesse that Olivia had to help support her family, but it did. "I was wondering, Liv, what did your father do for a living?"

"He was a carpenter before he took ill." She had a far away look in her eyes. He gave her a moment, but the suspense was killing him.

"Are you gonna look at what's inside those packages or make me wait all day?"

"Shouldn't I wait until after you leave?"

"No, you should not!"

Her green eyes twinkled with glee. "You're sure?"

"Olivia ..!"

As much as she loved teasing him, her curiosity was peaked. She pulled the string on the smallest package and smiled up at her husband before opening the wrapper. Inside she found two skirt lengths of fabric: a nice golden brown, with a light print for a blouse, and a deep shade of purple with a darker print for a matching jacket. Under the stack of fabrics were trims, buttons and threads to match. She was so pleased speech evaded her.

"Did I do all right?"

"Better than all right, these are wonderful! Thank you." As hard as she tried to ward them off, her eyes glassed over and then tears began to fall.

Jesse pulled her out of her seat and into his lap, quickly altering her mood with his moving fingers.

"Stop!" she screeched. Her feeble attempt to escape his hold failed, but that was just fine with her—she wanted him close.

He kissed her cheek. "Where do you think you're going in such a big hurry?"

"Don't tickle me, Jesse."

"Then no more crying. I didn't buy these things to make you cry. I was hoping they would make you smile. Besides, how can you sew if your eyes are all swollen?"

She had to ask, "How did you know I needed clothes so badly?"

"I asked the proprietor if she knew of anything specific Olivia Ordan could use as a sort of wedding gift from her husband."

Her expression was demure. How did one respond to such generosity?

"Come on, Liv, open the other package. Your lady friend's reserve would not allow her to help me pick these items out."

As Olivia digested his blatant admission, her flush deepened.

"Whenever Lizzy and I would shop together, I did a little

looking myself. I've longed for the day I could buy pretty things for my wife. I hope you don't mind."

If her apprehensions were not at an all time high, she would have kissed him. Fortunately, Jesse's excitement prevailed. She reached to open the ties.

He watched with pleasure as her wide eyes danced in delight, enthralled with every discovery. She loved the colorful ribbons and combs for her hair, the looking glass, comb and brush set, and she desperately needed the three new pairs of socks. She drank in the wonderful scent of lilac salts for her bath. When she picked up the soft flannels for nightgowns she rubbed them against her skin. Then she found a beautiful raspberry fabric for a warm winter dress and stood, holding it up against her frame.

"Oh, Jesse, it's so soft, and this color is lovely."

"I'm glad you like it." His greatest satisfaction came when she withdrew the last items in the package. She slowly fingered the intricate lace trims and delicate fabrics of the intimate apparel. A whirl of emotions spiraled through her—and him as well—when she turned her soft green gaze on him.

Did she know the way his heart was changing towards her? Did she feel the same way? For now he could only wonder, since pressing her was not an option.

She was pleased and yet astonished at the same time. Pleased that she would finally know what it was like to wear the dainty unmentionables, that up till now, she could only look at in the store, but astonished that Jesse would buy her such personal things. As understanding dawned, an overwhelming sense of timidity washed over her. Olivia, knowing these gifts were not given for her alone, forced herself to confront her own commitment to this union. Would she ever get beyond her anxieties and allow her husband to delight in seeing her in such things? Maybe if she could begin to place his needs above her own, she could then make a few bold moves that would help her to move beyond intimidation, and someday welcome his closeness.

Hesitantly, she pressed herself to make such a move and reclaimed her place on his lap. Wrapping her slender arms around his neck, she thanked him for the gifts, as she leisurely ran her long fingers through his thick brown hair. When that was not enough, she summoned the courage to caress his bristly cheeks and offered one sweet kiss after another.

Moments had passed when he breathlessly offered, "Olivia, feel free to do that any time you'd like."

The thoughts that transfused her mind induced a dreadful case of the giggles.

His confusion knew no bounds.

"What about in the morning when you're still a grumpy bear?"

He sighed audibly. "You start out my morning like that and I assure you the bear will no longer exist."

Olivia wasn't sure she could accommodate, though she would consider it. She kissed the tip of his nose and hopped off his lap saying, "We'll see!"

"So what's the verdict, Liv?"

She considered the unavoidable. "I suppose I'd rather you go now and get it over with."

"Tell me, can I count on you to help me skin and clean ..."

His words were halted when she closed her eyes, covered her ears and bellowed out, "La-la-la-la -la-la-la-la-la-la-la-la-la!"

As Jesse exploded with laughter, she cautiously opened

her eyes and ran out the door.

He collected the things he would need and was ready to bid Olivia farewell when she came back in. "Shall I take your reaction to mean you don't clean fish or butcher chickens either?"

Her fierce scowl told him exactly how she felt about his inquiry.

Jesse gathered her to him and held her gaze. "Let's make sure I have this straight, so I never have to bring it up again. You have no desire to know where the meat comes from as long as it is cleaned and ready to cook when I bring it to you."

Olivia smiled. "You're a very wise man, Jesse Somers."

His demeanor became solemn. "Put the bar across the door the moment I leave. And, no matter who comes, stay out of sight unless you're sure it's me. Don't leave the cabin for any reason, understood?"

"Yes ..." she said as her eyelids slid shut and then rose when she added, "you don't have to be such a grouch about it."

As hard as he tried, withholding a smile was nearly impossible. "Do as I ask and I won't be."

"Let me see if I have this straight." Jesse's uncompromising glare warned her to tread lightly. Her playful mind ignored it. "If anyone seeks entry, I should hide myself within the castle walls, because the daring knight who guards the lady of the keep is away on the hunt and will not allow her to bid the visitor enter."

All pretenses aside, Jesse pierced her with his narrowed glare. "If the lady of the keep does not adhere to the orders given, she will find out just how daring this knight is when he upends her across his knee upon his return."

With a flick of her hand, she dismissed him. When he did

not release her she informed him, "You're such a grouch, Jesse Somers. Now kiss me and away with you!" With a raised brow, she tauntingly added, "I shall bar the doors so I can try on all these pretty things while my generous knight is away and unable to see."

Shaking his finger in her face, he tweaked her nose and admonished with a smile, "You, Olivia Maryse Somers, are a terrible tease, and one of these days ..."

She interrupted his blathering with a flippant reminder, "Papa warned you of your plight before we wed, so don't threaten me, husband."

"He did, and that suits me just fine." Convinced this conversation could hold him up for hours, Jesse turned to leave. While Olivia had made every attempt to show him otherwise, her apprehensions were clear. He would do his best to hurry back.

After cleaning up the mess in the kitchen, she carried her packages to their room and slowly went through them again. Unable to resist, she tried on her unmentionables and was pleased with how well they fit. She tucked them away for another time. After spreading the new fabrics on the bed to get a closer look, she decided to start with the deep purple. She could use another skirt, and her white blouse would go nicely until she could finish the new one. Olivia folded the other fabrics, opened the large chest her father's hands had made, and carefully placed them inside with the extra notions.

Knowing her tendency to lose track of time while sewing, she went back to the kitchen and started dinner. The bread supply was low, but she could stretch it out for one more day if she made muffins or biscuits to go along with the soup. She filled the pot with water and added salt, pepper, dried celery, carrots and onions from last year's garden. When she reached for the bag of beans, she didn't take the time to measure and dumped way too many in the mixture. "Oh, brother!" she scolded herself. "Slow down, Olivia. Now you'll have to add more of everything. We'll be eating bean soup till it's coming out our ears!" Rolling her eyes, she diced the ham and potatoes, slid the pot onto the burner and stoked up the flame. After filling the kettle for tea, she added more water to the soup as well.

She couldn't resist peeking out the kitchen window. A small possum was waddling away from the barn toward the trees. Several robins were digging for worms, but nothing out of the ordinary was stirring, so she hurried back to the bedroom to gather her needle, thread, fabric and scissors. She cut the skirt out on their bed, and she had just plopped down in the chair that sat in front of the fireplace to begin sewing when she remembered the kettle on the stove. *Really Olivia, you're such a flibbertigibbet!* Most of the water had boiled out, but enough remained to fill her mother's small teapot. She added a bit of sugar, placed everything on the tray, stirred the soup and put the lid on the pan before she made her way back to the sitting room.

Her diligent efforts were paying off. She had just started pinning the waistband to the skirt when the sound of horses pulling a wagon up the hill drew her attention. Taking a deep breath, she cautiously moved to the window, wondering who it could possibly be. This cabin was out in the middle of nowhere. It wasn't as if neighbors would be dropping by.

Jesse's orders were clear, so she stayed out of sight, hugging the wall next to the window. She waited until they were closer before taking a quick peek.

A woman with snow-white hair leaned against a man with a full white beard and tan wide-brimmed hat. She couldn't be sure, but the elderly woman looked gravely ill.

What should I do? Jesse had warned her not to open the door for anyone. Surely he would make an exception for this elderly couple—wouldn't he? Not knowing what to do, she decided to let them make the first move.

When the gentleman pulled the team to a halt in front of the cabin, Olivia moved on silent feet toward their room.

Jacob Woods saw the smoke coming from the cook stove in the kitchen, so he knew someone was in the cabin. Why wouldn't anyone answer? After several knocks, he went around and tried the side door—nothing!

Desperate, he stood on the front porch, calling out to the occupants who were apparently reluctant. "If anyone is in there, I'm Jacob Woods. We're good friends of the Somers family. My wife has taken ill on our journey home. I'm sorry if we've frightened you in any way, but I really could use your help."

Olivia couldn't listen any more. At the risk of dealing with Jesse's wrath, she removed the bar and slowly opened the door. "I'm sorry I didn't come right away. My name is Olivia Ord ... Somers. My husband is hunting and left me with strict orders not to answer the door."

The elderly man's mouth dropped open. "Am I to understand that our Jesse has taken a wife?"

Olivia smiled as a delighted grin creased the gentleman's aging face. "Yes, he has. I'd be glad to help you get your wife into the cabin, Mr.?"

"Woods ... you can call us Grandpa and Grandma, Olivia. Jesse does."

"I'd love to!" Olivia moved toward the woman in the wagon. "Hello, Grandma, I'm Olivia, Jesse's wife." Anna looked to her husband for confirmation. Jacob nodded, so she turned back to Olivia.

"Well, I'll be! It's about time Jesse took a wife ... and look at you. Oh, Honey, you're lovely."

"Grandma, you don't look so good. We should get you into the house, and then we'll talk."

Olivia's concerns for the frail woman escalated as they walked into the cabin. "Grandma, I'd feel much better if you'd lay in the bed and rest until I can finish our noon meal."

"I think that's a good idea, Honey. I don't wish to be a bother, but I am a little under the weather."

Olivia had Anna sit on the edge of the bed so she could remove her boots for her. Olivia then helped her out of her dress, hung it from the hook behind the door and slipped the nightgown Grandpa supplied over her head. After tucking Anna in, Olivia offered, "I have a pot of tea made. It's not hot, but it is warm. Would you like some?"

"I would. Thank you."

Olivia, enthralled with this couple already, had to believe that Jesse would be glad she let them in. When she came out of the bedroom, Jacob's gaze was fixed on her. It pleased her to see him relaxing in one of the big chairs.

"Olivia, come over here and let me get a good look at you." As she neared, he slipped his large hands under hers and gave them a reassuring squeeze. "You're something else. Jesse is blessed to have you, but let me assure you he'll make you a good husband."

She couldn't withhold a smile. "He already is a good husband. Grandma wants a cup of my warm tea. Can I interest you in some, or maybe a cup of coffee?"

"If you have enough tea that sounds fine."

Olivia lifted the tray she had sitting on the end table and went to the kitchen. After filling their cups, she added two plates and put an apple muffin and a thick slice of cheese on each. She didn't know how far they had come without eating, and she didn't want them going hungry.

"Here you go," Olivia said, as she placed the tea and food on the small table next to Jacob.

"Thanks, Olivia, this smells wonderful."

"Dinner will be ready in about an hour. I hope you like bean soup. I think I made enough for an entire regiment!"

He chuckled. "Sounds grand."

"Good." Olivia nodded and took the remaining items on the tray in to Anna. "Do you think you could sit up and try to eat a little something?" Her skin felt warm to the touch. "Grandma, besides the fever, what are your symptoms?"

"My head hurts, my throat's sore, and I've been coughing. It's like I get a tickle, and it just won't quit." Anna's heart wrenched at the sight of tears flooding Olivia's eyes. "Oh, Honey, don't worry. I'm going to be fine. I've only been ill for a few days."

Olivia's relief was obvious.

Anna sensed a deep-set pain behind Olivia's tears and made a mental note to question Jesse later.

The blazing yellow sun flickered high in the sky by the time Jesse returned from his successful morning hunt. Hungry enough to eat a bear, his stomach churned as he neared the cabin. Olivia must be cooking. The aroma was growing stronger. *Beans and ham*, he thought.

He leapt up the back steps to let her know he was home, but when he lifted the latch on the back door and found it open, alarm slammed through him. Looking around, his distress was replaced with frustration when he realized there was no sign of forced entry. She had obviously disregarded his warning. Hearing movement in the barn, he headed that way. When Jesse came to the open door his wife was bent over a pile of straw filling a tick. Without a word, he moved to her side.

Filled with fear, Olivia's wide eyes flew up when Jesse grabbed her arm and swung her around to face him.

"Why are you out here?" he berated. His irritation was clear.

"Jesse!" Olivia exclaimed, surprised beyond further words, she wriggled to free herself from his grasp.

He had no more relaxed his grip when a deep male voice interrupted his thoughts. Jesse's mouth dropped open in shock when he turned to find Jacob Woods standing near one of the stalls.

"I know Olivia disobeyed you, Jesse; she told me as much. I don't wish to interfere, but you really should think this through. In the short amount of time we've been together, I have no doubt that our prayers have been answered."

"Grandpa?" Jesse was so perplexed.

"Yes, Jesse. Grandma and I arrived about an hour ago. The year you've been away has been long. We've missed you."

"Same here." He was still confused.

"Jesse, you settle things with your wife and then we'll chat. Keep in mind that a wise husband treats his wife with gentleness. Listen to her, talk things out, and then neither of you will have regrets." Jacob, understanding the young couple's need for privacy, left the barn and moved toward the cabin to check on Anna.

Jesse turned back to his wife. Feeling foolish, he led her to the bench and gently pulled her into his lap. The uncertainty in her eyes was too much for him to bear. "Olivia, I'm so sorry! Grandpa is right. I'm a fool for not letting you explain."

She accepted his apology, but the trembling would not cease—nor could she stop the flow of unbidden tears. As much as she would like to be alone to sort this out, she needed this resolved. Forcing her gaze to his, she could only stare.

"I've always thought of myself as a fair man, but I seem to be proving otherwise where you're concerned. I have much to learn about self-control and trusting my wife—don't I?"

"None of us are perfect, Jesse."

"Maybe you could start by telling me how you handled this. Knowing won't change what I've done, but it could help me to see that you're not impulsive."

"I heard their wagon coming up the hill. I stayed out of sight like you said, but Grandma didn't look so good. Grandpa knew someone was inside. He explained who he was and how he knew your family. When he pleaded on his wife's behalf, I couldn't stand it, Jesse. I had to let them in."

"It's fine, Liv, you did the right thing."

"Grandpa was really worn out, so I came to the barn with

him to unhitch the team and settle his horses."

A doubtful grin crossed his face. "You helped him?"

"Don't tease me, Jesse. It's not my fault if my husband hasn't taught me about hitches and such. I did the best I could with Grandpa's help. The wagon is behind the barn by ours. I put his horses in the empty stalls and fed them. I couldn't add another act of defiance to my list of many, so I didn't go to the creek for more water. I gave them what was left in the spare bucket." She shrugged. "You might need to give them more. I have no idea how much horses drink."

"That's fine. Do you think you could find it in your heart to forgive me?"

She peered into his hopeful eyes. "I can see why you reacted the way you did ... of course I forgive you, but you really scared me, Jesse." Olivia's eyes found their way to her lap.

A wave of doubt passed through him.

"I need to tell you a few things that I should have told you the night I got lost. If I had, I'm fairly sure none of this would have happened."

"Okay ..."

"We're bound to make mistakes. I expect that. Even so, I have to believe you have my best interest at heart. I made a decision to trust you the day we were wed, and with God's help, that will not change. Having you in my life, Jesse ... well, it gives me an overall sense of security that I desperately need with my parents gone. I have too much riding on this relationship to be careless. I think your grandfather is right: when your anger flairs like this, it shows me that you don't trust me. I would like to see that change, but I understand that these things take time."

He dried her damp cheeks with the palms of his hands. "Thank you for telling me. I'll work on it, Liv. I promise."

"I just have one question for you." Her cheeks flushed.

"What's that?"

"How will I ever look your grandfather in the eye again? I'm so embarrassed."

"Honey, I have much explaining to do, but you—you've done nothing wrong."

"But ..."

"Liv, Grandpa's only concern is for your welfare. He has prayed for years that God would bring the right woman into my life. I haven't seen him in almost a year, and how does he find me? Sinning against the woman we've prayed for. I'm glad he was here to stop me, but I have not heard the last of this. Grandpa is a fine Christian man and an elder in our church. He holds nothing back when he thinks I'm wrong—and boy, was I wrong. I know I'm in for a deep discussion about the benefits of being a loving husband who listens to his wife and never lashes out in anger." When Jesse dramatically shuddered, Olivia started to laugh.

"Personally, I think it might do you some good."

His brow arched. "Oh, you do, do you?"

"Oh, yes! Builds character, don't ya know?"

"You're the only character around here!" When his moving fingers came to her waist, she squealed, leapt off his lap and ran towards the door.

"Are you coming in for dinner, or are you afraid to face your grandpa?"

"Get in the house you sassy thing! I'll be in as soon as I water the horses and see to something else."

"What?"

"You don't want to know, remember?"

"Oh." As Olivia turned to go, she glanced back and smiled. Her heart was so much lighter knowing they had come to a peaceful resolution.

After checking on Jacob and Anna and finding them both asleep on the bed, Olivia moved back to the kitchen to finish the meal. The bean soup had thickened up nicely, so she started some corn muffins. While they were in the oven, she mixed up a batch of her mom's sugar cookies.

Everything was ready when she heard Jesse calling from outside. She wondered why he didn't just come in until she opened the back door and took one look at her husband. Horrified by what she saw, she ran towards him, screaming, "Jesse!" He was splattered with blood from head to toe.

"Liv, settle down. I'm fine."

"But ..."

"You don't want me to tell you about it, remember?"

"So, you're not bleeding ...?"

"No, I need some clothes and soap so I can get cleaned up in the creek."

"You could have warned me. I thought you'd been attacked by a pack of wolves!"

"Not this time." Without an ounce of concern in his tone, he pointed up the hill and said, "I have a friend up the way though. He has been watching my every move."

Olivia's gaze followed the direction his finger was pointing and stopped dead on a coyote. She had never seen one up so close. The sight of him made her shudder. "Jesse, you'd better come in the house. Won't it come after you?"

"I doubt it. For the most part, they're scared of humans; besides, he's only interested in the items I'm not allowed to tell you about." She laughed at the goading expression on his face.

"You're just lucky I'm not coming down to the creek with you, Jesse Somers, or I'd be dunking your ornery self in the water!"

"Ah, ah, ah! Watch those threats, or you'll be joining me, like it or not."

His tone told her he would follow through without a second thought, so she backed off, thinking, *Sometimes it's best not to tempt fate.* "Now would be a good time to go and get your clean things."

Nodding, he agreed, "You're a very wise woman for your fifteen years!"

"Almost sixteen," she muttered as she moved in the back door.

Olivia returned in short order with a stack of clean clothes in her arms, a big bar of soap and a large piece of toweling.

"Did you need anything else?"

"This should do."

"Jesse, I was wondering, were you saving the chocolate and lemon drops for anything in particular?"

"Nope!"

"Good, see you in a bit."

❀ ❀ ❀

"Grandma," Olivia softly called, as she tried to wake her.

Anna opened her eyes and, smiled. "Hi, Honey. Did I sleep through dinner?"

Olivia caressed her pale cheek and returned the smile. "No, Grandma, you haven't. Jesse's back. Would you like to join us at the table, or have your meal in here?"

"I have to get up anyway, Honey, I'm in your bed."

"While you're with us, consider it your bed." Anna was about to protest, so Olivia added, "Jesse and I won't take no for an answer. I've made us a straw tick for the floor, and I have extra bedding from my room at home. We'll be just fine."

"As long as you're sure. I'd like to join everyone at the table. Let me sit up and see how I feel."

"Take your time. When you're ready, I'll have Jesse help you to the table. Grandpa said you don't have your robe along, so you can wear mine."

"Oh, Honey, I don't want to be a bother."

"You could never be a bother, Grandma. I didn't know my own grandparents. I'm thrilled to have the time to spend with you. Besides, Jesse has an extra shirt I can use as a cover up."

Olivia had the robe wrapped around Anna when Jesse came into the room, sat down beside Anna and gave her a big hug.

"What's going on, Grandma? A little under the weather?"

"I'm afraid so." Anna reached for Olivia's hand and brought it to her lips. "But look who we found when we came to the door— an angel of mercy. Where on earth did you find this sweet girl?"

Jesse's eyes sparkled as they met his wife's. "She's certainly an answer to my prayers."

"Ours too, Honey."

Jesse smiled. It didn't matter to Anna if you were a man or a woman; if you showed her kindness in any way, you were *Honey* to her. "We'll take our time going out to the table. Olivia made us a feast. I've been out hunting all morning so I'm starving."

"Don't let him fool ya, Olivia. It wasn't the hunting that made him hungry. He's got a hollow leg. I wish you all the best trying to keep it filled."

"Thanks for the warning. I need to pour the drinks before we eat. Would you like tea or coffee?"

"Oh, tea, Honey. Always tea. I never did develop a hankering for coffee. Jacob said I would whenever I grew up, but he was wrong. Either that or I'm an eighty-three-year old child." She giggled softly, adding, "Now wouldn't that be something?"

Jesse slid his arm around her waist. "You're something all right, Grandma. Even Grandpa would attest to that!"

Chapter Eleven

Blueberry Pie

O LIVIA FOUND IT hard to believe that over a week had passed since Jacob and Anna's arrival. Olivia was pleased. Her new grandma had recovered quickly under Olivia's tender care. The color was back in Anna's cheeks, and her cough had eased considerably. While Olivia loved doting on the elderly couple and enjoyed them immensely, she understood their desire to be heading home.

Grandpa mentioned at breakfast that they would be pulling out tomorrow morning, so she racked her brain for a tasty dessert that would make their last supper together special. Only one thing came to mind.

Since Jesse had things he needed to do in the barn, she asked Jacob, who was still seated at the table, "Grandpa, it looks like there's a patch of berry bushes up the hill behind the cabin. I've got a hankering for pie, sound good?"

His mouth watered as he thought of the many delicacies Anna had created for him down through the years. "Sure would be a nice treat."

Her eyes brightened. "That's what I was thinking, but I have a problem."

"Anything I can help solve?"

"Jesse doesn't want me wandering off alone, so I was wondering ... would you mind sitting in the chair beside the cabin and watching me while I pick?"

"Be glad to. Should we go before the sun gets too hot?"

She nodded. "Sure, let me grab my bucket."

Olivia knew what she'd be up against the minute she stepped out the back door into the stifling air. As she began her trek up the steep hill, the sun beat down unmercifully. Still she trudged on, giggling as she recalled Jesse's offer to confiscate a pair of his brother's jeans for her. Her ascent would have been easier if she had them, but would she have summoned the courage to put them on? The way her skirt kept tripping her made her think she could. Fortunately, the berries would be reward enough for her efforts.

She was within feet of the crest when she spotted the first bush filled with plump blueberries. Sighing with pleasure, she thought, *my favorite*. She waved at Jacob to be sure he saw her and knelt to pick them.

Mmm! Olivia savored the sweet flavor as she shoveled the first handful into her mouth. Her father had a firm rule whenever they would come across such a find together—the first handful belongs to the laborer. The berry pickers need nourishment. *Oh, how I miss my parents. I know they're safest in Your hands,*

Lord, but will this ache in my heart ever ease? See to their needs and give them strength for their journey.

Emptying that bush, she moved on to the next and then to another. She set her bucket down in front of the fifth bush and heard her grandpa calling.

"Olivia ..."

Glancing down the hill, she could see him standing, looking her way. His tone was filled with concern, and his next words earned him her full attention.

"Olivia, don't panic, Honey. Come slowly towards me."

She would have questioned him further, but she heard a low growl behind her. Suddenly all else was obscure. As she turned to look, alarm slammed through her. She was staring into the pale green eyes of a ferocious snarling wolf—no more than eight feet away. Her father had said they travel in packs, so she scanned the area for others. Although none appeared, this one caused the hair at the base of her neck to stand on end. Jacob's advice escaped her frenzied mind. She ran for the nearest tree and scrambled up it. Unfortunately, her quick movement set the beast in motion. He lunged toward her sinking his teeth into her skirt, scratching the back of her leg as her feet left the ground. When the wolf lost his grip on her skirt, she climbed higher. As she pulled herself upward, her foot swung out, and he latched onto her boot instead. His sheer determination terrified her. It took every ounce of strength she could muster to ward off his assault. With great effort, she finally shook him loose. But, Olivia kept climbing. She had to be sure he would not reach her again.

It took her a moment to catch her breath. Her heart had barely begun to ease when she glanced down the hill; Grandpa was almost to the barn. *Jesse! He's going for Jesse. Oh no!* Her brain reeled. *Is the snarling wolf at the foot of this tree really the least of my worries?* Jesse would be furious and rightly so.

She put it out of her mind and tried to maneuver to a more comfortable position. Regrettably, her foot was stuck in a groove. All she could do is wait for her husband—and he was the last person she wanted to see.

Jesse came running toward her with his gun, yelling as he fired into the air. The wolf took off like a scared rabbit—she, on the other hand, was still caught in the tree. Olivia noted the muscles twitching in Jesse's neck and lowered her gaze. She could not bring herself to look his way as his dogged steps brought him closer and closer.

"What did I tell you, Olivia?"

Guilt washed over her as she met his narrowed glare. "I'm sorry. I should have waited for you. I thought ..." She could not continue. The disappointment in his eyes was unbearable.

"Can you climb down?" he asked through clenched teeth.

"My foot's stuck ... I can't get it out."

"Good!" he declared as he turned to leave. "Maybe if I leave you up there for a while you'll heed my warning next time." His angry words brought quick tears to her eyes.

"Jesse, please!"

He ignored her plea, picked up the bucket of berries and continued on his way.

Olivia's gaze never left Jesse as he made his way down the hill, stopped at the bottom, said something to Jacob while handing him the berries, and headed for the barn. Her concern mounted when Jacob made his way in the back door without glancing her way. Completely at Jesse's mercy, she had no way of knowing how long he would leave her there, but she would bide her time without complaint. After all, his anger was justifiable.

Only minutes had passed when he came out of the barn with the ladder, but it felt like hours. He was heading towards her again. What she wouldn't give to be able to disappear. She said not a word as he made his way up the hill, adjusted the ladder and climbed up to her. His calm visage left her feeling more unsettled than if he had lashed out at her.

"Olivia, lay across my shoulder so I can work your foot loose."

She complied—not at all comfortable with her awkward position. He struggled with her boot until it finally broke free. When they were on the ground again, he made sure she was stable, picked up the ladder, latched onto her hand and moved down the hill. As they neared the back door, she tried to pull away.

He held on tight.

"Jesse, please let me go. I have things to do ...."

"We have things to settle!"

Glancing nervously at her husband, she again tried to pull away from his grasp.

Not about to accept her refusal on this matter, he set the ladder down, slung her over his shoulder again, and took great strides toward the barn. When he passed it and headed for the creek, there was no doubt in her mind what would happen next.

Wrapping her arms around his neck, she begged him, "Oh Jesse, please ... I don't have any more clean clothes!"

"You should have thought about that before you climbed up that hill!"

"I'll wait for you next time, I promise."

He warned his dangling wife as he removed her boots, "Don't tempt fate again, Olivia. I might not be so kind the next time, understood?"

A small "yes" escaped just before he hurled her into the water.

Jesse's eyes never left her as he removed his bluchers, socks, and all but his under drawers before joining her.

Although the swimming lessons were paying off, her weighted clothes made it difficult for her to move freely in the deep water. He would not chance her going under.

When he came towards her in the water, his unwavering look irritated her. Lamentably, her every attempt to avoid him proved unsuccessful. She had no right to be annoyed with him—but she was.

Her reluctance brought a gentle smile to his face as he turned her to face him. "Liv, please look at me."

As kind as his tone was, she could not comply.

"We both know you were wrong, but like you told me several days ago, we're bound to make mistakes along the way. I forgive you." His heart beat several times before her shoulders slumped, and she melted in his arms.

"I tried to convince myself that you wouldn't mind as long as Grandpa watched me. Deep down I knew you would. I really am sorry."

"I appreciate your telling me the truth, and I'm glad that you're sorry, but I think you owe me more than words."

Her wide eyes, filled with doubt, met his. "What do you mean?"

"To begin with, that had better be the best blueberry pie I've ever eaten."

"And?"

"Several kisses would be a nice start." She laughed out loud when he sucked in his cheeks, made fish lips, and crossed his eyes.

"You can't really expect me to kiss a man who looks like a deformed fish. I'm sorry, Jesse, I just can't do it!"

His tone sobered and his fingers began to move. "I'd strongly suggest you try."

"All right!" she conceded and took him totally by surprise ....

Jesse helped Olivia out of her weighted dress so they could swim for a while, but her long list of unfinished chores weighed heavy on her mind.

"Jesse, our laundry is piling up, and I wasn't kidding when I said I have nothing else to wear. Even my nightgowns need washing."

"I'm sure we can find something in my things that will suffice until your clothes are dry."

She rolled her eyes, mentally going through his clothing, trying to picture what he had in mind. She gave up trying.

"Liv, would you like me to haul water, or should we do the laundry down here at the creek?"

She hadn't thought about that. "Are you offering to help?"

"Sure, sounds like fun!" She ignored her husband's playful wink and willingly took the hand he offered as they moved up the hill.

She was glad that Jesse had forgiven her, but now she

needed to make things right with her new grandfather. While Jesse retrieved the laundry tub, she went inside to collect the other things they would need. Olivia found Jacob in the sitting room and immediately went to him. His eyes were closed, and while she knew he might be asleep, she needed to speak to him. "Grandpa." Her touch startled him.

"Olivia! What happened to you?"

"I'm fine. That grandson of yours threw me in the creek. I'm sorry I put you in the middle of this. I tried to convince myself that Jesse wouldn't mind me going as long as someone was watching me. I should have checked with him first. Will you forgive me?"

"As long as I can steal a big wet hug."

She was happy to oblige. "Grandpa, Jesse said he'd help me do the laundry. Do you have anything besides the few clothes I saw in the bedroom?"

"That's it for now. Can I do anything to help?"

"No. You just relax for a while. I'll be back in to make dinner as soon as we hang the clean laundry on the line."

He nodded and Olivia made her way to the bedroom. She had a question for her grandma that simply couldn't wait.

"Grandma," Olivia asked, as she opened the door and found her awake. "I have a huge problem."

Anna's brow rose. "Do you think I can help?"

"I got myself in trouble today. Jesse forgave me for what I did, but he said the blueberry pie I'm making had better be the best he has ever tasted."

"So what's the problem, Honey?"

"I've never made one before. I looked through my mother's

recipes, but there's not one in there. Please tell me you know how."

Anna offered a reassuring smile. "I'm not normally one to brag, but my recipe for blueberry pie is the best I've ever tasted."

She hugged her. "Thanks, Grandma. You're a life saver."

"Glad to help. Honey, if you get me some paper and a pencil, I'd be glad to write some of my favorite recipes down for you."

"You know them by heart?"

Anna giggled. "Yes. I've used them so many times, they're forever written on my mind."

Olivia gladly did Anna's bidding before joining Jesse outside.

The warm summer day flew by in a whirl of activities. By the time the four of them sat down to the evening meal, Olivia and Jesse were exhausted from their efforts.

Jesse looked to Jacob and asked, "Grandpa, would you like to say grace?"

"I would love to." His eyes slowly scanned the table and then fell on his granddaughter. "Olivia, every meal we have had at your table has been delicious, but tonight you have outdone yourself."

"We've enjoyed having you. Jesse said it could be a while before we see each other again, so I wanted tonight to be special."

"We can't thank you enough for your wonderful care. I'm sure Anna agrees that we're blessed to have such a special new granddaughter."

Olivia nodded, saying, "That goes both ways."

"Let's bow our heads and thank the Lord for His goodness."

Jesse had just finished his last bite of rabbit stew when his eyes narrowed in on his wife. "Are you going to share that blueberry pie I've been smelling all afternoon or keep torturing us?"

"I suppose ...." Olivia went to the counter, dished up everyone a hearty portion, and couldn't help but smile as she placed Jesse's piece in front of him. She held her breath as he took the first bite. The twinkle in his eyes told her all she needed to know, although it was nice to hear his proclamation.

"Mmm! Mmm! Mmm! I'll tell you what! This is the best blueberry pie I've ever tasted!"

Olivia kissed his cheek, thanked him, and sampled it herself.

Anna smiled when Jesse sent her a corroborating wink, knowing this was not the first time he had savored this wonderful pie. It pleased her to know that he would keep their little secret for the sole purpose of encouraging his new wife and making her feel special—for, in fact, she was a special gift sent straight from the Lord.

Chapter Twelve

Created for Each Other

*J*ESSE WRAPPED HIS arm around Olivia as they stood in the meadow watching Jacob and Anna's wagon move slowly out of sight. His eyes beheld her with undeniable devotion. The tears trickling down her sunkissed face were stirring untried emotions that transfused him body and soul. Was he coming to love her? They were becoming more and more at ease with each other, and the way she had bonded with his grandparents warmed him deep inside—so much so he had considered following them home. While he desperately wanted to share Olivia with his family, the notion had no more entered his mind when he pushed it aside. They needed time—time to explore the other aspects of this wonderful covenant called marriage.

Although his grandparents would be missed, and his prayers would go with them, it was not them who held Jesse's thoughts captive. The desire to sweep Olivia off her feet and claim her as his own overwhelmed him. He had every intention of doing that soon, but he would not rush the day. For now he settled for drying her tears and claiming a passionate kiss.

"Do you have plans for the day, Jesse?"

He nodded. "I have a few things to accomplish ... won't take long. I'm looking forward to having some alone time with my beautiful wife."

Hearing tenderness in his tone, Olivia's wide green eyes rose to meet his deep blues. As they did, a wave of uncertainty swirled through her. His thoughts were written on his face. Was she prepared to surrender to his growing desire?

He smiled at his timid wife who turned away from his intense gaze and suddenly became very interested in the budding wildflowers. As the gentle breeze tussled her unbound hair, he tried to decipher why her mood had changed so suddenly—but nothing came to him. Instead of questioning her, he helped her gather a nice bouquet, hoping the gesture would relieve her mind.

They were back to the cabin when Olivia announced, " I need to get the bedding washed, or it won't have time to dry before nightfall."

"That's fine. Let me finish what I started in the barn, and then we'll go."

She shook her head. "Jesse, I don't need your help ... there isn't that much to do."

His eyes narrowed in on her. "You know what happened the last time you went off on your own. If you're in that big of a hurry, I'll haul water for you."

There was something about the way he said it that irritated her profusely! In truth, she thought he was being ridiculous, but arguing the point would do no good. He was just as bull-headed as she, so she said nothing and stormed into the house.

Women! Jesse thought as he headed down the hill. *One would think her confrontation with that wolf would have scared some sense into her.* He should follow her into the cabin and get to the bottom of her irritation, but he had no desire to fight with her. *Not today!*

Olivia found a vase on the pantry shelf, filled it with water and plopped the bouquet in it. Normally she would have delighted in arranging the lovely buds just so. Unfortunately, her dismal attitude had a way of taking the joy out of everything. As she placed the vase in the center of the table, a strange scratching sound coming from the bedroom drew her attention. Since it stopped when she neared the door, she could only presume her imagination was playing tricks on her. Thinking it was better to be safe than sorry, she opened the squeaky door just a crack and took a peek. Nothing! Sighing with relief, she pushed it the rest of the way open.

Her heart skipped a few beats when a squirrel darted around her and scampered into the kitchen. In truth, she thought the small creatures were adorable in the wild, but having one in the cabin was a different story. It was her fault. How could she have forgotten to close the window?

In her impertinent frame of mind, she was not about to ask Jesse for help. *Anyway, how hard can it be to get rid of the varmint? It's no bigger than a ... large rat!* She shuttered at the thought.

Summoning her courage, she reached around the corner leading to the kitchen and grabbed the broom. It would serve well as a weapon—if needed. She didn't think the bushy-tailed critter would come after her; however, she did think it was best to be prepared. She devised a plan—a feeble one, yet a plan nonetheless.

Beady brown eyes peeked out from under the table as she leapt towards the door and propped it open. She looked like a fool prancing across the room. Felt like one too! *No matter,* she thought, *who do I have to impress?*

Now all she had to do is run back to the entrance and shoo the thing out with the broom. If only the squirrel had read her mind. It darted! She screamed—twice, before she reached her destination.

When he stood at attention in the middle of the kitchen, rational thought evaded her. It was one thing to have it hiding under the table. Now, well, now the fury thing was looking at her!

Taking a deep breath to calm her nerves, she prayed that he, she, whatever it was, would make the next move. No such luck! Frustrated, she stomped on the wooden floor like a spoiled child—screeching her frantic war cry! The poor creature could take no more and scurried out the door.

She ran to secure the entrance and then the window. As she offered up thanks that the ordeal had ended, she giggled and twirled around. No doubt, she handled the situation badly. Somehow she could picture God laughing at her ... with her ... and the thought made her laugh all the more.

Unfortunately, when she went back to strip the dirty linens off the bed, her irritation with her husband again reared its ugly head. *What is wrong with me?* she asked herself, but she didn't have a clue as to the source of her annoyance.

Jesse had apparently finished what he needed to do in the barn because he was coming toward her as she stepped out onto the porch. Since she had nothing to say to him, she picked up the laundry basket and strode past him.

Confused, he asked, "Do I need to haul anything?"

A curt "nope!" was all she offered.

For the life of him he didn't know what he had done. When he reached the path that led to the creek, he stopped at the top of the hill and watched his wife. Her skirt and blouse had been discarded and she was standing on the bank in her shift. He smiled when she stuck her toes in and swirled them around testing the cool water. And, how could he not laugh when she lost her balance and fell in? Thankfully, she didn't hear him.

As Olivia regained her footing and stood, every curve of her slender frame held him spellbound. *She's so beautiful!*

Although the enchantment ended when Olivia reached for a sheet and moved back into the water, he could not bring himself to look away. She finished washing the first one and was reaching for another when it finally dawned on him. *She's angry because I didn't want her at the creek alone. Well, she'll just have to get over it!*

Since she did not seem to want his help, Jesse refused to offer again. Instead, he went back to the barn, grabbed his fishing gear and a small shovel to dig up worms. Olivia kept her back to him as he came down the hill and followed the creek until he came to his favorite fishing hole. As much as he hated the tension between them, he thought it was best to give her the breathing space she apparently needed.

After threading a nice big worm on each hook, he threw his

lines in and took a seat on the stump of a huge oak. A few years back a storm had come through and uprooted the aged tree. A large portion had fallen across the creek, stopping up the flow of the water, so he and Kaleb had worked for two weeks chopping it up for firewood and salvaging what they could for furniture.

He glanced down the path at Olivia and couldn't help the soft chuckle that escaped. While he hated to keep comparing the two of them, she really was like Elizabeth in many ways! For the most part his sister was a delight to be around, but she did have her moments. If she thought for an instant that he and Kaleb were being overprotective, her irritation would flare like Olivia's did earlier.

He would never go to the extreme Kaleb had, but to a degree he could understand Kaleb's desire to keep his sister from harm. Love really was a powerful driving force.

The ambiance of the babbling brook reminded him of the Huron and home. He longed to get back and see his family. It bothered him to think that his niece and nephew wouldn't remember him. Jesse wondered how much his little sisters and brothers had also changed in his absence. Ten months was a long time to be away.

In a way he felt guilty contemplating all that he had missed when he gained so much more than he could have ever hoped for. As ornery as Olivia was at the moment, he loved having her in his life. Would the love he and his family have to offer be enough to fill her void? He whispered a prayer that it would be so .... He also prayed that God would be with her parents, ease their pain, and heal them in body as well.

Jesse had three fish in the bucket when he saw movement

out of the corner of his eye. Olivia was placing the last damp sheet in the basket. He waited to see if she would ask for help, but when she took off with the heavy load and tried to make it up the hill—unsuccessfully—he set the poles down and headed her way.

Olivia realized that she was going to have to ask for help or carry the wet items up piece by piece. When she heard Jesse coming toward her, she opted for the latter. By the time she had the quilt on the line, he'd set the basket down and was standing behind her.

Jesse, astounded by her pluck, shook his head when she reached for the next sheet, completely ignoring his presence. All appearances told him a confrontation would be unavoidable.

Olivia's heart beat at a murderous pace. He was close—too close. She cringed when his large hands slid around her waist and turned her to face him. In her reluctance to look at him, she said what she thought he wanted to hear, "Thanks for bringing me the basket, Jesse."

He was all too aware that her words had cost her. "You're welcome." Since she was still avoiding his gaze, he pressed her, "Are you going to tell me what's wrong, or make me guess?"

He wanted to kiss her. She looked so adorable standing there, trying to look angry in her damp shift.

Flippantly she said, "I'm sure you already know what's wrong." When she tried to move away, he would not let her pass. She pleaded through gritted teeth, "Let me go ... I have work to do ...."

"Olivia." His tone was not unkind in any way, but her annoyance remained at the fore.

"What?"

"Do I need to take you down to the creek and throw you in again?"

His grip loosened.

She slithered out of his arms. Before he could grab her, she took off running toward the barn. Her determined heart raced out of control. Jesse was right behind her. At least he was until she cleared the barn door and raced up the ladder to the loft. For some reason, he slowed to a snail's pace. Never having been in the loft, she had no way of knowing she was trapped. It didn't take her long to figure that out. *Oh no!* Her mind reeled in desperation. *What am I going to do now?* A quick peek over the edge brought her husband's smiling eyes to hers.

"In a bit of a pickle, are you, Liv?"

She backed out of view, demanding, "Go away!"

"Not hardly, My Dear!" Jesse waited for a time.

She remained as quiet as a church mouse.

"Are you going to come down so we can kiss and make up, or would you like me to come up and join you?"

She wasted no time in setting him straight. "I wouldn't kiss you if my life depended on it!"

His brow arched. "Is that so?"

"Yes—so go away!"

"You forget too easily that I have ways of exacting compliance, Olivia."

Impudence oozed from her tone, "And they work like a charm ...."

That was it! He flew up the ladder and pounced on her before she had time to take her next breath. "Now what are you going to do, Mrs. Smarty Pants?"

She stuck out her tongue and turned away laughing.

"You know, Young Lady, if you were one of my students you'd be in really big trouble right now."

"Well, I'm not, so don't be such a grouch!"

"Grouch!" He choked on the word. "If I remember correctly, I'm not the one who has been stomping around having a temper tantrum for the last two hours."

"If you weren't so blasted irritating, I wouldn't have a reason to be mad!"

All too aware that this conversation was getting them nowhere, Jesse really looked at the half-dressed woman in his hold and wondered ... *Is she picking a fight with me on purpose? Is it possible that she's merely uneasy over what the night will hold?* Having no answers, he gave her an ultimatum. "You have a choice, My Dear. You can sit up and kiss me or land yourself back in the creek."

When she offered no reply, he threw her over his shoulder, descended the ladder and his long-legged strides had them to the water in no time at all.

Olivia didn't even try to put up a fight. In truth, the heat in the loft had gotten to her. She looked forward to cooling off. To her surprise, he didn't toss her in like yesterday. Instead, he kicked off his bluchers, cradled her in his arms, and walked slowly in. By the time he reached the center of the swimming hole, she had apologized for her anger, slid her arms around his neck and surrendered to his ardent kisses, one right after the other ....

"Jesse," Olivia asked as they stepped up onto the bank.

"Did you catch anything?"

His smile brightened. "Yes, Ma'am. Would you like to have

fish for dinner, or supper?"

"I was wondering ... would you mind having our big meal early today?"

"Fine with me." The light glistening through the trees twinkled in her eyes, and he could only speculate as to what she had on her mind.

"Any chance you'd settle for a picnic supper?"

There was something about the way she leaned against him before peering up that earned her his undivided attention.

Every nerve in his body came alive. "Where would you like to go?"

She smiled as she stood on her toes, kissed his cheek, and whispered, "I thought I'd leave that up to you."

For a long moment Jesse could only stare. He might be reading her wrong, but Olivia came across as being more receptive to him than she had been in days. His grandparents' presence could have attributed to her apprehension. Whatever had brought on this change, he was pleased. "Sounds like a fine idea. I'll be up to the cabin with the cleaned fish before ya know it."

Olivia nodded, offering a subtle smile as she turned and walked up the hill. She had much to do before they could leave, but she tried not to get ahead of herself. She spread the rest of the linens on the line, realizing as she did how nice it was to be out in the middle of nowhere instead of in town. The wilderness did have its advantages. Jesse didn't mind if she stayed in her damp shift, as long as it was just the two of them, so she took him at his word. She did feel a little odd to have so little on, but why sweat if she didn't have to?

Olivia opened the kitchen window, hoping the gentle breeze

would cool her while she did her baking. Firing up the stove on such a sweltering day would be unbearable, but it couldn't be helped. She had enough blueberries left to make muffins for dinner, and she had a real hankering for cookies. Her grandma had given her a few new recipes that she had already tested on Jesse and knew he loved them. They'd be a nice treat to take along on their picnic. The bread was getting low, but she had enough to make ham sandwiches.

By the time Jesse came in the back door with the fish, the last tray of cookies was in the oven. He set the meat on a plate and washed his hands before taking a clean towel from the shelf. After pouring his wife a glass of water, he dipped the towel into the cool bucket, wrung it out, and gently wiped the sweat trailing down her face. His gesture made her smile.

"Thanks, Jesse. I know you're hot too, but would you mind pealing some potatoes while I start the fish?"

"Not at all. I see you've been busy. Smells good." He stole a cookie off the plate and took a big bite. "Mmm ... molasses, my favorite."

She giggled as he shoved the rest of it in his mouth. When he tried to steal another, she swatted his hand. "You'll spoil your appetite, Young Man!"

"Hardly, I'm starved!"

The meal they shared was delicious as always. Olivia's talent in the kitchen never ceased to amaze him.

Jesse went to retrieve his Bible. He and Olivia were going over his sermon notes from a series Pastor Jamison had taught on the seasons of life. Opening his Bible he read Ecclesiastes chapter three.

As hard as it was for Olivia to hear these passages, she listened intently, knowing they would bring her comfort in the days and weeks to come.

"Pastor reminded us that we have to go through various seasons in life so we can grow. You know, Liv, when I think about all I've learned and the sweet fellowship I shared with the Jamisons over the last ten months, I realize how true these passages are. God was preparing me—showing me how important it is to walk in obedience. I could have ignored the inner promptings of my heart and stayed home. But, if I had done that, I wouldn't have you. I was discouraged when I thought I'd have to go home without a wife, but God had a plan. He brought us together when we needed each other the most." Tears were collecting in her eyes as Jesse added, "Pastor went on to say that these seasons we go through are out of our control. Although at times they can be confusing, God has a purpose for them, and we need to trust Him."

"I'm trying, Jesse. Knowing my parents are in the Lord's hands brings me comfort, but I miss them terribly. I'm anxious to get to Ypsilanti and see if I have a letter." Jesse pulled her out of her chair and cuddled her in his lap.

"I know you are. It's too soon, Liv. They weren't scheduled to arrive at their destination for two more days."

She found this news disheartening. "If that's the case, I won't get a letter for at least another week or two."

Not knowing what he could say to console her, he asked, "How are your new clothes coming along?"

"Grandma finished my skirts for me, and I'm working on the last blouse."

"Well ... how would you feel about leaving soon?"

"Are you serious?" Her swift mood change brought a smile to his face.

"Yes! If we get an early start Saturday morning, we might be able to make the church service on Sunday."

"Do you mean it?"

"Absolutely! Are you sure you can be ready?"

She rolled her eyes and squeezed him tight. "Does a rabbit have ears?"

"Last time I checked."

"Then I'll be ready!" A wave of doubt ran through her. "Are you sure ...?"

Jesse, noting the vulnerable look in her eyes, answered her question before she could finish asking, "They will love you from the moment they lay eyes on you—stop worrying!"

"How can you be so sure?"

He reached to caress her cheek. "Olivia, you're going to have to trust me in this."

"I'll try." She had so much riding on his familys' acceptance; she couldn't help being a little uneasy. She would have to leave her cares in the Lord's hands.

"Enough about this; you're getting yourself all worked up over nothing. Besides, I'm looking forward to this picnic. Go ahead, pack the basket and get ready. I'll haul water for our evening bath, saddle Shadow, and be back to get you soon."

She was about to question what he said when he flew out the back door.

By the time Jesse came back in, the linens were back on their bed, the food had been packed, and she was mending her holey socks. She gladly set them aside to join her husband.

"So are you going to tell me where we're going?" Olivia asked as they headed toward the clearing on Shadow.

"Nope!"

"Fine with me, I like surprises."

She was riding in front of him and didn't see the smile that crossed his face. His wife's admission was not very convincing.

"Jesse."

"Hmm?"

"You told me that Suzanne is thirteen and Louise is ten, almost eleven. How old are Jared and Joseph?

"Jared turned sixteen in February, and Joseph was fifteen in May."

"So they're my age?"

"That's right." When she grew pensive, he asked, "Does that bother you?"

"You don't think your family will mind that you married someone so young?"

"Not at all." Jesse saw the turn off for where he planned to take her and pointed up the way. "Look, Liv. Is that a view or what?"

Olivia's gaze followed his finger to a meadow filled with daisies, lilies, and a multitude of other blooming wild flowers in a variety of vibrant hues. In fact, there were so many, she would be hard pressed to name them all. Off in the distance a large drooping willow sat close to the creek. Jesse agreed that it would offer a nice amount of shade for their picnic, so they headed that way. What she wouldn't give for an empty canvas and a full pallet! The scene was breathtaking.

Husband and wife shared a wonderful afternoon, laughing, talking, and simply enjoying the many wonders of God's creation. Since so much of Olivia's life had been spent indoors caring for her ailing parents, everything was a fascination to her.

A small brown toad leapt in her path while they were exploring. Jesse stooped down, caught it, and placed it in her hand. The amphibian's spotted skin, as soft as velvet, fascinated her until the creature urinated on her hand. She squealed, and the poor thing went flying through the air. Chipmunks scampered about, racing up and down the trees. Jesse recommended that she stand perfectly still when a skunk meandered up to the water's edge, sniffed around, and nonchalantly waddled away. Olivia spotted a snake slithering about, even followed in its course, but deemed it prudent to keep her distance. This adventure could have held her captive for hours—days—possibly weeks, but Jesse had become preoccupied with his thoughts and no longer joined in her explorations.

She observed him from a distance as she gathered another bouquet. She could not look away. His tall muscular frame leaning against the tree was a sight to behold. His eyes, as deep as the bluest sea, followed her every move. Her heart rhythms increased with every shared glance. They were entranced in each other. If she were a mouse and he a hawk, she would have reason to fear him, but she did not. In fact, she had a few thoughts of her own that might surprise him. If only she could summon the nerve to share them. Growing uncomfortable under his vigilant watch, she was about to stroll away when Jesse called out.

"Olivia, we need to be heading back."

"So soon?" She would have balked at his suggestion, but

something in his expression kept her from doing so. Instead, she simply thanked him for bringing her as she packed up their belongings.

He held her close—too close as they journeyed home, and while she could hardly breathe, she never said a word. An unfamiliar presence hung between them that both frightened and excited her all at the same time.

Jesse kissed her cheek, lowered her to the ground and handed her the basket before he went to bed the animals down. She heard him fumbling around in the kitchen when he came back in, but she was so engrossed in the book she had finally begun to read, she didn't bother to check on him. He would let her know if he needed something.

Emotionally entangled in the story—rebel Indians had captured the heroine and she was being led into a village—when she heard her husband's call from the kitchen. "In a minute, Jesse ...."

He called again, "Olivia!"

"Give me a few minutes ... I have to see what happens ...."

He stuck his head around the corner.

Her eyes met his. She had no idea what he wanted, but the book no longer held such a powerful draw. Perhaps the woman in the novel was less at risk than she? Olivia swallowed hard past the lump now forming in her throat. "What are you up to, Jesse?"

He sent her a playful wink. The indisputable longing in her husband's eyes had its effect. She could not ignore her goose flesh, and the knot in the pit of her stomach would not let up.

"Come and see for yourself!"

Olivia's eyes widened as she rounded the corner and took in

the scene before her. "I've never seen a tub that big ...."

Jesse would have responded, but he was suddenly at a loss for words. Instead, he turned Olivia away from him, laid her hair to the side and slowly unbuttoned her dress.

The beat of her heart increased with his every touch.

"I've always thought that every married couple should have one of these to enjoy, together."

The full impact of his intent came to light. She thanked the Lord that he could not see her heated face. *Surely he doesn't want me to bathe with him ... does he?* Just as she was about to ask, he turned her back to face him.

"Olivia, I'll get the toweling while you undress and get in. I'll join you in just a minute."

As he was about to leave, she blurted out, "Jesse ..."

"Hmm?"

"I ... c ... can't ...."

His gentle hand lifted her chin, bringing her eyes to his. "Olivia, both of us love the water. Perhaps I'm wrong, but I thought starting out in a bath would be less awkward than the bedroom."

What would make you think that? Her thoughts were barely rational as she tried to sort this out. *His request is reasonable. He's given me enough time to adjust. I love being in his arms, find him desirable, and his kisses are amazing. My parents made it clear that I have nothing to fear, everything to gain. We were created for each other, so why—why the panic, Olivia? Jesse has done nothing to give me cause to distrust him. In truth, he has gone out of his way to show me that he cares for—even treasures—me. True, he hasn't declared his love for me. Even so, this door needs to be open—but now? Does it have to be now?*

Sensing her unease, Jesse whispered a silent prayer. Kicking his bluchers off, he abandoned his original plan and lifted his reluctant bride into his arms. Their gaze, the windows to their hearts never parted as he climbed into the tub with his wife—fully clothed.

Olivia giggled as they sank into the warm water, saying, "Jesse, you're so silly."

"So in love ... with my beautiful wife."

It was the most wonderful thing he could have said. The fear that had seized her loosened its hold. The gentleness of his touch as he caressed her face, his passionate kisses that came one right after the other were an amazing place to start. Forsaking all reluctance, husband and wife were swept into a whirlwind of mutual yearning and shared pleasures that took them swiftly into uncharted waters ....

Chapter Thirteen

Family

OLIVIA'S EXCITEMENT AS they drove the team into Ann Arbor encouraged Jesse's heart. She had been so quiet and thoughtful over the last few hours, he couldn't help wondering if he should have given her more time before bringing her home. Her face, now alight with pleasure, relieved his concern.

After pulling the team off to the side and setting the brake, he jumped down, reached for her waist, and slowly lowered her to the ground. Her dress was a mass of wrinkles from their journey, but his tender look, as she tried to push them out, told her all she needed to know. She looked beautiful to him. Suddenly his opinion was all that mattered.

Jesse offered his arm, and asked, "Are you ready to meet your new family, Mrs. Somers?"

Unable to resist, she stood on her toes and stole a kiss. "I am now."

Hand in hand, Olivia and Jesse climbed the steps and moved quietly into the chapel. The congregation's voices were being raised in worship, so they remained in the back until the last stanza had been sung. Jesse nodded in greeting when Pastor Williams glanced his way before making an announcement to the congregation, "We have some special guests who just arrived unexpectedly."

The small gathering of friends turned in their seats and followed their pastor's gaze.

"I would like all of you to take the time to welcome Mr. and Mrs. Jesse Somers, before we open the Word of God together."

"Jesse!" Elizabeth squealed the moment she saw him. She handed the baby to Kaleb and flew into her brother's outstretched arms.

"Oh, Jesse. We've missed you so!" Several seconds passed before Elizabeth realized that the woman she had been longing to meet was standing at her brother's side. "Oh my, Jesse, I'm sorry ... how could I be so rude ...." She turned to her new sister and without another word, pulled her into her arms.

There was nothing Elizabeth could have said or done that would have meant more to Olivia. Her simple gesture made her feel loved and accepted.

Elizabeth stepped back and took a long hard look at Olivia who asked, "You must be my oldest sister, Lizzy." Olivia's green eyes fell on Elizabeth's stomach and her smile went from ear to ear. "And you're going to have another baby."

"I am, and you could only be Olivia." Elizabeth's hands came to Olivia's cheeks. "And look at you. You're the very image of the woman my brother dreamed of marrying."

Her comment caught Olivia by surprise. She would have asked her to clarify, but the rest of the family was gathering about them. Everyone moved aside so a blonde-haired gentleman, slightly taller than Jesse could get through. In his arms were two small children: a handsome boy who resembled Jesse, and a darling baby girl who was a smaller version of Elizabeth. Olivia, noting the look that passed between Jesse and this handsome stranger, knew this could only be Kaleb.

Elizabeth took Brenae, Jesse plucked Cameron out of his friend's hands, and Kaleb wrapped his arms around the newest edition to their family. When he released her, Elizabeth said, "Olivia, in case you haven't figured it out, this is my husband Kaleb, and our children, Cameron and Brenae."

Olivia smiled as she turned back to Jesse and murmured her delight. "I have a niece and nephew, Jesse, and they're darling, aren't they?"

"I'll agree with you there."

Jesse and Kaleb shared a brotherly hug as Kaleb asked, "You are home to stay, aren't you?"

Jesse drew his wife back into the crook of his arm. Tears were streaming down her cheeks. She was apparently overwhelmed by his family's open display of affection. "Olivia and I are both home to stay."

Kaleb and Elizabeth had so many questions, but knowing they would have time to visit later, they stood off to the side, giving the rest of their family and church friends the chance to greet the newlyweds. After a time, everyone found seats and listened as Pastor Williams began to speak.

"I would like you to turn with me in your Bibles to Matthew chapter six. We'll be reading from verses twenty-five through thirty-four." Pastor's eyes scanned the small congregation. "As we read through and study these passages, I want you to ask yourselves this question: how much does worry weigh?"

Olivia's gaze met her husband's. Over and over again he had reminded her that she must leave her burdens at the cross—that worry is a sin. Now Pastor was reaffirming what Jesse had been telling her all along. He gathered her hands in his, squeezed them, and turned back to pay attention.

Pastor Williams made several points that Olivia found helpful. However, the answer to his first question was the one that stood out in her mind the most: worry weighs enough to cause you to take your future out of God's hands and put it into your own. No doubt this message would give her much food for thought in the coming days, weeks, and months.

The Whites and Somers were all standing in the churchyard getting ready to leave when Jesse really looked at his father. The change in him brought tears to Jesse's eyes. In fact George was so weak and short of breath, Jesse pulled Jared aside and suggested that they get their dad home.

Olivia had been visiting with his sisters when Jesse caught her eye and came near. "Are you ready to go?"

She offered a reluctant smile, unsure of how Jesse would respond to her request. "Would you mind horribly if I ride with your sisters?"

His brow rose.

Elizabeth tried to soften the blow. "Kaleb told me the two of you need a chance to catch up."

"Fine!" Jesse declared as his hands went in the air. He continued his ranting all the way to the wagon where Kaleb stood waiting. "I'm home for an hour and already my bride wants to leave me for my sisters. What's a man supposed to do, Kaleb?"

Kaleb laughed, but Olivia, unsure of whether her husband was angry or not, had followed him.

"Jesse, if you really want me to ride with you I will."

He leaned over and whispered in her ear, "I won't throw you in the river when we get home if you give me a kiss."

Her mouth dropped open. He was toying with her. Without an ounce of hesitation, she slapped his arm and strutted back toward her sister's wagon proclaiming, "You're dreaming, Jesse Somers! There is no way I'm kissing you in front of everyone!"

Elizabeth burst into uncontrollable laughter. Olivia not only *looked* like the woman Jesse described to a tee, but Olivia also appeared to be as sassy as Elizabeth herself.

Jesse glanced at his friend and grinned before nudging the team on. Once the women were on their way he sobered quickly. "Kaleb, I know how emotional Mom and my sisters can be at a time like this. I don't want to ask them, but I need to know, how long has Dad been suffering?"

"Since the cold weather set in last winter."

"That long?"

"Yes, at first Doc thought he had a bad case of dyspepsia. He had pressure in his chest, but the spells only seemed to come after he ate. He tried eating smaller meals, but the indigestion didn't get any better. The last two weeks have been bad, Jesse. I think he's been hanging on to see you and meet your wife."

Jesse's eyes glassed over. "How's Mom holding up?"

"She's struggling, but you know Dad. He encourages us to accept what can't be changed. He keeps saying that if God is calling him home, He has His reasons, and we need to trust Him."

"Had I known I would have come home earlier."

"When we got your letter, I mentioned going out to the trappers' cabin to get you." Kaleb shrugged. "He said you and your wife needed this time alone."

"He was right. You know, Kaleb, if I had come home before school let out, I wouldn't have Olivia in my life."

"Knowing you've found a wife to share your life with is a huge answer to all our prayers. Everything is as it should be. You heard what Pastor said: leave your worries where they belong."

"I just didn't expect him to be this bad ... so what else has been going on in my absence?"

"All in due time, Jesse. First things first! I need to hear everything about Olivia and how the two of you ended up together."

Olivia couldn't have been more pleased with her new sisters. She found it hard to believe that Suzanne, at only thirteen, was almost as tall as she, and Louise, at only eleven, wasn't far behind. No telling how tall she'd be. Elizabeth, on the other hand, couldn't be a speck over five foot two, and even with her rounding tummy Olivia could see the slenderness of her frame.

The women had been talking so much that before Olivia knew it, they were turning into the Somers' farm—her new home ....

Jesse and Kaleb arrived just after them, so Jesse came over to help Olivia out of the wagon, while Kaleb gave Elizabeth a hand.

For a time, Olivia simply scanned the farm, trying to take it all in. She could hear sheep off in the distance. Cows and horses were grazing in a nearby pasture. A butterscotch cat with white markings on her face was sprawled out in the sun, relaxing while her playful kittens romped about her. Olivia didn't know what to think. She felt so out of place—like a stranger in a foreign land. Their stay in the cabin had been a wonderful adventure, but never once did she feel like she was home. This piece of God's green earth is where she would begin her life with Jesse and hopefully put down roots that would run as deep as Jesse's seemed to. Her husband's arms came about her, interrupting her ponderings.

"What do you think, Mrs. Somers?"

"Oh, Jesse! It's wonderful. Her eyes followed his large family as they made their way into his parents' home. As far as she could tell, the original cabin had been added on to as the family grew or perhaps as time allowed. The porch in front would be a splendid place for gatherings. With a swing at both ends and chairs across the front she could almost see his family sitting around enjoying quiet evenings and chatting.

Father, thank You for bringing us safely home. Bless this family. Open my heart, Lord, as we come to know each other. Thank You for Jesse and all that You have given.

"Liv, would you like to join everyone?" When she didn't readily respond, he added, "or we could go for a walk."

She twirled in his arms and stole a kiss. "I would love to see the farm, but we're here to stay. Can't we do that later? I'm looking forward to getting to know your family better ...."

"I'm glad. Didn't want to overwhelm you is all."

"Jesse, your father is struggling for every breath. You don't know how much time he has. Be with him. Treasure each day that you have. I'm not going anywhere. Your father needs you right now. Trust me, Honey, I am fine."

He kissed her, reached for his hanky, and dried the tears trailing down her face. "Thank you for understanding."

"You're welcome."

In an attempt to lighten both their hearts, he lifted her chin and said, "I suppose I could overlook your impertinent display before we left the church, provided you give me another kiss."

Her brow rose. "My display? Jesse Somers, you should know better than to ask me to kiss you in front of a bunch of strangers!"

"Ah! Ah! Ah! You'd better watch yourself or you'll land yourself in the river!"

She quickly turned away. "You'd better not!"

"Kiss me again, and maybe I won't."

She complied, but only for reasons of self-preservation.

Kaleb came out the front door and helped Jesse unload the wagon. Since George could no longer climb the stairs, Jesse and Olivia would be taking his parents' old bedroom on the second floor.

Elizabeth gladly offered to help Olivia unpack while the other women finished the meal.

"Lizzy, do you and Kaleb live very far from here?"

"No ... five minutes on horseback, tops."

Olivia lowered her eyes and then lifted them to find her new sister's gentle gaze on her. "Jesse told me he sent a letter, but I'm not sure how much you know about me. He seems to think our personalities are very much alike."

Elizabeth giggled. "He said he'd never marry someone as sassy as me … must have decided he'd be bored if you were too agreeable."

"The first time we met I had fallen in the mud, and he came to my rescue. Since it was all over my face, he had no idea what I looked like."

"When was that?"

"On his way to Frenchtown almost a year ago. I never saw him again until the day my father introduced us." Elizabeth looked confused, so they sat on the bed together, and Olivia started at the beginning.

"So when he married you, he didn't know you were the same girl he had met?"

She shook her head. "No. I didn't think he'd want anything to do with that clumsy girl. My lips were sealed. Your brother made a huge impression on me when we first met. When I saw the man I had dreamed about and prayed for over the past year sitting in my mother's rocking chair, I was shocked. But I also knew that my prayers had been answered. God used our prior meeting to bring me comfort. My parents had to leave for the waterfront just after the ceremony. As difficult as it was to let them go, I've never doubted that God brought Jesse and me together when we most needed each other. In spite of our many faults, every day brings us closer together."

"You and I weren't ready for marriage when it was thrown in our laps, but I can honestly say that if I had it to do over again I wouldn't change a thing. Would you, Olivia?"

"No. I can't imagine my life without Jesse. I'm thankful he has a big family, too. I've only ever had my parents."

"Now we have each other. For so long I've wanted my children to have another Auntie who will love them." Elizabeth heard heavy steps coming up the stairs, so she wasn't surprised when Jesse stuck his head in the door.

"Well, you two, was I right?"

Elizabeth asked, "About what, Jesse?"

"Think you'll be friends?"

Olivia's eyes met Elizabeth's as she said with a smile, "For life!"

Elizabeth turned her sparkling blue eyes on her brother and saucily added, "I couldn't agree more, so get out of here. We have more to discuss while we finish unpacking your bags!"

Jesse pulled his sister into his arms and tickled her sides.

"Stop!"

"You're still as sassy as they come, Elizabeth!"

She glanced at Olivia and said, "I don't know, Jesse. Olivia seems to be holding her own quite nicely."

"Perhaps, but she pays the penalty for her crimes ...."

When Jesse turned and made his escape down the narrow stairs, Elizabeth stared at her sister-in-law, waiting for a confession. It wasn't long in coming.

"If I push him too far, he throws me in the creek or tickles me unmercifully!"

Olivia rolled her playful eyes, and Elizabeth laughed out loud.

"You are a character, Livia!"

"And you, Lizzy, have no room to talk."

Jesse had been visiting with his father, but George was dozing in the chair when Olivia and Elizabeth flounced down the stairs. "I'm glad the two of you finally decided to join us!" He wasn't surprised when Olivia plopped down on his lap and snuggled close.

"Did you miss me?" she asked.

"Immensely!" he responded as he kissed her cheek.

When Kaleb came out of the kitchen with Cameron hanging onto his leg, Kaleb's remedy for the situation caused Olivia's heart to skip a few beats. He reached down and swung the small boy onto his high shoulders before whispering, so as not to wake his father-in-law, "Dinner is served."

"Olivia," Jayne said as the entire family stood hand in hand in a crooked circle within the confines of the small kitchen. "You're an answer to all of our prayers. If there's anything we can do to make you feel more at home, please don't hesitate to ask."

Olivia scanned the circle of caring eyes. "The welcome I've received has blessed me beyond measure, but I feel it's only fair to warn you."

"About what, Honey?" Jayne asked.

Olivia caught Jesse's curious glance as she admitted, "I've lived in the small town of Tecumseh for as long as I can remember, so don't assume I know anything about the inner workings of this farm. Jesse was kind enough to teach me how to ride ...."

Jesse put in, "She's a quick study. In fact, I've come to the conclusion that Shadow's taken a shine to her. He's been grunting every time I get on him lately."

Overhearing their conversation as he walked into the room, George said, "It could have something to do with the extra weight you've put on, Son."

Jesse laughed. It pleased him to see that his father's illness had not robbed him of his humor. "Could be. You try staying slim while eating Olivia's cooking and lazing around at the cabin for several weeks."

George joined the circle by taking Olivia's and Suzanne's hands and turning to his new daughter-in-law said, "Thanks for not letting our boy starve. And don't worry about your lack of knowledge; we're a patient family."

She nodded. Uncomfortable being the center of attention, her gaze lowered as she softly added, "I ... I just thought you should know ...."

Jesse squeezed Olivia's hand, and while his tender gesture was comforting, her eyes flew up when Jared spoke.

"Don't you worry your pretty little head, Sis. Joe and I will be glad to break you in nice and slow."

She didn't know if he was teasing—not at first anyway—and his mischievous tone set her on edge.

Jared slapped Joe's back seeking affirmation, "Won't we, Joe?"

Joe nodded, but the warning look Jesse sent his way kept him from saying more.

When Olivia stepped behind Jesse, using him as a shield, he drilled his brothers with his narrowed gaze. "Just keep in mind, boys, this woman is my wife—not one of your friends from school. You'll answer to me if you don't have her best interest at heart."

Jared said, "Always the big brother, aren't ya, Jess?"

Jesse nodded.

And then Jared added, "Don't lose any sleep over it, Jesse. If she gets too feisty, we might throw her in the river, but we wouldn't dream of hurting her."

Jesse craned his neck to look at Olivia. Sharing a knowing glance, they burst out laughing.

When Olivia regained her composure, she said, "Apparently this consequence is common place in your family."

Jesse nodded and kissed her cheek.

Curious, Kaleb asked, "Is this a private joke, or can you fill us in on what's so funny?"

Jesse glanced at Olivia who rolled her eyes, saying, "Go ahead and tell them. They'll find out anyway."

"I'll just say that Olivia, being such an agreeable wife, became very familiar with the creek at the cabin."

Olivia saucily added, "Yea, but if I didn't lack the strength to accomplish such a task, I would have been throwing him in on several occasions too!"

Elizabeth put in, "You tell him, Olivia. We all know he's no angel!"

Olivia conceded, "True, but he is quite nice when he wants to be."

Pleased with the lighthearted camaraderie his family shared and pleased with his newest daughter, George looked to Jesse and asked him to return thanks.

He Loves Me!

Chapter Fourteen

Preparation for Eternity

HOPEFUL, OLIVIA ASKED, "Do you think Brenae would allow me to hold her, Lizzy? You look like you could use a break, and I'm itching to get my hands on her." Olivia had been sitting on the floor with Cameron for some time, rolling a ball back and forth. They were getting along famously. But when Jesse and Kaleb said they had things to see to in the barn, Cameron had trailed after them.

Elizabeth, exhausted from her busy day, had a favor to ask her new sister-in-law. "Actually, I was wondering if you'd mind taking her out for a walk while I lay down and close my eyes for a bit."

Olivia was delighted that she would ask. "I'd love to."

She's sleepy too, and the fresh air always relaxes her. You can bring her back in and lay her down in the crib in your new room when she's asleep. If you don't mind, I'll stretch out on your bed so I can hear her when she wakes up."

"That would be fine." Olivia held out her hands to see if the ten-month-old dolly would come to her. Brenae glanced her way but shyly tucked her face into her mother's shoulder.

"Olivia," Elizabeth suggested, "come with me to the door. If you step outside and I stay inside, I'm sure she'll come to you. She loves being outdoors."

"Oh, okay." Olivia was so amazed. A sweet smile covered Brenae's face as she reached for Olivia without delay. Enamored with the small wonder, Olivia snuggled Brenae in her arms, and they were off on their first adventure together.

Since the farm was unfamiliar to her, Olivia thought it best to stay close to the house. She spoke softly to the chubby little cherub in her arms as they wandered toward the coral outside the barn. Several horses were grazing. When a playful sorrel came their way and hung her neck over the fence, Brenae, completely unafraid, patted the horse's face and said, "Zy! Zy!"

"That's right, Brenae. Horsey." When the filly wandered off, Olivia kissed Brenae's pudgy little hand and moved toward the chicken coop. By the time they finished visiting with the chickens, sheep, pigs, cows and goats, Brenae was yawning. Cuddled against Olivia, she tucked her face into the crook of Olivia's neck. Brenae's eyes were already drooping when she strolled toward the beaten path they had ridden in on earlier. Hearing Jesse call out, she turned and waited for him.

Noting his drowsy niece, he whispered as he slipped his arm around his wife, "Who ya got there?"

"Isn't she the cutest thing?"

He nodded. "Hard for me to believe she's grown so much.

When I left for Frenchtown, she was only two days old."

"Cameron's adorable too. Such a little man already."

"When he was a baby he looked just like me. Now he's a miniature Kaleb with my hair color and blue eyes."

"Seeing them makes me wonder what our children will look like."

"All in due time, Olivia ... all in due time." Jesse slid his long fingers under his wife's chin, turned her face toward him and kissed her tenderly. The small bundle asleep in her arms never budged, but Olivia was stirred to tears.

Confused, Jesse asked, "Liv, what is it?"

She tried to move away, but he wouldn't release her.

"Tell me."

"Jesse, seeing your father like this ... I ... I can't quit thinking about my parents. Death is difficult enough when you have others around you that love you. If my mother goes first, my father will be alone. He'll have no one to share his final days with."

"It is tough, but we have to respect your father's wishes. Your coming to live with me in Ypsilanti was his choice. His faith is strong. I honestly believe he'll be fine. Besides, we can't get hung up on *what ifs*. Will fretting about them change anything?"

She shook her head.

"We have to trust the Lord. He loves our parents more than we ever could. Somehow He will give us the strength to get through."

"The three of them will never see our children—and our children will never know them."

"Their future doesn't look good, but we still have to trust the Lord, Liv. If God's calling our parents home, He has His reasons.

We need to trust Him."

"I'm trying, Jesse, really I am. I want to be strong for you and your family, but my heart feels like it's breaking in two."

"Oh, Honey, let me hold you."

She willingly complied. She had no more regained her composure, when Elizabeth flew out of the house, calling frantically from the edge of the porch.

"Jesse! Come quick!"

Olivia shooed him away. "I'm fine. Go see what's wrong. I'll get Kaleb and your brothers."

Olivia moved as swiftly as she dared toward the barn. She had no wish to wake her little niece. Cameron was petting the cat as she moved through the big door, so she stooped down to inquire, "Cameron, can you show Aunt Livia where your daddy is?"

Kaleb, hearing strain in her voice, came around the corner and asked, "Olivia, is something wrong?" Jared and Joe were with him, but Cameron seemed to be hanging on her every word, so she moved closer and whispered in Kaleb's ear. "Lizzy's upset. You and the boys should head in. Let me keep the children out here for a while. Come for us if we're needed."

Kaleb kissed her forehead and thanked her. "Pray, Olivia."

"Count on it."

"Cameron," Kaleb said as he ruffled his young son's hair, "I need you to do me a favor and show Aunt Livia around the farm. You'll need to be sure and tell her everything about how we take care of the animals."

Delighted, but confused, he asked, "She don't know, Daddy?"

"No, Cameron. She's lived in town, so Uncle Jesse says it's our job to teach her."

He reached for her hand, saying, "Come on, Auntie. I show you."

Olivia gladly held the dirty little hand Cameron offered, and her schooling began without delay. First he led her to the tack room where the grain, bridles, and saddles were kept along with many other grooming tools. She had no idea what most of them were for, but she didn't want to tax her companion's mind too much. Besides, he was pulling on her hand, ready to move on to their next lesson. Olivia couldn't help but smile. Kaleb was apparently the authority on everything, because every explanation Cameron offered ended in Daddy said. They went on to visit the pigs, the horses, and they were walking away from the chicken coop when Jared approached. She did not doubt he was fighting tears.

"Olivia, my dad's struggling for every breath. He doesn't look good. Before Kaleb goes for Doc, Dad wants to speak to all of us together. Olivia's hand came to her mouth, as her eyes filled with tears.

"Jared, I'm so sorry."

"Thanks. I know this can't be easy for you either." Sympathetic to her own parents' physical conditions, Jared wrapped his arm around his new sister-in-law and led her toward the house.

Olivia took her sleeping charge up the stairs and laid her in the crib before joining her new family in her father-in-law's room. Jesse was sitting beside his father on the edge of the bed holding his hand. She went to Jesse's side and was not surprised when he slid his arm around her and pulled her onto his lap.

"We're all here now, Dad."

George opened his eyes and glanced around at all the tearful faces of his loved ones. "I'll tell you what: I've never seen such a big group of gloomy gusses."

Jayne, who was sitting on the other side of the bed holding his other hand, reminded him, "We love you, George. How does a family say goodbye to someone they adore?"

Lifting his hand to caress her cheek, George said, "You don't, Honey. You say 'I'll see ya at the pearly gates'. This is one of those times in life when your faith will be challenged. Always remember what the Word of God teaches us: this world is just a training ground that's preparing us for eternity. God must think I'm ready for my Heavenly reward. We need to trust that our Heavenly Father knows best. Don't be sad for me; I'll be rejoicing with the Lord." His lids slid shut. Were it not for his labored breathing, his family would have thought that he had gone. After a long moment his eyes opened and he continued, "What we need to talk about in the moments we have left is how this family is going to go on living without me here."

Jesse squeezed his hand and said, "We'll manage, Dad, but you'll be greatly missed."

"I don't doubt that for a minute, Son. Let the good times we've shared help you get you through this time of sorrow."

"We will, Dad."

"Now, on a more serious note ...."

Jesse thought, *How much more serious can this get, Dad?*

Everyone's ears perked up when he called his four younger children to the foot of the bed. "I hope that all of you know how much you are loved."

They could only nod. Because the four of you are not adults yet, I need you to understand what I'll expect from you in my absence."

Jesse had no doubt that this conversation was stemming from one they had earlier that day and asked, "Is this necessary, Dad?"

"My children are my heritage from the Lord, Jesse. It's best that they hear this from me. Otherwise, raising four siblings could really tax your marriage, and I don't want that."

George smiled at his new daughter-in-law. Holding her tearful gaze he said, "Olivia, you may not always agree with Jesse's methods of parenting when it comes to his siblings, but I hope you'll support him and pray for him anyway." Olivia nodded, so he went on, "Being the head of a home isn't always easy. I want the four of you growing up happy, and part of that is respecting those in authority over you. I need you to understand that in my absence Jesse is in charge, and what he says goes."

All four of them glanced at Jesse and then back to their father who asked, "Jared, if you don't agree, tell me, Son, so we can clear the air."

"You know best, Dad."

"Joseph, are we in agreement?"

"Yes, Dad."

"Suzanne?" She lowered her eyes, reluctant to answer.

"Honey, can you do this for your dad?" George closed his eyes again, summoning what strength he had left. Every breath felt as though it would be his last. He knew what was troubling Suzanne, even without asking. She had always been such a private child, embarrassed to question him with everyone else in the room. Still, she would prefer knowing what to expect. The moment George's eyes opened, he said, "The answer is yes, Suzanne. When you or your siblings pull any of your shenanigans, you will answer to Jesse. Now keep in mind he would rather not have to go to extremes, so I'm hoping you won't put him to the test. He did make me a promise though, and I'll expect him to follow through. I don't want to be looking down from Heaven at disobedient children. Do I make myself clear?"

"Yes, but I don't have to like it."

"No, you don't, but I hope you'll respect my wishes and make Jesse's burden lighter."

Feeling guilty for pressing her dying father, she burst into tears as she flew to hug him, "I will, Daddy."

"I know you will, Honey ...." George waited for her to calm before calling out to his youngest daughter, "Louise?"

"Yes, Daddy. I'll obey Jesse, but you have to tell him ..." she hesitated when her father's chest heaved as he tried to catch his breath.

"What do I need to tell him, Honey?"

"That if he's going to tickle me, he has to stop when I need to use the outhouse!"

George looked at Jesse, trying to be stern, but he couldn't quite pull it off. He burst into laughter, and everyone in the room joined in. This was the way George Somers slipped into eternity: seeing that his children were well cared for, and then laughing and carrying on with the family he adored—like he had so many times before ....

✿ ✿ ✿

Word traveled fast. By the following morning, the yard was full of caring friends bringing food and coming to pay their last respects to a man who had left his mark on many lives. At George's request, Pastor Williams read Ecclesiastes chapter three—the seasons of life—and then Jesse came forward.

"Dad and I had a long chat yesterday morning. In his own way he wanted to help his family and friends get through the trying days ahead. He reminded me that there's a time for everything. This season of loss and mourning is beyond our control, and although we are confused as to why God would take him from us when he had so much to live for, we have to trust that God does have a purpose. God wants us to rely on Him in this life for everything, not on others or ourselves. Dad said God is testing us right now. He wants to see if we will trust that He knows best. My dad lived his life pointing others to Christ. He was careful in the choices he made and tried to make the most of every opportunity God placed before him.

"He told me that if anyone asks why God would take him so soon, tell them that life is only a stepping-stone, a preparation for eternity. Apparently Dad has finished the race. He has fought the good fight, and he has gone home to claim his eternal reward. Yes, we will miss him, but we will forever hold our memories in our hearts. In closing, I would like to read something that his children sat together and wrote last night. Since Dad's last breaths were taken while laughing with his family, we thought it only fitting that his funeral end the same way—with wonderful memories of a wonderful husband, father, grandfather, and dear friend.

"A tender romance that began over twenty-three years ago blossomed into so much more .... George and Jayne were married on a warm sunny day in June. They were blessed with six children. Elizabeth became Mrs. Kaleb White a few years back, and Olivia is now Mrs. Jesse Somers.

"While Kaleb had numerous stories he could tell, the one that stands out the most is the night Dad offered him Elizabeth's hand. He said, and I quote, 'I learned so much about parenting that night. The choices we make for our children are not always easy, but following God's lead is best in the long run. When I think of how God has blessed Elizabeth and me, because of George's decision to have us marry, I can do nothing but rejoice.'

"For me, most of my favorite memories of Dad revolve around fishing and hunting together. I'll never forget the first time I threw my line in, and it actually had a hook and worm on it. Every other trip I had only caught fish on Dad's line; but it never dawned on me that there was a reason for that, until I watched him remove the stone he had tied to the end of my rod and replace it with a hook and worm. When I asked him about it a few years later, he said that I needed to prove to him that I could get a hook in the water without taking myself with it. I started paying closer attention after that and found out he did the same thing when we went hunting. His gun was the only one that had firepower. Mine only clicked. He was always willing to go the extra mile to protect us kids, and we never doubted that we were loved."

Elizabeth said, "I would have to agree with Kaleb, but since he already shared that memory with you, I've opted for another. I had a very dear friend who would come to visit me when we lived on our farm outside of Detroit. I learned that Snowbird's family was moving to the northern territory. The day before she was to leave, I got ready for Sunday meeting like I was told but then snuck down to the river with my white pony. I was planning to move with her the next day, and I was sure that if I made my pony look more like Snowbird's, her family wouldn't notice me and send me back home. I proceeded to paint mud spots on my pony, not realizing I was getting dirty in the process. Now mind you, I was only five. Dad looked everywhere but couldn't find me. When he saw me coming up from the river, he had a look on his face that told me I was in really big trouble, but like always, he gave me the chance to explain what I was doing and why. He said he understood my love for my friend and that I would miss her, but he said he loved me too and that he and Mom would miss me more. He punished me for going to the river without permission and for getting my dress dirty, but I knew how much he loved me when he woke me up early the next morning and allowed me to ride alongside of my friend for several miles."

Jared, Joseph, Suzanne and Louise put their thoughts together and said, "We loved everything about Dad. We could always count on him no matter what was going on in our lives. He could walk into the room and brighten our day with his wonderful smile. His joyfulness during the holiday season had a way of making all of us laugh! We'll always remember sledding with him in the winter, his zany way of judging backwards-bareback races in the spring, and how could we forget our times of swimming together and making hay dunes in the barn.

"Though we will miss finding ways to fill his unquenchable sweet tooth and helping him navigate through each day—we will always treasure his delightful antics and his oh-so-silly ways. We couldn't be happier for our dad, knowing he is now at peace and walking in perfect health.

"Until we meet again in glory, we send him with all of our love."

He Loves Me!

Chapter Fifteen

Fitting In

*T*HE SOLEMN DAYS following George's funeral were emotionally draining on the family, but everyone made an effort to honor his wishes by going on with their lives. The quiet reverence that permeated their home seemed to be lifting as the week progressed.

For Jayne, her new daughter-in-law's consoling presence during this time of grief was a godsend. Jayne no longer wondered why her son agreed to take her as his wife when he knew so little about her. Olivia was a rare and special treasure—mature beyond her years. The hugs she offered so freely warmed Jayne deep within. Olivia's ability to take over in the kitchen, making sure breakfast was well underway before Jayne could even drag herself out of bed, astounded her.

She had spent every night since her husband's death crying herself to sleep, but the previous night, that was not the case; she had fallen asleep conversing with her Heavenly Father. Today she awoke determined to gain the victory over this terrible sadness that was keeping her bound—keeping her from her family who needed her as much as she needed them.

"Olivia," Jayne began as they cleaned the kitchen after breakfast, "the garden looks like we've been ignoring it for weeks. Would you mind helping me do some weeding and picking this morning?"

"I'd love to, Mom, but Jesse had a fit when he saw these blisters on my face. He told me not to be out in the sun any longer than I have to."

Jayne, after taking a better look at the skin across the bridge of Olivia's nose, admitted, "I can't believe I didn't notice this. I'm so sorry. You must think I'm horrible."

"You're hurting, Mom. I understand."

"Honey, we were so excited about your coming. Who would have known ... we weren't expecting ..." Jayne fought against the pain of her loss.

Olivia held her tearful gaze. "It's all right. Remember what I've been through with my own parents. I really do understand what you're going through. Saying goodbye to someone you love doesn't happen overnight. You need time. Don't be so hard on yourself. God has been so good to me. He blessed me with a wonderful husband and a loving family. No matter what's going on, I'm thankful to be included."

"We're glad to have you, Honey, but it's time for me to quit ignoring my family's needs." Jayne went to the pantry shelf and found the salve from Doctor Taylor that would soothe Olivia's skin.

Olivia used the small mirror on the wall and applied the salve to her burns, admitting, "Jesse said he's taking me to town as soon as he can." She curled up her nose when she added, "He thinks I need a sun bonnet. I'd make one myself, but the snippets of fabric I have wouldn't be suitable."

"If a bonnet is the only thing holding you back from helping me in the garden, I think I could fix you up."

"Oh?" Olivia looked up, trying not to snarl her nose again.

"Elizabeth left one here."

"Doesn't she need it?"

Jayne giggled for the first time in days. "No, Livia. Your big sister hates wearing bonnets. In fact, she put that one in her sister's drawer the day she got married. If she had it with her, Kaleb would insist that she wear it, and she wasn't about to do that."

Olivia's brow furrowed. "Did she say why?"

"They make her sweat ...."

This information made Olivia laugh out loud. When her hand came up to cover her face, Jayne had to know, "What's so funny?"

"Oh, Mom, the more I hear about Lizzy, the more I agree with Jesse. She and I are so much alike. Believe it or not, I feel the same way about hats."

Jayne shook her head. "You girls ... you make such a fuss over the silliest things."

"But it's not silly. My father used to make me wear one almost every time I walked out the door, as if I was only half-dressed without one. I thought I had escaped that torture. I've been in a panic all morning over your son's insistence that I start wearing one too. Why must men be so pigheaded about such things?"

Jayne's brow rose as she tilted her head and inquired, "Are you sure it's the men who are being pigheaded?"

"Well ... maybe I am to a degree, but there are some things ..."

Jayne interrupted, finishing her sentence for her, "I know, Livia ... that a woman would like to decide for herself."

"How did you know what I was going to say?"

Jayne's smile went from ear to ear. "I have three other daughters. I've not only used the phrase myself, I've heard the phrase come out of their mouths numerous times."

Hoping to relieve Olivia's mind, Jayne suggested, "Come upstairs with me. I have an idea that might make both you and Jesse happy."

"I'm all for that!"

Jayne retrieved the bonnet from Suzanne's drawer and the two of them went back into Lizzy's old room, which Jayne now claimed as her own. The night George had gone home to be with the Lord, she moved in here. The memories that filled her mind whenever she was in one of the rooms she had shared with her husband were wonderful, but those memories were keeping her from finding the rest she desperately needed. She was so relieved when Jesse offered to reclaim his old room off the kitchen.

Jayne took scissors out of her sewing box. "Livia, all you really need is the brim to keep the sun out of your eyes and the tie to hold it on, isn't that right?"

"I suppose."

Jayne proceeded to cut the back out of the bonnet and paused long enough to glance at her new daughter-in-law. "I never thought to ask, Honey, do you mind my calling you Livia?"

She smiled. "Not a bit. To be honest, my parents called me

Livia. I've missed hearing it."

"Good! We won't take the time to finish the seams right now ... you can do that when you have some free time this evening."

Olivia took what remained of the bonnet and thought as she put it in place that her mother-in-law was a genius. She told her as much, as they headed outside toward the garden.

Jayne, after allowing her eyes to scan their farm, glanced at Olivia. "Jesse said he and the boys are so far behind in their chores, it could take them weeks to catch up."

Olivia pointed at the garden, saying, "Looks like we have our work cut out for us too."

Jayne grimaced. "Sure does!"

"Mom, I have a confession to make."

"What's that, Honey?"

"My father did all the gardening at home, so I hope you won't regret having asked me to help. I'm afraid I don't know a weed from a plant."

Jayne winked. "Don't you worry about a thing. I'm a patient teacher."

"Good thing."

"I'll have you start here in the green beans, while I get the hoe from the barn." Jayne stooped down next to the first row they came to and lifted the side of the bush, showing Olivia the tender green beans sprouting from it. "Everything else you see growing around it is a weed that has to come out, or the weeds will choke off the plants. I brought you two buckets: one for any beans that are ready to eat and the other for weeds. Just be careful when you pull the beans off the plant. Hang onto the vine close to the bean or you'll uproot the whole plant. Any questions?"

Olivia shook her head, crouched down and started working her way up the lengthy row, wondering as she did if she would ever reach the end. It didn't take long to discover that the gardening her father had always taken such pleasure in was back-breaking work. In truth she couldn't comprehend what he found so pleasurable about the task. To Olivia it was drudgery. Although she felt guilty for doing so, an hour or so had passed when Olivia looked back at her mother-in-law who was still humming away as she loosened the dark soil around the plants and made her excuses. "Mom, I hate to leave you when we've barely put a dent in this, but if I don't get our laundry washed and on the line, it won't have time to dry."

Jayne saw right through her excuses and didn't mind, but then she remembered one small detail. "I didn't have the boys haul extra water, Livia. Can't you wait and do it tomorrow?"

"I got used to doing it in the creek while we were at the cabin. I'm sure the river's no different."

"Suit yourself. If Jesse comes in early from the fields, I'll send him down to help you."

Jared and Joseph stood on the upper bank watching Olivia without her knowledge. Her skirt and blouse had been discarded, and she was standing in her shift waist deep in the water, scrubbing at a spot on Jesse's jeans. Jared whispered to his brother, "Do you think our new sis can take a bit of tomfoolery?"

Joe shrugged and murmured back, "Suppose it's about time we find out."

"Jesse might have our hides, but it could be worth it." Jared acknowledged and then added, "I'll head upstream and sneak up on her, while you keep her busy talking."

"Works for me!"

Joe waited until Jared was out of sight before heading down the hill and making his presence known. "I'll admit, Livia, I've never seen anyone wash clothes like this before."

She looked up and smiled. "Suits me better than the alternative."

When Joseph sat down on the bank to remove his bluchers and socks she didn't think anything of it—but when he removed his shirt and jeans and waded into the water, she panicked just a smidgen. "What are you doing, Joe?" Although he was slightly younger than she and skinny as a rail, he had to be at least six feet tall. He could certainly overpower her. She didn't think for a minute that he would hurt her. At the same time, she didn't trust him not pull something devious.

"Thought I'd give you a hand."

She rolled her eyes, hoping he wouldn't notice her apprehension. "I think I have things under control. This is the last pair of jeans."

"Good! Then, what I have planned won't interfere with your chores."

His mischievous intonation did not sit well, and she was about to call him on it when something rubbed against her bare foot. She jumped.

Joe nonchalantly asked, "What's wrong, Livia. Got a turtle nipping at your toes?"

Her heart took flight. She scanned the water. "Turtles are in here?"

"Why sure. Snakes and muskrats too!" Terrified, she turned to flee, but Joe reached for her arm and said, "No need to leave. They won't bother ya ... too much."

"If it's all right with you, I'll get these things hung ...."

Olivia's words were cut off and she let out a blood-curdling scream when someone grabbed her ankles from underwater and flipped her backwards. Righting herself, she came up spitting and sputtering to find Jared and Joseph laughing their heads off. Apparently this little conspiracy had been planned and she was not about to let them off without some form of retaliation. Jared was the closest, so she leapt up, pushed firmly on her unsuspecting brother's shoulders and shoved him under the water before going after Joe with the same intent. He wasn't hard to catch because he was laughing so hard he could barely move in the murky water. After dunking him she headed for shore, calling back with a touch of satisfaction, "Good luck finding Jesse's jeans on the bottom of the river. If they're lost, you two can explain why he has nothing clean to wear tomorrow." On that note she picked up her laundry basket and headed up the embankment.

Olivia was hanging their clean clothes on the line when she saw Jesse coming in from the field. She waved and continued what she was doing, unaware of the disapproving look he sent her way. She had the last shirt in her hand when Jesse's scolding words reached her ears.

"Olivia, what are you doing?"

She craned her neck around and rolled her eyes. "What does it look like I'm doing?"

He swatted her backside.

"Hey! That hurt!"

"No more than it stung my hand." He kissed her cheek and said, "Liv, we're not alone at the cabin anymore. You can't run around in your shift. I have brothers."

She scowled. "I'm all too aware of that. Who do you think got me so wet?"

"Jared and Joe?"

"No, Clem and Pete ...."

"Olivia!"

"Of course, Jared and Joe. They are the only brothers you have, aren't they? And, about my shift ... aren't you the one who told me your sisters swim in their shifts all the time?"

"Well, yes ... but I don't think you should."

"So ... what's all right for your sisters is not necessarily all right for me?"

"Something like that ...." He turned away, knowing he wasn't being fair. He should have expected her to call him on it.

"Sounds like a personal problem to me. If you didn't want me in the water, you shouldn't have taught me how to swim."

He grabbed a hold of his feisty wife, secured her in his arms and kissed her thoroughly. "You'd better watch yourself, Mrs. Smarty Pants, or I'll throw you back in."

"I wouldn't mind at all if you were joining me."

He chuckled. "Maybe later ... I have a few odd jobs to accomplish before I call it a day."

Hearing voices, Olivia spoke her thoughts. "Wonder if your brothers found what they were looking for."

"Did they lose something?"

"Inadvertently." Olivia saw them coming up the embankment and said, "Speak of the little darlings ..."

Jesse found it difficult not to laugh. His wife's annoyance with his brothers could not be denied, and their guilty expressions told him all he needed to know. Jesse reached for Olivia's chin and brought her gaze to his. "Liv, go back to the house and put on something decent. I need a few minutes alone with my brothers."

She did as her husband asked, but inwardly she was trying to figure out why she allowed Jared and Joe to irritate her so. Jesse had warned her about their teasing—said they'd give her a hard time until she learned the ropes. Olivia had assumed he was talking about the inner workings of the farm. Could she have been wrong? Was he really referring to her becoming a vital part of this family? Could their antics be Jared and Joe's way of including her as one of them? If that were the case, she'd better rethink how she responded to them. Being accepted by Jesse's family meant the world to her. They were all she had.

Jared hung Jesse's jeans on the line, dreading the reproach that was sure to come. Jesse's calm surprised both of them.

"Ya know, boys. I'm sure you were just toying with my wife, but I have a feeling you owe her an apology."

Jared wasted no time protesting, "Oh, come on, Jesse."

"Come on, Jesse, nothing. If I remember correctly, I warned you about your shenanigans."

Joe confessed, "We only scared her a little."

"Oh?"

"Well maybe more than a little."

Jared maintained, "She needs to toughen up and quit tattling like a school girl."

"The only thing she said is that you two got her wet."

Jared and Joe looked at each other, taken aback.

"You know, boys, Olivia makes a scrumptious berry pie and enjoys eating it almost as much as we do. You bring her a few buckets of berries, and I'm sure she'll gladly overlook your earlier indiscretions."

Jared squinted, shading his eyes from the blazing sun as he glanced up at his older brother. "Sounds good, Jesse, but where are we supposed to find berry bushes that haven't been picked clean."

"The raspberry patch behind the old trading post is rarely touched."

"True. If it's all right with you, we'll take Suzanne and Louise with us."

"That's fine. Just keep a close eye on them."

Olivia peered out the kitchen window and saw her mother-in-law; she was still working in the garden. Filling a large tankard with water, she headed her way. Jayne's accomplishments were in plain view before her. "You're pushing yourself too hard, Mom. You really should come in out of the sun and sit for a while."

Jayne allowed the peppers she had in the folds of her worn apron to fall into the bucket before she gladly accepted the water Olivia offered. "I'm about done for the day. Suzanne and Louise won't be happy with me, but tomorrow I'll have them help. We should be able to get the weeds under control without too much effort."

"I take it they feel the same way I do about gardening."

"Not everyone enjoys the task as much as I do, but it is a necessary part of our survival, Olivia. Without the vegetables our garden yields, a family the size of ours would go without through the long winter months. Dried beans and rice may be filling, but they get real tiresome after a while."

"I can attest to that. Don't misunderstand me. I've never been one to shirk my responsibility, but after an hour of gardening, I was thankful I had laundry to do."

"Then maybe we can make a trade off. I hate doing laundry, so if you'll help me out with that, I'll spend the time out here doing what I love."

"Sounds like a fair trade."

"I don't know what I would have done this last week without you, Olivia. I wish you could have had the chance to spend some time with George. He was a wonderful man. He and Jesse are so much alike. I'm sure you would have enjoyed him."

"I don't doubt that. We haven't had much time to talk, but you should know, Mom, that son of yours has been something else. A real knight in shining armor from the first time we met."

Curious, Jayne asked, "Lizzy was telling me about a painting you gave Jesse after you were married. If I call it a day now, will you help me with dinner and begin filling me in on the details surrounding your marriage?"

"I'd love to. Besides, if the four of us go at this tomorrow, it won't be too unbearable."

Jayne went back for the buckets and said as she walked alongside of Olivia on their way back to the house, "Try convincing the girls of that tomorrow, will ya?"

Olivia sent her a playful wink. "If they choose to be

disagreeable, Jesse has a surefire method of exacting compliance."

Jayne smiled. "So I take it he's had to torture you on occasion."

Astounded, Olivia's gaze held Jayne's and giggles bubbled up from deep within. "You don't know the half of it."

Jayne's eyes brightened, "Then you must tell me everything from start to finish."

"I will, Mom, but let me tell you this: when I saw Jesse sitting in our parlor, I knew my prayers had been answered. Even though that first night alone with a near stranger was scary, it didn't take me long to realize that there was no reason to fear a man who would tickle his obstinate wife to amend her behavior."

"You have George to thank for that."

"Oh?"

"Kaleb and Jesse were left to oversee their other siblings quite often, but as the two got older, convincing the younger ones to mind was a challenge. George didn't think it was wise to allow the boys to punish them, so he gave Kaleb and Jesse free rein to tickle them as much as necessary."

"I'm surprised the kids never complained. I don't know about Kaleb, but Jesse can be relentless."

"The children never complained until Louise spoke up before George slipped away from us." Jayne paused and wiped at the tears that filled her eyes.

"Mom, you don't need to tell me if it's too difficult."

She shook her head. "I'll be fine. You see Jesse and Kaleb always gave the children a choice. They could tell their dad what they had done and chance a trip to the woodshed, or they could be tickled. Needless to say, they always chose being tickled."

"I can see why ...." A gust of wind swirled the sandy soil as

Olivia followed her mother-in-law up the steps and through the side door. The air had been so close and humid over the last few days; she wondered if a storm could finally be brewing. Time would tell.

With joyful anticipation, Olivia went to her room to retrieve the painting from under their bed. Upon arriving home, Jesse had been eager to share the story of their union with his family, but extenuating circumstances had altered everything. Olivia opened the brown protective wrapper and glanced at the painting. Her eyes welled up as memories of the day she had met Jesse flooded her mind. Fortunately, her resolve prevailed, not allowing anything to put a damper on this time with her husband's mother. Drying her tears, she bustled back to the kitchen.

Jayne loved the portrait. Staring at it for a while, she tried to take in every detail. "So is this Tecumseh?"

"Yes, it wasn't always so muddy, but the streets were a mess when Jesse came through the first time."

"I've seen portraits like this before in New York, but I've never known an artist, personally. This is incredible."

"God is amazing. Drawing and painting became an outlet for me when my parents were ill. At first you could barely tell who or what I was trying to capture. But the more time I devoted to the endeavor, the stronger my desire became and the better I got. The ability has definitely been a gift from the Lord."

"Every good and perfect gift comes from Him." Jayne smiled at her daughter-in-law and said, "Come on Livia. Let's hang this up in the sitting room before we start dinner."

"Are you sure you want it in there?"

"Absolutely! When God gives you a gift like this, it needs to be shared."

"That's what Papa would say every time he gave my paintings away."

"Your father is a wise man, but if you don't mind, we'll hang on to this one."

"I'm glad you feel that way, 'cause I don't think Jesse would part with it."

Olivia helped Jayne with preparations for their evening meal while Olivia began her rendition of how she and Jesse came to be husband and wife. The laughter and tears they shared brought healing to both of their ailing hearts.

A large pot of red stew was simmering on the back of the stove, and the rolls were formed and set aside to rise when Jayne looked at Olivia and admitted, "I haven't been sleeping well. I'm exhausted. Would you mind baking the rolls when they're ready, so I can take a short nap?"

"You go right ahead. I need to gather my laundry before it blows away, but I'll be back in plenty of time. Do you know where the girls are, Mom?"

"Jared and Joe took them riding. Should be back before too long."

Olivia ran out to the barn, hoping to find Jesse, but he was nowhere to be found. Surely he would come in out of the weather. She stopped to pet Shadow before collecting their clean clothes and heading back to the house with her heavy-laden basket. The bright sun had disappeared behind a dark, clouded expanse. The storm was moving in fast—too fast for her liking. She whispered a prayer that everyone would make it safely home before it hit.

After tucking their clean clothes away, Olivia sat down to finish the seams on her backless bonnet. She had a hard time concentrating on what she was doing and poked herself three times in the process. Where was her family? She added potatoes to the stew and had just closed the oven door, when Jared and Joe came in the back door, each with a full bucket of raspberries. Her curiosity peeked when they set them on the counter, came toward her, and took turns kissing her cheek. Jared was the first to speak.

"Jesse mentioned that you like berry pie. We're hoping you'll accept these as a peace offering. We were only playing with you, Livia. Hope you won't hold it against us."

She smiled, "Brotherly affection—or part of my initiation?"

Jared chuckled softly. "Maybe a little of both."

Joseph piped in, "I meant it when I said the snakes, turtles, and muskrats won't bother you. Truth is, we rarely see them."

"Good to know. So tell me, brothers, who's supposed to make this berry pie?"

Jared and Joe looked at each other and shrugged. Jared admitted, "Jesse told us that was your area of expertise."

"Oh, he did, did he? " Olivia turned to face the counter and busied herself with washing the few dishes in the basin, leaving her brothers in an awkward state of confusion. After a moment, maybe two, she wiped the grin off her face, craned her neck around and said, "I suppose I can make myself up a nice berry pie; maybe I'll even offer a piece to Jesse, Mom, and the girls. But ... since you two haven't mentioned liking" her eyes fell on the full buckets for emphasis, "raspberry pie, I won't bother to make you any."

Unbeknownst to Olivia, Jesse had come in the front entrance and overheard their entire conversation. Now standing in the frame of the kitchen door, he announced, "If she tried to con me like she's conning you two, I'd be throwing her back in the river."

Olivia's eyes flew up at Jesse and then back to her brothers who were moving toward her with ill intent. Thinking her chances were better with her husband, she flew around the table and ducked behind him.

"Jesse," she pleaded, "a storm is brewing. Please don't let them."

"What do you say, boys? I'm thinking you picked enough berries for at least three, if not four, pies. If she's willing to do the baking and share them, will you let her off the hook?" They both nodded in unison.

Olivia was not about to take this lying down. "That's blackmail!"

"And what do you call what you were doing to them?"

You're supposed to be on my side, Jesse Somers! she thought, but declared, "Giving them a dose of their own medicine."

"You wanted brothers, Olivia, and I gave them to you. Now it's up to you to decide where the sibling rivalry will end: in the creek or in the oven?"

She scowled at all three of them, conceding, "In the Oven!" When she moved around Jesse, she murmured, "But you three will get the sour one ...."

Jesse bellowed, "Olivia!

Irritated, she spun on her heals and spewed her response, "I'm not your child, Jesse Somers. Don't scold me!"

Jesse threw his hands in the air and said as he strode into their room, "She's all yours, boys. You decide on her plight!"

When Jesse firmly closed the door behind him, Jared and Joe each took an uncompromising step towards her. She made haste to offer her meek response.

"I'm sorry I made light of your peace offering. I will gladly make the pies, and they'll all be sweet ... promise!"

Joseph smiled and said, "Thanks, Olivia. If you need help, we're willing."

She offered a sideways grin. "Considering Jesse's skills in the kitchen, I think I'll pass."

Jared and Joe stuck around long enough to help Olivia clean the berries and collect the ingredients she would need for the pies. Suzanne and Louise were still in the barn and needed to be hurried along.

Olivia heard their bedroom door open, but she didn't acknowledge Jesse's presence until he came up behind her and slid his arms around her.

"Are you angry with me for making more work for you?"

"No ... I was angry because you wouldn't protect me from your brothers."

"If you really want to be accepted as one of the family, you're going to have to make your own way, Liv."

"Since when is three against one fair?"

"It's not, but you backed me into a corner."

Olivia turned in his gentle hold and stared at the man she was coming to love. "I suppose I have to learn to back off before it's too late. I'm sorry, Jesse, I shouldn't have put you in the middle."

She reveled in the tenderness of his touch as his long fingers slid along the soft skin of her face before weaving their way through her long silky hair. Then his amazing kisses stirred her blood, quickened the beat of her heart, and delighted her senses, making her feel so loved—so cherished.

He Loves Me!

Chapter Sixteen

Honesty and Trust

"OLIVIA," JESSE SAID as he pulled her into his lap, snuggled her close on the porch swing, and swayed back and forth. "With all this family's been through over the last week I hesitate to even bring this up, but I thought we should at least discuss it."

There was something in his tone that concerned her. She gave him her full attention. "Is something wrong?"

"No, not at all. Kaleb reminded me that the farmer's meeting in Detroit is next week. He and his father are going."

Jesse paused for a moment before he continued, "Dad and I have always gone together. They'd like me to join them."

"So, what's holding you back?"

"If I go, it would mean leaving you here for a little over a week. Do you think you could manage?"

Olivia was coming to love her new family and didn't doubt

that they cared; still, the thought of being without Jesse for a week gave her pause. "I suppose my going along is out of the question?"

"Sorry. If you're uncomfortable with me leaving, I'll stay home. There's always next year."

She shook her head. "No. With your father gone, the welfare of this family rests on your shoulders. We both need to make sacrifices. I'll miss you, but I'll be fine."

"You're sure?"

She nodded. For a time, husband and wife simply enjoyed being in one another's arms while they listened to the peaceful night sounds. Chirping crickets echoed each other's calls as leaves, rich in vibrant greens, rustled on the limbs that swung in the gentle breeze. A milk cow bellowed in the distance, and their big old tomcat purred in contented bliss on the seat beside them. Olivia grinned when Jesse tensed at the sight of a polecat waddling away from them. Apparently the potentially pungent critter had set up housekeeping under the porch. Her husband was not at all pleased.

"I should get my gun and get rid of the foul creature before he does any lasting damage."

Olivia's brow furrowed. "Leave him. He's not hurting anyone."

Jesse harrumphed. "You say that now. The first time you get sprayed you'll feel differently."

She snickered softly. "I take it you've had first-hand experience."

"Twice. I took a liking to their young when I was seven and got an itch to hold one. Let's just say his momma didn't approve."

"And the other time?"

"Kaleb and I were catching frogs in a small stream on the way home from school one day when I remembered Dad needed my help mending fence lines. He didn't like it when I kept him waiting, so I took off running through a field of high grasses and nearly stepped on a big old skunk. After regaining my footing, I hightailed it out of there but not fast enough." Jesse laughed in remembrance. "Dad made me burn my clothes and sent me to the garden for the last of the tomatoes. Frost came early that year, so those tomatoes were almost as rotten and rank as I was."

"I've heard they don't really get rid of the smell anyway."

"I'm not sure anything could."

Shuddering at the thought, Olivia slid her arms further around her husband and said, "Maybe you should get your gun."

He shrugged. "Too late now. He's gone."

"Tell me something."

Gazing into her twinkling eyes, he could almost see the wheels turning and wondered aloud, "What are you concocting now?"

Her eyes narrowed in on him. "You can lose the school teacher tone, Jesse Somers."

His burst of laughter altered her mood.

"I've been wanting to do something special for your family, but I'd like it to be a surprise. You know what it's like around here. I'd never be able to accomplish what I have in mind without someone peeking. So I was wondering ... how would you feel about me going to stay with Lizzy and the children while you're away? It would give us a chance to get to know each other better and allow me the time I need to work on the gift." When he didn't readily reply, she asked, "If you're hesitating because you think my place is here with Mom, then tell me."

"That's not it at all. Mom can manage with Jared, Joe, and the girls, but the thought of you and Lizzy spending a whole week together ... I don't know, Liv, it could spell trouble!"

She sat up, slapped his arm and scowled, "Jesse Somers, quit!"

"Now, now, now! If I know Kaleb, and I do, he won't be too fond of the idea either."

"He likes me just fine, and you know how I feel about Lizzy and the children." Her husband teased her so much of the time she couldn't always tell if he was serious or not.

"I do." Jesse squeezed her tight and smiled mischievously.

"If I agree to let you go, will you tell me what it is you're making?"

"Absolutely ... not!"

He tickled her, saying, "I'll wriggle it out of you ... you just wait and see."

"You'd better stop. You can wait just like everyone else."

"Oh, all right." he conceded.

"You didn't answer me, Jesse."

"If I agree, we'll need to work extra hard over the next few days to get caught up on the chores we've been lagging behind on."

She saw the sparkle in his eyes, and her own narrowed in on him. "No doubt you're up to no good, Jesse Somers, but I'll do what I can to help out."

"Good." He kissed her cheek and stood her on her feet. "Let's get to bed, Mrs. Somers. We've got a few hard days ahead of us."

Olivia overheard Jesse informing Suzanne and Louise that they were to finish weeding the garden and help their mother without complaint, or they would answer to him when he returned. Suzanne was so close to Olivia's age that it seemed odd to have her husband scolding her. In truth, it rubbed Olivia the wrong way. Her first reaction was to tell Jesse to lighten up, but then his father's dying words came to her, and she changed her mind. Jesse knew his sisters better than she, and he wouldn't be pleased if she were to countermand his orders.

When Jesse opened the door to their room, threw her a pair of Jared's jeans, and told her to put them on, her mouth opened and then shut. The look he sent her way dared her to defy him. On a normal day she might have challenged him, but not today. In the mood he was in, she could only imagine what awaited her.

Slipping her shirt on, Olivia pulled the jeans too easily over her slender hips and buttoned them. She had no more released them when they fell back down. Not even rolling the waist helped.

Impatience filled his words as Jesse stuck his head in the door and asked, "Are you coming?" He caught her reflection in the mirror. Noting her distress, he walked in and closed the door. "Honey, come here. Maybe I can help."

His tone, so soft, assured her that he was not angry, still, how could she let anyone else see her like this? She couldn't bear the thought. "Jesse, I know my pride's involved, but I feel like a fool. I can't go out in men's clothes. Besides ... you could fit two of me in these."

"Give me a minute, Liv. I'll be right back."

Why couldn't he just give it up and let her wear her skirt? She prayed that he would. However, when he came back in with smaller jeans and a leather strap for tightening them, she suspected protesting would do no good.

"Try these."

"I'd rather not."

"I can see that. I'm afraid this time I must insist." He tried not to laugh when her lip came out in a little girl pout. It just slipped out.

"Jesse, if you're going to laugh at me ..."

He playfully pushed her back on the bed, grabbed the bottom of Jared's jeans and slid them off. "I'm not laughing about your jeans, Liv; it's that protruding lip of yours."

"Oh ..."

He handed them to her, watched her pull them into place, and almost changed his mind about having her wear them. "Let me slide this piece of leather through the loops. It won't do to have them falling down."

"I don't know why you want me to wear these. I'd be more at ease running around in my unmentionables."

"Sorry, Dear ... that I can't allow." She had her shirt tucked in and Jesse pulled it out, needing to cover more of her ... "There, that's much better."

For whom? she wondered, as she glanced at her reflection. "Sure, now I look like a sloppy young buck instead of just a young boy."

"Look again," he berated, annoyed with her fretfulness. "With all those womanly curves and that face, no one could ever mistake you for a man."

Olivia took another peek and wished she hadn't. Her apprehensions heightened.

He noticed and said, "Enough! We've got a full day ahead of us and time's a-wasting."

She reached for her coat and was trying to slip it on when Jesse stole it from her, slung it on the bed and pushed her out the door. "It's too hot for a coat! You're being ridiculous, Olivia."

"No, I'm not." As humiliating as this entire experience was, she might have survived the ordeal if Jared and Joe hadn't been waiting for them as they moved out the door. They were mounted up, and despite the warning look Jesse sent their way, they whistled and carried on, deepening Olivia's flush even more.

"Ignore them," her husband whispered. When she headed toward Shadow, Jesse took her hand and led her to the sorrel she'd visited with on numerous occasions in the corral.

"I know you've formed an attachment with Shadow, but he is my horse. I'm thinking it's time you get to know your own horse."

Her eyes lit with pleasure. "My horse? I have a horse?"

Jesse chuckled. "Yes. She's a wedding gift from Kaleb and Lizzy."

Bemused, she asked, "And you're giving her to me?"

"Well, yes. How else am I going to keep you off Shadow? This little filly was Lady's first foal."

"Lady is Lizzy's horse, isn't she?"

"Mmm hmm. Lizzy has quite a flair for breaking horses. She's taken the time to make sure this little filly is a gentle mount for her children's new Auntie."

Quick tears filled Olivia's eyes and spilled down her cheeks. "She's so beautiful. How could Lizzy part with her?"

"She's got a big heart, Liv. She's had this planned since the day Guinevere came into this world." Pushing her tears away with the back of her hand, Olivia smiled.

"Her name is Guinevere?"

"Yes, so I suppose that means we should be calling Shadow, Lancelot."

"All right you two!" Jared interrupted. "I thought we had work to do."

Jesse's hand came up to forestall him. "Liv, you have the day to prove to me you can handle her. If you do, I'll show you the short cut to the White's farm so you can go back and forth whenever you please."

Olivia gracefully bowed in her masculine attire and said with an impish grin, "I shall not disappoint you, My Lord."

"Oh, brother!" Joseph declared, "I think I'm going to be ill."

Jared added, "Get over it, Joe. Before ya know it, we'll be the ones acting the fool with our own females."

"Not me," Joe threw back.

"I'm of the opinion that time will prove otherwise," Jared maintained.

Jesse gave his wife a boost up and made sure she was at ease with Guinevere before mounting Shadow.

Olivia had always wondered what it would be like to have her own horse. As reality seeped into her tender heart, she leaned over, wrapped her arms around her horse's long neck and patted her as she came back up. Looking at her husband, she said, "Thanks, Jesse. She means more to me than you'll ever know."

"Now you understand why I'm so attached to Shadow."

She nodded, asking as they rode away from the house, "What's the plan?"

"Moving sheep to start. Some kind of predator's been at the

flock that grazes in the north pasture, so until we have the time to get to the bottom of it, we'll need to move them closer to the farm. Jared and Joe will have enough on their plate without having to watch over the flock day and night."

A wave of guilt passed through her. "Jesse, are you sure you don't want me to stay home and help your family?"

His tender smile eased her mind. "They'll be fine. Besides, I'm glad you're going. You were right. You and Lizzy need this time together. My only regret is that I'll be missing out on all the fun."

"I'm so excited. It took me forever to fall asleep last night."

Jesse laughed.

"Well, it did!" she reiterated.

"I don't doubt that for a minute, but I can guarantee you'll sleep tonight after we get through with you."

"I'm not so sure I like your implication, Jesse Somers."

"Nothing bad, Honey. We do have our work cut out for us though."

She had watched the sheep from a distance a few days ago with Suzanne, but she knew nothing about them. Olivia dismounted. As she followed Jesse into the pasture, hiding her fear was not an easy task.

When she ducked behind him like she had done the first time she came face to face with Shadow, he reassured her, "Olivia, they won't hurt you."

Overhearing Jesse, Jared snickered, saying, "Don't let him fool you, Livia. The ones with the tan bodies are docile, but don't turn your back on the black ones. They'll nip ya when ya least expect it."

Cognizant of her brother's teasing, she stepped around Jesse and boldly informed him, "I'd watch myself if I were you, Jared Somers. With Joe's jeans on and these big clodhoppers, I could get ya!"

Jared's brow rose on her daring inflection, keeping his thoughts to himself. But when Jesse's hand connected with the seat of his new sister's britches, the irate scowl she flashed at her husband made Jared laugh out loud.

However, Olivia was glad she listened when Jesse pulled her close and whispered, "Think carefully before you speak, Mrs. Smarty Pants. We have a long day ahead of us for you to be working in wet jeans."

She kissed his cheek. "Thanks for the warning." Jared and Joe, seeing that they were no longer needed, went to check the perimeter.

Jesse reached for his wife's hand and answered her many questions as they moved among the flock waiting for their brothers to return. Unfortunately, Jared's voice interrupted what could have turned into a very tender moment.

"If you two lovebirds can quit gawking at each other, we're ready to get some work done."

"Oh, right!" Jesse said, smiling at his wife as he led her back to their mounts.

Had Jesse told her ahead of time that it would take the better part of the morning to move the flock, she never would have believed it. Sheep were passive creatures as he had said, but the way they wandered to and fro in constant need of guidance rankled her nerves. *Shepherding a flock,* she thought, *is definitely not my cup of tea.* In truth, she was beginning to wonder if there would be any aspect of farming that she would enjoy as much as horseback riding—or was farming all drudgery, like the gardening that she must learn to tolerate in order to survive. For a passing moment, she contemplated the things she missed about her simple life in Tecumseh. It didn't take her long to realize that her life without Jesse in it would be unbearable. She couldn't go back; she needed to go forward. Change was seldom easy to embrace, but it was necessary. Perhaps in time she would come to like farming as much as her husband—perhaps not, but either way, she would have to approach each task with a willing heart—and try to do it as unto the Lord.

After devouring the sandwiches she had brought along, the four of them worked at chopping down small trees and mending fences. By the time they finished that, Olivia was ready to collapse, and her earlier resolve was waning. She cringed when Jesse informed her that there was more to be done. Oh, how she wanted to moan and groan, tell him he was on his own, but how could she? She had promised to help so she could spend the week with Elizabeth. Finding no hope for her plight, she said not a word as she followed him to their next task. When they finally reached the barn and bedded the horses down for the night, the cool evening swim Jesse had promised was forgotten—at least by her anyway. She was so tired, she wasn't even sure she could sit through supper without falling asleep.

"Hi," Olivia said as she traipsed in the back door, looking like something the cat had dragged in. "How was your day, ladies?"

Jayne giggled and so did Suzanne. They were sitting at the table picking the ends off the beans when Jayne admitted, "Ours was busy, but apparently not nearly as exhausting as yours."

Olivia rolled her eyes, but she held her response until her husband had walked into their room and shut the door. Joining them at the table, she pleaded, "No kidding. If you girls love me at all, you'll help me get out of having to work with them tomorrow. I don't mean to be disrespectful, Mom, but I won't survive another day with that slave driver son of yours."

Jayne smiled and sent her a playful wink. "You leave it all up to me, Honey. I've been thinking the four of us ladies need to make a trip into Ann Arbor. If I know my son, he won't want us to be off gallivanting while he's away. I'll just have to convince him that the trip can't wait until he gets back."

Olivia's eyes glistened. "I've been wanting to check the post office for a letter from my parents."

Jayne reached for Olivia's hand and patted it. "That's not an excuse Jesse will buy. Our mail comes to Ypsilanti now."

"Oh ..."

"Don't look so worried. I have several things on my list that we can only buy in Ann Arbor. And besides, it's high time I started showing my new daughter off."

The room grew silent when Jesse opened his bedroom door and joined them. To their chagrin, he noticed and said, "If I didn't know better, I'd swear the three of you are up to no good!"

Olivia and Suzanne were struggling to keep their smiles under wraps, so Jayne spoke up, "Jesse Somers! You know better than that."

"I wish I did. Olivia, are you ready?"

Her weary heart dropped. "For what, now?"

"Our swim."

"Oh, Jesse ..." she whined, "I don't think I have it in me to walk down there."

He had his heart set on it and wasn't about to take no for an answer. "If you can't walk, I'll carry you."

She sighed in disgruntlement. "I sure would like to know where you get all your energy." He laughed as he practically shoved her out the door.

Suzanne watched them leave. She would have enjoyed going along, but she wasn't oblivious to her brother's desire to be alone with his wife. In truth, it pleased her to know that Jesse had finally found someone to love. There was no question in Suzanne's mind; Olivia adored him as much as he did her, and that was a good thing.

"Mom," Suzanne asked, "do you enjoy having Olivia around as much as I do?"

Jayne reached for her middle daughter's hand.

"Absolutely! I think this family needed her as much as she did us."

"I wish she would hear from her parents. I think she'd feel better."

"Jesse's praying that all is well, but it's not a good sign that they haven't written."

"I know how much I miss Daddy. I can't imagine what she's going through having both of her parents leave her on the same day."

"Pray for her, Suzanne. While her parents have breath in them, pray for their healing. God alone holds the keys to life and death."

"Daddy would say that God sees the greater picture, and He does have a plan. Isn't that right, Mama?"

Jayne pulled her hanky out of her sleeve and dried the tears that still seemed to flow so freely. "Yes, he would, Honey. We don't always understand what that plan is, but we need to trust that He knows best."

Suzanne squeezed her mother's hand. "Enough crying. So tell me, Mama, how are we going to get Olivia out of her predicament tomorrow?"

"Well, our reasons for going are legitimate; I do need several things ...."

"Olivia!" Jesse chided, when he came in the back door and found her sitting at the breakfast table with his mom and sisters. She was sipping at a cup of tea and still in her bathrobe and gown. "Why aren't you ready? The boys are saddled up and waiting." When his wife glanced at his mother, he knew something was up.

"Jesse. Your mom and sisters—"

Jayne interrupted Olivia's explanation. "Jesse, we were hoping you'd let us steal her away for the day. You'll both be gone for a week, and we'd like to show her around a bit. Besides, I have things we'll need from Ann Arbor."

"You do, do ya?" His tone was patronizing.

Olivia could barely hold his gaze when he turned to her. Although his scowl was ever so slight, she found it quite intimidating.

"If you're asking me, I think the women in my life have been scheming to get my wife out of another day of hard work."

Olivia couldn't believe her ears. How did he manage to figure this out? "I would like to go with them, Jesse." When the silence lengthened, she added, "If you really need me though, I'll get ready." Olivia cringed when Jesse reached for her hand, pulled her out of her chair, led her into their room and shut the door. Struggling, she said, "Jesse ..." but his hand came to her mouth to forestall her.

"What's really going on here, Olivia?"

She didn't like being found out, but more than that, she was mad at herself for not being honest with him in the first place. "I'm sorry. I should have told you instead of trying to weasel my way out of it. I've been dragging lately. Maybe it's just the emotional ups and downs, but I'm always tired. I can't ... I can't keep up with the pace you and your brothers set."

"Was it really that hard to tell me?"

"Yes ... you know me: I don't like letting you down."

"Liv, don't ever feel like you have to come up with excuses. We're not always going to see things the same way, but our relationship should be based on honesty and trust."

"I know. I'm sorry, I should have talked to you."

"So ... are you ready to make amends?"

"Amends?" Her eyes, wide with uncertainty met his. A pink flush kissed her cheeks as he slowly ran his finger along the trim line of her jaw. In her reluctance to answer, he asked again.

"Are you?"

While she couldn't be sure of what he had in mind, the look in his deep blue eyes told her she was about to be admonished—in the nicest way. There was nothing harsh about the words he spoke and his touch was ever so kind. So far, this was like nothing she had ever endured. Jesse's hand slid ever so gently into her long brown hair, stopping at the base of her spine. Her eyes slid shut as his lips tenderly brushed her neck on either side—the tip of her nose—before at last capturing her mouth.

"Oh, Jesse ..."

"Hmm?" He loved the dreamy look in her soft green eyes.

"I sure do like your kisses."

He chuckled softly. "I like yours too ... now, about this trip to town ..."

"You really don't mind if I go?"

"Not at all. Let me send my brothers on ahead. Grab some paper and come to the table. We need to make a list so it's not a wasted trip."

Olivia plopped down on the bed and smiled as she watched her husband leave. He really did have a way of helping her to see things differently. Bearing her soul was not always easy, but without honesty, trust would be forsaken in their marriage.

Chapter Seventeen

The Whites

"OLIVIA," JESSE YELLED up the stairs, "you need to hurry. Kaleb and Samuel are waiting on me."

"I'm coming." Olivia shivered with excitement as she packed the last of their things, said her farewells to Jesse's family and ran out the back door. Jesse had Guinevere and Shadow saddled and ready to go by the time she entered the barn.

When her twinkling eyes met his, he winked and said, "Come on, Smiley, let's ride."

She gave him a playful shove. "Don't tease me, Jesse. Maybe it sounds odd to you, but I've never gone to a friend's house to stay the night."

His brow furrowed. "You stayed at the cabin with me."

"True, but that was different. You're my husband."

"I hope I'm your friend too ...."

"Well, of course you are, but ... oh, forget it! I suppose you'd have to be a woman to understand."

He chuckled. "Was it because of your parents' illness that you never went anywhere?"

She shook her head and said as they moved out of the barn, "No. Papa wouldn't let me. He said he didn't know my friends' parents well enough to trust them with his only daughter."

"Liv, you lead. I want to be sure you know the way in case you need to run home for anything."

"All right."

"Back to your father. I'm a little confused. If he was so cautious, why did he offer me your hand after a few meetings?"

She grinned. "Now you know why I didn't hesitate to say yes when you asked me to marry you. I figured if Papa deemed you trustworthy, I was in good hands."

"Any regrets?"

For a moment she looked away before her gaze settled back on him. "What do you think?"

"I know I have none."

"Neither do I."

His features brightened. "I thought so, but it sure is nice to hear."

She nodded in understanding. "Your mom and I stopped to check the post yesterday. My parents still haven't written. I'm trying not to, but I'm getting concerned."

"We've talked about this, Liv. Is it going to change the outcome if you worry?"

"No ..."

"It's out of our control. Remember what Pastor said, 'Worry weighs just enough to take our future out of God's hands and put it in our own.' Enjoy this time with my sister and your niece and nephew and leave the future to God."

"I suppose you're right ... the reminder helps. Will you do something for me while you're away?"

"If I can."

"Will you close your eyes every night at eight o'clock no matter where you are and pray with me?"

"Absolutely! I'll even blow you kisses."

"Thank you, Jesse. Maybe it's silly, but it'll make me feel better—like you're right here with me, if only in spirit."

A sparkle tweaked his eyes as he asked, "So you'll miss me, will ya?"

"What do you think?"

"Not nearly as much as I'll miss you."

Her head lowered. "You'd better stop. You're going to make me cry."

He rode Shadow right up next to her and took Guinevere's reins. When he reached to slide Olivia over onto his lap she came willingly. Sharing a moment of tenderness, she said, "we really should be paying attention."

"Shadow knows the way. Besides, I need a whole passel of your sweet kisses, or I'll never make it through the week."

She was happy to oblige.

"Look at that!" Kaleb announced from where he and Elizabeth stood on the porch. Olivia and Jesse were riding into the yard, lost in the splendor of the moment. "I don't know, Liz, he might not make it through the week without her."

"Well look at her, she's no better off!"

Jesse, hearing his sister's voice, asked, "Who's no better off?"

"Looks to us like this week away could be a bit of a struggle. Are you sure you're up to it?"

Olivia's gaze held her husband's, and she kissed him one more time for good measure. "I'll be just fine ... now that ..." she flushed, somewhat embarrassed by her forwardness, "you know."

Jesse laughed as he lowered her to the ground and then dismounted himself. "Are you and your father ready, Kaleb?"

"Yes." Kaleb kissed his children, who were still clinging to him like glue. "You two be good for Mama and Auntie Liv."

Cameron's head bobbed up and down. "I will, Daddy."

"That's my little man."

Brenae peeked up at Olivia from Elizabeth's arms and said, "Hi!" And as if that weren't surprising enough, her pudgy little fingers waved in greeting. When Olivia held her hands out, her little niece came without hesitation, melting Olivia's heart.

"Hi to you too, Brenae." Olivia kissed her soft cheek, glanced at her sister-in-law, and asked, "Lizzy, when did she start talking?"

"She only says five words: *Mama, Dada, Ron* for Cameron, *Zy Zy* for horsy and *hi*."

"Well, that's a good start."

Samuel rode out of the barn, leading Kaleb's mount. He smiled as Jesse picked up Cameron, spun him around, and then tussled his soft brown hair.

Jesse entreated, "Make sure you tickle Auntie Liv and Mommy for me while we're away."

The mischievous glance Cameron sent Olivia's way told her he was up for the assignment; however, she thought it only fair to warn her smiling nephew, "Don't forget, Cameron, I tickle back." Her warning must have been even funnier to him than Uncle

Jesse's orders because Cameron giggled out loud.

As soon as the men were on their way, Elizabeth, Cameron and Brenae took Olivia to the barn so they could get Guinevere settled.

"Lizzy, Jesse told me that Guinevere was a wedding gift from you and Kaleb. I had never been on a horse before I met your brother. Having one of my own is something I could only dream about. You made that dream come true. I can't thank you enough."

"Well, I'm glad you like her. Guinevere and I spent many long hours together. I'm quite fond of her myself."

"I don't know the first thing about breaking horses. Was it difficult?"

Elizabeth smiled. "If you're open to new challenges I can do better than tell you. While you're here I was hoping to begin breaking Lady's second filly. You can help if you'd like."

Olivia's eyes widened. "If I won't be a hindrance, I'd love to."

"Good."

"Did you name her, Lizzy?"

"Not yet. Guinevere will be hard to top."

"I know what you mean."

Elizabeth's brow knitted together. "Let me know if you come up with one that would suit her."

Olivia nodded as she handed Brenae to her mother, removed Guinevere's saddle and followed Elizabeth to the tack room. After hanging her saddle from a long post, Olivia took a moment to look around. Someone had gone to great extremes to organize everything. She hadn't been inside many barns in her day, but this one was almost too clean. Thinking it would be rude to comment, she reached for a brush and went to give her horse a good rubdown. Olivia then led Guinevere to an empty stall. Noting how immaculate even that was, she closed the door, wondering as she did if Elizabeth and Kaleb's home would be the same way.

Elizabeth had been watching her new sister closely. She was pleased to see her progress with Guinevere and commented, "You've come quite a ways for a small town girl, Livia."

She smiled. "Thanks. I'm getting there. I do love working with the horses and the rest of the barn animals. Milking ... it's tolerable. The chickens can be scary at times, and the gardening ... well, let's just say it leaves a bit to be desired. But let me tell you, gardening is a picnic compared to working a day with Jesse and the boys."

The scowl that twisted Olivia's face gave Elizabeth a case of the giggles. "What did he have you doing?"

"You name it! Jesse was trying to help the boys get caught up before the trip, so maybe it wasn't an average day on the farm, but I was dead on my feet by the time we finished." She held her sister's gaze as she confessed, "I'm a terrible wife."

Elizabeth had a niggling suspicion she was over-exaggerating. Even so, her curiosity peaked. "What do you mean?"

Olivia snickered. "I begged your mom and sisters to find a way to get me out of working with the guys yesterday. They were very accommodating. Mom decided she and the girls needed a few things in town and asked Jesse if I could ride along with them."

Elizabeth was intrigued. "Did Jesse call you on it?"

Olivia rolled her eyes. "He saw right through our whole plan.

I really don't know how he does it."

"I do. Think about it. Look at your new sisters and brothers and Kaleb's sister Sarah. He and Kaleb have had years of practice putting up with all of our antics."

"I suppose .... I'm glad he found out. It saved me from my own guilty conscience."

"I know what you mean. I can't stand it when Kaleb and I are at odds."

Olivia followed her nephew's every move. He was so at ease as he interacted with the animals, and the barn cat weaving around his legs was no exception. However, when Cameron accidentally stepped on the cat's tail, the cat screeched, swiped at Cameron's little hand, and took off running. She was not surprised when he cried out in pain. Olivia stooped down beside him and lifted him in her arms. "Are you all right, Cam?" She found a scratch on his hand, but otherwise he was fine. Glancing at her sister-in-law, she asked, "Lizzy, should we head in and clean this up? I wouldn't want to chance it getting infected."

"True. I could use a cup of tea anyway, what about you?"

"Sounds good." They were climbing up the back steps, when Olivia heard a dog whining and suddenly looked up at Elizabeth. "Jesse told me about this monstrous dog of yours. Should I be scared?"

Elizabeth rolled her eyes. "He's just a big baby. Let him smell you. I'm sure you'll be the best of friends." She opened the door slowly and Olivia cautiously followed her in.

"Oh, my!" Olivia exclaimed. "He's huge!"

When Cameron, who was still in her arms giggled, she tickled him and said, "What are you laughing at little man?"

"You funny, Auntie!" Cameron wiggled until she put him down and he wrapped his little arms around the dog's neck, as if to assure her that there was nothing to fear.

Olivia held out her hand to the dog to let him sniff her, but his big old wet tongue came out to kiss her instead. *Oh, yuck!* It took great restraint not to overreact. "What's his name, Cameron?" she asked as she patted the massive head.

"Bwu-tis!"

Olivia glanced at her sister for clarification.

"Brutus is six months older than Cameron. Isn't that right, Buddy?" Cameron nodded as Elizabeth set Brenae down in a little wooden play area lined with blankets. She was content to play with the small toys scattered within.

Olivia asked, "Would you like me to clean Cam's wound or start the tea?"

"The kettle needs more water. Do you mind getting some first?"

"Not at all." Olivia took the kettle outside to fill it and asked as she came back in, "Who's the elderly gentleman coming out of your barn, Lizzy?"

"I don't know ...." Elizabeth peeked out the kitchen window and sighed with relief. "That's Mr. Ballard, the town carpenter. Kaleb and his dad are trying to decide if they should just add on to the existing barn or build another one. He said he'd be coming by to give them an estimate. Will you do me a favor and watch the children while I run out and chat with him?"

"Gladly ... would you mind if Cam and I make a batch of cookies?"

She glanced at her small son as she went out the door, "If you want special treats, Cam, help Aunt Livia find the things she'll need to make them." Cameron didn't offer a verbal response; one wasn't necessary. His smile said it all.

"So tell me, Cam. What kind of special treat would you like?"

"I show you." Olivia wasn't sure what he would come back with when he went to the pantry shelf, but he returned with what looked like his mother's journal. She sat down next to Cam as he leafed through the pages. It was the most thorough collection of recipes she had ever seen.

"Do you know what you're looking for, Cam?"

He nodded, saying "Yep!" and he did. The moment he came to the sought-after recipe, he pointed to it as he looked up at Olivia. "That's my specialist tweat."

"It is, is it?" Olivia scanned the page and realized it was a recipe for sugar cookies dipped in a chocolate glaze. "Sounds good, Cam. Shall we get started?" When he nodded, she asked, "Can you show me where the bowls and spoons are?"

Cameron immediately informed his mother of their efforts when she came in the back door. "Me and Auntie's making my specialist tweat, Mama."

"I'm glad, Honey."

All Olivia could see when Elizabeth walked in the door was her pale features and the letter in her hand. Immediately her heart stood still. "Is it from my parents?"

"Jesse was afraid this would happen. He asked me not to collect the post until he returned. Mr. Ballard didn't know."

"It's okay, Lizzy, really it is ... if Jesse were supposed to be with me, he would be."

When Olivia's eyes welled up, Elizabeth suggested, "Go

ahead and take it into my room and shut the door. As soon as this tray of cookies comes out, I'll take the children over to visit with Kaleb's Mom and Grandma."

Olivia took the letter from her sister-in-law's hand and did as she suggested. No matter what it contained, her tears might upset Cameron and she didn't want that. She couldn't bring herself to even glance at the envelope until she sat down on the bed. It was penned by her father's hand and as much as she wanted to rip it open, fear sliced through her with a vengeance. *What if ...*

Since nothing could change the reality of what she would find within, she took a deep breath and broke the seal. Sliding the missive out, she began to read.

Dearest Jesse and Olivia,

It is my prayer that this finds you both well and settling nicely into your new life together in Ypsilanti. I'm sure you enjoyed your time alone at the cabin, but harvest time is drawing nigh, so I'm assuming you are home. Give your family our best.

I can't begin to tell you how much the portrait has meant to us, Olivia. I sure do hope you have told Jesse by now. If not, don't wait. Your mother and I agree, He is the most gallant of knights and deserves to know.

This illness seems to have a mind of its own. I have both good and bad days, but as I feared, Mama did not fare well on our journey. The nurses here at the asylum are kind. Even with all their valiant efforts, she has been unconscious for three days now. Her breathing is very labored. She is not expected to pull through. It grieves my

---

heart to tell you this in a letter, but I promised to keep you informed. Remember what we talked about Olivia: God sees the greater picture. Never forget that He knows best.

I do not wish to get your hopes up, because there are no guarantees, but I will ask that you continue to pray. The doctors here have had some success with their patients. They informed me that while my lungs are weakened, they are not giving up hope. In the meantime I am doing everything they suggest. Most of my time is spent reading God's Word to your mother and taking long walks. I am told that while the fresh mountain air is healing to those with consumption, the common remedies such as smoking tobacco, vigorous horseback riding, and opium are not cures but are actually detrimental to one's health.

The mountain ranges surrounding the asylum are beautiful beyond compare, and I am richer for having seen them. The trees stretch into the clouded expanse and give the appearance of Heaven and earth joining as one.

While I miss the two of you, our home, our friends, and my garden in Tecumseh, I have come to realize that home is not about familiar surroundings. It is more of a state of mind—where your heart is. My heart is both here with Mama and there with the two of you. Know that I am with you in thought and prayer. Give each other a huge hug from us and by all means, write as often as you can.

With all our love,
Papa and Mama

Olivia's tears flowed freely as she read the letter over and over again. When she was almost through it for the fifth time, she heard a soft knock at the door before it opened. Elizabeth wasted no time sitting down beside her and enfolding her in her arms. For a time she just held Olivia and let her weep. "Mama had been unconscious for three days when Papa wrote. She's not expected ... to live."

"Oh, Honey. I'm so sorry."

"It's not like I didn't know she's dying, but it's still hard to accept."

"I know what you mean," Elizabeth said. "Seeing my father sick for so long was difficult, but not nearly as hard as it is now. He's in a better place, I know that, Olivia. Your mom will be, too, if she isn't already."

"Jesse and I talked about it this morning. He's been amazing through all of this."

"I'm not surprised. He's been an awesome big brother. Do you want me to have Jared or Joe go for Jesse? I'm sure if they ride hard, they can catch up with them before morning."

Olivia would love to be held in his arms, but her husband needed this time away, and she refused to take this from him. "No. We'll just have to stay busy. What are the children doing?"

"I'll need to pick them up before bedtime, but Mom and Grandma asked if they could have them until then."

"What about Cam's *specialest tweat*?"

Elizabeth smiled. "We'll finish them later and take a plate over to share. I'd like you to have a chance to visit with them anyway. Kaleb's grandma is a character, and his mom's a gem too."

"I'd like that. I'm sure the pot of tea I made is cold, Lizzy."

"No matter, I drink it cold all the time. How would you feel about working with that filly and then taking a nice cool bath in the creek after we finish our chores?"

"Sounds great! You know, Lizzy, we could eat that first tray of cookies before we go out. No one would be the wiser. There's plenty of batter left to make more for later. They don't have the glaze on them yet, can you live with that?"

Olivia smiled. "They're fine the way they are. I'll get too fat if I eat too many with chocolate on them."

Elizabeth rolled her eyes. "You could eat a batch a day for a month and still not be fat, Sis."

"Hardly! Jesse's been feeding me so well since we weremarried, I look in the mirror and barely recognize myself." Lizzy patted Olivia's hand and stood to her feet.

"When your tummy starts rounding out and you get as big as I'm going to, then I'll listen to your complaints. For now, let's go have a snack and see what we can do about training this nameless filly."

"So tell me, Lizzy, how will I know if I am?"

"Am what?"

"With child. Is there something I should look for?"

"I've been told that every woman is different ...."

"How so?"

"Well for instance ..." Elizabeth began as she poured the tea and Olivia set the plate of cookies between them.

The rest of the afternoon flew by in a whirl of conversation and all-out fun. Though her father's letter would come to mind from time to time, she refused to give in to despair. Instead, she'd whisper a prayer for her parents and reminded herself that they were safest in the Lord's hands.

Olivia was thoroughly impressed with Elizabeth's skill in handling Lady's frisky offspring. It took a while, but Elizabeth's gentle prodding paid off, and the filly eventually obeyed her commands. It wasn't long before she had Olivia accomplishing the same tasks with the young horse, and, in truth, Olivia enjoyed it quite thoroughly. Patience is a trainer's greatest asset, and these two women had plenty of that.

Elizabeth and Olivia shared a light meal while baking the rest of the cookies. After dipping the sweet confections in chocolate glaze and leaving them to dry on a cooling rack, they gathered their bathing supplies and clean clothes. When the animals were bedded down for the night, they headed down to the creek.

"I'm tired, Lizzy, but a bath sure does sound wonderful."

"I couldn't agree with you more. So tell me, did Jesse drag the big tub out at the cabin?"

Olivia giggled recalling the first time ....

"What's so funny?"

Olivia winced. "Let's just say that the first time he brought it out, I was a bit reluctant to join him."

"Was it a private moment, or can you share?"

"The night after Grandpa and Grandma left, I could hear him fumbling around in the kitchen, but I was so engrossed in a book I was reading, I didn't know what he was up to. When he called me out to the kitchen, he wanted me to get in the tub while he went for the towels, but I couldn't."

"If I know Jesse, he wasn't upset in the least. But he is persistent. How did he convince you to join him?"

"He lifted me in his arms, and we went in fully clothed."

Lizzy shook her head and laughed out loud. "He always did have a tender way of dealing with my fears. I'm sure he's even more patient with his wife."

"He is at that. Are Jesse and Kaleb alike in that respect?"

"For the most part. Kaleb knows that if he doesn't press me at times, I'd let my fears rule me, and then I'd miss out on God's blessings. I used to think he was overbearing to the point of being extreme—still do at times—but it works for us. He knows how to get me past my stubbornness so that I can see things more clearly."

"When we don't see eye to eye, Jesse threatens to throw me in the creek, and he actually has done it on several occasions."

Elizabeth smiled. "That form of correction runs in the family, so watch out!"

"I'm all too aware of that!"

Cameron squealed when Olivia came in the back door of his grandma's house with a plate full of his favorite cookies.

"You bemembered!"

"I did! How could I forget something so important, Cam?"

His little hands went palm up as he said, "I do-no."

"Cameron," Elizabeth said, "Aunt Olivia hasn't met Great-Grandma. Would you like to introduce her?"

"Auntie," Cameron said as he took Olivia's hand and pulled her along, "this is Gwate-gwama." Olivia went gladly into Naomi's outstretched arms. "It's nice to meet you, Ma'am."

"It's good to finally meet you too, Honey. You feel free to call me Grandma, the other Somers children do."

"Thanks, I'd like that," said Olivia as she turned to hug Ruth and Sarah. "Good to see both of you again."

Sarah nodded as Ruth said, "That goes both ways, Olivia. The kettle's hot. Could we interest you girls in a cup of tea to have with the sweets?"

Olivia glanced at Elizabeth who said, "Sounds good."

Naomi acknowledged as they all sat around the table. "You girls look exhausted. I hope you haven't been trying to do too much."

Olivia knew that Naomi and Ruth were concerned about her; she could see it in their eyes. Discussing her father's letter openly would not be easy, but she needed to expose the terrible grief welling inside her. Whom better to share her burden with than these caring women? Lowering her gaze, she said, "I want you ladies to know how much I appreciate your prayers today. My father didn't want to get my hopes up, but the doctors are encouraged by his progress."

Ruth acknowledged, "That is good news."

When Naomi agreed, Olivia looked up, trying to be brave, but unbidden tears flooded her eyes. As difficult as it was, she forced herself to go on. "Papa said Mama didn't fare well on the journey. When he sent the letter she had been unconscious for three days. She's not expected to ... live ...."

Naomi and Ruth went to her and just held her while she sobbed. After a time she calmed and Ruth offered, "We're so sorry, Olivia. We'll continue to pray for you and your parents, but don't you try to carry this burden. Give it to the Lord. We're here for you, too, even if you just need a shoulder to cry on."

"Thank you. Mama's a wonderful woman. I wish all of you

could have known her. She's suffered for so long. As much as I will miss her, I believe God in His great mercy is calling her home."

Naomi rubbed at her arm. "God loves her more than any of us ever could, Honey. He knows what is best and we need to trust Him."

"Keep reminding me of that, will ya, *Gweat-Gwama*?" Her playful words chased away their tears, and Olivia, having shared her weighted soul, knew much relief. Elizabeth poured the boiling water over the tealeaves and set the pot in the center of the table with the jar of honey and pitcher of cream.

The women smiled when Cameron, who had been as quiet as a church mouse while Olivia was upset, climbed up into her lap and announced, "I'm ready for my specialist tweat, Auntie." Olivia kissed his cheek and handed him two cookies.

"You've been very patient, Cam. I hope you enjoy them."

"Olivia," Naomi said, "I sat on the porch and watched the two of you with that new filly. She's coming along nicely, isn't she?"

Sarah was curious, "Did Lizzy tell you she's a gift for Suzanne?"

Lizzy reminded her, "We're not telling Suzanne though, are we, Sarah?"

Sarah giggled. "No ... but I'm praying Lady has twins next time. With Louise being older than me, it's only fair that she get the next offspring. That'll mean I have to wait two more years before I have a horse of my own."

"Did you tell them what we named her?" Olivia asked Elizabeth.

"We've been calling her Star. What do you think?"

Everyone agreed when Ruth affirmed, "A perfect name for

an ebony horse with a white star."

"Good!" Elizabeth declared, "Then Star it is."

"Elizabeth," Olivia asked, "how old does Guinevere have to be before we can breed her?"

Naomi put in, "Those wheels are turning in her head, Lizzy girl. You keep at your new sister. You'll make a horse breeder and trainer out of her yet. Jesse's small town gal is definitely a huckleberry above a persimmon in my book."

Bemused by Naomi's odd way of saying things, Olivia asked, "So ... do you think he'll mind, Grandma?"

Elizabeth shook her head. "That's not what she's saying at all. It's just, well, you know ...."

Olivia admitted, "I'm afraid I don't."

"You being a small town girl and all, we weren't expecting you to catch on to farm life and fit in so ... well."

Chapter Eighteen

Distraction

OLIVIA CLICKED HER tongue, and Star trotted obediently in circles around her at the end of a lead rope. Yesterday Star had accepted a blanket without protesting too much; perhaps tomorrow they would try the saddle. Who knows? By the end of the week she may even accept a rider. Olivia was hoping her sister would be willing to let her try riding Star, but whatever she decided, Olivia was thankful for the distraction. She missed Jesse something fierce and her parents ... well, she couldn't allow her mind to dwell on them or surely she would fall apart.

Unable to sleep well without her husband's presence alongside her, Olivia spent most of her long evening hours painting by candlelight. A few more restless nights and some of her paintings would be complete.

❀ ❀ ❀

Olivia stuck her head in the back door and said to her sister-in-law, who was splattered with flour from her baking efforts, "Elizabeth, I'm heading over to the village to see if Mr. Norris has mail for us."

"I was hoping to get you to help me with the laundry this morning. If we take it down to the creek, the children could play in the water while we work." Olivia knew what Elizabeth was doing. Her concerns were written on her face.

"I won't be gone long. We can see to the laundry when I get back."

"Olivia!" Elizabeth moaned, "You're going to get me in big trouble with my brother if you get a second letter without him here."

Olivia, understanding her duress, went to Elizabeth and hugged her. "How about this: if there is something for me, I'll give it to you. I won't even ask to read it until Jesse gets back."

"Are you sure you can do that?"

"No, but if I promise, I'll have to, won't I?"

Elizabeth smiled. More at ease she said, "If that's all you're doing in town, take Cameron with you so he doesn't wake up his sister."

"I would love to."

Elizabeth's eyes narrowed in on her. "You didn't promise."

Grinning, she exclaimed, "I promise!" When Elizabeth nodded, Olivia took her anxious nephew's hand and led him out the door.

"Auntie," he asked as they rode towards town, "we going to Hawk's, too?"

Olivia liked his shortened name for Hawkins House. His expression was so hopeful, how could she deny him? Tussling his dark brown hair, she teased, "You do have quite the sweet tooth, little man."

"Like Papa!"

"Yes, like Papa and Uncle Jesse, too!" Cameron giggled when she tickled his sides as they rode into town. The gentleman who had stopped by the house the other day greeted them after they dismounted.

As he shook the small boy's hand, he asked, "Cameron, who do you have with you?"

He looked up at the kind man and said, "Auntie!" as if he should have known already.

Olivia cracked a smile. "I'm Olivia Somers, Sir."

He nodded. "I heard Jesse got himself a pretty wife. It's a pleasure to make your acquaintance, Mrs. Somers. The name's Arden Ballard."

"I was with the children when you were by the White farm the other day. Lizzy mentioned that you're a builder. My father was a carpenter before my mother took ill."

"Well, if he's ever looking for work, you send him my way. I always have more jobs than I can handle."

Olivia's gentle smile concealed the awful sorrow swelling inside her. "I'll remember that. Enjoy this wonderful day, Mr. Ballard." Cameron tugged on Olivia's hand, pulling her toward Hawkins House the moment the white-haired gentleman moved away.

The trading house carried many necessities, but it was the frivolous items that tweaked Cameron's interest—more specifically, the jars that held various flavors of stick candy. As they made their way to the counter, a clerk Olivia did not recognize met them.

"Will this be all today, Ma'am?"

"Yes, thank you. Could you tell me if Mr. Foster is available?"

"He's having his meal in the hotel, Ma'am. My name is Douglas. Can I assist you in his absence?"

"Thanks, Douglas, but it's nothing pressing. We'll stop by again in a few days." Another customer came up to the counter, so Olivia took her leave. After collecting the mail from Mr. Norris, they headed home.

Olivia held in her sweaty palms two envelopes. She wanted to look in the worst way, but they were almost home before she summoned the courage to glance down at the top one. She breathed a sigh of relief; it was addressed to Kaleb. Afraid that she wouldn't be able to keep her promise to Elizabeth, she refrained from looking at the second. In fact, when Elizabeth, who had been waiting for them on the porch, came toward her in the yard, Olivia handed her the mail, admitting, "One of these is for Kaleb. I can't bring myself to look at the other one, Lizzy. Will you?"

Elizabeth nodded, but inside she was just as reluctant.

Taking a deep breath for courage, she scanned the envelope and sighed. "It's for Mom, from my uncle in New York. He must have gotten word about Dad."

"Should I run it over to her?"

Elizabeth shook her head. "Jared or Joe will be by to check on us later if I'm not mistaken. They can take it to her."

Olivia was confused and curious. "Why are they coming?"

Elizabeth rolled her eyes. "Do you really think Kaleb and

Jesse would leave us alone for a week without having our brothers check up on us?"

"I suppose not. If we need to get the laundry done, we'd best get started, Lizzy. Jesse doesn't like me running around in my shift in front of Jared and Joe."

Elizabeth scowled, "Please tell me you're not serious!"

Olivia held her gaze. "Wish I could."

"Well, don't let him get away with it. The Somers women have been swimming in their shifts for years."

"I called him on it, but ..."

"He'll get over it, or I'll get on him."

"If you're going to try your hand at breaking Star, Olivia, you have to wear these!"

"Oh, come on, Lizzy. Jesse made me wear jeans the other day. I really don't understand what men see in them. I spent the whole day tugging at them, trying to keep them up."

"That may be, but you'll be glad you're wearing them if you need to move quickly. Remember what I told you: Star's not going to take too kindly to having a rider on her back, not at first anyway."

Olivia groaned as she yanked them out of her big sister's hand. "Fine! I'll wear the silly things, but if it were up to me, I'd see to the task in my unmentionables!"

Elizabeth burst into laughter. Her sister-in-law was just as feisty as she in most areas, but where the jeans were concerned they did not agree. Elizabeth would wear them every day if her husband wasn't such a prude about her being in men's clothes.

"They fit fine—look at you, girl." Lizzy's hands rubbed at her protruding belly. "This body's been stretched out so many times, I'll never look that good again!"

Olivia shook her head. "But look at how God has blessed you and Kaleb. Cameron and Brenae are so precious."

"I know."

Olivia winked. "Who knows? Maybe I'll start getting round about the time you have this baby."

"Are you trying to tell me something?"

She shook her head. "Not that I know of."

"If you ever wonder, just ask, Livia." They were on their way to the barn when Jared rode into the yard. Olivia's heart sank when he dismounted and came toward them.

"You two look like you're on a mission. What are you up to?"

Olivia glanced at Elizabeth speculating as to whether she would tell him or not.

Elizabeth didn't so much as flinch when she said, "Olivia's taking a stab at riding Star."

Jared's eyes narrowed in on Olivia and then transferred back to Elizabeth. "Is Jesse aware of this?"

He was trying to intimidate Olivia and she wasn't about to let him. Her desire to accomplish this was too strong. "Jesse doesn't control my every move, Jared. I've been working with Star all week. Lizzy and I both think she's ready and so am I." He didn't look convinced so she added, "I need to do this."

"Olivia!" Jared declared incredulously. "You know zilch about breaking horses! Do you even know what you're in for?"

"Sort of ... besides, how will I ever learn if I don't try?"

"You know as well as I do that if Jesse were here he'd be stopping you."

"I'm not so sure he would. He admires my willingness to face new challenges—even encourages me to accept them. I appreciate your concern, Jared, really I do."

"You could get hurt ...."

"I could, but I refuse to let fear rule me." When he didn't appear ready to back down, she flatly stated, "I am going to do this, so please don't bully me. Be a nice big brother and offer suggestions that will help instead."

Jared nodded in acceptance. Although letting her proceed went against his better judgment, it wasn't his place to say more. After putting his horse in the barn, he took a seat on the top rail of the fence and just watched his sisters in action. It didn't take long to see that they made a fine team. He was impressed.

Olivia led Star into the corral and worked her out for a while before she and Elizabeth put the saddle on Star's back. The filly protested to a degree, but for the most part she was cooperative.

As Olivia was about to mount Star, Elizabeth's words stopped her, "Remember what I told you. Expect the unexpected. Don't let down your guard for anything."

Nodding, Olivia's calm amazed Elizabeth, but she asked just to be sure, "Are you ready for this, Livia? You don't have to, ya know."

Olivia glanced at her brother who was not at all happy with her. She then took a deep breath for courage and looked back at Elizabeth. "I'm ready!"

Jared slid off the fence and walked toward his sisters,

drawing their attention when he said, "Elizabeth, you get up on the fence and watch. I may not be able to talk this spitfire out of doing this, but you've got a baby growing inside you who needs protecting."

Elizabeth scowled at her younger brother. "I'll be fine, Jared."

"You'll be better than fine up on the fence, so don't give me a hard time."

Elizabeth, shocked by her younger brother's commanding tone, handed him Star's reins and climbed up on the fence to take a seat. As she did, she contemplated Jared's actions and how much he reminded her of her father—of Jesse. She smiled, wondering, *When did it happen? How did I not realize that Jared was a grown man?* Turning her attention back to the task at hand, Elizabeth saw her brother in a whole new light.

Olivia's apprehensions rose the moment Elizabeth walked away. She wasn't sure why, but Jared had a tendency to make her nervous. Fortunately, his softly spoken words soothed her every doubt.

"Livia, before you mount, I want you to lift your arms over your head and lean from side to side."

She rolled her eyes, thinking he was toying with her, but his look told her he had his reasons. "Now my shirt's un-tucked!"

"Exactly! I don't want anything binding you. Hold the reins in your left hand and hang on to the horn with the same hand. That'll keep you from jerking on Star's bit until she settles down. Put your right arm above your head to help you balance. When she throws you, roll away and stand as quickly as you can."

Olivia smiled and touched his arm. "Lizzy's been over this with me several times. Besides, Jar ... she might not throw me."

He shook his head. "Don't get too arrogant. Breaking horses has a way of humbling the most accomplished equestrian."

"I'll bet it's humbled a number of cowboys as well!"

He nodded. "It has at that. If you're ready, Sis, have at it!"

Olivia patted Star's long neck and soothed her with words before sticking her foot in the stirrup and trying to mount. When Star sidestepped, Jared gave Olivia a boost. To Olivia's complete stupefaction, she was back on the ground in seconds. She moaned as she stood, rubbed her sore backside, stretched her legs and was ready to go at it again.

Jared tried not to snicker as Olivia staggered toward him. "Are you sure you don't want me to show you how it's done?"

"No. If you do it, how is that going to help my confidence? I have to do this, Jared."

"Well, come on then."

This time Olivia lasted at least a minute, but when she hit the ground, the back of her left arm slid across the splintered fence. She could feel the wood digging into her skin; even so, she gave nothing away. She could remove them later. If Jared got wind of the slightest injury, he would stop her from trying again, and she wasn't about to let that happen. Not yet! She was about to mount for the third time when Jared informed her. "One more try and you're calling it a day."

"Nooo!" she protested. When Elizabeth agreed with Jared, her shoulders slumped in defeat, but she was more determined than ever not to fall.

At first, Olivia thought Star would never stop jarring her insides, but then Star broke into a canter, and Olivia was enthralled. Her heart soared as she led Star around the corral several times before the horse took a notion to protest again and threw her a good six feet. So much for her accomplishment!

Unfortunately, her left arm hit the fence again, hard. The pain was so intense it took her breath away. Olivia couldn't be sure if the slivers had gone deeper into her arm or if she had gained new ones, but she could feel them stabbing her. Whatever it was, blood was seeping into her sleeve.

Jared noticed, called out for Elizabeth to come and take Star, as he turned to Olivia and informed her, "Elizabeth can't handle the sight of blood, so I'll have to help you get your arm cleaned up."

"You okay with that, Livia?" Elizabeth asked as she led Star toward the barn. But she didn't wait for an answer. The thought of seeing Olivia's injury made her feel sick to her stomach.

Olivia looked up at Jared when he helped her stand and softly murmured, "I suppose I'll have to be." She worked at the buttons on her shirt as she and Jared made their way down to the creek. Pulling her good arm out, she hesitated and then said, "Jared."

"Hmm?"

"I can't get my bad arm out. Is the fabric hung up on the splinters?"

"Splinters?"

Olivia nodded, undecided if she should tell him more. Shame washed over her. Her brother was only trying to help. "The second time Star threw me, my arm slid along the fence. I picked up some splinters."

He grimaced. "You should have stopped then, Olivia!"

His heated words hit their mark, and tears filled her eyes as she turned away.

"Olivia."

"What?" she murmured, unwilling to face him.

"Did you pick up more splinters the third time?" When she shrugged, his irritation subsided. "We both know what you should have done, but we can't go back, can we, Sis?"

She shook her head.

When the silence lengthened, Jared laid a gentle hand on her shoulder. "Are you going to turn around and let me help you?" He sounded so much like Jesse, she came close to losing her composure but caught herself. Wiping away her tears, she swallowed her pride, and turned. Several seconds passed before she peered up.

"Jared, I'm sorry."

"No need to apologize. I'm just as bull-headed. More than likely I'd have gone at it again myself."

"Serious?"

"Serious!" Jared took out his knife and sliced at the fabric of her blouse until her arm was free of it. His gentleness could not be faulted, but the pain was so intense she found it difficult to remain standing.

Jared tried not to overreact when he saw the back of her arm. One look at his sister's face told him she was doing her level best to hide her anguish. He could see right through her facade. "Olivia?"

"Jared ... I don't feel so good." The color had drained from her skin. Having seen the look on Elizabeth's face several times before, he wrapped his arm around her, just in case she passed out. When she turned and lost her last meal, he held her hair and just waited.

"Are you all right?"

"I'm sweaty, Jared. Maybe I'd feel better if I sit in the creek."

A bit out of his element, Jared hemmed and hawed a bit, "Sure ... ah, let me help you with your ... ah ..." His cheeks warmed, and he let his words hang as he stooped down to untie her bluchers and tug them off. By then, she had loosened her own jeans and was pulling them off while he saw to his own. As awkward as it was to be helping his brother's wife undress, he reminded himself that Olivia was his sister and did what needed to be done. Holding onto her good arm, he led her into the creek, thanking the Lord that her shift and unmentionables were still intact. After lowering her into the shallow water, he said, "I need to run up to the house for a minute. Will you be all right?"

Olivia nodded, cringing as the wounds she could not see slid under the cool water. She didn't want to alarm her brother, but it hurt so badly she wondered if something was drastically wrong. "Hey, Jared!" she yelled as he turned to leave.

"Grab the soap and a towel. After rolling in the dirt, I could use a good scrub."

He nodded and worked his way up the hill.

Elizabeth heard Jared calling for her and came out of the barn. "How is she?"

"The swelling in her arm is bad."

They were walking back toward the house when Elizabeth said, "Then I'd better run home and get Joe. If there's a chance it's broken, Jesse would want Doc to see to her care."

"I'd take her into town myself, but I don't think she could handle the long ride. She got sick down by the creek. If you're asking me, she's in worse shape than she's willing to admit."

"More than likely. When she's done in the creek, have her lay on my bed while you work on those splinters. You need to get them out of her arm. I'll be back as soon as I can, Jared."

Olivia, still trying to conceal her anguish, cringed when Jared came toward her in the water and sat down beside her.

"Olivia, let's get one thing straight. I know you're in a great deal of pain, so there's no need for the brave front."

Her tear-filled eyes met his. "I wish Jesse were here."

He tenderly wiped away her tears and tried to reassure her, "I know you do. Afraid you'll have to settle for your big brother."

"My arm feels really heavy, Jar ...."

"I know .... Lizzy's heading over to get Joe ... he'll go for Doc."

"Are you mad at me for not listening to you?"

"How could I be? You proved me wrong. You're quite the horsewoman. Jesse would be proud."

"I hope he is, but if you're wrong and he locks me in my room, will you promise to let me out?"

He chuckled. "As long as you don't tell him who did."

"You can count on that." She watched Jared rub soap into the washcloth and thanked him when he handed it to her.

"I help Louise and Suzanne with their hair all the time. Do you want me to suds yours up?"

"If you don't mind."

"Not at all."

Olivia couldn't see where the splinters were on the back of her arm, so when Jared offered to wash around them, she let him. This was no time to be stubborn.

Olivia was changing in Elizabeth's room when Jared heard a rider come in. He hesitated going out in his wet skivvies, but thinking it was probably Lizzy, he went ahead.

"Well, well, well!" his brother called out. "Are you setting a new style, Jared?"

Jared laughed. "Boy, am I glad to see you, Jesse. We weren't expecting you until tomorrow."

"I missed my wife ... came back early. Is she here?"

"Yes, but there is something you should know." Jared was acting strange, so Jesse dismounted and listened as Jared filled him in.

"Olivia was determined to try her hand at breaking Star."

"Lady's filly?"

"Yes. She hurt her arm. I had her soak it in the creek, but the splinters are huge, and her arm's swelling ... could be broken. Lizzy's went over to have Joe fetch Doc. I'm sure your wife could use some help getting out of her wet clothes. Sorry, Jesse, I did what I could ... had to draw the line somewhere.

She's in Kaleb and Lizzy's room."

Jesse smiled and slapped his red-faced brother on the back. "Thanks for what you've done, Jared!" Jesse leapt up the back steps, went into the house and knocked softly on the bedroom door. He had no wish to startle his wife.

"I'm not ready, Jared."

Jesse turned the handle and said as he opened the door, "It's me, Honey."

"Jesse!" Olivia cried out. Her relief knew no bounds. When he carefully wrapped his arms around her and held her close, she let down her guard and allowed the tears to flow.

"Jared said you had an accident. Mind if I take a look at your arm?"

She nodded, but it was hurting too much to lift it, so she turned around. "Is it bad?"

"Afraid so. Let me help you out of your wet things. Honey, where are your night clothes?"

She turned to face him. "Jesse, it's barely noon."

Caressing her face, he said, "Sorry, Liv. I know you'll hate me for it, but I'm going to insist that you stay in bed for a few days, maybe longer. We'll see what Doc says."

"I'll be fine. Just let me change and I'll make you some coffee. I'll bet you're hungry, too." Her mistake was meeting his stern glare when he reached to unbutton her wet camisole. "All right," she conceded. "I'll lay down until Doc comes."

"You'll stay down until I say you can get up or I'll tie you to the bed."

Her sodden eyes flew up. "This is a fine way to treat your wife when you haven't seen her in days."

"If you weren't so stubborn ..." She was standing in the buff with a pitiful expression covering her face when he held her gown and presented an ultimatum, "Are you going to stayin that bed, or ..."

She knew what he was thinking—he would take her clothes without a second thought if she didn't comply! "Oh, all right! You don't have to be such a grouch about it."

He kissed her pouting lips. "I'm not a grouch. I just want my wife to get well."

Lifting her arm to get into her gown made her feel ill again. She broke out into another cold sweat and yelled, "Jesse, quick! Get me the chamber pot."

One look at his wife's pasty complexion said it all. "Sit on the edge of the bed, Liv."

She complied.

He reached her side just in the nick of time. After washing her face with a cool cloth, he got her settled in bed and encouraged her to rest until Doc arrived. It wasn't long before she drifted off.

After getting a better look at her arm, he decided Jared was probably right. When the splinters were removed they would leave big gaping holes that would need to be stitched. He would have to wait for Doc.

Jesse heard someone in the kitchen and ambled out to investigate. Jared was making a pot of coffee. "I sure could use some of that."

"I figured as much."

"Is Lizzy back?"

"I'm expecting her any minute. Can I do anything, Jess?"

"Liv got sick and it's all down my leg. She's asleep. Would you mind keeping an eye on her while I run down to the creek and wash up?"

"Go ahead. The sleep will do her some good. Did she tell ya she got sick down by the creek, too?"

"No," Jesse said. "The pain must be bad if it's making her ill."

"She did a good job of hiding it from me for a while."

Jesse nodded. "I'm not surprised. She's tougher than she looks."

"The bar of soap is in the kitchen, and just so ya know, I put Shadow in the barn."

"Thanks, I won't be long."

Lizzy stopped by her mother-in-law's to see if she and her grandma could keep the children for the night.

"Take all the time you need," Ruth said, "the children are fine. Grandma and I will pray." Elizabeth thanked Ruth as she went out the door with a basket full of baked goods.

"Jesse?" Elizabeth called out as she came out of the barn and found her brother coming up from the creek. "When did you get back? Are Kaleb and Samuel here, too?"

He shook his head. "Sorry, Sis. They had another meeting to attend, but I couldn't wait."

"Have you seen your wife?"

"She's sleeping. Jared stayed with her so I could get cleaned up." His sister's anxieties were written on her face.

"Accidents happen when you work with animals, Lizzy. This wasn't your fault."

"If I didn't let her try ..."

"Don't blame yourself. It happened and we'll deal with it. Tell me, how did she do?"

"She's a natural, Jesse. We really do make a good team."

"Good. Give her time to heal and I'm sure she'll be back at it. If you haven't figured it out, she's not a quitter."

Elizabeth smiled, feeling more at ease. "You're right about that. She got bucked off Star three times."

He shook his head. "So you finally named her."

"Olivia did."

"She's going to be sore for a while."

"I tried to tell her, but she was determined. Did Jared tell you he tried to talk her out of it?"

"No ... I'm not surprised she didn't listen to him. Could be because they're so close in age, but Jared has a tendency to get on her nerves."

Elizabeth giggled. "I noticed that." Jesse held the back door open and followed his sister in. Jared, who was pouring himself a cup of coffee, said, "She's still sleeping."

Jesse nodded. "I'm exhausted from the long ride. I'm going to lay down with her. Let me know when Doctor Taylor arrives."

Jared wanted to know, "Do you need me to stay, Jesse? Evening chores will need to be done. Joe's bound to be worn out from riding into town and back. Do you mind if I head home?"

"Not at all.

I'll be over in the morning to check on Olivia."

Jesse hugged his brother. "Thanks for all you've done."

"You're welcome. I'm not positive, but Olivia could be changing her mind about me."

"What do you mean?"

"She didn't refuse my help down at the creek."

Jesse's brow rose. "Give her time, Jared. She's never had siblings before."

He grimaced. "She likes the girls and Joe just fine."

"True, but they're not her older brother, are they? It makes a difference."

"You could be right. I'll be praying for her." Jared was at the door when he turned back and said, "Jesse, she hit that arm twice in the same area. She came clean while we were down at the creek. The first time she picked up most of the slivers. She was afraid I wouldn't let her get back on, so she didn't tell me. When she flew off the last time, she hit it hard."

"I'll let Doc know."

Olivia moaned when Jesse lay down beside her in the bed and snuggled her close, but she did not waken. He could only presume the movement brought her pain. He had missed her so much he wasn't sure he could ever leave her again. After pouring his heart out to the Lord, he gave into his weary body and fell asleep, thanking the Lord that she was back in his arms. Jesse wondered how much time had lapsed when Elizabeth nudged him.

"Jesse, Doc's pulling into the yard."

He Loves Me!

Chapter Nineteen

Too Much to Endure

AMBLING INTO THE kitchen in his stocking feet, Jesse poured himself a cup of coffee and went to the door. "Thanks for coming, Doc."

"How is she?"

She's been sleeping for hours now. Her arm looks bad. I know she's in pain, she's been moaning off and on, but I was afraid to mess with it."

Doc looked up at Elizabeth and asked, "How are you and the baby growing inside you doing?"

"Just fine. It's my new sister I'm worried about."

"I'll take good care of her, Lizzy. Can you get me a small cup of water?" Doc turned to Jesse and said, "The laudanum I'm going to give her will take the edge off ... I'm afraid there's not much else I can do to kill the pain."

"Just do what you can. Something's better than nothing."

Doc followed Jesse into the bedroom and pulled a chair up next to the bed where his patient lay sleeping.

"Olivia," Jesse softly called from the other side of the bed, "I need you to sit up and take this medicine for me. Doc's here to tend your wounds." She shook her head and dozed back off. Doc examined her arm before he tried to wake her again.

"Olivia, I need you to sit up and take this for me." His raspy voice did the trick. She opened her eyes. However, when she tried to sit up, the pain was too intense. Jesse had to help her. The moment the cup was drained, he laid her back on the pillow, and she was asleep in seconds. Doc, needing to give the drug a chance to take effect, went for a cup of coffee and Jesse followed.

"What are you thinking, Doc?"

"Could be a bad sprain. Most likely it's broken, Jesse. Won't know until I check the bones. What was she doing that would cause that much damage?"

Elizabeth spoke up, "She was helping me break Lady's filly. She did real good until Star threw her for the third time."

Jesse added, "Jared told me she got some of the slivers the second time she was thrown."

Doc reaffirmed, "So she injured the arm twice?"

Jesse nodded.

Doc harrumphed. "Well, she fits right into this family, mulish streak and all!"

Jesse and Elizabeth laughed, and Jesse admitted, "Had to go all the way to Tecumseh before I found a wife with the Somers' spirit!"

Doc nodded, took a long sip of his coffee and said as he stood to his feet, "I'd best get to work, or I won't make it home in time to snuggle with my wife."

Elizabeth let them know, "I'll start dinner. If you need me, holler, but I'm hoping you won't."

"Jesse," Doc said as they moved into the room, "I need you to lay almost on top of her and hold this arm down so she doesn't move quick. She'll be dopey from the laudanum, but it only numbs the pain."

Olivia woke immediately, and though her voice was slurred, she wasted no time protesting, "Jesse ... get off me!"

"Can't, Honey, Doc's orders. He has to get those slivers out."

"Nooo! Leave me alone ...."

Doc pulled the first one out, and it took all Jesse's strength to keep her still. As Doc proceeded, her agonizing screams mellowed into sobs that tore at Jesse's heart. Unfortunately, there was nothing he could do to ease her distress. Over and over again Jesse kissed her cheek. "I'm sorry, Liv. He'll be done soon, just hang in there."

Doc set the tweezers down on the table beside him and said, "The slivers are out, Olivia. A few more stitches and I'll be done."

"Hurts ... Jesse ..."

"I know, Honey ... it's almost over." Jesse watched Doc tie the last stitch and cut it off before allowing his fingers to trace the bones in her arm. Jesse held his breath, hoping and praying that it would be fine. When Doc suddenly stopped and stared at him, his heart faltered. "Is it what I think?"

Doc nodded.

Jesse, needing to console his wife before Doc proceeded, lay next to her on the bed. He tenderly dried her tears and pushed her damp wisps from her face. "I know you're hurting, Liv. Can you be brave just a bit longer?"

"Jesse, I can't give her more laudanum yet. It's your call, but the longer I wait to do this, the harder it will be to set."

"Did you bring a splint?"

"It's on the seat in the buggy." Doc turned to his patient and asked, "Olivia, if Jesse gets up will you lay real still so I can bandage your arm?" Her brain was so foggy, it took a bit to process what he was saying, but when she finally agreed, Jesse went to retrieve the splint.

Jesse stood on the porch and thanked Doc as he drove away, but Olivia's screams haunted him long into the night. After three attempts to set her arm, her bone finally slipped back into place. Mercifully, Olivia passed out during the second attempt. Three hours had passed since, and although Jesse's concerns were many, Doc assured him that she was breathing normally. The pain had been too much for her to bear. While Doc didn't think she would wake up until tomorrow, he suggested that Jesse give her more laudanum for the pain if she did. For hours Jesse sat beside his wife, bathing her face with a cool rag and praying.

I know this is beyond my control, Lord, but will her suffering never end? Help us both to learn what you're trying to teach us through this affliction. Elizabeth told me about the letter from her father. If her mother is still with us, ease her suffering, Lord, and be with Josiah and Olivia as well.

Exhausted, Jesse surrendered his weary bones to the bed and awoke to the sun's brilliant rays streaming in the bedroom window. Glancing at his wife, he smiled when her puffy eyes met his. He reached to caress her face. "How are you, sweetheart?"

"Better now that you and Doc quit torturing me."

"I'm sorry about that ... couldn't be helped."

"Jesse, I need to use the outhouse."

"Sorry, Hon, the chamber pot will have to do," but she was shaking her head. "Liv, you've been through quite an ordeal. You need to stay still."

Her eyes fell on the odd looking splint. "My arm is not going anywhere in this contraption. If it makes you feel better, I suppose I can let you come with me."

"You're not a very good patient, Olivia Somers."

"Sorry!"

"I will carry you to the outhouse, but after that you're coming right back to bed, understood?"

She nodded and grinned. "Right after tea and breakfast!"

"Olivia Somers!"

"Jesse Somers! After all you put me through last night, you owe me."

"What I put you through? Ha! What about what you put me through? My ears are still ringing. And besides, you gave me quite a fright you know."

"You sat on me!"

"Fighting ... I suppose that's a good sign!" Elizabeth spoke from outside the closed door.

Olivia and Jesse burst into laughter, and Jesse stood to open the door.

"She's in rare form, Lizzy! She wants me to carry her to the outhouse and then she wants breakfast before she'll consent to going back to bed! What's a man supposed to do with such a defiant wife?"

Elizabeth giggled. "Love her."

"You would say that, seeing how you're just like her! Where is Kaleb when I need someone on my side?"

"He'd better be on his way home! I miss him something awful."

Jesse pulled his sister into the crook of his arm. "He was only a day behind me. They should get here sometime tonight."

"All right, you two!" Olivia interrupted. "Your patient is desperate!" *And the horrible pain in my arm is making it worse.* Her thoughts, though true, were not about to be revealed.

Jesse helped Olivia into the sling Doc had left behind and then lifted his wife in his arms. When she moaned out loud, he went to put her back in bed, but she refused to let go of his neck.

"I'll be fine, Jesse. It's bound to hurt for a few days."

They were on their way out the back door when he asked, "Do you want more of that medicine Doc left?"

"No ... it makes me feel strange. Fogs up my brain."

"Maybe that's a good thing."

The outhouse door creaked open, and the foul aroma wrenched her empty stomach. She rolled her eyes when Jesse insisted on following her into the cramped space, but when she tried to maneuver things with one hand, she was glad he had come. Husband and wife were moving through the back door when Olivia admitted, "I don't feel so good, Jesse. Maybe you were right." She closed her eyes and laid her head on his shoulder. Her movement, or was it the pain in her arm that made her feel so dizzy and light-headed? Before she had time to decide, he had her back in the bed.

Elizabeth poked her head around the corner. "Olivia, I have

a pot of sweet tea made. Sound good?"

"Yes ... please." When Elizabeth went to the kitchen, Olivia turned her pleading eyes on her husband. "My stomach's a mess. Would you mind butchering a chicken? Maybe if I eat some soup it would help."

"That's fine ...."

"Here you go," Elizabeth said as she came back into the room and handed Olivia's tea to Jesse.

After just a few sips, Olivia laid her head down, admitting, "So tired ..." And she was asleep.

Doc came by to check on his patient, and while he knew she was in a great deal of pain, Olivia refused to take more of the laudanum. He didn't press her.

Olivia had seen the effects of using such drugs too freely, and she wasn't about to chance becoming addicted like her mother had. Doc tried to tell her that a few doses wouldn't matter, but she stuck to her guns, knowing the pain would eventually pass.

That afternoon, Elizabeth's chicken soup was a taste of Heaven. After several small bowls throughout the evening hours, Olivia was pleased to be regaining her strength. Kaleb and Samuel had returned just before dinner. When Olivia suggested that she and Jesse head home so Elizabeth and Kaleb could have their bed back, they ignored her.

Doc had said she was not to travel for three more days. He didn't want to chance the bone dislodging on the bumpy ride. Since Doc's word was final, Jesse and Kaleb insisted that they were staying. In truth, she was glad.

"Elizabeth!" Olivia called from the bedroom the next afternoon. When no one came, she sat on the side of the bed, cracked the door and tried again. "Lizzy!" She knew the men would be in the barn, so there was no sense calling for them. It wasn't long before she heard footsteps and Elizabeth appeared.

"You look bored!" Elizabeth teased. "Want to join me in the kitchen?"

Olivia smiled. "Jesse told me to stay put until he comes back in, but if I don't get up, I'll never sleep tonight."

Elizabeth's hand came up and slapped at the air. "Don't worry about Jesse. I'll take him to task if need be. Let me pull the rocker and foot stool into the kitchen. I'll be right back to help you into your robe."

"Thanks, Lizzy!"

She winked. "What are sisters for?"

Olivia smiled. "So much more than I could have ever imagined."

Elizabeth had been sharing memories from her childhood with Olivia throughout the week, and this morning was no different. In fact, Olivia was laughing and didn't hear her husband come in the back door. Jesse's brow knitted together as his eyes narrowed in on her. She glared right back when he scolded, "I told you to stay in that bed, Young Lady!"

Elizabeth, noting how his words intimidated Olivia, took him to task as promised. "You leave her alone, Jesse Somers. She's bored being stuck in that room all by herself. Besides, I needed the company."

Jesse's hands went in the air as he glanced back at Kaleb and asked, "What am I doing wrong? I thought a wife was supposed to obey her husband."

Kaleb admitted, "I'm probably not the best person to ask,

Jesse. If you really want to know what I think, I'd say love her a bunch and maybe ... just maybe she'll come around!"

Jesse leaned over and kissed his wife. "I suppose I can manage that. How's the arm, Liv?" He was pleased to see that she at least had it propped up with pillows.

"The same. Are you really mad at me?"

He leaned over and whispered in her ear, "You will pay for your crimes later, My Sweet."

She grabbed the front of his shirt with her good hand and pulled him close for another kiss. "How was your hunting expedition?"

"Successful, but you don't want to know about it, remember?" When she laughed out loud, Kaleb's curiosity peaked. He sent his friend a probing look.

Jesse happily explained his wife's aversion to such things. In truth, Kaleb wasn't surprised; Elizabeth shared Olivia's revulsion.

"Lizzy," Olivia asked. How long before supper is ready?"

"The potatoes are almost done. You hungry?"

"Yes, but I've been wondering. Are you and Kaleb familiar with the game of patience?"

Elizabeth nodded. "It's like solitaire, right?"

"Yes. My parents and I used to play it together all the time. It's great fun, but Papa called it peanuts when you play in teams. Instead of playing alone on your own cards, all the aces go in the center, and both teams can play on them. It can get kind of wild, but as long as we play in teams, I shouldn't have to use my gimpy arm."

Elizabeth looked up at Kaleb who nodded in approval. She wondered if he would be too tired from his long journey, but apparently not. "Sounds like fun."

"Good. I brought one deck of cards along with me. Do you have another?"

"Yes, they're in the top drawer of our armoire."

Kaleb piped in. "Since you girls are making plans for our evening, I'll head down to the creek for a cool bath before supper. Coming, Jesse?"

"Sure, might as well get it over with."

The laughter and rivalry ensued around the table as the women played against the men and won the first two games. When Elizabeth suggested they call it a night, Jesse and Kaleb wanted no part of it. They were convinced that they had the game all figured out, and besides, they weren't about to go to bed as losers. The men won the next hand but lost the two after that, and the only way they would agree to call it a night was if the women agreed that the competition would continue tomorrow night. Olivia and Elizabeth agreed, knowing if they didn't, their husbands would have them up all night.

"Jesse," Olivia asked as she lay down in the bed, "my body's really sore. I'm not sure if it's from Star jarring my insides or fighting you and Doc. Any chance you'd haul water so I can soak in a warm bath tomorrow?" He was sitting next to her on the bed. Untying his bluchers, he kicked them off, turned the lantern down low, and his large hand caressed her warm cheek. "I'd be glad to. If you think you can turn over, I'll try to rub some of the kinks out."

She wasn't really sure what he had in mind, but she was so stiff and achy she had to let him try. Seconds later she admitted,

"You could do this every night for the rest of my life and I'd never complain, Jesse Somers."

"Is that so?"

"Umm, Hmm!" It was less than a minute later that his wife drifted off.

Jesse pulled an envelope out of his pocket and tucked it down into his boot. He prayed for Olivia as he lay down beside her—her father too. The letter he received from Josiah today was not good news. Maryse had gone home to be with the Lord. His heart ached. He hated knowing his father-in-law would be alone in his grief, but there was nothing that could be done. At first he was torn about telling Olivia. He didn't like keeping things from her, but at the same time, she needed to get her strength up before facing this. He knew all too well how hard it was to say goodbye to loved ones. Perhaps he was wrong for not telling her, but he was determined to give his wife the time she needed to heal. They would be staying with Elizabeth and Kaleb for one more night. As long as she was doing better, he would tell her after they were home. For now he was convinced it would be too much for her to endure.

He Loves Me!

Chapter Twenty

A Time to Celebrate

OLIVIA GLANCED AROUND the table as she savored her last few bites of apple muffin and thanked the Lord for the blessing of friends. Jesse and Kaleb were discussing plans for the new barn that Kaleb and his father would be building in the fall. They were so receptive to each other's council. No doubt, the time they had spent together down through the years had formed a bond as strong as any brothers. Olivia loved knowing that she and Elizabeth were fast becoming friends of the dearest kind. God's goodness never ceased to amaze her. In truth she hated to leave, but life must go on. The reprieve had given her much to look back on. Her husband and brothers had a farm to run and their home was with his family.

The look Jesse sent her way told her he was ready, but she couldn't leave just yet. "Kaleb and Lizzy, I'm so glad we've had this time together."

"So are we," Elizabeth returned. "Thanks for all your help with the children and Star."

"I'd like to continue helping you with Star's training."

When three sets of eyes narrowed in on her, she quickly amended her statement. "Not until Doc gives me the go ahead, of course."

Jesse informed her without delay, "He'd better not give it too soon, or you'll have to contend with me."

Then Kaleb added, "And I'm next in line."

Olivia glanced at Elizabeth and asked, "Did they gang up on you like this while you were growing up?"

"All the time!"

"You poor thing!" Olivia smiled demurely as she stood and moved slowly from the room. When she returned with a painting in her hand, the room went silent. Before turning the canvas over she said, "This is just a little something I thought you might enjoy having in your home—a thank you gift of sorts. Kaleb, you'll have to make a frame for it. Woodworking was my father's specialty, not mine." She laid the painting in the center of the table so Kaleb, Jesse and Elizabeth could take it in at the same time. She stepped back to watch their reactions. The tears that filled their eyes told her just how much her efforts would be cherished. It was a perfect image of George and Jayne facing each other. Their eyes held each other in a warm embrace.

Elizabeth was beside herself. "Oh, Livia. How could we ever thank you enough?"

Kaleb added, "This is amazing. You've captured him exactly. Even the love that always filled their eyes for each other. But how did you do this from memory?"

"I'm not real sure. When I begin to draw or paint, I close my eyes, and I can recall scenes or my subjects in great detail."

"Have you always had this gift?"

"No. This is definitely a God thing. I began to draw when my parents took ill and started painting soon after that. Papa said that this gift was God's way of channeling my inward thoughts—taking my sorrow and turning it into something that can bring joy to others and myself. I suppose I'll always be in awe of what He can do through willing vessels."

"I think all of us would agree with you there, Livia."

Jesse turned to Kaleb and asked, "Didn't you see the portrait she did of the two of us on Shadow? She saw me once through mud-smeared eyes before she did the painting. It really is something."

"I heard about it, but I haven't seen it."

"Mom hung it in the sitting room, but ... I have a feeling the other one I have sitting around the corner will soon take its place."

Elizabeth's head tilted as she asked, "Are you going to show us or keep us in suspense?"

"I don't know," Olivia teased. "Maybe I should make all of you wait until after Mom sees it."

Kaleb glanced at Jesse. "What do you think? Is she up to being tortured?"

"She's certainly tempting fate!"

Elizabeth spoke up when the men took a step toward her new sister, "Olivia, trust me, you don't want to press them. You'd better give over. Besides, it really isn't fair to tell us about it and then not share it!"

"I suppose .... Jesse, if you'll pick up the one on the table, I'm sure Kaleb won't mind helping me with the other."

Kaleb smiled. "I'd be glad to help, especially if it means I get the first glimpse." Elizabeth and Jesse stood aside so Kaleb could lay it on the table.

"I was able to finish this one when I couldn't sleep at night, which as you can see was quite often." Since the three of them were stunned speechless by what they saw, Olivia went on to explain her thoughts. "I debated who should be in this, but I didn't want anyone to know what I was doing, so I couldn't ask. At first I was going to do just the Somers family, but then I couldn't leave Kaleb and the children out. That's when I decided everyone who was a part of the family before Dad went home to be with the Lord should be included." When no one said a thing, she asked, "Do you think Mom will mind?"

Jesse slid his arm around her and held her tight. "I think there's nothing you could have given Mom that she'll treasure more."

Kaleb and Elizabeth couldn't have agreed more, and Kaleb asked, "Do you mind if we come home with you? We'd like to see Mom's reaction when you give this to her."

Olivia's eyes twinkled as she smiled at her husband. "We would love that, wouldn't we, Jesse?"

"Certainly!"

Kaleb kissed his wife's cheek. "Liz, you run over and get the children while I hitch up the wagon."

When Samuel and Ruth heard what was going on, they joined the small caravan along with Grandma.

Olivia felt like a small child being coddled by her father. She wanted to ride Guinevere home, but her husband would not hear of it. Instead, he lifted her into the back of the wagon and insisted on padding her on every side with blankets and pillows. "Jesse, please quit and go away. I'll be fine. You're embarrassing me." She felt as if everyone was staring at her. Little did she know, Jesse was not the only one concerned about her traveling so soon after her injury.

Jesse held her face in his hands and tenderly informed her, "I've waited a long time to have a wife to dote on, so put your bad arm on top of this pillow and don't give me a hard time, or I'll climb into the wagon and ride back here with you."

Her brow arched. "I don't know. That could be fun."

"Behave yourself, Young Lady. Your nephew is hanging on your every word."

Olivia glanced at Cameron, who was sitting at the foot of the wagon bed and smiled. "Cam, come on over here and keep your Auntie company."

He gladly obliged, chattering with her the entire way.

Suzanne, standing at the counter finishing up breakfast dishes, turned to her mother and said, "Jesse and Livia are back, and it looks like the rest of the Whites came along." Jayne had been kneading bread dough. Dusting the flour from her hands, she covered the bowl, removed her apron, and moved out the door with Suzanne.

Kaleb had just let himself in the front door, and since his hands were full, Jayne took the time to greet everyone else.

She was pleased to see Olivia up and around. The way her son doted on his wife made her smile. She thanked the Lord for his goodness, thinking, *There's nothing like a man in love.*

Jayne asked of the crowd at large, "To what do we owe the pleasure of your company?"

"Well," said Jesse as he stepped forward, "Olivia has a gift to present to the family."

"Oh?" Jayne turned to Olivia and asked, "What have you been up to beside breaking horses and your arm?"

"Much, but you'll have to wait until we're in the house to see. Kaleb already carried the gift in, so I suppose we should join him." Glancing around, she asked, "Where are Jared and Joe?"

"Louise," Jayne called out to her youngest daughter who was deep in conversation with Sarah.

"What, Mama?"

"Louise, Jared and Joe are in the barn. Tell them to come in. Olivia has something she wants to give the family."

"Sure ..."

When everyone was assembled, Jesse and Olivia led them into the sitting room where they found Kaleb standing with a huge grin on his face. The painting was turned toward him so no one could see it. Olivia had asked Jesse to present the gift, so he moved to stand next to his friend.

"I think most of you are aware of my wife's special gift. It would seem that while I was away she didn't sleep much, but let me assure you she put her sleepless hours to good use. Lizzy brought along a painting Olivia did for her and Kaleb, so she'll share that one with you in just a bit." Jesse turned to his mother and held her gaze, "Mom, this painting is really for you, but I am sure all of us will cherish it in the years to come."

Jesse moved to stand beside his mother and slid his arm around her as Kaleb turned the portrait and set it on the mantel.

Needless to say, though his family was elated, mesmerized, and taken aback by the gift, tears flowed freely. George was in full color before them and seeing his likeness brought back a flood of wonderful memories.

❀ ❀ ❀

"Olivia, come to bed."

"I will in a minute, Jesse. Let me finish this letter so you can mail it while you're in the village tomorrow. Something is wrong; I can sense it in my spirit. Papa would have written by now if he were able, I'm sure of it."

"Give him time. I'm sure he will, as soon as he can." Guilt washed over him. The days of his wife's recovery had folded into weeks. Three had past and still Jesse couldn't bring himself to tell Olivia of her mother's passing. He wrote to her father and let him know about her injury. He even mentioned that he would wait to tell Olivia about her mother until she was doing better. Olivia had asked him last Monday if she could go into town and check the post. When he told her he didn't want her riding until the splint came off, she wasn't happy, but she accepted his decision. This also meant that her visits with Elizabeth and the children were few and far between. While this was not his original intent, it couldn't be helped. Jesse knew she was restless to be out and about. While he understood, he had too much to accomplish before the cold weather set in. He had to keep moving.

Olivia's birthday was coming up, and Jesse was planning a big surprise party for her. All their friends would be coming. Jed had mentioned that he'd bring along his fiddle, Bruce his Dulcimer, and with Duke leading on his guitar, the singing, dancing and merriment would go on for hours. Jesse could hardly wait to introduce Olivia to others in the community.

The crops were harvested, and many families were looking forward to this time of celebration just to relax and enjoy one another before the winter winds began to blow, and they were once again snowbound.

What could a few more days hurt? Jesse didn't like keeping this from her, but at the same time, her happiness was important to him. He would tell her soon—very soon ....

Jesse blew out the lantern, and as his wife slid under the covers and snuggled up close. "Olivia, I was wondering, is there something specific you wanted for your birthday?"

"If I told you it wouldn't be a surprise, and I love surprises."

A moment passed. "I understand that, but there are so many things you need before winter. I'd just as soon get you what you want instead of guessing. When she remained silent, he suggested, "You could make me a list of several things I can choose from."

"If you really want me to ... I suppose I could ...."

He wasn't convinced she liked his idea. When the scant light from the shadowy moon exposed her protruding lower lip, his wiggling fingers altered her mood.

"Jesse, quit!"

"Only if you'll be honest with me." He propped himself up on one elbow, watching her intently. Her changing mood had him somewhat baffled.

"I'm not a child who needs to have my own way all the time, Jesse."

"Did I imply that you were?"

"No ... my parents had their way of doing things, and you

have yours. Our traditions were different, but who's to say I won't like your way better?"

This gave him pause. "Would you like to tell me how your family celebrated birthdays?"

"Maybe someday. I'm still struggling, Jesse. Change is good; it helps me to focus on what I have left, instead of what I've lost. Maybe someday it won't hurt so much."

"Just so you know, I'm open to change, too."

"I don't doubt that for a minute. You married me without the benefit of time to get to know me first."

"We needed each other."

"Still do ..."

"Always will, My Love ..."

❀ ❀ ❀

"Jesse," Olivia softly called as she entered the kitchen. The moment his sparkling eyes beheld her, she twirled before him like she had the day they were married. "Do you mind if I wear this?"

"How could I mind? You're irresistible!" She smiled with pleasure and stole a kiss before whining just a bit. "Too bad I still have to wear this ugly splint."

He touched the tip of her nose. "I heard you tell Elizabeth the other day that you're itching to get back to training Star. So, no complaints about the price you're paying, or I won't even consider letting you try again."

She sent him a coy look, murmuring as she turned away, "Who said I was asking, Mr. Smarty Pants?"

"Olivia! You're not too old for a birthday spanking, ya know!"

"Well, you're too young to be such a grouch—especially on your wife's birthday!"

"If you don't want me to be a grouch, then promise you won't try breaking anymore horses until we're in agreement about it."

She turned back to face him and nodded ever so slightly.

"If you don't mind, I'd like to hear the words from your mouth."

She rolled her eyes. "Oh, all right! I promise. Satisfied?"

"I will be in a minute." He pointed to his lips, expecting a kiss.

There was something about his tender expression that she could not resist. She was happy to comply.

"So, are you going to tell me where we're going all dressed up?" Olivia overheard her sisters talking that morning and knew they were going to Kaleb and Lizzy's for her birthday, but her husband was unaware of her newfound knowledge.

"Nope!"

"Well, I hope Mom plans to bring along that cake she won't let me see. I could smell it cooking earlier, and it's killing me. I want a piece."

"All in due time, Liv. I've got the buggy ready. Let's go."

"The buggy ..." she protested, how is everyone else getting there?"

He chuckled softly. "I don't think you need to concern yourself with everyone else."

"They're my family, too, Jesse. I want them with us."

He shook his head. "They're coming, Liv. They wouldn't miss your birthday party."

"Good. So we're having a party, are we? I love parties. Do I need my shawl? How long will we be gone?"

"Enough!" With a firm hand on her back, Jesse led his inquisitive wife out the door. "You know, Liv, for someone who likes surprises, you sure do ask a bunch of questions."

"I'm curious. Can't help myself."

Turning her to face him, Jesse smiled as he gathered in his hands the face of the woman he loved. "Well, I can't help myself either," he admitted as his lips tenderly claimed hers, exposing only a smidgen of the yearning in his heart.

Olivia, silenced by her husband's passionate display, allowed him to lift her into the carriage. He handed her his hat, which the wind had dislodged from his head, and a pillow on which to rest her arm. Her eyes never left him as he climbed in beside her and reached for the reins. The gentle breeze tousled his coffee brown hair. Jesse finger-combed it back off his face, reclaimed his hat and settled it on his head before leading Mable in the opposite direction of Kaleb and Lizzy's.

In the worst way, Olivia wanted to question him, but she refused to pry more than she had already. Perhaps he was taking her for a stroll in order to give the rest of his family a chance to reach Kaleb and Lizzy's before them. As difficult as it was, she settled back against the seat and did her best to relax and enjoy the ride. It was so seldom that she and Jesse could scrape a few minutes alone. His workload never seemed to end, and with this broken arm, she felt useless most of the time. He made sure her paint and supplies were ample. She'd been working on several scenic views that she hoped to sell in town when they were complete. A number of folks had mentioned that they would love to have family portraits done, but with Jesse not wanting her riding with the splint, and too busy to take her, she was often stranded at the house.

The sweltering humid weather that typically pervaded July had carried through the month of August, but now September's gentler days and cooler nights would soon lead into fall, Olivia's favorite season of all. Closing her eyes in wonder, she could almost envision this rolling landscape clothed in autumn's vast array of vibrant shades. She could hardly wait to partake of its splendor.

"Jesse, where are we going?" she asked when she realized how far out of their way he had gone.

"You'll see."

"Are we going to pick up someone?"

"No, Honey, we're not." She was beginning to regret not using the outhouse before they had left home. If they had only been going to Kaleb and Lizzy's, she would not be in such a desperate state. Growing more uncomfortable by the minute and somewhat frustrated, she insisted, "Then we're going the wrong way."

A single eyebrow arched. "And how would you know that?"

She grimaced. Regretting her outburst, she merely said, "A pair of birds were speaking too freely ... I overheard."

He laughed out loud, knowing exactly whom she referred to. "You see, Liv, that's where you went wrong. Every other member of this family is on to my little sisters. They can't keep secrets, so we've learned to feed them false information."

"You lie to them?"

He shook his head. "Not really. We tell them something different every time they ask, and they know why."

"Oh ... If we have much further to go, I won't make it. My needs are pressing in."

When he led Mable close to a line of trees, Olivia had her answer. She hated knowing he would have to help her, but some things couldn't be helped. If she were to fall and do more damage to her arm—well, she couldn't allow her mind to go there. Instead, she swallowed her pride and followed her husband into the thicket.

They traveled for at least another hour before Jesse skirted around Ann Arbor and headed slightly northwest. When they finally arrived at their destination, she was clueless as to where they were until Grandma and Grandpa came out of the house. Her heart leapt at the sight of them. "Is this their home, Jesse?"

He grinned as he pulled the team under a nearby tree and jumped down. She wanted to jump down herself and run to Jacob and Anna, but she waited until Jesse helped her.

"Welcome. How's our birthday girl recovering?" came Jacob and Anna's voices from the porch.

"I'm fine, Grandma. It's so good to be here. How are you doing?" Hugs were shared all around before Jacob answered her.

"We're doing well. I'll tell you what, Olivia, I've had an awful hankering for some of your blueberry pie. Suppose I'll have to wait to see if we can find another patch next summer, won't I?"

"Afraid so," Olivia affirmed.

Jesse kissed Olivia's cheek and suggested, "Grandma, if you'll take the birthday girl inside and keep her busy for a while, Grandpa and I can get to work."

Anna reached for Olivia's good hand and squeezed it in her own as they moved toward the house. They were almost to the porch when Anna craned her neck around and said, "Don't you worry about us, Jesse. Olivia and I have lots of catching up to do."

Jesse and Jacob began setting up make shift tables for the wide array of foods that would arrive with every family coming to join in their celebration. These potluck affairs were a wonderful place to share family favorites, and everyone benefited from the group's efforts.

"So, tell me, Jesse. Has Olivia received any news from her parents?"

Jesse, unsure of his grandpa's reaction, hesitated before saying, "She received a letter from her father while I was away. Her mother had been unconscious for several days and not expected to live."

"I'm sorry to hear that. Has she heard since?"

"Well ... yes and no. We got a letter, but I haven't had the heart to tell her yet. I wanted to give her time to heal before facing her grief."

Jacob's head lowered. Several seconds ticked by before he looked at his grandson. "How long have you known?"

"Too long. I'm going to tell her, Grandpa. I wanted to give her this time to celebrate first."

Jacob shook his head, his brow furrowing. "Don't wait, Son, or this could backfire on you. Olivia trusts you, but she won't if you continue to mislead her. She'll feel betrayed instead of protected."

"Pray for us, will you?"

"Grandma and I do every day. That won't change. But God called Maryse home on His appointed day. God's timing is everything. Never forget that. Trust Him, Jesse. He knows what is best for Olivia. He loves her more than you ever could."

"I know you're right. I'll tell her soon." Jesse pointed toward the trail leading in from town. "Our guests are arriving." And indeed they were. Within the hour the musicians were in rare form, and the guests were enjoying the festivities.

Jesse, reaching for his wife's hand, offered a gentlemanly bow. "Mrs. Somers, might I have the pleasure of a dance?"

A soft blush kissed her cheeks as Olivia nodded and went willingly into Jesse's outstretched arms. The waltz he had chosen was one of her favorites and brought a flood of wonderful memories of celebrations gone by. So many times she had danced this same waltz with her parents—safe in the circle of their arms— and now she was finding that same security in the arms of her husband—the man she adored.

"Happy Birthday, My Love," Jesse whispered before indulging in a tender kiss.

He Loves Me!

Chapter Twenty-one

A Time to Mourn

"*THIS CAN'T BE!*" Olivia exclaimed when she found a letter her husband had apparently hidden from her. *Why, Jesse? Why would you keep this from me?* She glanced at the postmark on the envelope, and the tears that had been pooling in her eyes fell freely. The letter had to come two or three weeks ago. She was crushed.

Jared had brought their clean basket of laundry into the room before he left. She was reorganizing Jesse's clothes and putting them back in his drawer when she found the letter tucked underneath his last pair of jeans. It was addressed to both of them from her father, so why would he not give this to her? She could understand his reluctance when she had first injured her arm, but what was he waiting for? No doubt he had read it—it was open. More than likely it was devastating news, but still that was no excuse to keep it from her. As she contemplated his actions, a wave of emotions transfused her, with anger and betrayal at the fore.

At first she was determined to go to Jesse and give him a piece of her mind. Then she thought better of it. Knowing Jesse, he would try to make light of her anger. His excuses were not something she could abide. Not now! Not yet! The more she thought about it, the stronger her need to flee became. She had to distance herself—needed to get away—give herself time to let go of her anger and think things through. And she knew the perfect place to go.

Olivia couldn't bring herself to read the letter from her father right now. Best to wait until she arrived at her destination. Reading the words would only confirm what she already suspected, but words were so final ... like death itself ....

Bursting into tears, she reached for her hanky, paper, inkwell and pen. Wiping at her clouded eyes, she scribbled out a quick note, put it on Jesse's pillow and threw a few necessities into a bag along with her paint supplies and empty canvases. If she couldn't sleep, she could always paint. Using this gift had a way of soothing her despondent heart, drawing her ever closer to the Giver of Life.

Thankfully, her mother-in-law and sisters were off visiting with a friend. The men wouldn't be back until supper—the supper she was supposed to make. Today they would have to fend for themselves.

In a way she felt like a criminal trying to make a quick escape, but she couldn't stay. Perhaps it wasn't fair to run off like this. Her husband would be worried—perhaps angry. Too bad, he had brought this on himself. She trusted Jesse—depended on him.

How could he betray her like this? Since thinking about it made her feel sick inside, she tried to put it out of her mind as she headed for the barn. Saddling her horse could be a challenge with one arm. If she had to ride bareback, she would. Her determination was unwavering. She might calm down and feel differently later, but for now getting away was her only thought.

Olivia took Guinevere out of the stall and ended up putting her right back in. Her horse's fiery mood and her own unrest would not be a good mix. Shadow was predictable. She would need predictability for the long ride.

Hearing Jared and Joe's voices coming in from the field, Olivia mounted Shadow and led him cautiously out of the barn. If she took off with a start like she wanted to, they would know something was wrong and alert Jesse. She decided it was best not to even let them see her, so she hid on the far side of the barn and waited—hoping they wouldn't go in and notice Shadow was gone. She breathed a huge sigh of relief when they headed toward the house instead. They would find her missing and wonder where she was, but by then she would be long gone.

Moving slowly until she cleared the farm, Olivia patted Shadow's neck, nudged him with her heels and rode hard for the first few miles.

※ ※ ※

"What do you mean, she wasn't in the house?" Jesse was furious. "Did you look for her or just assume that she was fine?"

Jared and Joe glanced at each other and shrugged. The three of them had been working hard all day. They were dripping with sweat in spite of the cool breeze, and neither of them were in the mood for Jesse's interrogation. At the same time, they understood his duress, so Jared answered his questions.

"We just assumed she was busy in some other part of the house or outside."

"You're probably right. I'm sorry," Jesse said. "I didn't mean to jump down your throats. I suppose I've got too much on my mind that needs dealing with. After a quick dip in the river, I'd best get to it. Obviously, it's affecting me more than I realized."

Joe nodded. He didn't have a clue as to what Jesse was talking about, but he did accept his apology.

Jared asked, "Is there anything we can help you with?"

"No, but thanks for offering. This is something I've been putting off too long. Learn from my mistakes, boys. Procrastinating when the Lord tells you to do something only makes dealing with a situation that much more difficult. You could pray that it won't blow up in my face."

Jared put his hand on his younger brother's arm. "We'd be glad to, wouldn't we, Joe?"

With a slight nod, Joe offered, "Hey, guys, I'll grab the soap, collect our things and meet you at the river."

Jesse and Jared thanked him and headed down the embankment toward the cool relief waiting for them at the bottom.

Storm clouds were moving in as Jesse neared the house, and the team was still sitting out in front. Apparently, his mother and sisters had supplies that needed to be unloaded, but first things first. Olivia was his top priority. Jesse opened the front door and moved toward the kitchen, expecting to find his wife cooking. Instead, he found his mother and sisters trying to throw together a meal that Olivia was supposed to make. "Where is my wife, Mom?"

With concern in her tone, Jayne shrugged. "Don't know, Jesse. You'd better look for her. It's not like Olivia to slough off when there's work to be done."

Jesse stuck his head in their room. Finding it empty, he yelled up the stairs. When no answer came, he went to the barn. His heart faltered. Shadow was missing. Dread washed over him as he ran in the back door. Ignoring his mother's questions, he went straight to his armoire where he had put the letter. When that too was missing, his eyes scanned the room, stopping when he saw the note on his pillow. Closing the door, he collapsed on the bed. Aching to hold his Olivia, tears filled his eyes as he read the desperate words written by her hand.

Jesse,

How could you?

You had no right!

I wish I understood, but I don't.

Perhaps I will feel differently in time, but for now I need to be alone. I have to sort this out. If I stayed to talk, you would not have let me go. Besides, I can't bear the thought of looking at you right now. Not yet.

Don't try to follow me, Jesse. Try not to worry. I am safe. I will write when I can do so without anger in my heart.

Olivia

He could feel her pain and sensed her anguish as regret washed over him. How could he have been such a fool? He wanted to go and find her. His mind raced, thinking of all the places she could be, knowing that because of him, she was alone in her grief.

Forcing himself to calm, he prayed that she would arrive at her destination safely. He thanked the Lord she had the sense to take Shadow. With her broken arm, Shadow would be easier for her to handle. If she happened to get lost, he was certain Shadow would bring her home.

The thought of not having her with him tore at his heart, but he understood her anger—her need to be away. He would feel betrayed if she had kept something so important from him. What was he thinking? *How could I have been so heartless?*

Falling on his knees before the Lord, Jesse cried out. If only he had listened to that still small voice and told Olivia the day he had received the letter. It would have been difficult for her to deal with her mother's death, but at least she would still be here with him instead of trying to face her sorrow alone.

Help us both, Father God, to lean on You, the source of all comfort. I know how wrong I was to withhold this from her; forgive me. You know I love her, Lord. Strengthen her, keep her safe and bring her home soon.

After sitting his family members down and explaining Olivia's disappearance, Jesse headed for the barn. Exposing his sin was not easy, but Olivia was hurting because of him, and he had to know his family would be praying for her.

Jesse, needing to talk to Kaleb and Elizabeth, headed over to the White's farm. Like his adopted grandfather, Jacob Woods, Kaleb had a way of helping Jesse to look at his struggles through different eyes. As hard as it was to accept, he was fairly certain he needed to honor Olivia's wishes and give her some time alone. He had every intention of following God's lead, but seeking Kaleb's advice couldn't hurt. If nothing else, Jesse would find comfort in knowing that others were praying.

"How are you, Jesse?" Kaleb asked, as his friend rode toward the house. "What brings you out so late in the day?"

Jesse was almost to him when Kaleb realized something was wrong.

"Is Lizzy here?"

"She just took the children over to my parents. Grandma made a cake and wanted to share."

"I'll bet Cameron's depressed about that."

"No kidding. When he left, the little rascal was grinning from ear to ear."

Jesse dismounted and tied Guinevere's reins to the front post. "Is my sister coming back, Kaleb?"

"Not for a while. Do you want me to go get her?"

Jesse was about to say yes and then changed his mind. "God doesn't make mistakes. Maybe I'm only supposed to discuss my circumstances with you."

Kaleb's brow furrowed. "Are you all right?"

"I've been better."

"Coffee's brewing. Come on in and we'll talk. Where's Livia, Jess?"

"That's part of why I came by." Brutus greeted Jesse with his normal vigor, but Jesse merely patted his big head.

"Oh?" Kaleb poured their coffee and joined Jesse at the table.

"She left me, Kaleb." Jesse's words were so matter of fact;

Kaleb was taken aback.

"Can you tell me why?"

Jesse's head lowered. "I got another letter from Olivia's father almost three weeks ago. Her mother passed away."

"And, let me guess: you wanted to give her wounds time to heal, so you didn't tell her?"

Jesse's shoulders slumped. "Am I that transparent?"

Kaleb ignored his question and asked, "Did you learn nothing from my mistakes with your sister?"

"I was wrong not to tell her. I know that, but now she's gone and doesn't want me coming after her."

"Did she say that or are you just assuming that's what she wants?"

Jesse pulled the note out of his pocket and handed it to Kaleb. "I found this on my pillow when I came in from work.

Believe it or not, I was coming in to tell her about the letter. Unfortunately, she found it first."

Kaleb read Olivia's desperate words, laid the note on the table, and put his hand over his friend's. "A few years back I would have told you to go find her and drag her back at any cost. I've learned the hard way that my way isn't always best. You know you were wrong, Jesse. She sounds like she needs time to sort this out, but that's something you'll have to decide for yourself. Let's commit it to prayer."

For a time they did pray together, as they had so many times before. Kaleb assured Jesse that for now, he agreed with his decision not to look for Olivia. "If she turns to Him, God will heal her wounds over time, but right now they are enflamed and raw. I'll pray that she won't allow bitterness to keep her from all that she has left. She'll have to work through her grief in her own way, Jess."

"Pray that she'll find it in her heart to forgive me. Instead of helping her through this time, like I promised I would, I've added to her grief."

"Place her in His hands. Give her time. God can rebuild the trust you once shared; I know that from personal experience. As much as we want to protect our wives, we can't fight their spiritual battles for them. Grieving is a process. Learn what God is trying to teach you through this time of waiting. Allow Him to heal your marriage, His way."

"I'm trying. I suppose I should get back home in case she changes her mind and comes back. Tell Lizzy for me and ask her to pray, will you?"

"Of course." Kaleb hugged his friend and sent him on his way.

The following days crawled by. Jesse prayed without ceasing and kept himself so busy that when he'd fall into his bed at night, he would sleep from sheer exhaustion.

Ten days had passed without a single word from his wife, and still Jesse did not feel as though he should go looking for her. He did, however, have a peace that she would eventually forgive him and come back home. When she did, he wanted their house to be well underway, so he drew up the plans. He and his brothers were spending every spare moment felling trees and preparing the ground.

Kaleb stopped by and found Jesse, Jared, and Joseph doing just that. Kaleb had been into the village and checked their mail. Sure enough, there was a letter from Olivia. Finally! Jesse turned to his brothers as soon as Kaleb left, and said, "Boys, I need to head over to the house for a few minutes. I'd like to begin laying the foundation before the sun gets too hot, if you're not too tired."

"Go ahead and read your letter," Jared said. "We'll keep working."

Jesse,

I hope this finds you and your family well. I am settling in nicely where I am staying and quite content. Facing my mother's death has not been easy, as I am sure you already know. My dear friends have been such a blessing, offering the spiritual and physical support I need at this time.

I wish I could tell you that I am ready to come back, but I am not. If I am wrong, I pray that God will show me. For now I have to stay.

I spend my days painting. You might be pleased to know that I've found a few outlets for selling my work. It feels so good to be financially independent for the first time in my life. The income has helped. I don't wish to be a burden to the folks I am staying with, and my earnings have surpassed what they will accept.

I can offer you no promises at this time, Jesse. I am sorry, but what you did still makes me feel ill inside. I will write again in another week or two. In truth, the only reason I am sending this is to appease the couple I am staying with.

You and your family are in my thoughts and prayers. Give them my love.

Olivia

Jesse folded up the letter, stuffed it into the envelope and threw it into the stove. His heart ached for having read it, and he refused to allow his family to see what had become of his wife—the woman he loved and wanted back more than anything in the world. Her resentment was so woven into her words, he could hardly bear it.

Father God, he cried out in desperation. *Please tell me that I haven't lost her. I need her—as much as the air that I breathe. Help me to accept Your will in this. Guide my steps. Use the people she is staying with to point her to You. If You want me to go to her, show me, Lord.*

Jesse prayed every day for Olivia. He half expected God to give him a peace about going to find her, but five weeks had come and gone since her hasty departure and still that assurance did not come.

Needing to get his mind off the house he was building for his estranged wife and the responsibilities that came with running the farm and raising a family, he took the wagon into Ann Arbor for supplies. He wasn't sure why, but he was convinced the trip would do him some good.

When Jesse walked into the bank and saw the owner's portrait hanging on the wall, his steps slowed considerably. He didn't doubt for a minute that this was his wife's work. Moving closer, he found her signature at the bottom.

"Excuse me," the teller asked, "is there something I can help you with, Mr. Somers?"

"When did you hang this up, Mr. Johnson? I don't recall seeing it before."

"The banker contracted a young woman just this last month.

She's quite talented, don't you think?"

"I couldn't agree more. You don't happen to know where she's staying, do you? I'd like to speak with her."

"Don't quote me on this, but I'm pretty sure I heard the banker say she's staying with the Woods'."

Jesse rubbed at his chin. "You don't say ...."

The gentleman's head tilted. "That's part of the rumor going around town anyway."

"Oh?" Jesse exclaimed, playing devil's advocate. "You don't happen to know the other part, do you?"

Mr. Johnson leaned over the counter and whispered, as if gossiping out loud was completely beneath him, "Now mind you this is hearsay, but it would seem the young woman lost her husband to influenza recently, and she has come to Ann Arbor to recover from her terrible loss. She's quite a looker, Mr. Somers. You should check her out. Heads are turning, I tell you. If the single gentlemen in this town have anything to say about it, she'll be a bride again before her proper grieving time has past."

Jesse couldn't believe the teller hadn't put two and two together. Did he not look at the signature on the painting? "Perhaps I'll take your advice and run over to the Woods' and see for myself if she's a looker as you say."

"Oh, she's a fine one, Mr. Somers. Even the wife agrees. Wouldn't have believed it if I hadn't seen her with my own eyes."

Drawing out the funds he would need, Jesse stepped out the door and murmured his thanks as he moved down the street with a confident bounce in his step. He was sure God was giving him the go ahead. After stopping by the country store for his supplies, he headed toward the Woods' home. He hadn't seen them in weeks. Couldn't hurt to stop by and check on them. After all, they were his adopted grandparents.

Jesse's spirit took flight as he neared the farm. The anticipation of seeing his wife filled his heart with joy. However, knowing how she felt about him, he opted not to be too brash in his approach. He wasn't willing to chance her slipping out of his grasp again. Feeling a tad bit ornery, he pulled the team to a halt just before the turn off into the farm and decided a game of cat and mouse was in order. Of course, he had already decided that he would be the cat and she the mouse.

After a moment of silent prayer, he moved cautiously along the trail. As he neared the clearing he could hear a feminine voice and stood perfectly still, watching from a distance. Olivia was in the corral brushing Shadow and talking to him as she would a friend. His wife loved his horse, so this did not surprise him. Jesse wondered if she was getting him ready to go somewhere, but he wasn't about to wait around to find out. He snuck around the backside of the corral and came up behind her. Needing to be closer, he ducked under the fence and was standing only inches away when he tenderly admitted, "I've missed you, My Love."

Frightened, Olivia darted across the corral, ducked under the fence and ran around the backside of the barn.

Jesse dogged her every step, but he wasn't quite as agile getting under the fence and lost sight of her when she rounded the corner. When he got there she was nowhere to be seen. His heart faltered. *Where could she be?*

"Olivia!" he called out. "We need to talk."

The silence lingered ....

Jesse went back the way he had come, hoping she had gone

all the way around, and he'd eventually catch up with her. That was not the case. He slithered through the crack in the barn door and gave the interior a thorough inspection. Regrettably, he came up empty there as well. Contemplating where to look next, he heard a swishing sound coming from the loft. As Jesse flew up the ladder Olivia darted toward the hay drop but not fast enough. He had her in his grasp before she took her third step. Taking care not to bump the arm she had injured, his own slid around her, drawing her flush against him.

His touch, so warm and inviting, confused her, but then the memory of his betrayal came rushing in. Her hand clenched at her side. She squirmed in his hold, demanding, "Let me go, Jesse Somers."

"I'm sorry, Olivia. I can't do that, not yet. We have things to discuss."

"I told you in the letter, I'm not ready to see you." Tears thickened her voice—clouded her eyes.

Although his heart was filled with compassion for his wife, he was not about to accommodate. Instead, he humbly confessed, "Olivia, I was wrong to keep the letter from you. I can't take back what I've done, but I'm hoping we can find a way to move past this."

"I'm happy here with Grandpa and Grandma. Why can't you leave me alone?"

"You're my wife. You belong with me."

She shook her head. "Maybe I did ... not anymore. You lied to me, Jesse."

While the truth in her words tore at his heart, he needed to confront the real struggle going on here. "We took vows for life, Liv. Those whom God hath joined together, let no man put asunder. Are you telling me that because I'm human—because I betrayed your trust this once that you're going to walk away from everything we've shared? This doesn't sound like the Olivia I married, the same woman who said she was willing to look beyond her loss and focus on our future together. Please tell me you can find it in your heart to forgive me."

"I trusted you!" she sputtered.

"I never claimed to be perfect. I'm going to fail you from time to time, just as you'll fail me, but God never will. That's why we have to lean on Him for stability." When the silence lengthened, he added, "It would break your father's heart to see what has become of our union ... like it's breaking mine."

"I have every right to be angry ...."

"I agreed with you for a while, but hanging on to anger will only destroy you, Liv. We need to get beyond this and go on with our lives." The seconds were ticking by when he gently added, "God's Word says that if we don't forgive, He won't forgive us. I'm sure that's not what you want, is it?"

"Fine," she snarled, "I forgive you. Are you happy now?"

She sounded all too much like a spoiled child admitting her wrong after a firm scolding. But when she crumpled to the hay-covered floor in a whirlwind of painful tears and emotions, Jesse sat down beside her and attempted to draw her into his arms. At first she fought him—pushed him away. Then, her shoulders slumped, and her wall of defense slowly began to crumble. He knew that it had fully collapsed when she latched onto him as never before. Although he had no idea what she was thinking or what the outcome would be, his hope was renewed. He understood her turbulent thoughts. His weren't exactly steady either. The longer he sat listening to her sobs, the more determined he became. This time away from each other did not have the effect he was hoping for. If anything, they were drifting further apart. One thing became perfectly clear: he would not leave without his wife, even if he had to force her. Again he tried to draw her close. This time she did not pull away, and that encouraged him.

Moments passed before Olivia took in a shuddering breath and sat up. Pulling her handkerchief out of her sleeve, she dried the last of her tears and blew her nose. "I'm sorry," she said as she rubbed the front of his shirt, "I've gotten you all wet."

His soggy shirt was the least of his worries. When Jesse realized that she could still not bring herself to look at him, he reached for her chin and lifted her gaze to his. "I am so sorry, Olivia. I never meant to hurt you, but your accident ... and then the days ... they passed too quickly. Believe it or not, I had just confessed to my brothers that I'd been putting something off far too long ... I was heading in to tell you when I found you missing ...."

Her eyes filled again with tears. Hanging on to her resentment was so much easier without him near. Jesse's love for her was unconditional—he was ingrained in her soul, a part of who she was. Denying him access to her heart was no longer possible, but neither was she ready to expose all.

"I can't believe Mama is gone. She keeps calling out to me in my sleep, but when I open my eyes, she's not there. I miss her so much. I never knew it would feel like this ... the loss ... I'm so numb inside."

"I understand, Sweetheart, really I do ... I miss my father too."

"I know you do, Jesse ... my loss is no greater than yours."

"The only difference is that we shared the loss of my father together. I never meant for you to have to face this alone."

She peered up at him. He really did care. How could she have been so wrong? "Grandpa and Grandma have been wonderful." She reached to caress his prickly face and admitted, "They're not you, though. I tried to convince myself that I didn't miss you—that I could go on without you. I'm beginning to understand what it really means to be one. A part of me has been missing. For several weeks now I've convinced myself that losing my mother was the cause. Now that you're here with me, that void is dissipating ... already. I do need you, Jesse. I'm sorry. I'm lost—so lost without you."

"Oh, Liv ... I've missed you too." When the inches separating them were too much, he pulled her into his lap. She came willingly and surrendered to his ardent kisses that came one right after the other.

"The nights were so long and lonely, Jesse. My tears, they had a will of their own. I didn't think I could ever forgive you ... but I ached to have you hold me. It made no sense. The Lord has been showing me some things. I'm so thankful His love isn't contingent on my obedience because I've failed both of you miserably."

"So have I, Liv."

"This time without you has been difficult, but I'm learning to lean on the Lord for comfort like I never have before."

He chuckled softly, "That makes two of us."

"I should have given you a chance to explain. It hurt me to think that you would keep this from me. I just had to get away. Can you understand?"

"Of course I can. I've been over this a thousand times.

There's no way around it. I was wrong to keep the letter from you, Liv."

"I judged you too harshly ... and for that, I'm sorry. I should have realized that you were only trying to protect me."

"Can you promise me something? I hope nothing like this will ever happen again, but if it does will you come to me?"

She looked straight into his deep blues and smiled. "It's okay, Jesse. I know you're holding back. You can say what's on your mind."

"And what, might I ask, do you think is on my mind, Mrs. Somers?"

She flushed before him. "Don't tease me ...."

"Sorry, Honey. It's part of who I am."

"How well I know ...."

His tone sobered. "You won't leave me again, will you?"

Her eyes glistened. "If I do, don't listen if I tell you to stay away."

"I suppose I can live with that." Jesse stood to his feet and helped his wife up. After dusting the hay off her skirt, he slid his hands around her waist and immediately noticed how much her body had changed. "Looks like Grandma's feeding you well. You were too thin, Liv. I'm glad to see you filling out."

Embarrassed, she took a few steps away from him. When she turned back to face him, her arms were spread apart and her eyes lowered as she took in her own appearance. "Look at me. I'm getting fat. All the dresses I brought with me are snug. I don't know what's wrong. I've never put on weight so fast ...."

Thoughtful, he smiled, reached for her hand, and spun her around so he could get a closer look. "You look perfect to me, Liv."

"You're prejudiced. What will your family think?"

A curious thought touched his mind. "Any changes in the way you're feeling, Honey?"

"Besides being moody and hungrier than usual ... no."

He rubbed at his chin, taking in her appearance before he pulled her towards him and turned her around so he could feel her tummy. "ave you noticed how round your belly is getting? If I'm not mistaken, I'd say you've got a bun in the oven, My Love."

She looked up at him and started to laugh. Her husband was grinning like a possum. "Wishful thinking, Jesse Somers. Your wife is just getting plump. Get used to the new me."

"Ya know there is a way to find out for sure."

"I'd be thrilled if I was, but I'm not pregnant, Jesse. A woman would know these things, don't you think?"

"Not necessarily. If I'm right, you owe me a good back scrub. You've been gone far too long, Liv ... you had me spoiled."

She stopped for a moment and really looked at him—the same yearning filling Jesse's eyes had plagued her from the moment she had left him. He had her spoiled as well. What had she been thinking? How could she have considered leaving the man who loved her so? There was no denying it; her grief was debilitating and his betrayal blinding. Still, how could she have disregarded everything else they shared? Feeling lighthearted at the moment, she frowned as she denied his request in a teasing manner. "Not hardly, Mister, that creek's too cold!"

"There's always the big tub I bought for our new home."

She giggled softly. "Jesse Somers, are you telling me you

bought a bath tub, and our house isn't even started yet?"

He winked playfully. "Suppose you'll have to come home and find out for yourself."

"Maybe I'm not ready to come home yet."

"Olivia Somers, you're going to land yourself in the creek if you keep that up!"

"If you throw me in that cold creek, I won't speak to you for a month!"

His big blue eyes narrowed in on her. "If you think for a minute that I'm spending another night alone in our bed, you'd better think again. You're coming home, woman!"

She grinned mischievously. "Kind of bossy, aren't ya, Mister?"

"You'd best believe it! The way I hear it, the single men in this town have taken a shine to my wife. It's not safe for you to be wandering around without me."

His insinuation was too absurd. "What are you talking about?"

"Rumor has it that if the young men in this town have anything to say about it, the lovely young widow living with the Woods will soon be a bride again."

She scowled. "You're making that up."

His brow rose into his hairline. "Heard it strait from the teller's mouth."

"Mr. Johnson at the bank? He's no gossip!" she offered in the teller's defense.

"He was very discreet when he leaned over the counter and whispered."

Perplexed, she spoke her thoughts, "I can't believe they don't know I'm your wife. I signed the painting."

"It is possible the man can't read."

"Now you're being silly. Have you met the banker? He's very meticulous. Rest assured, he would not hire an uneducated man to run his bank."

"Then perhaps the teller has taken a fancy to my wife ...."

"He'd better not. He's a married man, and besides, his wife is one of my new friends." He made a funny face and she laughed. It felt so good to laugh again. "I haven't laughed in weeks, Jesse. I'm so glad you came. Is this what Pastor meant when he said I needed to begin releasing my grief?"

"There is a time to mourn, Liv, but we need to accept what can't be changed and concentrate on what we have left."

"So it's okay to laugh?"

"More than okay. If we keep our eyes on God and not our circumstances, He has a way of turning our mourning into joy."

She nodded as her hand splayed across her belly. Could Jesse be right? Oh, if he were, it would be so wonderful. A baby? She was afraid to get her hopes up.

"So, what do you think?"

"About what?"

"If I'm right, are you going to scrub my back?"

"Your back, your hair, and ..."

Jesse grinned when his wife blushed to the root and turned away. "And what, Liv?"

"A lady never tells all, Sir ...."

He Loves Me!

Chapter Twenty-two

An Extra Blessing

THE AFTERNOON SUN winked sporadically as the churning clouds raced across the turbulent sky. The stiff breeze following Jesse and Olivia into town was gaining momentum by the time he pulled the team up in front of Doctor Taylor's office.

"Getting dark awfully fast, Liv, could be a storm's on the way. We won't be able to stay long."

For a moment, her gaze rose to the heavens. No doubt something was brewing, but her own swirling emotions took precedence. "Long enough to find out who's right and who's wrong, I hope."

His impish smile matched her own. "Forgive me .... This time, I'm hoping you're wrong, and I'm right."

"Me too!" Although doubt pulled at her heartstrings, she hid it well. Jesse could be right. After all, they had been living as man and wife for months. It was possible.

Setting the break, Jesse jumped down, reached for Olivia's waist, lowered her to the ground and led her up the steps. His tender expression made her smile.

Doc saw them from where he stood at the window, opened the door, and ushered them in. "Jesse and Olivia! Welcome!" Glancing at Olivia above his spectacles, Doc offered, "I was sorry to hear about your mother."

"I appreciate your saying so. She'd been ill for a number of years."

"Martha and I will keep you and your father in our prayers. No matter how prepared we are, losing a loved one is difficult."

Since her emotions were still too raw to allow further comment, Olivia nodded.

"So tell me, what brings the two of you out to see me today?"

Jesse, anxious to get to the bottom of why they had come, spoke up, "Doc, my wife and I could use your help solving a minor disagreement. She seems to think she's just getting plump, but I'm thinking it's something entirely different."

"Let me guess. You're eager to find out if you have a little one on the way."

Jesse winked at his wife and asked, "How'd you know, Doc?"

"Let's just say, I've seen a few hopeful men in my day." Doc led his patient into the back room with Jesse trailing close behind. "Tell me, Olivia, how have you been feeling?"

"As I told Jesse, other than being moody and hungry, I'm fine. If you ask me, we're wasting your time."

"Time spent with friends is never a waste."

His kind words eased her mind.

After several questions Doc examined her, but he was baffled by his findings. "You are going to have a baby ... there's no doubt about that." He paused, scratching his head. "Now when did you say you consummated the marriage?"

Jesse reaffirmed what Olivia told him, but Doc still had a bewildered expression on his face, so Jesse asked, "Is something wrong, Doc?"

"Not wrong ... unless I'm mistaken, you're too big for my calculations, which could only mean one thing: you're carrying more than one baby."

Her eyes widened as she sat up. This was too much to take lying down. Turning to her husband she asked, "Twins?"

They both looked back at Doc who shrugged. "At least two, maybe more."

"More?" This was too much for Jesse to process. Weak kneed, he took a seat on the table next to his wife.

"But how did this happen?" Olivia questioned.

Doc tried not to chuckle but couldn't quite pull it off. "The same way it happens when you have one, Livia."

She rolled her eyes and blushed to the root. "That's not what I meant."

Jesse kissed her cheek, fully comprehending her confusion.

Doc offered the only explanation he could, "God's way of giving a couple an extra blessing, I suppose."

The stunned couple managed a nod.

"I'll have to monitor you closely, Livia. And I'll be expecting you to take special care of her, Jesse."

His blue eyes sparkled with mischief. "That will be my pleasure."

Doc patted Olivia's arm as he issued orders that he expected to be followed to the letter. "I don't want you doing anything to excess. When you're tired, rest. Your body is going to be taxed more than the average pregnant woman, but you'll be fine if you heed my warning."

She looked up at him and smiled. "Does this mean you'll take this splint off so that I can finish breaking Star before I get too big?"

Jesse didn't wait for Doc to respond. "Olivia Somers!"

She giggled. "I'm kidding ...."

"You'd better be," Doc firmly stated. "I've never delivered a set of twins or triplets, and I'm counting on the experience to be the highlight of my career."

Olivia wasn't too sure how she felt about that, but she did want to know, "Can you take this contraption off while I'm here, Doc?" She had been in to see him a few times before, but every time he insisted on giving her bones more time.

Were it not for her pleading eyes, he would have denied her without a second thought. "I won't make any promises, but I'll give it a look see."

It wasn't what she wanted to hear; nonetheless, it was better than the alternative. Olivia's arm was scarred where the deep slivers had been. Although its appearance troubled her, she whispered her thanks when Doc agreed to leave the splint off. Unfortunately, he added a single stipulation: she would have to wear the sling for two more weeks.

"Two weeks!" she protested.

"Olivia!" Jesse chided. "Be thankful the splint's off."

She pouted, "Easy for you to say. You're not the one whose

arm has been bound up for weeks on end."

He slid his arm around her and squeezed her tightly. "You knew the chance you were taking when you mounted Star."

Her shoulders slumped. He was right. She opted not to tell him how much she longed to get back at it, but the babies would have to come first. With Jesse breathing down her neck, she had little choice but to concede.

The sling was back in place and they were coming out of the back room when the Wilson boy stormed in the front door and breathlessly called out, "Doc!"

"Now slow down there, Howard, and tell old Doc what's got you all riled up."

"It's Mama, Doc. Papa's riding circuit, preaching, and Grandpa went to deliver supper to the shut-ins. That drifter we have boarding is drunk again. Mama went upstairs to collect the dirty laundry. He has her trapped and won't let her go. My sisters and me are scared, Doc, real scared. If he caught me sneaking out, he would'a skinned me for sure."

Jesse glanced at Olivia. "You keep the boy here until I return, Liv. See if Martha has some cookies for him. Doc, can you get Henry?"

"Sure, we'll meet you over there. Be careful, Jesse. He's making a habit of pulling stunts like this—no telling what he might do."

"Mr. Somers," Howard informed him, "I left the back door open."

Jesse reached out and tussled the boy's hair. Howard was tall for his age, but the vulnerable expression on his handsome face exposed his youthfulness. "Thanks! Don't you worry, little man, we'll do our best to get your mama out of there safe and sound." Jesse leaned over and kissed his wife before hustling out the door.

Doc led Olivia and Howard down the hall to where his wife was sitting in her rocking chair knitting a tiny sweater. He filled Martha in on Rena's predicament and then headed over to the sheriff's office.

Olivia's concern for her husband and Doc were well founded, but at the same time, she knew they had to go.

"Olivia, I've been hoping we would find the time to have a nice visit, and here you are. And Howard, look at how you've grown. Your mother must be having a time keeping you in clothes that fit."

"She says it's 'cause I eat too much."

Martha smiled at Olivia and asked, "Any chance I can interest the two of you in some supper? I'm hungry and there's no telling how long Doc will be."

Olivia glanced at the young lad. "Are you hungry?"

"Yes, Ma'am! I'm always hungry."

Martha stood and took his small hand. "Then we'd best try to fill you up."

Jesse entered the back door of the Wilson home without knocking. Their four other children, Emily, Geraldine, Carrie, and Ethelyn were huddled together in the corner of the parlor, frightened half out of their wits. The minute they saw Jesse they sagged with relief. His finger went to his mouth to silence them. When their heads bobbed up and down, Jesse winked at them and moved cautiously up the back stairs. Rounding the corner, he heard a commotion in the third room on the left. Slipping off his bluchers, he moved soundlessly down the hall. The door was closed. Turning the handle, he peered in through a small crack. Sure enough, Jed was holding Rena like a shield in front of the window. Were it not for the knife pointing at her side, Jesse would have barged in. Instead, he simply watched and waited.

"Jed," Rena tried to rationalize, "if you just let me go, no one will be the wiser."

Jed's words, though slurred, came across loud and clear, "Nooo, Ma'am. You're not fooling ole Jed this time. If Ireland steps foot in this room, someone's gonna get hurt. Not gonna be me this time."

Jesse wanted to laugh, but he restrained himself. Henry had mentioned that most of the regulars at the tavern called him Ireland, but Jesse had never heard it himself.

Not wanting to frighten Jed, Jesse had an idea and headed back down the stairs. When he got to the bottom, he yelled back up, "Hey, Rena. If you don't come down and put these rolls in the oven, they're going to be ruined. Old Jed won't be happy if you don't have a plate full of his favorite cinnamon rolls on the breakfast table."

Jed tightened his grip, frightening Rena.

"Who is that?" Jed murmured.

"Jesse Somers must have stopped by to tickle the girls."

"Oh ..."

She could feel him relax and tried to press him a little further. Knowing Jesse was in the house gave her an extra measure of courage. "Jed, I suppose you have to decide. You keep this up, you'll land yourself in jail, and there'll be no cinnamon rolls for anyone come morning."

"Well ..."

"You need to decide, Jed. The cinnamon rolls will be ruined if you don't let me go soon."

"Can't have that ... Ireland must be busy."

"That's right. So give me the knife, and I'll let you get some rest."

Jed handed her the knife, crawled back in his bed, rolled over, and the ordeal was over—for now anyway. When Rena came down the stairs, the girls flew to her. She sat down on the sofa and took the time to console them. She had just begun to tell Jesse what had happened when Doc and Henry came in the back door, so she filled them in as well.

Henry asked, "Do you want me to arrest him, Rena?"

"No. I'm sure he'll be out tonight. With my Jesse being gone, I'd appreciate you stopping by in the morning and letting him know he needs to find another place to stay. My children should feel safe in their home, and his binges keep us on edge. We never know what he's liable to do next."

"That's not a problem. I'll see you in the morning. Save me one of those cinnamon rolls, will ya?"

Rena smiled. "That's the least I can do."

Jesse stood to leave. Doc joined him and said, "I'll send Howard home when we get there. You take care, Rena. Let me know if you need anything."

"I will. Thanks for everything."

In unison the men replied, "You're welcome."

After sharing a pot of coffee and a light meal with Doc and

Martha, Jesse and Olivia headed back to Ypsilanti. Fortunately, the brewing storm had blown over. Jesse couldn't have been more pleased with all that had transpired. He was going home with so much more than the supplies he'd come for. Learning about their extra blessing definitely overshadowed all else. His heart, as light as a feather, was brimming with happiness.

Olivia chattered on and on as the reality of what was taking place inside her body came to rest. Thoughts of motherhood filled her with joyfulness. *Babies!* "Oh, Jesse, I'm so excited! I never thought it would happen so soon, did you?"

"I don't know what I thought, but it is starting to sink in. Our babies are growing inside of you, Liv."

Her hand slid tenderly over her stomach. "Isn't it wonderful?"

"A miracle!"

"I have so many unanswered questions, but I didn't want to bother Doc with them."

"Like what?"

"Lizzy's the only pregnant woman I've ever been around. How will I know what to expect? My clothes are already tight. So I'll need to know how much to expand them. And then we'll need clothes for the babies and diapers. I have no way of knowing how many I'll need and ... oh, no!" Her hand came to her mouth.

"What's wrong?"

"In all our excitement we forgot to ask Doc when the babies would come."

Smiling at his flustered wife, Jesse suggested, "Liv, you really should calm down. We have plenty of time. We'll make a list of questions for the next time we see Doc. Besides, Mom and Lizzy should be able to answer most of them for you."

"I suppose you're right." For a time the silence lengthened, but Olivia's thoughts rambled on.

Jesse, noting how pesky the flies were, glanced up at the darkening sky, but he saw nothing worth fretting about.

Pensive she asked, "will your family forgive me for leaving the way I did?"

"There's nothing to forgive. I betrayed your trust and you needed some space; it's as simple as that. I told them what I had done. My family loves and misses you. They told me as much."

"You're sure?"

He chuckled softly. "In this, My Dear, you can rest assured."

"If they're awake, can we tell them about the babies?"

"If they're not, we can wake them up if you want to."

"No ... that's all right. We can wait till morning."

For a time she snuggled against her husband, entranced in the vibrant shades of autumn that were mellowed by the iridescent glow of the moon. "Jesse."

"Hmm?"

"Have you heard from my father again?"

"Three days ago. I wrote to him after your accident and told him I was waiting a while to tell you about your mother."

"What did he say?"

"He told me he understood my reasons, but not to wait too long. You had a right to know." Olivia ran her fingers along his arm.

"We're both going to make mistakes. It's what we learn from them that matters—right?"

"Right!" Jesse could see that the long journey was having its effect on his pregnant wife. *My pregnant wife!* Even thinking about it stirred his heart.

"Olivia."

"Hmm?"

"Why don't you grab the blanket behind the seat and use my leg for a pillow? Your eyes are drooping. You're exhausted."

She would have protested, but she was so sleepy her eyes were burning. He settled the blanket around her shoulders, and she smiled up at him, welcoming the relief her weary body was begging for. Darkness was upon them, covering the heavens in thick velvety softness, and stars—millions of them—twinkled in the vast expanse. A thick slice of moon illuminated the trail with the towering oaks, maples, and pines dimming its shadowy glow. At first she found it beautifully peaceful, but that all changed when the trees thickened. Even though Olivia's eyes were weighted by the time they reached the Huron, she fought slumber. How could she sleep now?

The ambiance surrounding them plucked every nerve in her weary body. The calming effect the river normally brought had dissipated with the light of day. A foggy mist now hovered above the ever-moving waters and held an ominous aura. She found it creepy yet exhilarating. The wind whistled through the swaying limbs. The horse's hooves slapped tersely along the muddied banks. When an owl hooted in a nearby tree, she reached the end of her endurance. Sitting up, she clung to her husband as if his presence alone shielded her from the great unknown. Fortunately, they were almost home. She'd had enough stimulation for one night. All she wanted was to be safe and snug in their bed with her husband's comforting arms about her ... oh, how she relished the thought!

❀ ❀ ❀

The Somers awoke to the wonderful aroma of cinnamon rolls baking, bacon frying, and coffee brewing. Since the one early riser in the Somers' household had been missing for weeks, there could only be one explanation. Olivia was home!

Jayne was the first to find her in the kitchen slaving over the hot stove. "Olivia," Jayne exclaimed, smiling as she drew her daughter-in-law into her arms. "I'm so glad you're home, Honey. Jesse told me about your mother. I'm sorry for your loss."

"Thanks, Mom. I shouldn't have run off the way I did."

"Don't worry about that. You had your reasons, Honey. You're home now and that's all that matters."

Jesse ambled into the room looking all bedraggled. Allowing himself a great big stretch, he smiled at his wife and then backed up his mother's comment. "Isn't that the truth, Mom?"

Jayne grinned at her son, pleased to witness his blissful expression. "You look well rested for a change, Jesse."

He sidled up behind his wife and slipped his arms around her for a gentle squeeze. "There's nothing like having my wife back where she belongs."

Jared sauntered in. "Welcome back, Livia. Sorry about your mom."

"Thanks, Jar." Joe came in next, kissed her cheek and offered his condolences as well. It was Suzanne and Louise's welcome that set her playful nature in motion. Of course they were elated to see her, yet when Olivia removed her apron to join everyone at the table, the girls' mouths dropped open in shock. Olivia could feel a warm flush creeping up her neck, and she suddenly realized that the rest of the Somers had noticed her thickening frame as well. Finding no hope of hiding her uncomfortable situation, she stood to her feet and spun around, exposing the extent of her plumpness. Her tone was somber as she sought to reveal her condition.

Jesse, noting her intent, covered his upturned mouth with his hand and listened as she went on. How she kept from laughing was beyond him! She really was the queen of drama.

"I know I'm getting fat, but I can't help it. I'm hungry all the time. As much as I'd like to blame it on Grandma for feeding me too well, I cannot tell a bold-faced lie. I've talked to Doc about it. He agreed that Jesse is just as much to blame for my condition as I am, but I'm afraid there's no cure. Doc seems to think I'll get much worse in the coming months, so I hope all of you will bear with me. You should be proud of your brother. Even though part of the cause lay at his feet, he's been wonderful about it. He doesn't seem to mind my chubbiness." A quick peek at her brothers told her they were going to have to leave the room or explode with laughter. Her taunting nature ached to see them squirm a little more, so she spoke directly to them, "Joe and Jared, I'm sure you'll be just as kind if the woman you marry goes through such a time." A quick glance at Jayne revealed a jovial smirk, which told Olivia that she was on to her game. Truth be told, Olivia was about to burst into laughter herself. When her twinkling eyes turned to her husband, he shook his head and took the reins.

"Jared, Joe, please! Tell me you're not falling for her balderdash again!"

Joe's mouth dropped open.

"Olivia!" Jared admonished as his big brown eyes narrowed in on her. "You're going to land yourself in the cold creek! Now what is going on?" Had she not been looking at him when he bellowed, she would have sworn Jesse had spoken instead of Jared.

A small giggle escaped, before her lips tucked inside her mouth. She glanced at her husband and said, "I'll let you tell them."

"You sure?"

"Completely." Olivia scanned the table. His family, sitting on the edge of their seats, turned their inquisitive eyes on Jesse.

"We're not sure when, because in all our excitement we forgot to ask, but we are expecting a little one some time in the spring."

"Olivia ..." Jayne said and then paused. She had no wish to come across in an accusatory fashion, but something was amiss. She could not bring herself to ask in front of the other children.

Olivia, understanding her mother-in-law's confusion, sought to ease her mind. "I know I'm much bigger than I should be, Mom. Doc seems to think there are two babies growing inside of me, if not more."

"Twins?" Louise asked, wonder filling her tone.

"Maybe even triplets!" Suzanne exclaimed with a hopeful grin.

"Wow!" Jared put in and then Joe added, "You'll certainly be a novelty in this community, Livia. Your size alone will give folks something to chatter about. How big does Doc think you'll get?"

Olivia didn't know what to say, but her wary expression did not go unnoticed.

Jayne's heart filled with compassion for her. She knew all too well how huge she had felt toward the end of her pregnancies, and she had only ever carried one baby at a time.

"If God is giving you more than one baby, Olivia, He will help you through ... and so will we."

"I really haven't had time to think all this through. We just found out last night."

Jayne asked, "Did Doc give you any special instructions?"

Jared warned, "I'd better not catch you trying to break any horses!"

Olivia smiled. "Don't worry, Jared. Doc and Jesse already covered that. Doc seems to think delivering twins will be the highlight of his career. He doesn't want me taking unnecessary risks."

Jayne smiled and said, "God is so good. He gave Kaleb and Lizzy the first grandson and granddaughter, and now He's giving Jesse and Olivia a first as well."

"Mom," Olivia said, "I hope you're planning to help me get ready. Loving these babies will be my joy, but I know little else about caring for them."

"We've got plenty of time to fill you in, Honey."

"You and Lizzy," Olivia said as her eyes fell on her husband, who read her mind.

"Let the boys and me finish our chores before we head over to the Whites'. They'll want to hear about our extra blessing."

Jayne, missing her grandbabies, made a suggestion, "Olivia, if we make a picnic dinner, all of us could head over.

Mind if you have a few tagalongs?"

Olivia's soft green eyes were pleading when she turned to her brothers and said, "I haven't had fried chicken in almost a month. Any chance ..."

Her words were cut off when Jared stated, "Consider it done, Sis! Sounds great to me too."

He Loves Me!

Chapter Twenty-three

The Many Faces of Love

*J*ARED AND JESSE had been working on Jesse and Olivia's new home for weeks now and their diligence was paying off. The walls had been up for days. The men, having been at it since dawn, had the roof well underway. Jesse could hardly wait to begin the finishing work inside. He wanted Olivia to have plenty of time to get settled in her new home before their little ones arrived. The men were coming close to calling it a day when they heard their mother calling from the foot of the ladder.

"Jesse, I hate to bother you, but something has come up that needs your attention. Could we talk?"

Jesse turned to his brother. "Do you mind finishing up by yourself, Jared?"

"Not at all."

Jesse descended the ladder, reached for his mother's hand and gave it a squeeze as they moved back toward the house.

"What's up, Mom?"

"The girls' teacher stopped by to check on them. Apparently Suzanne has been skipping school for over a week now, and today Louise didn't show up. Needless to say, he was concerned."

"And rightly so. Have you talked to the girls?"

"No ... truth is I needed time to cool off. They know he was here. They're looking guilty as sin, but I didn't say a word. I thought I'd let them squirm for a while. Maybe they'll think twice before pulling something like this again."

Thoughtful, Jesse said, "If Joe were in school instead of helping at the Woods', I'm sure he would've talked some sense into them."

"If Joe were here, they wouldn't have pulled something like this. I'm missing him. Have you heard how Jacob's doing?"

"Grandma seems to think he's on the mend, but Doc doesn't want him rushing his healing. I saw his leg. The bruises are fading; still he's pretty sore from the tumble he took. Joe may need to stay another week or two."

"Then we'll just have to get along without him. So tell me, Jesse. How do you propose we handle your sisters' rebelliousness?"

He turned to face her. "I'll talk to them."

Concern furrowed her brow. "You're going to have to do more than talk, Jesse. I understand that Suzanne has been struggling with your father's death, but that's no excuse for this kind of behavior. She's been at it for over a week, and now Louise is taking part in her shenanigans." Jayne shook her head. "I'm almost afraid to find out what they've been up to."

"I know what you mean."

"We can't let them off with just a warning. Not this time.

I love them with all my heart, but they're testing us, Son. They know what your father expected of them. Be honest with me. If you don't think you can follow through with your promise, I'll take care of this myself. Love has many faces. Disciplining an unruly child is one of them. I'm afraid this part of parenting is never easy, but it is necessary."

Pensively, Jesse glanced out over the farm. His father would be pleased with the changes he and his brothers were making. Even so, he would not be pleased with the way Suzanne and Louise were trying him lately. Up till now a firm scolding had brought them around. His mother was right. This was outright defiance. His father's words from the day he died played over and over in his mind. *I'll be counting on you to be the head of this house in every respect, Son.*

Jesse had grown complacent. He prayed that this day would never come, but here it was hovering like a weighted cloud. He could be firm with the boys, and in truth they respected him for it. The girls were a different story. Tickling them was one thing. He adored them and wanted God's best for them, but could he ...

Scripture entreats fathers to train a child up in the way he should go. His father had passed that responsibility on to him. Could he follow through or should he pass this burden on to his mother? Glancing at his mother, he saw the apprehension etched in her face and knew he had his answer. "I'll handle this, Mom, but I need to know you're going to back me no matter what my decision is."

Her relief was apparent. "I was hoping you'd say that. I trust your judgment, Jesse. Your father did as well or he would not have asked this of you. You love those girls, so I know you'll do right by them."

He nodded. "Go ahead and help Olivia with dinner. I'll find the girls and get this over."

Jesse was moving toward the front door when Jayne said, "They're probably upstairs."

"Thanks ..." He passed by Louise's room. She was sitting on her bed sulking, but he didn't stop. Instead he went to his room, washed up and took a few minutes to pray. By the time he knocked on Louise's open door, he was ready to face her. However, there was no doubt in his mind she was not pleased to see him. Scared skinny would better describe her untoward expression. Before he could say a word, her confession blurted out.

"I'm sorry, Jesse. I was supposed to be in school. I shouldn't have gone, but I had to see for myself what Suzanne has been up to." Her hand came up to her mouth to stop the flow of words. She hadn't planned to say that much.

Jesse sat next to her on the bed and reached for her quivering hand. "So, did you?"

"Did I what?" Louise was so distressed she could not bring herself to look at him.

He cupped her little chin and lifted her gaze to his. "See your sister?"

"Oh ... only for a minute."

"Louise, the need to appease your curiosity is not an excuse to disobey. You were supposed to be in school."

Her lids slid shut as she humbly concurred, "But I only did it once ...."

His resolve remained steady until long blonde lashes swept up, and she cast her sad, blue puppy-dog-eyes on him.

He weakened. Just as he was about to let her off the hook, his father's voice came to him. *I'll be counting on you, Jesse.* And his malleable mind began to firm. Once his feet were back on solid ground, he informed her, "You knew what the consequences would be and you disobeyed anyway, didn't you, Louise?"

"Yes, but ..."

"No excuses. You will take what you have coming without giving me a hard time or you'll have extra chores to do for a month."

Her shoulders drooped as she softly murmured, "Yes, Sir .... So much for Suzanne thinking we had nothing to fear."

"What do you mean, Lou?"

"She said you're soft-hearted—that you love us too much to ever paddle us."

"It's because I love you too much that I have to paddle you. You heard Dad before he left us. He doesn't want to look down from Heaven and see a bunch of disobedient children running around."

"Oh ... I forgot about that."

"Is Suzanne in her room?"

She shook her head.

"Do you know where she is?"

Louise nodded in the affirmative.

"Are you going to tell me where she is?"

Again she shook her head, although this time in the negative.

"Did she tell you not to tell me?"

Again she nodded, to affirm his suspicion.

Jesse understood her need to remain true to her sister, but he also understood there was a time to break through that barrier, and this was such a time. Grabbing on to her hand, Jesse tried to pull her along. When she sat down on the floor and refused to come, he slung the sweet little darling over his shoulder and headed for the barn.

Jared was on his way to the house when he crossed paths with Jesse and Louise who was pounding on Jesse's back, demanding that he put her down. When Jesse swatted her backside, she stilled, but Jared wasn't about to question him. He was just glad it wasn't him having to deal with her.

Jesse took the paddle off the hook, sat down on a bail of hay, and turned Louise over his knee. Pantalets flailed in every direction as he struck her once. She howled but calmed quickly. He informed her, "You have five swats coming for your punishment. However, the count does not begin until you tell me where your sister is. So I'll ask you again, where is she, Louise?" When the silence lingered he struck her again. This continued three more times, before Jesse heard Suzanne cry out from where she had been hiding in the loft.

"Enough!"

Ignoring Suzanne's frantic plea that Jesse stop spanking her sister, he leaned over and asked Louise, "Are you ready for the count to begin?"

She nodded.

So he went on ahead.

By the time Suzanne had climbed down from the loft, Jesse was holding Louise close in his arms, kissing her damp cheek, and saying, "I do love you Louise, but you have to obey."

Slowly, her sobbing eased. "I know, Jesse. Sorry I hit your back. Will you forgive me?"

"No question about that. A nice backrub later will make up for your outburst. Louise, now you need to go talk to Mom and let her know you're sorry for what you did. This can't happen again. Do I make myself clear?"

"Yes, Sir."

Suzanne, listening to the sweet conversation between her sister and brother, regretted putting Jesse in this position. She could see it in his face: punishing Louise was harder on him than it was on her sister. Now he had no choice but to follow through with her. How could she have done this to him?

Louise slid off Jesse's lap, glanced up at Suzanne, and said as her hands slid over her sore bottom, "Guess you were wrong, Suz."

"About what?"

"Jesse's not soft like you thought; he hits way harder than Daddy ever did."

Thanks for the warning! Suzanne hugged her sister and whispered in her ear, "Then we'd better be sure we don't cross him again, don't you think?"

"Wish I thought of that sooner." Jesse, noting Suzanne's reluctance to have Louise leave, put an end to their conversation. "That's enough now, Louise. Head back to the house and see that you talk to Mom right off."

"Yes, Sir ...."

When the barn door shut behind Louise, Jesse turned to Suzanne and got right to the point. "Where have you been going for over a week, Suzanne?"

She took a step back, needing to put some distance between them. "I don't have a good excuse, Jesse."

"I'd like to hear it anyway, if you don't mind."

Had she known how awkward it would be to face her brother, she never would have defied him. Guilt ate away at her, intensified by her brother's look.

"I'm waiting, Suzanne."

"Oh, all right," she conceded and plopped down on a bail of hay across from him. Fidgeting with the fabric of her dress she peered up. "You're not going to like it."

"I am losing patience, Suzanne."

His jaw was clenched; she'd best not to press him further.

"I'm sure you heard that Amy's father died of pneumonia last month."

He nodded. "I was sorry to hear that, but what does her father's death have to do with you skipping school?"

"Amy and I are friends, Jesse."

"I thought she was Lizzy's friend."

"She's mine, too."

"Get to the point, Suzanne."

She cringed at the thought of telling him. When her hesitant gaze met his stern glare, she just blurted it out, "Amy had a crush on Tom Bemis, and she's been asking me to act as chaperone for a few weeks now. I knew you wouldn't let me do it in the evening, so ..."

He buried his face in his hand, unsure about hearing the rest. "Why, so both of you would be in danger instead of just her? Amy needs a wake up call if she's wasting her time on the likes of Tom Bemis. Until Tom makes a conscious effort to change, he's not going to be good for anyone. I've tried where both Jack and Tom are concerned, but Amy can't change them any more than I could. They have to want to change themselves. Until that happens and God gets hold of their lives, she's best to steer clear of them. I'll expect you to do the same."

Suzanne rolled her eyes. "That shouldn't be a problem. Tom showed Amy his true colors today. If I wasn't there, God only knows what could have happened."

"Helping a friend is always commendable, but if you hadn't offered to go with Amy, she might not have gone in the first place."

Suzanne hadn't thought of it that way.

"Did you know your sister was trying to follow you today?"

"I saw her hiding behind a tree, but she took off." Suzanne shrugged. "I assumed she went back to school."

"Well, she didn't. She was wrong to try to follow you, but I know you, Suz. You would have been blaming yourself for months if she had gotten hurt wandering around alone in the woods all day."

Suzanne only peered up at him and stared.

"The effects of our sins touch others around us. Your teacher and Louise have been worried about you all week. Today your sin touched even more lives. I don't think I need to tell you what could have happened to you, Amy, or Louise. We all make mistakes, but you need to start thinking about the consequences of your actions."

"I know it sounds feeble, considering what I've done, but I really am sorry, Jesse."

"I'm glad to hear it."

"Taking Dad's place isn't easy for you. I wish for your sake I could go back and undo what I've done."

"Dad always said that in discipline there is hope. Your family loves you, Suzanne. I know you've been struggling with Dad being gone, but don't use it as a crutch to make bad choices. Come to me when you feel like doing something crazy. I'm always willing to talk. Defying me won't bring Dad back no matter how much you want it. As difficult as it is, we have to accept what we can't change and go on."

The second she nodded Jesse leapt to his feet and began pacing. In truth, he looked more worried about what he had to do than she felt to have to receive it.

"You're going to have to help me here, Suz. You're not so little anymore. Manhandling Louise is one thing. I hope you plan to take what you have coming without making a fuss. If you ask me, the sooner we get this over with, the better .... Tell me, how would Dad have done this, Sis?"

When Suzanne stood, calmly picked up the paddle and placed it in Jesse's hand, his frantic heart eased just a tad.

When she leaned over the double-stacked bails, he closed his eyes and whispered a prayer of thanks. She was going to be cooperative.

Suzanne had been lying across the hay for the longest minute of her life, but her brother made no move her way. As much as she'd like to avoid this whole experience, it was inevitable, so she hurried him along, "If you don't mind, Jesse, I'd just as soon get this over with too."

"Oh ... sure ...."

When he made a sudden shift towards her, her words came out in a rush, "Dad always told us how many swats." Louise had gotten one for being uncontrollable, four for not telling on her and then five more for skipping school for one day. Suzanne did the math and held her breath, wondering what Jesse would say. Five swats times five days added up to too many. If he did that, she wouldn't be sitting for a month of Sundays.

"I'll let you choose. Ten and extra chores for a month or twenty-five and the four you waited before sparing your sister of them."

Some choice! "What are the chores?"

"They're not negotiable and they must be done without complaint, or the rest of your punishment will be carried out." Growing impatient with her silence, he added, "Pick now, Suz, or I will choose the twenty-nine."

"I might be better off if you did, but I'll do the chores without complaint."

Jesse nodded and the count began. Suzanne never made a sound the entire time. He assumed she was withholding her tears. Jesse had done the same on numerous occasions, so he didn't think much of it until she walked toward the open window, and he noticed the way her shoulders trembled.

She heard him coming toward her and frantically begged, "Oh, Jesse. Please go away. I'll be fine, I promise."

But he did not go away. His hands slid around her waist. When he turned her to face him, he drew her close, wrapping his strong arms about her. He said not a word as he held her for the longest time and let her weep.

She felt so secure, like she had always felt in her Daddy's arms. Oh, how she missed him! Her father had a way of making her feel safe and loved in the oddest of circumstances.

Misunderstanding the reason for her tears, Jesse admitted, "I wish I didn't have to do that, Sis, but you know you were wrong."

She peered up at him.

He brushed back her wispy hair that had gone astray.

"I know, Jesse. You've been more than fair. I'm not upset about being punished. I deserved it and then some."

"Then tell me, what is it?"

Seconds ticked by. "You know how Daddy was with us girls. Always hugging us, holding us in his lap and kissing our cheeks, like you did with Louise."

"I remember. Dad had a tender spot for his kids, especially his girls, but he wasn't as soft as you thought I was ...."

"It isn't the first time I've been wrong, Jess. I'm sure it won't be the last." The way she shook her head and the way her eyes rolled up into her lids made Jesse laugh.

"All of us knew how much we were loved."

"I miss the man himself, but more than anything I miss his touch." When she burst into tears all over again, she was unable to say more.

Jesse scooped her up into his arms, went back to the bale of hay, sat down, and held onto her for a while, relieved to see her finally releasing her terrible grief.

How, Jesse asked himself, *could I have been so blind? Why did I not see the way the changes in our life have affected her before now? Just because she's tall for her thirteen years doesn't mean a young girl does not still reside within her slender frame—a girl who needs a father's touch—to know how much she's loved. Her needs did not magically disappear with Dad's passing. Parenting involves so much more than I realized. Food, clothing, shelter, teaching, and discipline are important. They're a big part of raising children, yes, but without the tender aspects of love being woven into a child's heart, all else is inconsequential.*

This revelation was too vital to sweep under the rug. He would have a talk with Joe and Jared as well. They needed to be aware of their sisters' need for affection. Hugs, kisses on the cheek, and playfulness had been missing from their lives since their father's passing, and that needed to be remedied. He had no wish for his sisters to be lacking—not when he could do something about it. Between the three of them, they should be able to make the girls feel safe and secure. Their father would be counting on them. Their sisters would as well.

Father God, in Proverbs I've learned that it takes wisdom to have a good family, and it takes understanding to make it strong. Give me wisdom, Lord, in the days, weeks, and months ahead. Make us a strong family once again. Thank You for opening my eyes before my little ones arrive. Help me to never forget that love is a gift—a seed You want us to plant and sow in others' lives. You never meant for us to keep it inside. Love must be shared or it will never grow. It will simply wither and die.

Somewhere in the midst of Jesse's thoughts and prayerful remunerations, Suzanne had cried herself to sleep. After gently drying her remaining tears, he lifted her in his arms, carried her into the house, up the stairs, and laid her on her bed. She didn't so much as budge when he covered her with the afghan at the foot of her bed. Kissing the tip of his fingers, Jesse transferred that kiss to Suzanne's damp cheek and quietly left the room. This experience had touched him deeply within. There was a new tenderness in his heart for this young girl, his sister, who resided within a young woman's frame.

Jayne met him at the bottom of the stairs. "Is she okay, Jesse?"

"She will be, but I need to hold her up before the Lord more often than I do. I hope that she'll soon learn to seek her comfort from Him. Until she does, we need to go out of our way to let her know how much she's loved. You were right, Mom. She is missing Dad, but I've gained a better understanding of how my brothers and I can help to fill that void."

"Praise God!"

"So, where is our other little moppet, Mom?"

"In the kitchen. She told Olivia she smacked you real hard. She needed to make you a special treat."

Jesse's grin went from ear to ear. "Then I'd best stay out of there so she can surprise me?"

"Probably a good idea, Son."

Olivia and Jesse were sitting at the game table playing a game of checkers when Jesse saw his disheveled, puffy-eyed sister coming down the stairs. After three losses to his wife, it was time to fight back.

"Suz," Jesse said motioning for her to come near. "I'm in desperate need of some advice. Mind helping your brother out?"

Suzanne had a strong suspicion she knew what he was about to ask, but she played along. Perhaps the time had come for her brother to polish his skills. For years they had been sadly lacking. "What do ya need, Jess?"

With a slight tug on her hand she landed awkwardly in his lap. He had to be sure she would not try to escape.

Suzanne listened intently when he leaned close and spoke for her ears alone.

"What do you say, Suz?"

She glanced at Olivia, wondering if she would mind, but Jesse must not have wanted her to gain Olivia's input and managed to distract his sister quite thoroughly. Suzanne squealed in delight when Jesse's wiggling fingers came to her sides. "All right! Quit! I might as well! You've been an embarrassment to the Somers family for too many years."

"Suzanne!" he warned as he tickled her more.

"Jesse, stop!"

"Are you ready to be merciful?"

"I suppose. It's past time to remedy the problem anyway."

"That's my girl. Now you're talking."

The game ensued, and while Jesse made all the moves, he didn't so much as blink without the advice of his sister. As they continued to play, it became apparent to Jesse that his father had passed on more skills about the game to Suzanne than he had to any of his other children. He was very thankful that unlike his wife, Suzanne was willing to share her wisdom. For the first time since their marriage, Jesse beat Olivia. His heart soared. Swollen with pride, he squeezed his sister and kissed her cheek before he stood to his feet and flaunted his triumph with a knightly bow. His dear sweet Olivia simply laughed out loud.

Jesse led his wife to the couch and pulled her into his lap. His mom, sitting in her cozy rocker working diligently on an embroidery creation, Jared, engrossed in his latest book, and Louise, determined to master her latest crochet project, didn't so much as flinch when they joined them. Olivia had barely regained control of her emotions when Jesse, out of the blue announced, "I'm not sure what's wrong with me, but I've got a terrible sweet tooth."

His wife replied, "You're out of luck, Mister. I'm too tired to do any more baking tonight."

Jesse winked at Olivia when Louise set her work aside, disappeared into the kitchen, returned in short order with a huge piece of peach cobbler, and handed it to her brother.

"Mmm ... this looks yummy! Where'd you have it hidden, Sis?"

"In the pantry. Olivia helped me make it for you." Louise leaned over and whispered in his ear, "Sorry I hit you, Jesse."

"If you're ready to give me that back rub you promised, I'll eat this peach delight, and we'll call it even."

She gladly did just that, but when the rest of her family headed for the kitchen, she reminded them to save her a piece of cobbler.

"Jesse," Olivia said when they were finally snuggled close in their bed, "the suspense is killing me. When are you going to let me see how the house is coming along?"

"Soon."

She didn't understand why it had to be a secret. "When do you hope to be in?"

"If the weather holds up, the roof will be finished in a couple of days. I'd say, no later than Christmas."

"Christmas! That's so far away. If you'd let me help it would go so much faster."

"Sorry, Liv. Not this time."

Annoyed, she turned away. "And I suppose you're working tomorrow?"

"Yes, Ma'am. I've got Suzanne working alongside of me for the next month. I intend to work her so hard she'll never think about crossing me again."

"She told me what you said and did. Are you sure you're not being too hard on her?"

"The choice was hers to make."

"Hardly what I'd call a choice. Would you really have hit her that many times?"

"Think about what she did, and then you tell me what I should have done. Truth is, I was counting on her choosing the chores. I'm not sure what I would have done otherwise, but I had to be fair to Louise."

"I suppose you know best. I'm just glad it wasn't me out there in her shoes."

"I'll bet you were a handful at thirteen."

"I was an angel."

"I find that hard to believe, but I have no room to talk. If it wasn't for Kaleb's influence, I'd have gotten myself into a heap of trouble."

"God knew you needed him."

"He knew we needed each other."

"You still feeling okay, Liv?"

"Just sleepier than normal."

"Doc said that's to be expected." Jesse heard Olivia yawn and knew he should let her find her rest, so he did. Unfortunately, his mind would not allow him to join her.

Father, today I realized that parenting is a greater challenge than I would have ever imagined. Have I only scratched the surface? When dealing with the human spirit there are no pat answers, are there, Lord? Fortunately, Your Word gives me guidelines. Without love I know I am nothing, and while love is the key that unlocks the heart, that key has many faces—faces that must be planted and nurtured by others. Several seeds of love come to mind. There is compassion, counsel, correction, confidence, enjoyment, challenges, and even consistency. Father, may I always keep this before me. Help me to be an example of Your love, so that the lives I touch will come to understand the many faces of love—Your love, made perfect in me.

Chapter Twenty-four

Choose Joy

*S*UZANNE AWOKE TO relentless knocking on her bedroom door. "It's Saturday—go away," she moaned to her thoughtless intruder. Saturday means sleeping in. Surely, not even the rooster had crowed yet!

"Go away!" she demanded again with an outraged snarl. When the hinges creaked, she turned away and buried her head beneath her quilt. Whining, she mumbled with all the gumption she could muster, "I said go away, and I meant it!" When moving fingers tickled her sides, they aroused her anger instead of a smile. Sitting up, she removed her shroud and turned to give the culprit a piece of her mind. When she came face to face with Jesse, the bold words sitting on the tip of her tongue slid back down her throat. Her shoulders slumped and her fury dissipated.

"Get moving, Suz," he said as he handed her a stack of her

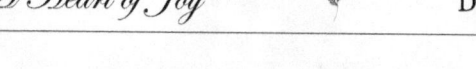

brother's clothes. "Put these on and be down to eat breakfast in five minutes."

"Oh, Jesse, why so soon? I'm too tired."

His gaze narrowed as he pointed to the door, reminding her without an ounce of reserve, "Without complaint or we head out to the barn. The choice is yours."

"Yes, Sir," she meekly droned, "without complaint." She could not, however, release her scowl. She was way too sleepy to put on a smile.

In her bedroom slippers and robe stood Olivia in front of the stove, scrambling eggs, when Jesse came in and slipped his arms around her. As he kissed her soft cheek, she peered up at him and smiled. "You're cheerier than normal this morning, what's up?"

"You read me too well, Mrs. Smarty Pants."

"I've had time to practice, Mr. Smarty Pants."

"I woke Suzanne up. She's just as grumpy as I used to be in the morning."

"Maybe someday she'll be blessed with a spouse who wakes her up with tender kisses, like I do you."

He squeezed her just a bit. "Your kisses, I will admit, have worked wonders, My Dear."

"I know."

Jesse poured a cup of coffee, added cream and sugar, and took a long sip.

"I'm heading over to spend the day with Lizzy and the children, Jesse. Do you need me to tell Kaleb anything?"

"No ... he'll be by this morning to help with the house.

I'd like you to do me a favor though."

"What's that?"

"I'd feel better if you and I switch horses until after the babies come. Do you mind?"

She craned her neck around, pulled him close, and stole a kiss. "I don't mind as long as you promise not to turn into a worrywart like Kaleb did!"

His warm hand covered her cheek as he kissed her again, tenderly. "God is able to protect you without my help, Liv, but that doesn't mean I'm not going to take extra precautions with my wife and my babies."

Her brow arched. "Oh, so they're your babies now, are they?"

He squeezed her tight and groaned. "Our babies, you sassy thing."

"Well ... I suppose I can put up with Shadow for a few months. Of course ..."

His eyes narrowed in on his wife. "Forget it, Liv. I know you like him, but he's still my horse. We go back a long way."

Shadow was a gift from his father. She understood his attachment, but ... "Jesse, do you realize how disturbing it is to have you read my mind like you do?"

"Shouldn't bother you, Liv, unless, of course, you have something to hide."

She zigzagged the wooden spatula slowly through the pan of eggs and softly murmured, "Maybe I do, and then maybe I don't ...."

"Now you're being silly. I'll saddle Shadow and leave him in the barn until you're ready to go."

Oh brother, she moaned internally. Her back was to him, so he missed the way she rolled her eyes. "I think you're the one being silly, not me, but if you must."

"I must and then some. Do I have enough time to haul water before breakfast?"

"Maybe one load."

"All right. Be back in a few ...."

Olivia heard the creaky stairs and seconds later Suzanne, dressed in her manly garb, ambled into the kitchen, heading straight for the back door.

"Morning, Sis." Olivia's long, drawn out playful whistle lifted Suzanne's spirits. She threw Olivia a slanted grin.

"You look adorable today, Suz. What's the occasion?"

"Your husband's idea, not mine. I'll be back to help in just a minute. The outhouse is calling my name."

Olivia loved being with her husband, but working alongside of him was no picnic. In truth, she didn't envy Suzanne in the slightest. She would have to remember to pray for her throughout the day.

❀ ❀ ❀

Elizabeth was stretched out on the bed to give her swollen feet a rest before the long trip into Ann Arbor. When she heard Olivia ride into the yard, she went outside to greet her. "Can I get you anything to eat or drink before we head out, Livia?"

"I'm fine. Where are the children?"

"My mother-in-law offered to keep them. I hope you don't mind ... thought it would be nice to have the day to ourselves."

Olivia's eyes never left Elizabeth as she mounted Lady. "Lizzy, should we take the wagon instead? You don't look so comfortable."

Elizabeth giggled. "I'm fine." But Olivia did not look

convinced. "Being pregnant is old hat to me. I've done this twice before—remember?"

"I know, but ..."

"Don't worry. I'd never do anything to bring harm to my baby."

"As long as you're sure ...." Olivia expected Kaleb to appear at any moment to offer his firm counsel before they took off, but he was nowhere to be seen. "Where's Kaleb?"

"Last I saw him he was heading over to help Jesse."

"Oh ... I'm surprised we didn't cross paths."

Elizabeth's hand slapped at the air. "Knowing him, he took the short cut."

They were riding away from the farm when Olivia realized what Elizabeth had said. "I didn't know there was a short cut."

Elizabeth giggled.

"What's so funny?"

"I know where it is, but Kaleb would have a fit if I ever went in there without him. Jesse, on the other hand, would be mad if he knew I was even telling you about it."

"Why?" Her curiosity was peaked.

"When Kaleb and Jesse were boys, they were chased out of there by a bear. Took them forever to chance using it again. They said there's a clearing somewhere in the middle of the woods with a small lean-to. Now mind you, I'm not sure if it's true, but they told me outlaws have been known to use it for a hideout."

Olivia harrumphed. "If you ask me, they're probably the only outlaws who know about it. More than likely it was their boyhood fort, and they don't want anyone else in there."

"Could be. Tell me, Livia, has my brother told you any of his scary stories yet?" When Olivia started to laugh, Elizabeth knew he had. "Which one, did he tell you?"

"The first night we were married, he warned me that there were creatures living in these forests that devour only the first person they come to when they open the door."

"Well, their hideout is the forest he was referring to when we were little."

"I was ready to choke him for telling me that."

Elizabeth's twinkling eyes met hers. "So tell me, Livia, where did you sleep?"

"What do you think? On the side furthest from the door!" They burst into a fit of giggles.

"Be thankful he spared you the ones about the abominable snow men."

"What about them?"

"Trust me, you don't want to know. Besides, we really should change the subject, or we'll be hightailing it home instead of going into town."

Olivia shivered. "I know what you mean. I already have goose bumps crawling up my arms."

They had no more reached the clearing when Elizabeth gave Lady full rein, allowing her to stretch her legs, and Olivia wasted no time following suit. Although the temperatures were milder than they had seen in days, the cooler temperatures had already had their effect on the area. Autumn's colorful array of vibrant browns, reds, oranges, yellows and gold had graced the rolling hills. The view was spectacular.

Out of concern for her friend, Olivia slowed their pace. "God sure did think of everything when He created the changing seasons, didn't He, Lizzy?"

"The wild flowers and new growth in the spring are a sight to behold, but nothing can top this—God's special blessing before a long cold winter."

"No doubt about that."

The women had been riding along at a comfortable pace when they heard riders coming up behind them, galloping at a breakneck speed. Glancing at each other, Elizabeth said, "Olivia, follow me. We shouldn't take any chances. You never know who they could be."

Olivia followed her into a thicket of trees where they waited silently until the riders passed. "Is my imagination playing tricks on me, or was that our husbands?"

"No tricks, Lizzy. If I was a betting woman, I'd say they're coming to check up on us."

"Did you tell Jesse what we were doing?"

She rolled her eyes. "Of course not! "

"You're a wise woman. It would serve them right if we just turned around and went back home."

"Or," Olivia said as she fixed her deviant gaze on Elizabeth, "we could just go and visit with Grandpa and Grandma before we do our shopping. That would certainly throw them off our trail."

"Oh, you little stink!"

"Me! Like you have any room to talk. If memory serves me correctly, you've led Kaleb and Jesse on a wild goose chase or two."

"True enough, but like you, I had good cause. They were always picking on me."

"I'm not sure what's going on in Jesse's head, but he'd better have a good reason for checking up on us."

"I hate to disappoint you ...."

Olivia grimaced. "What's wrong with him? It's not like we're in any danger."

"He's a man in love whose wife is carrying his first babies. Give him time, Livia. He'll relax after the first one. Kaleb was worse than Jesse, and he did."

"I hope you're right."

"So tell me, are we heading over to the Woods'?"

Olivia grinned mischievously, "Yes, and I can hardly wait to tell them about the babies."

Kaleb and Jesse were long gone by the time Olivia and Elizabeth took to the trail again and veered slightly north. Within the hour, they were sitting at the table with Jacob and Anna, chatting over a cup of tea.

Jacob, thinking it strange that Elizabeth and Olivia would show up without their husbands, asked, "What brings you ladies so far out of your way today?"

"We had shopping to do in town, but I have some wonderful news to share with you. I was hoping Jesse would be with me when I told you, but ..." Her words came to a screeching halt when Jesse's voice rang out, startling both Elizabeth and Olivia. Dumbfounded by their husbands' presence, their mouths gaped open.

"The truth, Olivia!"

Her eyes rose to meet his, along with her stubborn chin. "It is the truth. How did you find us ...?"

Ignoring her confusion, Jesse asked, "Why didn't you tell me you wanted to come to town? I would have brought you."

Disgruntled, she murmured, "Exactly why I didn't tell you."

Kaleb, standing behind Jesse, offered his input, "If you ask me, they're up to something. Isn't that right, Elizabeth?"

With a tilt of her head, Elizabeth's tone held a hint of sarcasm as she admitted, "That's about the size of it."

Jesse piped in, "Grandma and Grandpa, will you excuse us for a minute? We need to speak to our wives."

"That's fine, boys. Take your time; we'll get some coffee brewing."

"Sounds good." Jesse held his hand out, expecting Olivia to take it. "Come on, Liv."

And then Kaleb did the same. "You too, Liz."

When neither of them moved a muscle, the men scowled and took a daring step towards them. Olivia and Elizabeth glanced at each other, their thoughts running along the same vein, and they darted around the table, using Jacob for a shield.

Jacob found their actions quite funny, but he knew that if Jesse and Kaleb were determined to have their way, there was nothing he could say or do to stop them.

Hoping for a hint of sympathy, Olivia leaned over and whispered in Jacob's ear. Her words had apparently altered his mindset because Jacob's demeanor changed, and he glared at his grandsons like he never had before.

"Now, you boys need to leave Olivia and Lizzy alone. You're going to have to accept that sometimes secrets are necessary, and this is one of those times."

"Grandpa!" Jesse, exclaimed, but he wasn't given a chance to say more.

"Grandpa nothing! I'm pulling rank on you this time. Take a seat."

Although stunned, Jesse and Kaleb did as they were told. Never having seen Jacob interfere in marital squabbles, they were curious as to what would make him start now.

"I've got plenty to keep you boys busy, if you want to hang around here until your wives get their shopping done. However, I forbid you to question them about their reasons for coming to town."

"Grandpa!" Kaleb mildly scolded. "This isn't like you to meddle. They're our wives, and we have a right to know what they're up to."

"Under normal circumstances, I'd agree. Not this time, and you are going to have to trust me on this. Now," Jacob's eyes narrowed in on them as he stated, "if I hear that either of you have given them a hard time about this, we'll be having one of our nice long chats."

Kaleb glared at Elizabeth and Jesse did the same with Olivia, but the women were not about to give in to intimidation. Not when they had Jacob on their side. Almost in unison, they stuck out their tongues at their defeated husbands.

Kaleb and Jesse were flabbergasted, yet quite ready to give their wayward wives a piece of their minds. But when Jesse's pointing finger came up to rebuke them, a stern look from Jacob stopped him.

Jacob glanced up at the young women standing behind him, needing to see for himself if something was amiss. Their expressions were as innocent as newborn babes'.

Anna, on the other hand, had witnessed the entire exchange.

It wasn't easy, but she managed to contain her laughter until she walked the girls outside. "You girls would be in duck soup if Jacob had seen what you did."

Worry etched Olivia's brow. "You won't tell him, will you, Grandma?"

Anna giggled. "No, Honey. To be honest, I admire your pluck. I wouldn't trade my Jacob for the world, but he can be annoying at times. I'm sure it's no different with your men."

"Grandma, what are we going to do with them? We're grown women. There's no need for them to be fretting about us."

"Grown women don't usually stick their tongues out at their husbands."

Elizabeth rolled her eyes. "Sorry you had to see that. Hard to say why they're even here. Kaleb was fine about me leaving until after he talked to Jesse. We heard them following us and decided to take a detour. I don't know how they found us so fast."

"Don't let it spoil your fun. I'm glad you came—whatever brought you. Gets lonely out here. So tell me, Olivia, what's the news you were about to share before your men arrived?"

Olivia quivered with elation. "I'm not just getting fat like I thought, Grandma. We're expecting babies."

"Babies?"

"Doc says there's more than one, but he won't know how many until they're born."

Anna was all smiles. "And look at you all pert. I'll bet Jesse's pleased as punch."

"He is, but he's a bit over zealous."

Elizabeth, knowing time had to be getting away from them said, "Olivia, don't you think we should get moving?"

"I suppose ... we can talk more when we come back, Grandma. We're going for the supplies we need to start our nosy husbands' Christmas presents."

"I figured it was something like that. I'll put a pot of soup on the stove. Plan to eat with us before you head home."

Elizabeth hummed. "Sounds good."

They were riding away when Anna called out, "No hurry, girls. Jacob will make sure the boys don't have time to miss you too much."

Olivia nodded. "Thanks, Grandma."

"You're welcome."

Olivia was weary by the time the four of them headed back toward Ypsilanti, but thankful she and Elizabeth had taken the time to get away. The country store had a nice selection of yard goods and soft wools for her to start knitting small sweaters and booties for the babies. She and Elizabeth had also acquired the supplies they would need to begin working on Christmas gifts. Olivia could hardly wait to begin knitting the sweater she planned to send to her father. The thought of him being alone for the holidays was unbearable, but taking the time to make this for him would show him how much he was loved. He rarely even mentioned how he was doing. She knew he was trying not to get her hopes up. His last letter gave nothing away, but his silence did not affect her faith. Until God told her otherwise, she would continue to pray for a miracle. Her father had told her often enough that God alone held the keys to life and death. She harbored no doubts that if her father were meant to be here, God would heal him of this dreadful disease. *How I would love to see him, Lord, to have him be a part of this wonderful new life You've given me.*

Olivia knew that as tired as she was, if she didn't get her mind on something else, she would be bawling in seconds. She was learning the hard way that dwelling on things she could not change only brought her sadness and despair. She had so many things to be thankful for, she needed to dwell on them instead.

Kaleb and Lizzy were a ways in front of them when Olivia caught her husband's attention. "Jesse."

"Hmm?" He reached out for her, and the tip of his fingers ran down her arm. "Honey, you look so tired. Let me ride with you, so I can hold you."

How could she argue with him. He was right. When Kaleb and Elizabeth saw what they were doing, they followed suit.

"Grandma and Grandpa were pleased that we visited. You and Lizzy have had a busy day. Grandma appreciated all the cleaning you two did when you got back. I'm not surprised you're tired."

"I was angry that you and Kaleb came after us at first, but we wouldn't have been able to stay if you didn't."

"I should have known the two of you would be fine. I'm not even sure why I followed. I just ..."

"You're not worried that I'll leave again, are you?"

"A little ...."

"No need, Jesse. Running away from my problems didn't solve them. Didn't even make me feel better. Made things worse."

"You coming this far without me makes me ..."

Her slender fingers covered his mouth, effectively stopping

the flow of words. "I would never take unnecessary risks with our children, Jesse. They're a gift from the Lord. Surely you know that I wouldn't, don't you?"

"It's a comfort hearing you say it."

Olivia grew pensive. "There are times when the weight of our loss is almost too much for me to bear."

"I know what you mean. I know how much my mother misses my father, and she has all of us. I keep praying that God will surround your father with other believers to help him through his sorrow."

"You've told me over and over again that grief is a process that doesn't happen over night. I have so much to be thankful for; we're so blessed to have each other and family."

"Yes, we are."

"Jesse, I forgot to tell you, but while I was staying with the Woods', I asked the Grants if they'd be willing to take some of my paintings on consignment."

His brow arched. "What did they say?"

"At first they were reluctant. Mr. Grant said he'd give them two months to sell ... they were gone by the second week.

The proceeds paid for the items I purchased today, and we still have a credit with them."

"So much for me providing for my wife's needs."

"Do you mind?"

Jesse shook his head. "If painting makes you happy, then by all means keep at it."

"I'm glad you feel that way, 'cause the Grants were so pleased that they want me to keep them coming." Jesse's brow furrowed, worrying her just a bit.

"I know you're excited, Liv, but you can't do this for the money. You should paint because you love it."

"I know .... Papa always said that too." She would heed her husband's words. Even so, her heart was rejoicing. Painting was her special gift from God to share with the world. Knowing that dream was being realized brought her so much joy.

"Did you see the one I did of Grandma and Grandpa?"

"I can't fathom how you come up with these ideas, never mind bringing them to life on a blank canvas. Even my stick figures leave a bit to be desired."

Olivia giggled. His mother had shown her some of Jesse's artwork from his younger years. It was best that he had given it up.

"Grandpa said he's been telling everyone about his newest granddaughter's talent. He has you pegged as the next Leonardo de Vinci."

"A wonderful compliment, however, highly over-stated."

"Leonardo was probably his own worst critic as well, My Dear."

"I suppose." For a time, Olivia relished the warmth radiating from her husband's body. As much as she wanted to sleep, she could not. Her senses took over, making her vividly aware of how fast her surroundings were changing. The whirling winds rustling the colorful leaves had chilled the air considerably as the evening shadows slowly faded and darkness settled over the rolling hills. Barely a sliver of moon could be seen among the gathering cloud cover.

Jesse could feel Olivia shivering against him, so he untied his saddle blanket and wrapped it around her. "We could be in for a storm before long, Liv."

Her eyes scanned the heavens and found no comfort there. "Jesse, we could ride faster if we rode alone. I'm already chilled. If it rains ..."

"Hey, Kaleb," Jesse called out. "Take a look at that sky.

We'd better get a move on."

"You could be right."

Jesse saw the path that led to the Huron and they parted ways, but he kept Olivia on Shadow with him.

The rain began to fall moments before they reached the farm. "Liv, I'll drop you off at the house with the packages."

"All right." Suzanne heard them come in and was waiting on the porch to help them with their purchases. "Thanks, Suz!" Olivia said as she followed her into the house.

Jared and Joe took the packages from Olivia, Louise bent down to unbutton her sister's boots, and Jayne was waiting with a dry sheet of toweling for her damp hair. Olivia couldn't help but smile. The apprehension in their eyes was a sight to behold. She didn't know if their concern was for her, the babies, or a little of both. One thing she knew for sure, this family loved her, and the knowledge of it warmed her deep within.

Suzanne reached for her hand and led her up the stairs. "Let's get you out of those wet things, Livia."

"I am cold."

"Jared's adding wood to the fire, and Mom's making a pot of tea. We'll have you and Jesse warmed up in no time."

"How'd your day go, Suz?"

"Good—once they got me off the roof."

Olivia scowled. "Why were you on the roof?"

Suzanne shook her head and laughed. "Jesse had me working on your roof. I was fine until I had to use the outhouse."

"Coming down's scary, isn't it?"

"Scary would be putting it lightly. Every time I got near the edge I could feel the blood drain out of me." Suzanne finished unbuttoning Olivia's dress and went for her nightclothes.

"How'd they finally get you down?"

"Jared was great. He stood behind me on the ladder until I made it down. They wouldn't let me up there after that."

"I wouldn't recommend telling Jesse they let ya quit early."

Suzanne shook her head. "We didn't quit. The boys have been teaching me how to use the saws and planer. I've been making shelves for your pantry all day. I never would have thought being a carpenter could be so much fun. Truth is, I can hardly wait to get back to it."

"That's a good thing, Suz. I'm the same way with my cooking and painting."

"Do you think Jesse will mind that I like it so much? I mean ... well, you know. Extra chores were supposed to be part of my punishment."

"Suz, you know Jesse only has your best interest at heart. He'll be pleased to see you enjoy what you're doing instead of dreading it."

"I hope you're right."

"I know I am. Happiness is a choice, Suz. If we allow our grief and trials to make us bitter and resentful, we'll miss out on all the wonderful things God has given us. Choosing to find joy in the midst of our overwhelming circumstances can be quite freeing ... don't you think?" Olivia fastened her robe, stuck her feet in her slippers, and they headed back down the stairs. When they entered the kitchen, Mom was pouring water into the pot.

Suzanne was smiling as she poured all of them a cup of tea and commented, "Could be you're right, Olivia, but I can think of a few situations that would be difficult to find joy in."

Olivia knew exactly what she was referring to. "Ask yourself what God protected Amy, Louise, and you from that day. Find joy in knowing things didn't turn out worse than they did."

"I suppose."

"My parents could have died and left me alone to fend for myself. Trust me, Suz, I don't doubt my parents' wisdom in wanting to see me wed. They knew I would need someone, and because of that, I have Jesse and all of you."

Chapter Twenty-five

A Night to Remember

OLIVIA STOOD AT the picture window, taking in the peaceful glow of winter. A thick blanket of sparkling white flakes covered the great expanse as far as the eye could see, and beyond. Olivia's brothers and sisters had gone sledding. As much as she wanted to join them, she didn't think it was wise. Climbing up steps was difficult enough. Walking back up the sledding hill in the deep snow would be an even greater challenge.

Olivia had given up asking Jesse when he was going to show her their new home. She didn't understand why this had to be such a big secret, but neither did she wish to be a nag. Today, being Christmas Eve, she was busy with holiday preparations in her mother-in-law's kitchen. Jared and Joe had gladly helped Jesse move all of their belongings into their place without his wife's knowledge. That evening after supper, Jesse asked Olivia to take a stroll with him, and she found herself being carried across

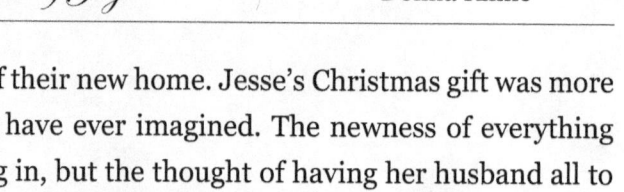
the threshold of their new home. Jesse's Christmas gift was more than she could have ever imagined. The newness of everything was still sinking in, but the thought of having her husband all to herself again was wonderful. After spending a peaceful evening together, Olivia was exhausted from all her endeavors and fell fast asleep soon after her head rested against her pillow.

Worn out himself, Jesse wasted no time joining her.

Jesse woke abruptly! His wife's shrilled screams transfused the darkness.

"No! No! Get away!"

A quick look around the shadowy moonlit room revealed nothing amiss. Jesse pulled Olivia into his arms, but she did not wake. His ill-fated attempt to calm her made her worse. "Olivia, it's me."

Trembling, fighting, and bellowing, with her arms flailing at his chest, she was trying desperately to get away from something, but what? She had to be dreaming. He lit the lamp, sure that the brightness would snap her out of it. He was right. The very second light pervaded the blackness—all was silent.

Her wide, clouded eyes searched their room. Something was wrong, but she had no idea what. "Jesse, what happened? I'm soaking wet."

"You were dreaming. Do you remember what it was about?"

She was quiet for a moment before understanding dawned. "Some kind of animal was attacking you. More than likely those creatures you told me about."

"Creatures?"

"Yea, the ones you said come out of the woods at night. Lizzy and I were discussing your warning the other day. They were attacking you. I kept trying to help, but someone was holding my arms. They were biting you ... I couldn't get free. It was horrible!"

Jesse began to laugh—a deep husky laugh. Just as she was about to berate him for making fun of her, he tried to explain, "I was holding your arms, Liv. You kept screaming—you were beating me up."

Her hand flew to her mouth, and the laughter they shared lightened their hearts.

"Jesse," she said, lightly slapping his arm, "can't you see? It was all your fault. You're the one who kept me from helping you. I could have saved you—you know that, don't you?"

"They never attacked me, Liv."

She grinned playfully as she softly murmured, "They did in my dream. It was very real."

"Are you all right?"

"I'm fine," she said in a frustrated drawl, "but now I need a bath. I'm all sweaty. I feel nasty."

"You're not taking a bath in the middle of the night. You'll be ill."

How did I know you would say that? I'm already wet—what's the difference? Olivia wisely kept her thoughts to herself. "I at least need to change my gown."

"All right, but hurry up. I've got a full day ahead of me."

She scowled intolerantly. "You're not very understanding, Mister."

"Sorry! I can't imagine what I was thinking." He rolled over on his stomach and stuck his head under the pillow to shade his eyes from the light.

As Olivia slipped into a dry gown, she realized how wide awake and giddy she felt. Her husband was lying there so vulnerable and unaware. How many times would she have an opportunity like this one? Soundlessly, she crept to Jesse's side. Her only ambition was to see if he too was ticklish. He must have heard her approach because the second her fingers touched his sides, he rolled her over onto the bed so fast her head was spinning. Her plan had gone awry. Instead of her tickling him, he was tickling her.

"Jesse," she protested amongst the laughter, "This is not fair! You always win."

"That's right, so give it up."

"One of these days, Jesse Somers, I'll devise a plan that will work. Then you'll be sorry!"

"No, you won't! Now get over here and let me hold those arms in case they start swinging at me again in my sleep." He blew out the lamp, drew her snugly against him, and pulled the quilt around them. "Go to sleep!"

Jesse's demanding growl ruffled her feathers—and besides, she wanted to talk. "I'm sorry I woke you up. I should have warned you about my nightmares. You might not believe me, but this is the first time I beat anyone up."

"You can find a way to make amends tomorrow."

It was quite evident that he wanted to sleep, but she had to question him further. "Jesse, do you mean to tell me that you won't just forgive me?"

"I'm thinking it's time for you to start paying a penalty for some of the trouble you cause." She gasped in perturbation.

Olivia didn't see him smile or she would have let it drop.

"Jesse, you know full well I was sound asleep."

"That may be, but you caused a big ruckus, and that should cost you something."

"I suppose you have something specific in mind."

"Of course I do. When a man's married to a spirited woman like you, he has to have a plan or he'd never survive."

"And when am I supposed to find out what this penalty is for my great sin?"

"In the morning." Though she tried to pull out of his hold, he was ready for her revolt and would not let her go.

"You have to tell me now, or I won't be able to sleep."

When Jesse said nothing, Olivia added, "I won't let you sleep either."

"You can't stand any form of suspense, can you?"

She wasn't about to justify that comment with a verbal response. "Let me up, Jesse. I need to use the outhouse."

He sighed in disgruntlement. "Are you just saying that so I'll let you up?"

"I couldn't be more serious. Now let me go." Her tone was filled with annoyance, so he dragged himself out of the bed and followed her.

"Where do you think you're going?" she questioned indignantly. "I think I can handle this alone, Jesse Somers." That he would not let her go out alone at night came as no surprise, but she couldn't resist giving him a hard time. Olivia wasn't really angry, but this big brute had a tendency to annoy her at times, and she didn't always know what to do with him—so she made herself a bit of a nuisance.

"You're not going out in the middle of the night alone."

"Fine!" For a change, he said nothing about her manner as they stuck their arms into their coats, feet into their boots, and headed for the door. Olivia was in front of Jesse and felt him place his knit hat on her head. She waited until she opened the door before throwing it back at him and scooting outside. Her bellowed name only served to heighten the exhilaration as she shuffled through the snow all the faster. Giggling—her heart was racing and she was fully expecting retribution.

"Olivia! You've been sweating!"

She ignored him and kept on. The outhouse door creaked as she entered. The disgusting aroma made her stomach churn. She quickly saw to her needs and nonchalantly stepped back out—cautiously heading for the side door. The babies must have sensed her unease because she felt them flutter.

Jesse, being the way he was, would not have left her alone, but right now he was nowhere to be seen. This could only mean one thing—he was up to no good. She shivered in anticipation. It was creepy being out in the middle of the night, but she so loved a good intrigue, and this was nothing less. While the snow offered some light, it was not enough for her liking. She scolded herself unmercifully. *If you were going to bait him, Olivia, you should have brought the lantern. What were you thinking?* Nervous and excited all at the same time, she crept on. If she could just clear ... this last patch ... of trees ... she would be home free.

But Jesse leapt out from behind a tree and growled like the bear that he was, effectively causing Olivia to feel like she had jumped out of her crawling skin. Her shrieking screams were so loud, Jesse was sure the neighbors could hear her a mile away.

He felt like a creep—she was terrified! What was he thinking? "Liv ... Honey, I'm so sorry! I thought you'd be expecting me to do something." His eyes never left her paled sober face as she bent over, picked up a huge wad of icy flakes and proceeded to wash his face. For seconds he stood in shock, but the shocked man quickly became defensive. "Now wait just a minute here. Now you've crossed the line!"

"Oh yeah! What line is that, Mr. Smarty Pants?" Her words taunted him, dared him, all-out begged him to do something about it. And her fierce scowl was so adorable, he wanted to kiss her, but the stage had been set—the play must go on. These night games with his irresistible young wife were interesting, to say the very least. Now wide-awake and up for the challenge, he scooped her protesting body into his arms and plopped down in the cold wet mound. As he scanned the length of her coated frame, he allowed his piercing glare to linger, putting her on edge—exactly what he intended. His words, though firm, were delivered with every ounce of playful vengeance he could muster. Grabbing handfuls of frigid clouds, he began to bathe her squirming body with the chilling white snow. "You did say you wanted a bath tonight, didn't you, My Sweet?" First he washed her face and neck, before proceeding to fill her coat. This was no one-sided endeavor; she returned his gifts of ice over and over again—with great pleasure.

After moments had passed, he pinned down her flailing limbs—completely disarming her with his oh-so-satisfying kisses. When she went limp in his arms, he gazed into her amazingly beautiful eyes; they shared a heartfelt smile. "Are we ready to get some sleep—or would you like to play some more?"

"Sleep, but you just ruined my last dry gown."

"You're welcome to put on one of those outfits I saw in your drawer this morning. Since they're not very warm, and they won't cover your belly, I'd be glad to snuggle you close and alleviate that problem."

"Maybe I will and maybe I won't ... now if you were to kiss me again the way you just did, I might be able to make up my mind."

He chuckled softly, happy to comply. "I'm so glad you like my kisses, Liv, 'cause I love yours."

Olivia smiled in delight, pulled herself up to his lips, and boldly stole a kiss of her own.

"I think I had better get changed before I'm sick and someone makes me stay in bed for a week. I thank you for the bath, kind Sir. I have to admit—I enjoyed it quite thoroughly."

"You're welcome." Jesse stood to his feet, reached for Olivia's hands, and pulled her up. "This has definitely been a night to remember, wouldn't you say?"

"Quite fun, if you ask me."

The last thing she remembered when they were snuggled back in their bed was the mantel clock striking five times.

Chapter Twenty-six

Winter Doldrums

*O*LIVIA PEERED OUT the kitchen window and waved at her husband who had apparently been standing there in the billowing snow, watching her at work in her new kitchen. When he came in the back way, Olivia was leaning on the frame of the pantry door.

Jesse shook off the worst of the snow, hung his coat from the hook and sat on the bench to remove his bluchers. Smiling at his wife, he said, "Kaleb made it into town yesterday, Liv. We got a letter from your father."

"What did he say?"

"I don't know. I thought I should wait so we could read it together."

"I wonder if he knows about the babies yet?" She couldn't help being a little anxious. Too much time had gone by since the last one. She wanted to take the letter from Jesse, but she was in her stocking feet, and that snow sprinkled all over the floor was cold.

Jesse reached for her hand, led her into the sitting room, and pulled her into his lap. For a long moment he only stared.

"What's gotten into you, Mister? Open the letter."

"I will in a minute." But he didn't; he just sat there ogling her.

"Jesse Cameron Somers!" The most tender of kisses silenced her protestations. Although she did wonder where all this was leading, instead of inquiring, she surprised him by asking, "Want to do that again?"

He chuckled. "In a minute. I have something for you."

"Besides the letter?"

"Something you should've had a long time ago. If you did, the young men in town would have known you were already taken."

"Jesse Somers, like another man would even look at me in my condition."

He shook his head. "Still just as sassy as you were the night we married."

She stole a kiss. "Did you really want me to change?"

"No, but I was kind of hoping you would have shared your feelings for me before now."

"But, you know how I feel without me telling you ...."

"That may be, but the words would be nice to hear."

Olivia grew pensive for a long moment, as if reciting words in her mind before she could speak them freely. "How can I reveal my heart without first recalling the day my daring knight rescued me from the dreaded bog. When I was sure nothing could save me from the depths of despair that following year, my chivalrous knight returned, like a gift sent straight from Heaven to comfort me and make me his wife. Not only did I gain a wonderful husband, the father of my children has become my dearest friend, an amazing lover, but more than anything you will always be my gracious knight that I love with all of my heart." She paused for several seconds. "Is that close to what you were hoping to hear?"

Jesse smiled and drew her close. "Three little words would have been enough, but I have to admit, I love your unique way of telling me things."

"I do love you, Jesse. I think I've loved you since the day you plucked me out of the mud."

"You made quite an impression on me that day, too. I know true love expects nothing in return, but I've longed to hear you say the words. I love you too, my sweet, whimsical wife."

"I know ...." The silence stretched on and on as they held each other's gaze. Entranced in the wonder of this tender moment, a rapt expression settled on Olivia's face as her long finger slid across her husband's silky lips. *He loves me—he really loves me—and I love him too!* They were truly becoming one, just as God intended, and the awareness of it thrilled her soul.

"Are you going to tell me why you're not showing me the letter?"

"Your father sent two envelopes: one addressed to me and the other to both of us."

"Oh?"

"Before we read the letter, I'd like you to open this." He handed her a small package wrapped in a delicately tatted handkerchief tied together with a lilac ribbon—not unlike the one she wore on their wedding day.

Gazing into his glorious blue eyes, her elation was more than apparent. She loved surprises and beamed as she leaned to steal a kiss before slowly pulling on the end of the lilac bow. Within the small box she found two rings—one, a golden ring with a diamond delicately set in the center of it. She held it between her fingers and took a closer look. "Oh, Jesse. How lovely. When did you ..." her words trailed off as her eyes fell on the golden wedding band still sitting in the box. The etching was too unique not to be ... her mother's. She fought them, but it was no use. Tears flooded her eyes and spilled down her cheeks in great abandon.

As she held her mother's ring, a mixture of reflections swirled inside her. There were joyful memories—memories that represented the years her parents had spent loving and caring for each other, but then she knew that were it not for her heart-wrenching loss, her mother would still be wearing this golden band.

Jesse handed her the hanky that had been laid aside. "Now you know why I was hesitant to give it to you, and why I wrapped this gift in a hanky."

"Having my mother's ring means the world to me, but ..."

His fingers touched her lips. "I understand, Liv. Don't try to say more. Do you like the one I got you?"

She nodded. "It's lovely, Jesse."

"Would you like me to put them on you, or do you need time before you can wear your mother's wedding band?"

"No ... wearing Mama's ring will remind me of the love they shared and my loss, but the ring from you will be a reminder of all that God has given me."

Jesse slipped them on her finger and cuddled close while he read the letter.

Dearest Olivia and Jesse,

A grandfather? How wonderful! My friends were pleased to hear that the lovely young couple in the portrait is going to have a child. The possibility that there could be more than one is exciting. Remember, God sees the greater picture. He knows best. Both of you enjoy this time of discovery. A miracle is growing inside of you, Livia. The way your mother's body changed when she was carrying you filled me with wonder.

Take care of yourself, Livia. Listen to your husband when he tells you to rest or when he asks you to take extra precautions. Jesse loves you and a man in love will need to take special care of his wife during this time.

"See … what did I tell you, Liv. Your father understands me better than you do."

She elbowed him in the stomach.

"Hey!"

"I understand you, Jesse. I just don't want you getting carried away. I will try to heed your advice, but I'll make no promises."

His wiggling fingers came to her sides.

Squealing, she demanded, "Stop … finish reading the letter."

The mountains are exquisite during the long winter months. The white-blanketed-stillness presents a breathtaking view. The dense snow does keep us indoors, but this gives me the time I long for to study God's Word with my sick friends, to visit with them and to pray. Many have come, and several have gone home to be with the Lord, but the few who leave this place well are forever changed by the sweet fellowship we've found amongst these caring people.

If only we as believers could live each day as if we were dying and see each day as a gift from the Lord. How much more, I wonder, would we accomplish for the Kingdom of Heaven?

I have known for years that Jesus Christ, the innocent Son of God, died to pay the price for my sins. But, never have I seen this more real to a man or woman than on his or her deathbed. The peace that passes all understanding covers those who know Him like a blanket. As they walk through the valley of the shadow of death, fear is not on them, because the King of Kings and Lord of Lords is with them.

I hope you enjoy having Mama's ring, Livia. That was her last request before she passed into eternity.

I received a package from you for Christmas. I hope you don't mind, but I'm waiting to open it. Having something to open will make this time special.

Know that you both are loved. Tell your family in Ypsilanti my thoughts and prayers are with all of you. Have the merriest of Christmases. We have much to celebrate.

With all my love,
Papa

"He still doesn't say how he's doing, Jesse. Why do you suppose that is?"

"Maybe he doesn't know. Continue to pray for his healing, Liv. Isn't that what we agreed?"

Olivia wrapped her arms around her husband and squeezed him tight. "Thank you for the ring, Jesse. I'll love having both of them."

"You're welcome. I'll feel better knowing you're wearing them."

Olivia, hearing Suzanne screaming out Jesse's name, jumped off her husband's lap and ran to see what was wrong. Olivia had no more opened the door when Suzanne flew in and ducked behind Jesse. Jared was hot on her trail, and the look on his face revealed much.

"Oh, Jesse. Please don't let him ..." Suzanne begged.

Jared, now glaring at Suzanne, took a daring step toward her, but Jesse stopped him.

"Slow down there, Jared. Winter doldrums got you two at each other's throats?"

Jared turned around and pointed to the back of his head. "Look what she did!"

Jesse tried not to laugh, but he couldn't help it. "As haircuts go, Jar ... I'll give it interesting. Maybe you should explain what happened before you come any closer."

"I was sitting at the table having a cup of coffee, minding my own business, when the little twit informed me that I needed a haircut."

"Well, I kind of agree with her, Jared. You are a bit overdue." Jesse peeked over his shoulder. Suzanne was staying as quiet as a church mouse.

"That may be, but I didn't give her permission to go hacking at my head."

"Oh? Then how did she take what she did?"

The mouse suddenly found her tongue. "Jared, I'm sorry. I didn't expect you to move like that. It was an accident. I'm sure I could fix it, if you'd only let me try."

He scowled and then snarled, "And chance having my whole head look like the back? No, Little Missy. Now it's my turn to take a chunk out of your head!" Jared moved around Jesse and grabbed her arm.

"Jesse, please don't let him."

Thinking he'd better put a stop to this quick, Jesse insisted, "Jared, let her go."

"She has to learn she can't take matters into her own hands, Jesse."

"I agree with you."

Suzanne's eyes grew wide and she paled instantly. "You can't let him."

"Be still, Suzanne, or I will. Jared, Liv is quite good at cutting hair, and I'm sure she'd have no trouble fixing yours. She does mine all the time."

"That's all well and good, but ..."

"I know, Suzanne needs to make this up to you, and I think I have a suggestion that would better suit both of you." Jesse pulled Jared off to the side and whispered his suggestion.

Jared's brow rose and worried Suzanne just a tad.

"I like it," Jared said out loud, his eyes never leaving Suzanne.

"Good. Are you going to tell her, or shall I?"

"I think I'll tell her, but thanks for the offer."

"You have three choices, Suzanne: extra chores for the week, with me ...."

Her mouth dropped open. "Jesse!"

"Hear him out, Suz."

"... Submit to a haircut of my choosing ..." Jared grinned, satisfied that she would not be tempted to choose this form of punishment.

"Jesse?"

"Listen closely, Suz. This is your last choice. You might not want to miss it."

"Or ..." Jared winked at his sister and said as he rubbed his hands together and licked his lips, "this is my favorite one ...."

"I can only imagine what it is ...."

"Seven days in a row you will make me my favorite dessert!"

"No way!"

"Then it's the scissors or working at my side for a week. What will it be, 'cause you're going to pay for your crimes, Dear Sister, one way or another."

"I'd leave home before I'd give you the satisfaction of cutting my hair. Jesse, I can't believe you think this is fair. It was an accident."

He was shaking his head. "No it wasn't, Suzanne. You may have had the best of intentions, but you've no right to cut someone's hair without their permission. Be thankful he settled for a week; I would have given him a month."

Without thinking, she stomped on Jared's toes.

In retaliation, he slung her over his shoulder and swung her around, laughing until she said the magic words.

"Jared, you have to stop ... I'm going to be sick." He quickly set her down.

"So tell me, Suz, will you be doing the baking? My stomach's already rumbling just thinking about the selections I'll make."

"You'll get your sweet tooth filled on one condition."

His eyes narrowed in on her. "You are not in a position to be bargaining, Sis."

She stomped her foot. "Jared, I want to learn how to cut hair." She started to giggle. "Someday I'll want to marry, and I don't want my husband's hair looking like that." She was pointing to the back of his head.

"I can see why."

"If you let me do the cutting, I promise to follow Olivia's instructions to the letter."

Jared turned to Olivia who said, "I will gladly teach her."

"All right, but this had better be the best haircut I've ever had or you'll be making my favorite sweets for a month instead of a week!"

"Agreed!" Suzanne hugged Jared tightly, while Olivia went for the scissors.

Olivia was beginning to wonder if Elizabeth was ever going to have her baby. Her own belly had surpassed Elizabeth's in size weeks ago. In fact, she was so big Jesse was concerned about her plans to help Elizabeth, but she desperately wanted to be available for whatever her sister needed.

Finally on the tenth of January, Samuel came by to let her and Jesse know that their newest niece or nephew was on the way. Unfortunately, Jesse wanted to go with her, and the animals needed to be fed first. By the time they arrived, sweet baby Chad had already arrived.

Kaleb placed him in Olivia's arms, and instantly her heart filled with love for her precious nephew. She couldn't help but smile as she took in his features. He was the spitting image of his father, except for his dark crop of hair.

Olivia stayed for three nights. On the fourth day, Jesse came by and insisted on her coming home to catch up on her sleep. Unaccustomed to all that motherhood entailed, she was exhausted from her efforts. The overwhelming desire to hold her own babies was setting in, but she would have to be patient. She still had three months to go.

He Loves Me!

Chapter Twenty-seven

Joy Cometh

Spring 1832

"MORNING, SLEEPY HEAD!" Olivia said as she leaned to kiss her husband's bristly cheek. While Jesse's eyes were not open even the slightest crack, she had a sneaking suspicion he was feigning sleep.

There was one sure way to find out, but she needed to give her lumpy self a good head start, so she opened the door and stepped out of the room before she said, "Jesse, the mud is drying up, the air is warm, and I'm sick of being stuck in this house. I'm saddling Shadow and heading over to the Whites'. Your breakfast is on the back of the stove—see ya later!"

As expected, he flew out of the bed and captured her before she took her third step. Jesse wrapped one arm around her as far as he could, cupped her chin with his free hand and lifted her tentative gaze to his. "You, Young Lady, are not going anywhere alone in your condition."

"Then come with me. I'm going crazy, Jesse. Winter was long and hard. I love being in our own place, but spring is here and I need to enjoy it. When the babies arrive I'll be stuck inside again."

"Oh, all right! While I get dressed, you fix yourself a cup of tea. We can talk about it while I eat."

She nodded. Another cup would be nice.

Jesse ambled into the kitchen a few moments later. After buttoning his shirt, he sat down at the table across from her. "I'll need to let my brothers know what I'm doing, Liv. They won't be happy that I'm not pulling my weight, but I suppose they'd do just about anything for you."

"Thanks for understanding."

"You're welcome. Did Doc say when he wanted to see you again?"

She peered up at him, wondering if he would deny her request if she told him too much.

"Olivia!"

She jumped. "Don't startle me, Jesse."

"Then tell me what he said."

She rolled her eyes, admitting, "He'll be by tomorrow. He doesn't want me coming into town anymore."

"And ..."

"And what?"

"Olivia Maryse Somers! Tell me or we won't be going anywhere."

If I tell you, we won't be going anywhere!

"I've been thinking about names for the babies, Jesse and I have an idea I'd like to run by you."

His hand came to his mouth to hide his smile, but not soon

enough—she had noticed. "Olivia, you have till the count of three to tell me what he said!"

"Or what? You can't toss me in the creek; the cold water would throw me into labor. And if you tickle me, I might pop. So tell me, Jesse Cameron Somers, what are you going to do if I don't tell you?"

His tone and look grew stern. "Make you stay home."

"Oh ..." It took her a long moment, but she finally came clean. "He's coming by here tomorrow, and he said I'd better be home." Where they came from, she did not know, but tears pooled in her eyes and spilled down her cheeks. Jesse reached across the table to console her, but her emotions were too scattered to accept his sympathy. Ignoring his pleas, she went back to the room, lay on the bed, and curled in a ball around her massive stomach and pillow.

Feeling like a heel, Jesse went to her. He didn't understand her changing moods, but Doc had warned him. He had even said that it was perfectly normal. *Whatever that meant.* Lying down beside Olivia, Jesse drew her close and just held her for a time. Unfortunately, nothing he said seemed to console her, until he asked, "Do you still want me to take you over to the Whites'?"

"Mmm ... hmm ..." She took the hanky he had dried her tears with, and blew her nose.

"If I make you a soft bed in the back of the wagon, will you lay down until we get there?"

She took in a shuddering breath and managed a nod.

"Honey, just lay still and close your eyes until I come back for you."

"All right," she conceded. "Maybe my back will quit hurting if I do."

His eyes widened. *Your back hurts? You didn't tell me this. I wonder?* "Is anything else bothering you, Liv?"

"I'm as big as a barn, Jesse. This morning I've been to the outhouse five times, most of which were false alarms. I'm not even sure what normal is any more. So, yes, everything is bothering me."

Jesse heard what she was saying and started to panic, but he forced himself to calm. He had no wish to make her cry again. Instead of discussing her condition further with Olivia, he ran back to his mother's house to enlist his family's help.

Jared was sitting at the kitchen table when Jesse flew in the back door. "Jared, can you go get Doc? Could be a false alarm, but we're not taking chances. Where's Joe?"

"Upstairs." Jared stepped into his bluchers, grabbed his coat, and put it on as he headed out the door.

Jesse went to the stairs and called out to the rest of his family. Joe came down first, so Jesse sent him for Elizabeth.

His mother, Suzanne, and Louise followed fast in Joe's footsteps.

"What's going on?" Jayne wanted to know.

Before Jesse answered, he glanced at his sisters and said, "Girls, I don't want all of us to bombard Olivia at once. Can you stay here and just pray for a while?"

"Sure," Suzanne gladly agreed. In truth, she had a weak stomach, so the thought of being around when Olivia was giving birth did not set well.

Louise, on the other hand, didn't like being left out, but she did as her brother asked.

Jesse and Jayne were on their way to his house before he got around to doing any explaining. "Mom, she's complaining of a backache. I had her stay in bed. I know she's had one for weeks now, but she keeps feeling like she needs to use the outhouse. Could she be in labor and not know it?"

Jayne's smile was tender. "She's never had a baby, Jesse. Anything's possible. Let me talk to her and see what I can figure out."

"Fair warning—she's been a basket case this morning. Tread lightly."

"I wouldn't dream of doing otherwise." The strain in her son's brow spoke volumes. "This is no time to start worrying, Jesse. Pray for her. First babies rarely come easy like Lizzy's did. She'll need your strength to carry her through."

Jesse's eyes, filled with apprehension, were fixed on his mother. "I was kind of hoping I could let Doc handle things and stay out of his way."

"Jesse Somers!" Jayne berated. "Your father was with me through every delivery. I needed his moral support more than anything. Don't you even think of leaving her! She needs you now. Don't forget, it's partly your fault she's in this state ...."

He held his hand up to stop his mother's triage. "Point taken, Mom. I won't leave her."

"Good!" Jayne crossed the threshold of her son's new home. When she walked into their bedroom and found Olivia sound asleep, she didn't disturb her. She would need the rest.

Instead, she put Jesse to work collecting the things they would need for the delivery, just in case.

At first Olivia thought she was dreaming. The pain in her stomach was unbearable. Her back felt as though it was ripping apart. When she realized it wasn't a dream, but reality, she cried out, "Jesse!"

"I'm right here, Liv. I'm not going anywhere."

She opened her eyes to find her husband sitting beside her, caressing her damp face. "You have to get Doc. The babies. I think they're coming."

"I sent Jared for him hours ago."

"Oh ..." Olivia looked up and saw Jayne standing in the frame of the door. "Mom, my back is killing me. Any suggestions?"

Jayne walked into the room. "You've been laying there for a long time, Honey. Let's get you out of your clothes and into your gown. We'll see if you can still walk around. Sometimes the change in position helps."

Jesse unbuttoned her dress while his mother went for her gown. Ensconced in her faded blue nightgown, he helped her to her feet. She held on to her husband's arm in case another pain hit.

"I need a glass of water. Your mother was right. The pressure isn't so bad now that I'm up."

"Good. Just take it slow."

She smiled up at him. His concern was genuine, and she loved him for it. "I really am fine, Jesse. Women have babies every day—remember?"

"But none of those other women are my wife."

"Just pray for me"

"Continually, My Sweet Liv."

"All this time we've been waiting. We're finally going to get to hold them, Jesse." His long finger tenderly brushed her fly-away strands of hair back from her rosy face.

"Soon, Liv. Take this in stride. You'll need your strength for the long haul." Jesse poured her a glass of water, and while she took several sips, he pulled her hair back in a loose braid and tied it off at the end.

"Is it hot in here, or is it just me?"

"Just you. Would you rather put on one of your light weight shifts?"

"Not right now. How long did I sleep?"

"A good four hours."

Her forehead crinkled. "That long?"

He chuckled softly. "Yes, Honey. You needed it; you haven't been sleeping well for days."

"I suppose." Setting her glass down, Jesse led her into the sitting room to join his mother, but she paused when another cramp hit.

Jayne glanced up at the mantel clock, noting the minute hand. For a while, the three of them sat talking about the farm and all that would still need to be done before the planting season began. The long winter had given them ample time to rest and make preparations for the season ahead. Spring was a time of awakening, and as much as they were glad that it had arrived, long days of hard work were ahead.

"Olivia, your pains are coming about five minutes apart. Do you feel like they're getting stronger?"

Surprised by his mother's words, Jesse asked, "How did you know she's having them, Mom?"

"Her brow furrows just a bit."

"Oh ..." Jesse reached for his wife's hand, capturing her gaze. "Are you all right? Need anything?"

She smiled. "I'm fine, but I would like to use the outhouse before Doc arrives."

Jesse glanced at his mother who shook her head, so he suggested, "Honey, maybe you should use the chamber pot until this is over."

"I'll be fine, Jesse."

"It isn't you I'm worried about ...."

"Oh! I suppose you're right ... the babies."

Jayne, aware of the strange look on her daughter-in-law's face, asked, "What is it, Olivia?"

She reached for Jesse's hand. "I don't feel so good. Maybe I should ...."

"Should what, Liv?"

"Maybe if I walk around a while it will pass."

He helped her to her feet and whispered in her ear as he led her toward the kitchen, thinking she was embarrassed to talk in front of his mother.

She giggled. "No, it's not that, Jesse. Just lots of pressure."

"Well, what would I know? I've never had a baby before."

She sent him a lighthearted wink, hoping to ease his mind.

"We're in the same boat, neither have I."

He squeezed the hand he was holding. "From the looks of things, you won't be able to say that for long."

"I suppose skipping this step is out of the question."

"Sorry, Honey." Jesse was contemplating taking her outside for a walk when her knees buckled against the pressure she was feeling. He was about to lift her into his arms and insist that she go back to bed, when a gush of water splattered against the dry wood floor. "I think you just sprung a leak, Liv."

She slapped his arm. "Don't make me laugh, Jesse Somers!"

Jayne retrieved the toweling from the shelf, and as she bent down to clean up the mess, suggested, "Jesse, can you help Olivia get out of her wet things while I take care of this?"

Determined to help her mother-in-law, Olivia stooped down, until another pain racked her body. This one was much more intense than the others had been. "Wow!" she breathlessly exclaimed when it finally eased. "That one took me by surprise."

"My pains always got more intense after my water broke, Livia."

"If this one was any indication of what's to come, I'd better get changed before the next one." Jesse ushered her back into the room, but another one hit before she was out of her wet gown and then another when she stuck her arms into her dry shift.

Elizabeth came in the front door and found her mother mopping up the floor. "Her water broke?"

"Yes, Lizzy. Go ahead and get a stack of toweling for her bed. Her contractions are coming harder now. See if she wants to lie down."

Hearing a light knock on the bedroom door, Jesse opened it.

"I hear we're going to have some babies soon," Elizabeth said as she smiled affectionately.

"Oh, Lizzy. I'm glad you could come. Where's Chad?"

"He's with Kaleb. He'll bring him over when he gets hungry."

Jesse put in, "With the way he's growing, that could be real soon."

Elizabeth stuck out her lower lip. "He's only three months

old, but he'll look huge next to your babies."

Olivia started to giggle, but another pain stole it away.

Spreading the towels out over the bed, Elizabeth and Jesse helped Olivia sit down, but she learned quickly that lying down was not an option for her. The pain was too intense. And she was sick in her stomach—a condition she could not abide. Jesse and Elizabeth had their patient propped up with pillows against the headboard when Doc came in. They all breathed a huge sigh of relief.

"You're having them a day earlier than I thought, but that's just fine with me. How you doing, Livia?"

"Since my water broke, they're coming closer and harder."

"Can't stand to lay down, can ya, Honey?"

"No, Sir. Makes me feel sick."

"You haven't had any room in there for a couple of months. I'm not surprised."

Olivia smiled for the last time that night. Her labor pains came in tidal waves all night long. Several times, Jesse had to leave the room. It tore him apart to see her in so much pain.

Her strength was fading fast by the time the sun peeked up above the clouds, and he wasn't sure how much more she could take.

Jesse gathered his family members together, and all of them got down on their knees to petition the Lord on behalf of Olivia and his unborn children. They had been praying for some time when Jesse heard Doc calling him back into the room.

"Jesse, sit with your wife. I can feel the cord wrapped around a baby's neck. If I can get it unwound, she's ready to deliver."

"Did you hear that, Liv?" She nodded, but that was all she could manage.

Doc was right. After untangling the cord and three good pushes, the first baby came out screaming at the top of his lungs. "Would you look at that, Jesse? It's a handsome boy, like his papa."

Olivia peeked up and smiled at her son, but the next baby was coming fast.

Jayne was taking her grandson from Doc's hands, when her next grandchild made an entrance. "It's a girl, Livia—one for each of you. And she's so adorable ... isn't she, Jesse?"

"They're both fine-looking babies and listen to them holler, Liv." Jesse was wiping Olivia's face with a damp cloth when her eyes grew huge. "Doc," Jesse called out. "Something's not right."

Olivia screamed out in anguish and then passed out from the pain.

"Is she still with us?" Jesse asked with tears in his eyes.

Doc checked her pulse. It was fine, and she was still breathing, so he felt her stomach. Thirty minutes later, Jesse was thanking the Lord that Olivia was unaware of what was happening—no doubt, God's mercy. A third child was born to them—another girl, but something was terribly wrong: her breathing was labored. She was much smaller than the other babies. Her little chest heaved as she took in every breath.

Doc shook his head. "I'm sorry, Jesse. I wish I could tell you differently, but she's not strong enough to make it. Would you like to hold her while she's still with us?"

Jesse didn't hesitate for a minute. He wrapped a blanket

around her tiny form and covered her little face with tears and kisses as he prayed for her. He did not doubt that God could heal her. But, as difficult as it was to accept, he had a peace about letting her go.

"Mommy and Daddy love you, Sweetheart. You're a special gift from the Lord. I don't understand why you must leave us so soon, but it's not my place to question. I have to trust that God knows best. We love you with all of our hearts, Honey, but God loves you more. We entrust you into His care, Sweet-Baby-Love." Jesse kissed her sweet mouth as she took her last breath. She was gone. Not since the day he married Olivia had he experienced such inexplicable joy and heart-wrenching sorrow in the same hour.

With her granddaughter between them, Jayne wrapped her arms around her sobbing son. "Jesse, I know it's a horrible thing to lose a child, but we need to trust that God knows best. Can you let me and your other siblings take her and prepare her for burial?" Jesse drew her close and kissed her little brow again before relinquishing his child to her grandmother's care.

"This sweet baby, born of your love, is with the Lord. He'll take care of her, Jesse. Your wife and other children need their father now. Try to focus on all that you have left, Son. Loving your other children doesn't diminish your love for this little one. She'll always be a part of both of you. God has blessed you abundantly this day. Keep your eyes on what you have here and not on what you have lost."

"I've told Olivia that so many times."

"Listen to your heart, Jesse. Those two babies in there need their daddy to shower them with I-love-you kisses too.

This little dolly is in the presence of the Lord. If it helps, think of Dad and Maryse loving on her now."

"I'll try. Thanks, Mom. You're an amazing woman."

"And you're a wonderful son, husband, and now a father."

As hard as it was to walk away, Jesse did, and the sight of his two babies, snuggled in his sister's arms, chased his gut-wrenching tears away.

"What do you think, Lizzy?" Twinkling blue eyes met his.

"I think they're beautiful .... I'm so sorry for your loss, Jesse."

He leaned down and kissed her cheeks before taking his babies from her. "Thanks, Sis."

She stood and said, "Jesse, here. You sit while I help Doc get Livia cleaned up."

"How is she, Doc?"

"I'm thinking she's just worn out, Jesse."

"Did the bleeding slow up?"

"Yes. Everything seems to be normal. Give her time. She'll wake up when she's ready."

Jesse looked down at his children and asked, "What about them? Won't they need to eat?"

"Not to worry. They'll let us know when they're hungry.

I'm curious, do they have names?"

Jesse looked up at Doc and grinned. "They do, but I'd like Olivia to tell you."

Two hours later, Olivia awoke to the sound of her babies crying. Feeling quite spry for all she had been through, she asked, "Who's pinching my babies?"

Jesse's grin went from ear to ear as he nuzzled their babies. "Would you look at that? Mama woke up just in time to feed you."

Doc decided this was a good time for a cup of coffee.

Elizabeth, after helping to prop Olivia up with pillows, followed Doc, shutting the door on her way out so that her brother and his wife could have some privacy.

The proud papa sat down on the side of the bed and handed Olivia the babies one at a time. Doc had suggested that he wait to tell Olivia about the third baby until tomorrow. Jesse had agreed, as long as she didn't ask.

"How are you, Honey?"

"I'm fine, now. Oh, look at them, Jesse. They're ours to love for as long as the Lord allows."

"Yes, they are. You've been sleeping, so I've had a few hours to enjoy them. They're something else. Open the blankets and look at their tiny fingers and toes."

She did as he suggested; her heart so filled with love.

"Are we agreed on their names, Liv?"

"Oh, yes .... George Jesse Somers, and Maryse Olivia Somers."

"George and Maryse." Jesse liked the sound of it, but more than anything he loved knowing that the babies' grandparents' memories would be kept alive by the names he and Olivia had chosen for them.

Jesse watched as she kissed them over and over again.

He understood, he could hardly resist himself. He hated to interrupt such a tender moment, but he needed his wife's undivided attention while the babies were still content.

Leaning to kiss Olivia, Jesse paused, holding her tender gaze.

"These babies are a result of the love we've shared, Olivia. I'm sorry this was so hard on you, but thank you."

"It's me who should be thanking you, Jesse. If you hadn't

answered my father's letter, I wouldn't be holding these little miracles."

"I'm so glad I did. I love you with all of my heart, Olivia Maryse Somers."

"I love you, too, Jesse, so indulge me, if you will, with a kiss of a man in love, and then I shall feed these little darlings."

Jesse sighed contentedly, more than happy to oblige ....

Daisytales

He Loves Me!

Epilogue

*O*LIVIA PUT WHAT would probably be the last of the wildflowers for the season in front of George and Sweet-Baby-Love's graves. Jesse had told her about their third baby the morning after George and Maryse were born. As hard as it was to accept, Jayne was right, thinking of their daughter in Heaven with her grandparents doting on her brought Olivia a measure of comfort.

After Jesse told her everything he had said to their daughter before she slipped into eternity, he asked if she would like to name their baby before they buried her next to her grandfather. In response, Olivia shook her head and said, "You already named her, Jesse."

"I suppose I did, didn't I?"

"Sweet-Baby-Love is a perfect name. She came into this

world because of the love we shared, and now she's in the arms of love."

Olivia could hardly believe how quickly time was passing. Having two babies to feed and care for had completely altered her life, but if she had it to do over again, she wouldn't change a thing.

Her father was thrilled to hear about George and Maryse's arrival. Olivia had sent him a sketch of the four of them, and he went on and on about how precious they were. He still evaded the subject of his health, and in many ways that troubled her. Jesse kept saying that her father would inform them if his time were short. "Trust, Liv. God holds the keys to life and death. Leave your father in the Lord's hands where he belongs. Worry is a sin, My Love." He was right, but leaving her father in God's hands was something she had to do daily.

She wanted to go and see her father; she had even brought it up to Jesse. The babies, he thought, were too small to take on such a lengthy journey, and she had agreed with him. Still, the longing to see her father plagued her at times. *If only* ... It was useless to even allow her thoughts go there. *Your will, Lord, not mine. I know You have a purpose for this time of waiting. Help me to be content with all that you have given. Help me to rely on You. Be with my father, Lord. Heal him in body if it be Your will .... You know my heart, Lord. Is it too much to long for? I have to believe that nothing is impossible with You!*

"Olivia ..." Jesse called. He was walking towards her with George and Maryse wiggling in his arms. They loved being outdoors. He had them all bundled up in their warm woolen coverings that his wife and mother had just finished. The moment the babies saw Olivia, their arms and legs started moving as they squealed in delight. "I would say they're happy to see you, Liv."

She kissed their little cheeks. Looking up at Jesse, she noticed that his pouting lip was sticking out. Feeling merciful, she kissed him too.

"Are you getting hungry?"

"For hours I've been smelling that roast you put in the oven. It's killing me!"

She giggled.

"The children and I are going to see the horses. Do you think you can manage without us for a while?" Jesse gave his bundles a squeeze.

Olivia kissed their little noses. "It will be difficult to cook without them pulling on my legs, but I'll try to manage."

He smiled. "See ya in a bit."

Olivia had the corn muffins in the oven and the rest of dinner ready to put on the table, but Jesse and the children were still in the barn. She had heard a rider come in about ten minutes ago, but didn't think much of it. Kaleb and her brothers were always coming and going.

Thinking she had enough time to change the babies' bedding before the muffins were finished baking, she went into their room. When she heard Jesse come in the back entrance, she hurried along.

"Liv," he said as he came to stand in the bedroom door.

"We have an unexpected guest. Did you make enough food to share?"

She finished what she was doing before she looked up at him and smiled. "If it's Kaleb, we'd better make some more."

"It's not Kaleb, this time."

Her brow furrowed. "Who is it, Jesse?" Her husband's look was unreadable.

"Just come and see ...."

"Give me a second. I'll be right there."

Jesse hurried back to the kitchen. He wanted to see her face when she came around the corner, and he was glad that he had. Her expression was priceless.

"Papa?" Olivia softly murmured, as tears flooded her eyes.

Jesse took the babies from Josiah so that he could go to his daughter who was too stunned to move.

"Yes, Honey. I can see that I've surprised you." Josiah wrapped his arms around his Olivia and did nothing to stop the flow of tears that fell from his eyes. He had dreamed of this day, prayed for it, but he had refused to come until he knew for certain that he was well.

Needing to look at him, she stepped back and touched his face. "Oh, Papa, look at you. You're the picture of health. How?"

"God's using Doctor Jennings' knowledge of the disease to heal many, Livia."

She glanced at Jesse and asked, "Did you know he was coming?"

"No! I'm just as surprised as you."

She stood on her toes and kissed her father's cheek. "You won't leave me again, will you, Papa?"

He chuckled softly. "Not until the Lord calls me home. I'll have to see if I can find a place to live, and I'll need to work if I want to eat."

Olivia was just about to speak, but Jesse beat her to it.

"You'll stay here with us, Dad. And, as far as making a living, there's enough work right here on the farm to support six more families."

"You're sure I won't be in the way?"

"Absolutely certain! Truth is, I could use the help. The upper floor isn't finished yet, but it's on my list of things to do this winter. We can finish your room before we start on George and Maryse's." Jesse glanced at his wife and grinned. "Liv says they're getting too big to be in our room. She thinks my snoring wakes them up."

"She might have something there, Jesse."

"Oh, no!" Olivia shouted. "The muffins!" She grabbed the hot pads, opened the oven and pulled the burnt muffins out. "So much for filling my craving for corn muffins."

Josiah offered, "I can whip some more up in no time if you're willing to wait."

"No, Papa, the rest of the food is ready. A twinkle lit her Eyes. Knowing how much her father loved them, she suggested, "We could have the leftover cinnamon rolls from breakfast."

"Mmm! Sounds great to me. I haven't had your cinnamon rolls ..."

"In far too long, Papa."

"Yes ... far too long."

"As soon as we're done eating, we'll have to introduce you to Jesse's family. And tomorrow if you're feeling up to it, we can head over to the Whites' so you can meet the rest of them. Then on Sunday you can meet our church family."

"I'd like that, Livia. I am tired from my travels, but nothing a good night's rest won't fix."

"First things first, Liv. Let's feed the man so he has the strength to keep up with all these outings you're planning."

"Oh ... sure." She knew she was rambling, but she couldn't help it; her heart was filled to overflowing.

❦ ❦ ❦

Spring 1834

In awe and wonder, Olivia stepped out onto her front porch for a long moment and just stood there drinking in the warmth of the sun's shimmering rays. Spring had come again to Ypsilanti, and the evidence of it was all around her. What a welcome relief! Many of her feathered friends had returned from their southern havens, squirrels were playfully scampering about, the trees were budding, and as far as the eye could see new life was sprouting.

Olivia smiled as her hands splayed across her tummy. Doc had informed her and Jesse just last week that they had another little one on the way. He offered no guarantees, but he suspected this would be a normal pregnancy with one baby, not three. Olivia and Jesse were relieved by his prognosis, and their family was elated with the news.

Mark Norris and his sweet wife, Roccena, were hosting the annual pre-season barn dance. Folks would be coming from miles around for this potluck affair, and the Somers were no exception. Everyone looked forward to this time of celebration before the planting season got underway.

Olivia's father had approached Jesse last week and admitted to a growing fondness for Jesse's mother. As odd as it was for Jesse to have her father asking permission to court his mom, he could appreciate the gesture. Since Jesse had already seen the attraction between them, he gave Josiah his blessing. Jayne gladly accepted Josiah's offer to escort her to the barn dance. Everyone in the family loved Josiah, and was even glad to see their mother forming an attachment to him—that is, everyone except Suzanne.

It was evident: Suzanne had been erecting a carefully guarded wall around her heart toward Olivia's father since the first time they had met. Olivia, wanting to understand Suzanne's struggle, had questioned her about it. Suzanne was convinced that accepting Josiah as an integral part of her mother's life would be a betrayal of her father's memory. Josiah was Olivia's father, and that was all he could ever be to her. Suzanne believed that soon her mother would realize this as well. Unfortunately, Suzanne's struggles didn't end with her mother's growing fondness for Josiah. She had told Jesse last week that if he didn't insist on it, she wouldn't even bother going to church. She enjoyed visiting with her friends when they were in attendance, but she wasn't sure how she felt about God anymore.

Jesse and Jayne were at a loss as to how to handle her despondency. As much as they would like to help her through, Suzanne's relationship with the Lord was personal. She would have to make her own peace with God. In the meantime, they would continue to show her how much she was loved.

Lord, Olivia prayed, *we all have our problems, don't we? Help Suzanne to understand what You've been teaching me: to everything there is a season, and a time to every purpose under Heaven. There's a time to be born and a time to die, a time to weep and a time to laugh, a time to mourn and a time to dance. Help her, Father, to release her grief so that she can dance again. You've shown me over and over how huge it is to accept what cannot be changed and to focus on what I have left. I know how easy it is to become bitter when we're hurting. I allowed my own bitterness to separate me from my husband. Whatever it takes, Lord, help my sister to turn back to You, the source of all comfort. You do everything right and on time, isn't that right, Lord? I entrust her to You.*

Jesse was coming out of the barn and saw his wife on the porch. He came to her, captured her hand, and pulled her into his lap on the swing. "Wool gathering, My Lady?"

"You might say that." As always, her husband read her too well.

"Care to fill me in?"

"Just praying for Suzanne. It's hard to see her struggling so."

"We all have things to go through, Liv, but God does have a purpose in the different seasons." The knowing smile that passed between them warmed each other's hearts.

"Do you ever sit and think about the circumstances that brought us together, Liv?"

"Yes ... how can I not?"

"Amazing how God blesses us when we're willing to step out in faith ... isn't it?"

"Absolutely!"

"Even in the midst of our sorrow, He has given us a heart of joy."

"God had a plan, didn't He? Twice He sent my knight in shining armor to rescue me: once from a terrible plight, and then again from the depths of utter despair."

"You rescued me as well, Liv, when you agreed to be my wife."

"Any regrets?"

"Not a one."

"Then kiss me, my chivalrous knight, and bestow upon me a glimpse of what is yet to come ...."

Tenderness and passion, the joyful celebration of a man and woman in love ....

✿ ✿ ✿

He Loves Me!

The Michigan Chronicles

Donna's signature series, *The Michigan Chronicles*, is fiction at its best, with purpose.

As one reader tells us:

> *"Donna Rhine has a gift for writing stories that entertain and warm your heart, while teaching moral and Biblical principles. Her works may be fictional, but she has a real relationship with the Lord, as evidenced in every book she writes."*
>
> K. MacDonald

Book 1

A Decision of the Heart

He said her heart was a gift that only she could give ...
Could she?

Not just a moving story of faith rising above suffering, slander, and life's circumstances, it's about a tender love that begins with a decision -

A Decision of the Heart

www.amazon.com/dp/0615455336
6x9 Paperback: 478 pages
Kindle Book

The Michigan Chronicles

Book 2

A Heart of Joy

When her impending loss plunges her into an uncertain future, her faith will be tested as never before ....

A moving saga of overcoming faith, it's also a heatwarming romance filled with adventure that ultimately leads to:
A Heart of Joy!

www.amazon.com/dp/0615466060
6x9 Paperback: 450 pages
Kindle Book

Book 3

A Heart Takes Flight

Will exposing the truth send her back to jail or into the arms of love?

A life changing story of God's abounding Grace and love's powerful influence - filled with intrigue, romance, and so much more ....

www.amazon.com/dp/0615486665
6x9 Paperback: 464 pages

The Michigan Chronicles

Book 4

A Heart Set Free

Her trials led to surrender. Could they also lead to her greatest blessings?

An an intriguing love story that evokes the heart's greatest passions, exposing the degradation of abuse in the light of God's Word — the power of God's redeeming love.

www.amazon.com/dp/0692021906
6x9 Paperback: 411 pages

Quick Note from Donna,

Thank you for all your continued support.

If this book has blessed you please let me know. Your comments and insights are both encouraging and enlightening. So often your input comes at a much needed time.

My hope and prayer is that my books have helped you get a little closer to the awsome God we serve.

My email: **donna@daisytales.com**

Other Works by Donna Rhine

In addition to Donna's popular series, **The Michigan Chronicles,** she has co-authored other books. Some of these titles include:

- **Still Dancing** - Gabriel Ford's autobiography shares the inspirational details of her life as a way of encouraging others yo move beyond their struggles and know that anything is possible.

- **Silent Tears, Loud Victory** - This heart wrenching story of one little girl's survival of abuse and her jourrney to become a woman of God. Edith Eddins reminds us that with God in our hearts, not only can we overcome horrific tragedy, we can forgive even the most deplorable sin and shine in the world as an example of His all-encompassing love.

You can find these and other works by Donna Rhine on Amazon.com by typing her name (Donna Rhine) in the search bar. Additional titles are in development, soon to be released.

Armoury House Publishing

Armoury House Publishing is dedicated to equipping of the saints through the printed word and other electronic media. Our mission is to draw all people one step closer in their personal relationship with Jesus Christ

Other Titles published by Armoury House Publishing:

Old Paths Series by John Charles Ryle

JC Ryle's conversational style of writing is easy to grasp and understand. Deep enough for the oldest of saints to find healthy portions of meat but lean enough to feed the new born Christian.

INSPIRATION of the Bible

How was the Bible written? Where did it come from ... Heaven? or of man? To what extent is God's word really God's Word? What do we mean when we say the Bible is inspired by God? How do the answers to these questions impact the way we live?

www.amazon.com/dp/1497476283
5x8 Paperback: 64 pages

OUR HOPE - The 5 Marks of a Good Hope

How do you distinguish a good hope from a mistaken hope that ultimately ends in a lie? Bishop Ryle gives us five characteristics of a good hope to follow.

www.amazon.com/dp/1499229798
5x8 Paperback: 48 pages

C.H. Spurgeon Works

PLAIN ADVISE FOR PLAIN PEOPLE

The wit and wisdom of one of the greatest men of the 19th century. Formerly published as "John Ploughman's Talk."

Spurgeon spans the denominational lines. His focus being that *"good wisdom is that which will turn out to be wise in the end; seek it, friends, and seek it at the hands of the wisest of all teachers, the Lord Jesus."*

John Ploughman

www.amazon.com/dp/1796309044
6x9 Paperback: 165 pages

These and other Armoury House Publishing books are available on Amazon.com and other on-line book distributors.

Thank you.

Armoury House Publishing
P.O. Box 60
Carleton, MI 48117   USA

No god is like you, O Lord.
No one can do what you do.

Psalm 86:8

GOD'S WORD Translation

www.ingramcontent.com/pod-product-compliance
Lightning Source LLC
Chambersburg PA
CBHW021330070726
47496CB00016B/134